Some content within this novel may be disturbing or triggering for some readers. Reader discretion is advised.

Subjects include mental illness, trauma, childhood abuse (physical and emotional), body shaming (by a parent to their adult child), parental rejection, bullying, instances of homophobia/biphobia, and discussions of suicide. This book contains graphic sexual scenes, intense sequences of BDSM, graphic violence, and strong language.

Any character depicted in a sexual scene is at least 18 years of age.

This book should not be used as a reference or guide for safe BDSM practices. Some activities depicted herein contain significant risk of injury and bodily harm. While all sexual scenes depicted are consensual, some scenes depict consensual non-consent (CNC) roleplaying. Other kinks include erotic degradation and humiliation, bondage, electrostimulation, domestic discipline, impact play, knife play, bodily fluids (including blood), public play, pain play, voyeurism, and pet play. Please be aware that this list is non-exhaustive.

If you have any questions pertaining to these warnings, please contact the author, Harley Laroux.

LOSRS

PART 1

HARLEY LAROUX

Editing: Zainab M. at Heart Full of Reads Editing Services
Cover Design: Ashes and Vellichor
Formatting: Chelsea Timm

A NOTE FROM THE AUTHOR

My dear reader,

I assume that if you've gotten this far, you've already perused that content note on the prior page. If you haven't, and you have any concerns about content that may be potentially triggering, I highly suggest taking a moment to go back and give it a read.

Losers has been an incredible story to write, but it also required me to pour out a lot of pain, trauma, and anger on these pages. Topics like homophobia/biphobia, abuse, and familial rejection are incredibly difficult for me to write, and I understand how difficult they can also be to read, especially for those who have experienced these things firsthand. While I have done my best to be thorough in my warning, as someone with triggers myself, not everything can be encompassed in a list. If you have any questions about any specific trigger, I welcome readers to contact me.

One last thing before you go on. If this book inspires you to explore the world of BDSM and power exchange, I cannot stress enough to seek out educational, non-fiction resources if you want to learn more. Many of the kink activities depicted in this book contain significant risk of bodily injury, and while we all love the smutty fictional filth (I mean… that's why you're reading this, right?), what we DON'T love is folks getting hurt by delving into the deep end of BDSM without taking the time to learn. So be risk-aware, be responsible, and do your due diligence for yourself and your partner/partners.

Now, on to the fun stuff!

Happy reading!

-HARLEY

To the losers, the freaks, and the outcasts.
Keep chasing sunrises.

1

JESSICA

High School - Senior Year

"Let me make one thing clear. The only way Manson Reed leaves this school tomorrow is on a stretcher, got that?"

There were nods of affirmation from the boys gathered around Kyle's red Ford Raptor. The parking lot was nearly empty; even the principal's Mercedes was gone. If it had been any other group of five boys lingering in the lot after school hours, the security guard would have dispersed them already. But it was quarterback, Kyle Baggins, and his teammates, and they could do no wrong.

Except they could, they did, and they were going to again. And this time, it was entirely my fault.

"It was just a kiss, Kyle," I muttered, hanging out the passenger side window. I had my cheerleading uniform on, and even in the crisp autumn air, my skin was sticky with sweat from practice. We'd been arguing earlier, and he'd made me so upset I'd blurted out the one thing I knew would hurt him.

I'd kissed Manson Reed, the school outcast, the freak, the boy everyone loved to hate.

"Fuck that." Kyle shook his head adamantly, his hands gripping the truck bed as if he wanted to tear through the metal. His jaw was clenched, his broad shoulders rigid with tension. "Unless you're trying to tell me you fucking enjoyed it, Jessica."

I huffed and sat back in my seat with my arms folded, staring straight ahead. There was no reasoning with Kyle when he was like this. I didn't dare tell him the truth.

I'd enjoyed it. I'd wanted it. Manson never would have laid a finger on me if he thought I didn't want him to. He never would have kissed me if I hadn't kissed him first.

But admitting what I'd done — what *we'd* done — was social suicide. It had slipped out to Kyle, because I was so angry he'd left me for Veronica Mills, only to come sauntering back a month later. What better way to hurt him than to tell him I'd kissed the boy he'd bullied relentlessly since freshman year?

Kyle's friends dispersed, and he got into the truck, turning it on. The engine roared as we sped down the road, whipping up leaves in a flurry behind us as he took me home. I was gripping my cell so tightly my fingers ached, knuckles gone white.

Kyle was Wickeston High School's star talent on the football field, the dream boy, handsome, and popular. My mom adored him, and his parents thought we were destined to be married right after we graduated. The idea filled me with dread. Behind his blue eyes and charming smile, Kyle was temperamental, jealous, and prone to fits of anger that would have us screaming at each other for hours.

He was also a damn cheater.

"Jesus Christ, would you stop sulking?" he snapped, his hand twisting on the steering wheel like he wanted to strangle it. Or like he was imagining strangling someone else.

"You can't keep doing this," I said. "You're eighteen. You have scholarships. If you end up with assault charges, it'll ruin everything."

"Reed is eighteen, too, isn't he?"

He was. His birthday had passed only a month ago — October 11th. But I wasn't about to piss Kyle off more with my knowledge about Manson's birthday.

He smirked at my silence. "Besides, do you really think they're going to press charges over *him*? Who's going to do it, Jessica? You think that freak's old lady will stay sober long enough to care if he's dead in a ditch somewhere?" He chuckled, like it was the best joke he'd ever heard. "If she isn't housing her bastard kid, then she has more money for booze. Sounds like a win for her."

My stomach felt like it was being yanked tight between two fists. I kept my arms folded so he wouldn't see them shaking. When he reached out and gripped my leg, I wanted nothing more than to swing my fist over and bash his face.

"I'm looking out for your honor, Jess," he said. "That scrawny freak isn't going to get away with this."

As if he knew a damn thing about honor.

Mom was in the kitchen when I got home. The scent of parmesan and garlic wafted through the house. She said something to me as I ran up the stairs, but I didn't have time to answer. The clock was ticking.

I had to warn Manson.

I didn't bother to shower; I just switched out my black and silver uniform for jeans and a hoodie. Dad poked his head out from the dining room as I rushed back down the stairs, my bag bouncing over my shoulder as I headed for the door.

"Why the rush, sunshine?" he said, his forehead creased with concern. "Your mother just finished up dinner. Won't you join us?"

"Can't tonight. Sorry, Dad!" I called to him as I slipped out the door. "I promised Ashley I'd help her with a project."

I wasn't sure if he heard the tension in my voice. Dad had never been a very discerning parent. His brain worked best in numbers and neat spreadsheets, where everything made sense and followed a logical sequence.

My BMW still had that new car smell, the engine purring softly as I sped down the dark country roads. It had been a birthday present from my parents, given to me right before the semester started. White exterior, red leather seats. My dream car. One more status symbol to hold my head a little higher when I walked through the halls of Wickeston High.

We owned that school, Kyle and I. The star quarterback and the cheer captain, a match made in romance heaven. Jealousy and desire followed us like a cloud. The haters and the wannabes couldn't keep our names out of their mouths. Every day was another rush of drama, an ego-feeding frenzy as the kids who had it all lorded it over those who didn't.

It wasn't as if I was unaware of it. I could look at myself in the mirror and point out every point of toxicity I carried, laugh about it, and carry on. Why care? Why change? I had everything I was supposed to want.

But our heavenly romance could swiftly descend into hell. When the King and Queen squabbled, pawns were sacrificed.

Not this time. It had to be different this time.

I took a slow drive past Manson's parents' house first, scanning the junk-covered yard for a glimpse of his lifted Bronco. I was glad not to see it there. If warning him meant walking up to that big dilapidated house and seeing one of his parents, I didn't think I could do it. His dad gave me the creeps.

I hoped my next destination would be correct. My tires crunched in the weeds as I pulled over beside the vacant lot, located at the end of a dirt road hidden by trees. The house that had once occupied the land had burned down years ago, leaving behind only a charred framework and a concrete foundation. Hope mingled with anxiety in my chest when I spotted two vehicles parked there: a dirty gray Ford Bronco on massive tires, and a midnight black El Camino.

I took a long, slow breath. The Bronco meant Manson was here, which was a relief. But the El Camino meant Lucas was with him, which probably meant Vincent and Jason were here too.

A whole gang of freaks, and me. The girl who had purposefully tormented them throughout every year of high school thus far.

I rummaged in my purse until I found a stick of bubblegum and chewed it viciously. Maybe it would help control my tongue when I went up there. I wasn't on good terms with any of these boys. It was simple — they hated me, and I despised them. That was the hierarchy. Yes, I'd made out with Manson, and I'd had some *very* close encounters with the rest of them. But that didn't mean we got along.

It also didn't mean I wanted Manson to walk straight into the ambush that would be waiting for him tomorrow.

I slammed the car door and shoved my hands into the pockets of my hoodie as I traipsed through the overgrown lot toward the back of the house's burned frame. The night air smelled like bonfire smoke and sour marijuana. The clatter of skateboards hitting concrete landed sharply in my ears as I rounded the house and laid eyes on the empty pool the boys liked to skate in. The concrete sides were covered in graffiti, and the area was illuminated only by the fires that had been lit in two large metal drums.

Vincent Volkov spotted me first. Perched on the gray bricks of an old wall, he had his long legs crossed beneath him. His joint went slack in his mouth when he saw me. He didn't say anything as the smoke slowly curled from his lips, enveloping his face and his long, messy hair.

It was Jason Roth who gave away my arrival. He'd always been the quiet one, the good kid. But his life had imploded over the summer, when the rumor went around that he and Vincent were dating. It shouldn't have mattered to anyone, but unfortunately, there were plenty of people in Wickeston with a stick up their ass who clutched their pearls at the very thought of two men being together. Including Jason's own family.

Some people claimed his parents kicked him out, others

said he'd gotten himself emancipated from them. Regardless of what was true, Jason had shown up senior year with his hair buzzed off, dyed bright blue, and his earlobes stretched with large black tunnels. The new look seemed like a giant middle finger to everyone who'd tried to make him feel ashamed.

"Fucking hell." Jason's blue eyes fell on me with such cold hatred that I didn't dare take another step toward the pool. He had his laptop open, playing "Awful Things" by Lil Peep from the crackling speakers. But he snapped it shut, cutting off the music. There was a screech of polyurethane wheels and Manson popped up from the pool, with Lucas close behind him.

"What the hell are you doing here, Jess?" Manson's voice was deep — a vicious baritone as dark as the black band tattooed around his upper arm. He usually spiked his hair into a mohawk for school, but the dark locks he kept in a long strip at the top of his head were loose tonight.

"I was looking for you," I said, as if that wasn't already obvious.

I didn't want to linger in the dark with them any longer than necessary. I had power in daylight, in the fluorescent halls of Wickeston High, where my status and Kyle's backing gave my words weight.

But this was their turf. I wasn't foolish enough to think I had a level playing field here. Especially not with Lucas staring at me as if his dark eyes alone could cause me to spontaneously combust. The only smile he ever wore was the stick-and-poke happy face tattooed under his right eye. His fists were clenched, his hands scarred from the fights that had gotten him continually suspended and eventually expelled.

"Kyle is out for blood, Manson," I blurted. His expression didn't change; he looked spectral in the flickering firelight, the flames making his cheeks hollower and his jaw sharper. "He found out."

"He *found out*, or did you tell him?" Only the shift in Manson's breathing showed his fear. I knew what he looked like when he was afraid, nervous, angry. His locker was right next to mine, and I'd spent enough time pushing his buttons to know what each and every emotion looked like.

"It doesn't matter how he found out." I folded my arms, chewing my gum faster as my nervousness rose. Vincent hopped down from the wall, tugging his black beanie lower on his head as he came to stand beside Jason. "Don't come to school tomorrow. Give him time to cool down."

Manson laughed bitterly. "No. We're not going to be catering to your boyfriend's tantrums anymore."

I threw up my hands in exasperation. "You're walking into a death trap, Manson! He wants to hurt you!"

"Kyle has another thing coming," Lucas said, and his voice sent a chill up my back. "If he thinks he's going to touch my boy…" He shook his head slowly. "That's not going to happen anymore."

"You're literally banned from school property," I said. "What do you think *you're* going to do?"

He didn't answer me, instead giving me a look that could have curdled milk. Manson was haunting and creepy in his quiet manner, but Lucas was monstrous. Everything about him had been built for violence; his lean body honed by years of fighting his father and anyone else who dared cross him.

Manson would wait for you in the dark and you'd never see

him coming; while Lucas would come in broad daylight, smash your windows out, and set your house on fire.

"Fine," I snapped. "Deal with it yourself."

I turned to go, flicking my blonde hair over my shoulder. But someone's fingers closed around my upper arm and jerked me back.

Manson pulled me against his chest, his body warm in the cold night. He smelled like cigarettes and something deep and dark, an enigma of hormones and anger. Heat shot from the pit of my abdomen to my cheeks.

He'd tasted like peppermint gum and tobacco when I'd kissed him. He'd felt like corruption, like a sin. He'd put his hand around my throat and squeezed when he kissed me, and ever since I'd been unable to shake that feeling of his fingers digging into my flesh.

I wanted to feel it again, feel it harder. I wanted to rip open his viciousness and take it all in. I wanted to ride this man like a goddamn rollercoaster and then take his friends for a spin too.

But a girl like me wasn't supposed to be with guys like them.

"What did you tell him?" Manson said softly. There wasn't anger in his voice, but his question hung by a dangerously thin thread.

I pressed my lips together. I'd made him promise not to tell, but I'd been the one who betrayed our secret. All for a ridiculous fight with Kyle.

I shook my head. "I didn't lie."

"Are you sure about that?" He lowered his voice even more, a whisper he left right in my ear as his lips brushed against it. "You wanted that as much as I did. Don't fucking lie about me."

He let me go, and when I didn't step back immediately, he widened the space between us. The sudden cold made me shiver, and without another word, I made my way back to the car. The hairs on the back of my neck stood on end as they watched me go.

I'd done everything I could. I'd warned him, and that was more than most people would have done. What happened now wasn't any of my business. If Manson would stay away like I told him, Kyle would eventually calm himself down and get over it.

I started the engine and turned up the heater, trying to chase away the chill in my hands. I could still feel Manson's heat on my chest. That weirdo. That freak. Why did he get to live in my head rent-free like this? They were all supposed to be beneath me, lower than gum on my shoe. Instead, I felt obsessed, like I couldn't stop. Couldn't stop looking at them, taunting them, seeking them out.

I couldn't stop wanting them.

"Get it together, Jessica," I said, clicking my seatbelt into place. I glanced over to check my side mirror before I put the car in gear —

And shrieked at the sight of Lucas looming outside my window.

"What the hell are you doing?" I rolled down my window but quickly realized it was a mistake. He gripped the opening, knuckles flexing against the inside of my door. "Move it, Lucas, seriously."

"You don't tell me what to do."

His voice was sharper than a knife's blade. My mouth hung open in shock, but the anger on his face was stifling.

"You know you went too far this time, Jessica. You fucking *know* you did." He leaned in, and my entire body tensed as I stared him down. "You thought you needed to warn Manson? How about you warn that fuckboy you open your legs for? Warn him there'll be hell to pay if he tries fucking with any of my boys again." His face was so close to mine, but he didn't touch me. Lucas never touched me. His eyes alone were enough — how they dragged over my skin as harshly as teeth and nails. "Fuck with one of us, you fuck with all of us."

Then, so quickly I hardly realized what was happening, he pulled the bubblegum from my open mouth, fingers brushing over my lips like an electric shock. He tucked the wad into his cheek, and with the first wicked grin I'd ever seen on his terrifying face, he gave me a two-finger salute and stepped back from the car.

He chewed, blowing a bubble that audibly popped, before he said, "Get lost, Jessica."

Dread was stifling me as I arrived at school the next morning. Manson didn't even look at me as he shoved books into his locker, no matter how hard I tried to catch his eye.

Finally, I hissed, "Manson, go home. *Please*."

"Save it, Jess." He slammed the locker shut, hauling his ragged backpack over his shoulder. His mohawk was spiked up, a rigid spine on his shaved head. He wore the same tattered jeans he had on every day, the same worn lace-up leather boots and denim jacket. "Don't start acting like you care. Being a bitch suits you better."

He turned his back on me, stalking down the hall. He usually kept his head down, shoulders hunched; a smaller target. But something was different today. His chin was up and his long strides were aggressive.

Trying to fight Kyle would only make it worse.

I hesitated at my locker, guilt gnawing in my gut as Manson

went into the men's restroom. *It doesn't matter*, I told myself, clicking my locker shut.

"Wow, tense in here today, isn't it?" My best friend and fellow cheerleader, Ashley Garcia, squeezed out of the crowd to stand beside me. "Have you seen Kyle yet?"

"No." My mouth was dry, and I didn't know what to do with my hands. God, all this stress was going to make me break out. "Do you have your flask on you?"

"Of course, girl." She reached into her bag and withdrew her "flask," a water bottle filled with vodka and clear soda. I took a generous gulp, hoping it would settle my nerves.

I handed it back as I spotted Kyle approaching, flanked by three of his friends. Alex, Nate, and Matthew were all part of the jock crowd and they followed Kyle around like loyal dogs. I waved to him with the best smile I could manage — which wasn't great. It felt cold and plastic on my face. But instead of coming to walk with me to class, Kyle and two of his boys went into the restroom. Nate, a linebacker the size of a grizzly bear, posted up outside with his arms folded. The message was clear.

No entry. Kyle needed his privacy.

My heart plummeted into my shoes. I needed to do something, tell someone. Get the principal, a teacher, the security guard, anyone.

But I just stood there.

Someone brushed against my arm, and Ashley and I looked over to find Vincent standing beside me. He stretched his arms over his head with a lazy groan before tucking his hands into the front pockets of his hoodie.

"Ugh." Ashley looked away, lip curled in disgust. "Volkov."

"Garcia," he responded in kind.

"Kill any small animals lately?" she snipped.

"Only the squirrel whose blood I drank for dinner last night."

"God, shut *up*." I turned to him, flinging my arm toward the bathroom. "Aren't you going to help him? Or are you too stoned to care that your best friend is going home in a casket?"

Vincent snickered. "You think Manson can't handle himself?"

"I think it's three against one, numbskull!" I shoved his arm, my pink acrylics digging into his skin. "Kyle has never had a problem beating him one-on-one, let alone with his friends!"

"As if you've ever cared." Vincent's smile wasn't so lazy anymore. It was bitter, frozen on his face. "I don't think this concerns you anymore, Jess."

Someone yelled from inside the bathroom, followed by a bang loud enough that I wondered if Kyle had ripped one of the stalls' metal doors off its hinges. Students looked around in confusion, some gathering closer to the bathroom, but keeping their distance from Nate. Cell phones were out, everyone eager to record the latest drama.

No one cared enough to interfere. It was entertainment, another opportunity to upload a good fight video and rack up the views. If someone got hurt, even better. An injury could shoot a video to virality faster than anything else.

The bathroom door slammed open, and Nate nearly plunged forward into the crowd as Kyle stumbled out. His eyes were wide, and people hurriedly made way for him as he panted, pointing a finger accusingly back into the bathroom as Alex and Matthew hurried out after him.

"Knife!" he yelled. "Reed has a knife!"

It was instant pandemonium. Suddenly, teachers were present, yelling for people to clear out. Two security guards showed up, flustered and red-faced, as Kyle kept babbling, "He tried to stab me! He tried to fucking stab me!"

I covered my mouth in shock as the rushing crowd pressed me, Vincent, and Ashley against the lockers.

Ashley was breathless with disbelief. "Holy shit."

"It shouldn't have come to this," Vincent said, his face somber and his voice barely discernible in the chaos.

My guilt was like a beast trying to claw its way up my esophagus, thrashing and gnawing. I crushed it under pride and blind self-assurance.

The security guards emerged from the bathroom, with Manson between them. Each of them kept an iron grip on his arms, leading him through the crowd as students tried to get shots of him with their phones. He wasn't fighting them, and he wasn't hurt other than a purple bruise on his cheek and a dribble of blood that streaked from his busted lip. They led him toward the principal's office, directly past me.

Manson nodded to Vincent first, silent words passing between them. Then his eyes fell on me and his lips parted to give me a wide, bloody smile.

It was feral — a beast's grin. Wild, reckless and, finally, victorious.

2

JESSICA

The morning after The Dare…

Everything changes after high school. *Everything.*

You're an adult now — or so people say. It's time to get it all figured out. Life, love, career. You're supposed to have a plan. The rest of your life is waiting for you.

But instead, you're flailing in the rising waters of adulthood as time ticks away, overwhelmed and underprepared. How the hell was I supposed to plot out the rest of my life when it had barely even begun? I was doubting the person I'd believed myself to be, doubting every decision, and the dreams I'd once had.

I'd changed. I didn't know myself like I thought I did.

I stared at my reflection in the diner's scratched bathroom mirror, using a makeup wipe from my purse to clean away my smudged mascara. But I couldn't wipe away the deep red hickey on my neck. I couldn't get the smell of sex out of my hair.

I couldn't forget last night. Neither did I want to.

Straightening my ponytail, I stepped back to take a better look at myself before I left the restroom. I should have brought a change of clothes or at least some pants to the Halloween party last night, because my angel costume was little more than glorified lingerie. At least the hoodie I wore was long enough to cover my short skirt.

The hoodie smelled like him, like Manson. It reminded me of the autumn leaves outside, cloudy days, and bonfires.

What the hell was I doing? What had I *done*?

I rejoined Ashley at our table in the dining area, glad to find that our food had already arrived. She was groaning over her plate of pancakes, resting her forehead on her palm.

"I'm never drinking again," she said miserably. I smiled and reached across the table to pat her head in sympathetic disagreement. It was the hangover talking. She'd be drunk again next weekend.

It was strange not to be hungover with her. But barely drinking anything had been far from the strangest thing to happen at the party last night. Seeing Manson in attendance, a year and several months after he'd been expelled, hadn't been the strangest part. Even seeing Jason, Lucas, and Vincent again hadn't been as strange as what came after.

What I'd done — what I'd finally let myself do — was so bizarre I didn't dare bring it up.

Maybe I'd screwed up, and last night had been a massive mistake. People would find out. They'd never look at me the same.

Videos of me playing that Drink or Dare game with Manson were going to be plastered across social media. But what had come after the game, what had happened in the dark, was what truly scared me.

I'd lost myself in the lust that had been building ever since those men first came into my life.

I didn't feel like the same person I'd been yesterday. I felt fake, like I'd been dropped into a mannequin's body and had forgotten what pose I was supposed to hold.

I didn't know what the hell I wanted anymore.

Except the big plate of biscuits and gravy in front of me. I wanted that in my stomach immediately.

"Girl, what even happened last night?" Ashley gazed at me with a little frown. "You took that weird dare from Manson and disappeared. Did you, uh…" She popped her lips with a little smile. Not even a hangover was going to stop her from getting the whole story. "Did you finally hook up?"

"*Finally*?" My voice squeaked. "What do you mean, finally?"

She rolled her eyes. "Oh, come on. I get it, okay? He's weird and dangerous. It's the whole bad boy thing, right? That's kind of fun." She pierced a piece of pancake with her fork, rubbing it through the syrup across her plate. "By the way, I ran into Jennifer at the party. She said that Vincent and Jason, and uh…" She snapped her fingers as she tried to remember.

"Lucas," I said softly, and she clapped her hands.

"Yes! Lucas Bent. She said she saw them all last night. Dressed like clowns, the fucking weirdos. *I* didn't see them. I can't believe they were invited." Her piece of pancake was completely drenched at this point. I stuffed my mouth with biscuit and country gravy in a last-ditch effort to buy myself time. "But she mentioned she saw you with them."

The biscuit felt like glue in my mouth. I swallowed slowly. "Yeah, uh…" Paused again. Took a sip of orange juice. "They're friends with Manson." Useless information. She already knew that.

"Riiiiiight." Her eyes were locked on me. Syrup dripped from her pancake onto the cheap diner tabletop. "Close friends, I've heard."

"Really close," I muttered and instantly regretted it, as she sucked in her breath. "Look, let's drop the subject, okay?"

"Ugh, Jess, *come on*! I wanna know! It was only a one-night stand, right? It's not, like…" She snickered, as if what she was about to say was completely ludicrous. "It's not like you're going to *date* him, right? Can you imagine? I think your mom would literally have a heart attack." She laughed, and I tried to join her.

My phone buzzed, and my heart rocket-launched toward my shoes when I saw his name pop up. Manson Reed.

Ashley tapped her fork repeatedly on her plate as I snatched up my phone.

What do you say to breakfast next Saturday? the text read. **It can be just us, but I think the boys would like a chance to get to know you in a better setting. We can debrief on all the craziness.**

I swallowed hard. My head throbbed and not from any hangover. Ashley was watching me like a hawk.

"Soooo," she said slowly as I clicked my screen off and set the phone aside. "Is that him? Did he text you that quickly? It's been, what, an hour since we left the house?" She giggled. "Knife boy seems a little obsessed."

"It wasn't him," I said quickly. "It was my mom. I doubt I'll hear from him again." I cut another piece off my biscuit, then kept cutting. Piece after piece, decimating the biscuit as it drowned in gravy. "It was a one-night thing. Just a little fun. It's not like we'd ever work together."

She nodded, my dismissive words finally calming her interest. The status quo remained. Manson, Lucas, Vincent, and Jason existed in their world, and I stayed in mine.

It wouldn't work. It *couldn't* work. My mom would freak out. My dad would never understand. My friends would think I'd lost my mind.

There was nothing there but lust, and what had happened at the party was a result of that.

Never mind that I'd never felt so free, so wildly *alive* as I had last night. Entrusting myself to those boys in the pursuit of pleasure had awakened a part of me I never knew existed.

God, I'd even let the word "Master" roll off my tongue as I'd said my goodbyes to Manson.

It made my heart beat fast and my palms sweat thinking of them as if every inch of me ached for their presence, for the slightest touch, for the breathtaking experience of being surrounded by the four of them in the dark, all of their attention on me and me alone.

I'd been dared to do a lot of things last night, but this morning, my bravery was gone. I had years of college ahead of me and a reputation to uphold.

What happened in the dark had to stay there.

3

MANSON

Present – 2 Years, 8 Months Later

I woke up feeling like the world was caving in around me.

My heart was pounding, adrenaline pumping through my veins. My fingertips were cold and tingling, but all these symptoms were familiar. Maybe a floorboard creaked, and it prodded an old memory, or perhaps one of the boys had raised their voice and my brain latched on to the potential danger. Whatever it was, the anxiety had wrenched me out of my sleep.

I'd been dreaming, and although I rarely remembered my dreams, this one was fresh in my mind. It was a memory really, dug up from the recesses of my brain and replayed like a shitty childhood VHS tape.

I'd dreamed I was sitting against the back wall of Wickeston High between the dumpsters. I could smell the stink of rotten food, and there was something sticky under my hand, squashed against the concrete. My abdomen ached, my diaphragm was spasming, my arm curled around my stomach as I held down the urge to vomit. Getting punched in the gut sucked no matter what, but Kyle could hit particularly hard, even in dreams.

But he and his friends faded into the background; their presence inconsequential to me. I didn't care about them or the pain they caused me. I only cared about *her*.

Jessica stood over me, arms folded, her legs looking a million miles long in heels and a tight plaid skirt. Her blonde hair was so long it brushed her waist, and I imagined wrapping it around my hand to pull her head back and hear her moan.

Did she think Kyle was impressive because he could push me around? Did it turn her on? Did it thrill her? I wished I knew what was happening behind those bright green eyes.

In my dream, she stood over me with her hand leaning against the wall over my head. She whispered, "Don't let the loser forget his place."

Yeah. My place was here, on the ground, staring at the woman I couldn't have. She was so fucking beautiful. Heartlessly perfect. The cruelest joke life had ever played on me.

I would have rather not woken up. I wanted to linger in that fantasy. All I had left of that woman was gut-wrenching memories and wild dreams.

With a heavy sigh, I sat up in bed, rubbing my face. The sun was a hazy glow through the metal blinds covering my window, and I picked up my phone, groaning when I saw the time. It was even later than I'd thought.

I brushed the used tissues from last night off my bedside table and grabbed the bottle of lotion to take back to the bathroom. But my real shame was the crumpled fabric next to the tissues — a lacey thong stiffened with cum because I'd jacked off with it, *again*.

It was Jessica's. I'd wash it in the sink later, there was no way in hell I was putting it in the regular laundry and risking one of the boys finding it. I'd never get it back.

It was too hot already, the air sticky with humidity as I stumbled into the bathroom. I splashed cold water on my face and shoved back my hair as best I could. It was getting too long; I needed it cut. The world was a little clearer once I had my contacts in, clear enough to grab my bottle of pills off the shelf and swallow two.

After about forty-five minutes, maybe an hour, the tight feeling in my chest would mellow out like melting butter. I'd be able to breathe again. I'd be in control.

I filled my diffuser and switched it on before I headed out. Chamomile, lavender, and lemon wafted into the air in a gentle mist, covering the stale old smell of cigarettes that clung to the walls. Kathryn Peters, my former social worker, suggested I try aromatherapy when I was living with her family, and the habit had stuck. Without Kathy, I would have ended up on the streets. Another kid on probation who should have fallen through the cracks. Instead, she gave me a safe place to stay until I had a house of my own.

I still called her often to talk, and I'd gotten close with their son Daniel too. But Daniel lived overseas now, so when I moved out, Kathy and her husband James sold their house in Wickeston and started traveling. She was on a cruise headed for the Alaskan coast when she called me last.

I made a mental note to text her today. There weren't many people outside my household that I considered myself close to, but Kathy had saved my life. I'd never forget that.

The room closest to mine was Lucas's, but the door was open and his messy bed was empty. He was probably in the shop working, already pissed that I'd slept in. Vincent's room was in the attic and Jason's was further down the hall, although he spent most nights in Vince's room anyway. The house was big enough for all of us with a bedroom to spare, but that extra room stayed shut and locked. It was used for storage now, nothing more. No memories, no ghosts in the walls. Only a room.

If I told myself that enough, I'd eventually make it true.

The smell of fried food and weed greeted me as I went down the stairs toward the kitchen. Jason was at the stove, frying sausage patties as my pit bull, Jojo, shoved her wet gray nose demandingly against his leg. The shower down the hall was running and Vincent was loudly singing from within.

"Damn, took a while for you to haul your ass down here." Jason glanced back at me as I walked in, his shaggy blue hair damp and a towel slung over his shoulders. "Are you hungry? Don't let that beggar fool you. I fed her already."

"I could eat." I flopped down on one of the mismatched chairs next to the table as Jason scooped the sausage out of the pan. Jojo decided I was a better target to beg and came over with her tail wagging so hard it whipped her sides with every swing. I grasped her big head in my hands, shaking her back and forth in a little dance that made her whine excitedly as she tried to lick my face. I wasn't hungry, not at all, but if I didn't eat, I'd have the damn shakes in a few hours.

"Toast and eggs, too?" Jason said, hand poised near the refrigerator door.

"Please."

The shower turned off and Vincent came out singing, obnoxiously loud and completely naked. His long hair dripped water on the floor as he snatched a sausage from the plate and took a bite before heading up the stairs, shouting, "God, Manson, put a shirt on! You can't be walking around half naked!"

"Has Lucas texted you yet?" Jason said. He slid a plate of food to me as he took a seat on the opposite side of the table. I shook my head, drenching my eggs with hot sauce before I dug in. "He's on a good one this morning. Pissy as fuck."

"I'll talk to him," I said. Jojo shoved her nose against my hip with an eager whine, and I slipped her a piece of sausage beneath the table. "We were up late in the shop. That Ford was way worse than we thought it would be. Engine sludge thick as fucking molasses."

Jason made a face of disgust. He worked as a programmer, but he spent enough of his free time in the auto shop to know his way around, pitching in when Lucas and I got too swamped with repair jobs.

"Just a few more months and things will change," he said. "No more shitbox cars once you get the next shop set up."

I nodded in agreement. We were only a few months away from being able to list this old house for sale and get the hell out of Wickeston. Once we moved, Lucas and I planned to set up our next place as a true tuner shop. I took a hell of a lot of pride in my work and I couldn't settle for being merely another community mechanic. No more fucking around with Granny's slipping transmission or Uncle Pete's blown engine. We wanted to be known for what we loved — building fast cars that could smoke the competition without fail.

As difficult as it was to eat, the food did settle my stomach. I cleared my plate by the time Vincent came back downstairs, finally fully clothed. He sat down beside Jason, smirking.

"Missing something this morning, J?" he said.

Jason gave him a long look. "Probably."

"Something like your lighter, maybe?"

Jason shook his head with a sigh. "Let me guess — it's behind my ear?"

Vincent opened his mouth in an exaggerated shock as he completed his favorite magic trick and pulled Jason's lighter from his ear. "Damn, J, why are you keeping your lighter in your ear?" Jason groaned, and I hid my smile behind the last bite of toast.

As I was putting my plate in the sink, the front door creaked open, and Lucas poked his head inside. "Manson. Need to talk to you."

"Hey, at least get some breakfast!" Jason said, but Lucas stalked off again as quickly as he had appeared. I glanced over at Vincent, who shook his head.

"He's in a *great* mood today," he said.

"He'll calm down," I said. "I'll go see what's up."

I walked outside, squinting in the glaring sunlight. The property was large, most of it covered with trees and weeds. We had cleaned up the front yard when we moved in, hauled away the junk, and repaired the big metal garage built on the side of the property. That garage was now our shop; its exterior walls emblazoned with Vincent's paintings. My parents had allowed this place to waste away when they owned it, but I'd inherited it a little over a year ago and already we'd done more work to the place than my dad had in all the years he lived there.

I couldn't guess where my dad was now. When Mom passed away last year, he only showed up to make a fuss about the will before he disappeared again. For all I knew, my old man was dead too, and good riddance to him.

Lucas was pacing the yard, a deep frown fixed on his face as he smoked. His hands were dirty from working at the shop, streaked with oil and grime. The garage was manned by the two of us, and we worked it seven days a week, sometimes twenty-four hours a day when we got busy enough.

Our other dog, a little snub-nosed mutt that Vincent had named Haribo, lay nearby with his head resting between his paws. As I left the porch, the dog gave me a look that clearly said, *this guy is stressing me out.*

It was clear to me anyway. Lucas probably would have disagreed with the interpretation.

"Did you know Alex McAllister is going to that party next week?" Lucas's voice was low.. Every muscle in his throat was tense with the effort to control his volume.

It took my brain a second to catch up with what he'd said. "You mean the bonfire? On the 4th?"

"*Yes*, at the fucking bonfire." He took a long drag on the cigarette, his body one rigid mass of nervous energy.

I'd known him for years and he'd always been like this. Quick to anger, slow to forgive, moody as hell. He was either horny enough to fuck night and day, or so withdrawn he didn't even want to be touched.

But we understood each other in a way no one else could. We'd bonded through trauma, clinging to each other when the hopelessness of our teen years had felt like it would never end. It was a bond that wouldn't break.

The four of us had chosen to build our lives together, and that meant dealing with each other even at our worst.

"I didn't ask about Alex," I said, remembering the dick who'd punched me in the face right before I threatened to slit his throat from ear to ear. There was nothing quite like being bullied until you're ready to kill someone. But I'd never forget how fast that fucker's expression had changed from smug to terrified when he realized I'd fight back. "I figured he'd be there though. Considering it's a holiday, I doubt he'll be staying home. Hell, Kyle could show up for all I know."

"And that wouldn't bother you?" Lucas stubbed the cigarette out under his boot. "That wouldn't fucking bother you to see that asshole's face, after he did this —" He tapped my jaw with his knuckles, right where a scar remained. "— and this?" Another tap, another scar, and his attitude was starting to raise my blood pressure.

If he'd touched my face like that a few years ago, I would have swung without thinking. It had happened before, because Lucas had no impulse control when he was like this, and I had no control over those fight-or-flight spikes that inevitably leaned toward *fight*.

I'd gotten better, I'd *made* myself better. Pills, meditation, therapy, whatever it took. I wasn't going to continue the cycle my dad had roped me into.

"Lucas, you gotta chill." I shoved my hands in my pockets to keep them under control. "You're a level ten right now, man. You have to bring it down. Otherwise I can't talk to you."

He exhaled furiously as he paced, then rubbed his hand over his buzzed hair. After a moment, he stood still and took another deep breath.

"Right, right, sorry," he said. "I'm sorry, Manson, you know, I — You know I'm sorry."

He fell silent, giving himself a few moments to get his thoughts back in order. Haribo came to sit by my foot, and I reached down, giving him a scratch behind the ears.

"There's plenty of people in this town I don't like seeing either," I said. "But we'll all be there. Who's going to fuck with all of us together?"

"Some asshole who doesn't know what's good for them, probably." He shook his head, but the tension had drained out of his face.

"Then, you'll still come?" He gave me an uncertain look, grimacing. "Come on, I know you don't want to sit at home and sulk."

He shoved my shoulder with a laugh. "Fine, fine. I'll go. But no guarantees that I'll be well-behaved. Are you going to get your ass to work soon or what?"

"Yeah, yeah, I'm coming. Let me go grab yesterday's mail first. Some assholes have been stealing it again." He just waved his arm at me over his shoulder as he stalked back into the garage.

A narrow dirt road led past our house, shaded by walnut trees. I followed it to the main road, Route 15, wiping the sweat from my forehead. I couldn't wait for summer to be over with; I wasn't built for this heat. I was looking forward to the cooler, drier autumn days.

"Goddamn it," I groaned when I found the mailbox knocked over on its side, its wooden post splintered in half, the metal box mangled. It looked like someone had slammed into it with their truck — likely on purpose.

"Motherfuckers." I picked the mailbox out of the weeds and leaned it against what remained of its post. Yet another thing we'd have to find time to fix. I wrenched open the door, breaking it off in the process and tossing it away. The mail was gone too. Fantastic.

Another fine day in beautiful, welcoming Wickeston.

4

JESSICA

B eing back in my hometown was strange, especially considering I never thought I'd live here again. Wickeston billed itself as "a charming slice of Western Tennessee," but as I drove through downtown, it was hard to see the charm. A few cute historical buildings and 1950s-themed cafes didn't change the fact that this place was dull.

We had a few big box stores and chain restaurants, nothing like the plethora of options I'd had while living in Nashville the past couple years. Most people were so damn bored that they entertained themselves by getting into everyone else's business.

Like my mother, for example. I'd only been in town for a week and she had honed in on my love life with single-minded focus. Why the *hell* was I still single? Forget work, forget unpacking, don't even *think* about taking a breath after moving halfway across the state. I needed to get back out there and meet a potential husband, regardless of how many volunteer events she had to foist on me to make it happen.

It was like high school all over again. Mom was right back to putting my entire life on her precisely timed schedule, and according to her, I was running late. I'd wasted all my time getting an education when I should have been pursuing my true calling of becoming a trophy wife and grandbaby-producer as quickly as possible.

It wasn't like I could tell Mom no. Her house, her rules.

It was a sweltering, humid day as I pulled into the parking lot at her church. I hadn't attended a service in nearly twelve years, but that was irrelevant to her. Her worship group was hosting a car wash fundraiser for the upcoming 4th of July Festival, and there was already a line of cars forming when I arrived.

God, this was going to give me horrible tan lines. Mom had insisted I dress "modestly" — most specifically, "no little booby tops and hussy shorts."

Well, that was exactly what I was wearing. A low-cut top and cute frayed denim shorts. To be fair, they were the longest shorts I owned and *did* cover my entire ass. Barely. Honestly, Mom should have been grateful I'd put on a white t-shirt instead of only wearing the bikini top I had on underneath.

Unfortunately, she looked anything but grateful as I walked up to meet her, under the canopy sheltering volunteers from the sun.

"I should send you home," she muttered, tugging at the hem of my shorts. Her long hair was teased up into a big pile of wavy blonde locks, perfect as always despite the humidity. But she used enough hairspray to withstand a tornado. "And you're late. I told you to be here at ten."

"I was working, Mom." I sighed, taking a water bottle out of the cooler and running it over my neck. She waved her hand dismissively.

"That little internship is taking up so much of your time," she said. "And they're hardly paying you. You're getting so pale being inside all day."

I resisted the urge to cover my face with my hands and scream. My "little internship" was with the Smith-Davies Architectural Design Firm, one of the best on the east coast. I spent my mornings in the gym before I came home and got to work, filling out spreadsheets and answering my boss's emails. It was all remote work and it didn't pay much, but at least it was getting my foot in the door. If I could nail my six-month review, there was a good chance I could turn this part-time internship into a full-time career.

I had to do *something* to get myself back out of Wickeston. Smith-Davies' main office was in New York City, and if I was brought on full time, I'd move there in a heartbeat.

Trying to tell Mom this went in one ear and out the other. She spotted someone across the parking lot and waved, leaning close to me to say far too loudly, "Oh, look! That's Julie's oldest son. You remember him, don't you? Robert?"

"I literally haven't seen him since first grade," I said, staring at the tall, vaguely familiar guy helping direct the younger kids working the car wash line. "He threw up at my birthday party because he ate his cake too fast."

Mom made a disgusted face. "Mm, that's right. I forgot about that. Well, he has a younger brother. Joshua, I think. Oh, there's Julie. She and her husband are talking about getting a divorce again, bless her heart. Hi, Julie! Honey, so good to see you! How's the family?" And just like that, Mom was away, off to play matchmaker while I very alluringly washed cars.

I couldn't explain to her the real reason I was so disinterested in dating. But the bar had been set for me in the worst way possible, and now I didn't feel satisfied with anything less.

If a guy couldn't play with my masochism as enthusiastically as he played with my pleasure, then I didn't want it. There simply wasn't a nice way to tell your mother that you wanted a guy who could spank you as well as he could fuck. A man who was as comfortable with whips and chains as he was at candlelit dinners. Someone who wasn't afraid to take control but wasn't going to make the relationship feel like a cage.

Was I asking for too much? Probably. But I'd been demanding too much for my whole life and I wasn't going to stop now.

Problematically, I'd already found people who met those qualifications. Four of them, actually, and they were all still here in Wickeston.

If explaining my kinky desires to my mom was bad, then broaching the subject of these four men would probably get me disowned. Tattooed guys with bad reputations and some *slight* criminal history would not be good enough for her little girl.

It didn't matter anyway. I hadn't spoken to any of them since the day after that Halloween party.

I glanced back under the canopy where Mom was talking loudly on her cell phone, a list in one hand and her iced latte in the other, her phone tucked between her ear and shoulder.

"I already told Annamae that Red, White, and Blueberries was the theme year before last," she said. "Bless her unimaginative little heart, but we're not repeating a theme."

I'd had enough of roasting in the sun. I stripped off my t-shirt and tossed it over one of the plastic folding chairs nearby. All these nice church ladies were going to have to live with some titties if they wanted me to keep scrubbing. I paused for a water break, guzzling down half a cold bottle and pouring the rest over my arms and shoulders.

Another car pulled up, a blue Subaru WRX with a large wing on the back. The engine purred, and the windows were tinted so dark I could barely see inside.

It was a familiar vehicle, but I couldn't place my finger on why until I rapped my knuckles on the driver's window to collect their money.

The window rolled down, and I froze. My breath stilled and my heart hammered, a tight feeling swelling in my chest until it stoppered my throat.

Vincent sat in the driver's seat, holding a ten-dollar bill folded between his fingers. He looked as surprised as I was, his dark green eyes wide as he looked up at me.

"Jessica?" Jason stared at me from the passenger seat, his shaggy blue hair curling around his face in soft waves. His eyes were the same color, preternaturally bright.

My mouth gaped open and closed before I managed to choke out, "Hi."

Hi. That was it; that was all I was capable of. Damn, real smooth there, Jessica.

But my greeting got a smile out of Vincent. His long brown hair was tied back into a messy bun, his bare arms covered in tattoos. He smelled like summer; like citrus, weed, and very bad decisions.

I was instantly aware of every inch of my flesh they could see, my skin heating even more.

The last time I'd seen them, I'd been on my knees giving the most terrifyingly erotic blow jobs of my life. *Awkward* didn't even begin to describe this roiling feeling inside me that was half panic and half excitement. Excitement for what, exactly, I didn't know.

"Back in town for a visit?" Vincent said. He was still holding out the money, but I hadn't taken it.

"Yeah. I mean, no, not exactly. I'm here temporarily." The two of them exchanged a look as I stammered. Good God, girl, get it together. "I'm not visiting. I moved back home. Temporarily."

Saying it felt like admitting defeat. I'd dreamed of getting a job straight out of college, starting my life somewhere new. Instead, I was right back where I started.

"Damn, back home with Mom and Dad," Jason said, shaking his head. "Must be weird for you."

"Weird is putting it mildly," I said softly. I hated feeling like I'd been caught unprepared. My nerves shot into overdrive, and when I got nervous, I got mean. It was often a struggle to try to control my tongue.

"Uh, Miss Martin?" one of the youth group boys called to me, looking at the car with uncertainty. "Should we start washing, or...?"

I still hadn't taken Vincent's money. I reached for it, but he pulled it back slightly, and in a lowered voice said, "You know, I'm kind of particular about my car. Maybe let the kids do the next one and you take care of us yourself?"

Jason smirked, pretending he was focused on his phone. He didn't even have an app open; he was just randomly clicking around his screen. I plucked Vincent's money out of his hand, tucking it into my bikini top.

"Turn the car off," I said. "And roll your windows up, unless you want to get wet."

"I wouldn't mind getting wet."

I ignored him, grabbing the bucket of soapy water and sloshing it over the car. He still managed to get his window up in time, but I could see him grinning at me through the windshield. Jason wasn't pretending to look at his phone anymore as I leaned over the hood, scrubbing a sponge over the bright blue paint.

"You guys get the next one," I said, shooing the kids away. They could deal with the minivan that was next in line instead.

The WRX was mine.

Jason and Vincent both stared as I reached as high as I could on the hood, my chest brushing against the wet metal. I was thorough, but I tried to move quickly, because the last thing I wanted was for my mom to get off the phone and start scolding me for not having a shirt on. As I moved around to the passenger side, Jason rolled down his window slightly and said, "Don't forget the wheels. They're pretty dirty."

I grit my teeth as I knelt, scrubbing the black rims. Once I'd finished, I stretched up on my tiptoes to get the roof. It put me right in front of Jason's window, and I knew he was staring, but I didn't mind putting on a little show. Pressed so close against the glass, I could see Vincent reach over and lay his hand on Jason's obvious bulge, squeezing.

It was unbearably hot and I was sweating like a sinner in church. It was a disturbingly accurate allegory, considering my present circumstances.

Right as I was finishing up, I caught my mom's furious gaze. Oh, she was pissed and ready to be petty, especially as I'd pulled a total Paris Hilton — all I was missing was the messy burger. I hurriedly rinsed the car and gave the window a knock when I was done.

Vincent was smirking as he rolled it down.

"World class service," he said, handing me another ten-dollar bill. "I usually avoid giving to the church, but you might make a believer out of me."

"Believe it or not, I'm not here for the church," I said, tucking his very generous donation into my bikini beside the other bill.

Jason's eyes widened in mocking shock. "No? Really? I never would have guessed."

That bulge in his pants was catastrophically distracting.

I stepped back as Vincent started the car; the engine coming to life with such a roar that several of the women under the canopy began to complain. The way Vincent looked at me, eyes lingering at all the right places, made me feel like he was stripping my clothes off without even touching me.

"We'll see ya' around, Jess," he said, his tone making my stomach do a ridiculous little flip. His engine popped with a backfire as he pulled onto the road, a brief flash of flames bursting from his tailpipe as he sped away.

5

VINCENT

The last time I'd seen Jessica, she'd been on her knees begging to suck my cock. It was a particularly heady memory, the kind of thing I recalled far too often as my go-to wank material.

That Halloween party was almost three years ago. The universe would give and take as it pleased, so when Jess ghosted after that night, I took it as a sign. It simply wasn't meant to be. Regardless of history, longing, or whatever the hell else existed between me, my friends, and her, fate worked its mysterious ways and drew us in opposite directions.

I could usually accept that. When the universe flows, flow with it. Let fate take its path.

But damn, sometimes the universe surprised me. Sometimes

its signs were subtle, and sometimes they were massive, flashing, and undeniable.

Today was one of those undeniable signs; I could feel it.

Jess had always been poised, dripping with confidence. The type of woman who could intimidate you with a glance. But today, she'd been flustered, uncertain, distracted.

I couldn't help but wonder if she thought about that night like we did? Did it haunt her, lurking in the corridors of her mind? Did it come out in the dark? Did she touch herself to the memories?

We did. We *all* did. Jason would scoff at the idea, Lucas would vehemently deny it, and Manson would claim she never even crossed his mind. But they were all liars. Manson still had her thong, although he thought he was sneaky about it. I'd caught Lucas stalking her social media several times.

The deep scowl on Jason's face for the rest of the day proved he couldn't get her out of his head. He got all sulky and broody when he was faced with a problem he couldn't fix, and Jess was exactly that.

A damn problem that none of us could figure out.

"I doubt she'll be sticking around long," Manson said. When I mentioned we'd seen her, he looked like I'd slapped him before he quickly buried the expression. "She'll be gone again before summer is over."

Lucas looked pissed off, as usual. "Good riddance to her. This damn town doesn't need any more issues."

As if he was one to talk. Lucas had more issues than Playboy magazine.

I was sure they were wrong. Shit like this didn't just happen —

it was a *sign*. There was a change in the air, a little more heat in the thick summer breeze. The Fates were weaving a new pattern into our lives, every thread tangling us a little closer to inevitable destiny.

Or maybe I was overthinking and waxing poetic. I was just pleased to be getting a little excitement in the midst of the summer doldrums. Watching Jess lean all over my car in those sexy little shorts and barely there bikini top had gotten my brain churning.

Whether or not Jess was here to stay, I needed to work out a little frustration.

I caught Jason when he was coming out of the shower, pinning him against the wall in the hallway with a towel around his waist and his hair still dripping.

"Oh, fuck." His breath hitched as I gripped him through the towel, teeth grazing over his neck. I caught his ear in my teeth, biting softly at first, but then harder as I moved my mouth down his throat. His arms twined around my neck and tangled into my hair, pulling it when I bit down hard on his shoulder.

"I need you upstairs," I said.

"One second, I'll —"

My arm snapped up, gripping his throat. I pressed my forehead to his so he couldn't avoid my gaze and snarled, "No, *now*."

That got a grin out of him.

I shoved him on the bed the moment I got him into the attic. I climbed on top of him, and he shoved his hands against my chest, trying to wrestle his way on top. I was taller, but he was doubtlessly stronger than me. The time he spent at the gym had honed his muscles to perfection.

Perfection in my eyes; he'd probably protest that declaration.

But strong as he was, he let me pin him. He needed to be overcome; he craved it. Held down, used and dominated, spared the struggle of being in control.

Not unlike Jess. The two of them were more alike than he cared to admit.

"You've been brooding for hours," I said, leaving the words in kisses and bites on his chest as I held his wrists pinned at his sides. He sucked in his breath sharply when I moved my mouth low on his abdomen, tracing my tongue below his navel, then biting him again. His muscles were rigid, veins swollen. When I tugged the towel away and tossed it aside, his cock was already hard. Long and veined, with a striking redness when he was erect. It made my mouth water for a taste of him.

"Haven't been brooding," he muttered, but the words died on his tongue when I took him into my mouth.

I preferred him a little dirty, but fresh out of the shower was nice too. His hips twitched as I took him deep into my throat, savoring the struggle of consuming his entire length. I curled my tongue along his shaft, popped him from my mouth, and said, "You don't fool me. Jess has been on your mind all day."

He stiffened, eyes opening wide as he gave a vehement shake of his head. "No, she hasn't. I don't care what she…what… she…fuck…"

I rose up, hunching over him as I wrapped my fingers tightly around his throat, and he gripped my arm. The black paint on his thumbnail was chipped from how much he'd been obsessively chewing. I pressed myself between his legs, forcing them apart, watching the storm rage in those blue eyes.

"You don't need to hide it from me," I said as his throat bobbed with a gulp and his heart hammered against my palm. I'd told him that so many times, and doubtlessly, I'd tell him many more. "You've been having dirty, sinful, perverted thoughts about her, haven't you? Tell me."

He gave a jerky nod, and I squeezed the sides of his throat, growling out a warning, "Don't move until I tell you."

I retrieved a coil of rope from one of my hooks on the wall. The attic was both my bedroom and my studio. Whether I was making art with paints and canvas or flesh and blood, I had plenty of space to work. I grabbed a blindfold too, a red bandana that I tied over Jason's eyes before I took my time tying him.

He relaxed as I moved him, binding the ropes around his arms and chest to secure his wrists behind his back. It was an intricate tie, but I wasn't in a rush. With every knot, my fantasies delved a little deeper.

What I wouldn't give to tie Jason and Jess at the same time, binding them until they could do nothing more than wiggle, then suspending them from the rafters to suffer for me.

"You've been thinking about her too." Jason's voice was muffled against the blankets, face down as I tightened a final knot. He tested the restraint, muscles tightening, grunting slightly when he strained against the rope.

"You're right." I squeezed his ass before I gave him a smack, smiling as the redness blossomed on his pale skin. "Want to hear what I've been thinking about?" He gave another nod, and I gripped his hair, pulling his head up from the bed. "*Words*, boy, use your words. Answer me."

"Yes, sir, I want to hear what you've been thinking about."

He sounded a little too snappy for my taste. I grabbed one of the pillows and placed it beneath his hips. He began to struggle again, but another smack stilled him before I gripped his ass and spread him. He gasped sharply when I buried my face between his cheeks. I stroked my tongue over his hole, rimming him until his thighs clenched and he was thrusting mindlessly into the pillow beneath him.

"Feeling a little more compliant?" I said.

"Yes, sir." His fingers were curling and flexing with restless energy. "I want to hear what you've been thinking. Please."

I loved hearing that desperation in his voice. I reached for the lube in the bedside drawer, coating my finger and then spreading a generous amount on him.

"I've been thinking about how much fun it would be to have you and Jess tied up side by side," I said, swirling my finger over his anus before I pressed inside. He groaned, muffling his mouth against the blanket again. "I could finger you both at the same time, see which one of you starts shaking first." He was already shaking and stiffened for a moment as he tried to stop himself. "Stretch you both until I can fist you. I'd love to have a brat impaled on both hands."

"It won't happen," he said, the words quivering. "You know it won't ever fucking happen."

"That's what you told yourself about me too, wasn't it?" I loved forcing him to keep talking when he could barely get out two sentences. I probed him, pumping my finger in and out as I added a little more lube. "And see how that turned out."

"She ghosted," he huffed, dissolving into a moan as I slowly added a second finger. "She doesn't...fuck...she doesn't want us..."

"Yes, she does." The way his ass squeezed around my fingers drove me wild. I wanted to bury myself inside him, hear him cry my name as I bottomed out. "She wants it, Jason. She wants you. Wants us. You really think that girl hasn't been obsessing over that night ever since it happened? After the way she acted today?" I curled my fingers inside him, pressing down against the small, firm bump of his prostate. "Do you remember how sexy she looked on her knees for us? How good her mouth felt around your cock?"

His fingers clenched into fists, desperate sounds punctuating his gasping breaths. He thrust against the pillow again, unable to stroke himself with his hands tied. I kept fingering him, massaging over that walnut-sized bump.

"I'd tie you both up," I said, my voice growing rough the more worked up I became. "Bend you over side by side, make you watch each other's faces while I edge you." I smacked his ass again, chuckling at his struggling. "Stop wiggling so much. You're not going anywhere."

I added more lube and a third finger. He pressed his mouth against the blankets and yelled, the sound sending a pleasurable shudder over my entire body. I leaned over his back, my fingers thrusting into him as I gripped his hair with my other hand.

"Tell me what you were thinking about all day," I said, my voice tight. It was getting harder to wait. My cock was straining against my jeans. "Tell me, no matter how embarrassing it is, no matter how much it makes you squirm. You're not getting up until you do."

"Goddamn it, please…" He arched back, pressing against my fingers. He never used to be very vocal in the bedroom, cringing in humiliation every time I made him talk about what was in his head. "She was fucking teasing us at the car wash, sir. I wanted…"

"Keep going," I whispered. "What did you want?"

"God, I wanted to pull down those tight little shorts and fuck her right there over the hood. Have the whole damn church watch us."

There it was. That's what I wanted to hear. I stretched my fingers inside him until he whimpered, demanding, "Mm, that's right. Fuck that pretty little cunt until she squirts all over your cock."

"Fuck, yes," he gasped. "I'd bend her over and make her suck you off while I fuck her. Pound her until her legs shake —"

He cut off with a cry as I pulled my fingers out of him. I couldn't wait anymore. I spread the lube onto my cock before I pressed against his entrance, the puckered hole still resisting. I went slow as I eased the first couple inches inside him.

"Make it hurt," he said, his voice vicious with need as he arched his back. I was happy to oblige.

I pressed fully inside, and he cried out again, his toes curling, struggling against the ropes that kept him helplessly restrained.

"Yeah? You'd fuck her until her legs shake?" I tugged his hair, gripping it hard as he squeezed around me. "You know she likes it rough."

"She was so fucking wet when she was on her knees for us," he said, his words bringing the memories back with stark clarity. I released Jason's hair, gripping his hips and pulling them up so I had a better angle. I reached around and stroked him, fucking him in unison with my hand. I was too worked up. I wasn't going to last long when he felt so good.

"I want to fuck her while you fuck me," he said, the words ragged, his thighs clenching. Every stroke of my hand made him shudder. "God, I want to feel her come on my cock. I want to see her smile like she did after she sucked her own juices off your fingers, sir." He drew in his breath sharply. "Fuck, you're going to make me come."

The image of Jess sucking my finger into her mouth pushed me to the point of no return. My pace increased and Jason brokenly cried my name, his cock pulsing in my hand as spurts of cum ribboned across the blankets beneath him. The ecstasy that overtook me was like a blackout. Nothing remained but our bodies throbbing in unison until I was spent, collapsing beside him with my cock still inside.

I pulled the blindfold off him, nuzzling my face against his neck. Maybe he was right. Maybe Jessica wasn't meant for us, and this lust — this longing — meant absolutely nothing. But I couldn't let it go. I hated the thought that I could feel so much, that I could be so ridiculously desperate to have her, and yet it would lead to nothing.

"I love you." His voice was rough with exhaustion, a drunken smile on his face as he floated through the afterglow.

"I love you, too." I gathered him closer, holding him tight against my chest for a few moments to catch our breath before I began the work of untying him.

I didn't like being told something was impossible. *Nothing* was impossible.

Our entire universe was barely organized chaos, the eternally echoing aftermath of an explosion at the beginning of time. Yet Jessica kept being brought back into our lives. Somehow, out of all the paths of destiny she could be drawn toward, this was where she ended up yet again. She'd pushed away but been pulled back.

So maybe Jason was right. Maybe seeing Jess today meant nothing at all. Or perhaps it meant that the Fates hadn't finished playing their messy little games.

It wouldn't be the last time we saw her. That much I knew with certainty.

6

JESSICA

I couldn't sleep at all that night.

I still hadn't gotten used to being back in my old bed, but it wasn't only that. I tossed and turned, drifting off into fitful half-sleeps before abruptly waking when strange dreams crept into my mind. By 1 am, I was simply staring at the ceiling, clutching one of my throw pillows against my chest, telling myself that the dreams meant nothing.

It was them. Jason and Vincent. The fact that I'd seen them, merely *talked* to them, had completely thrown me off.

It had been almost three years since I'd spoken to them, but that didn't mean they hadn't been occupying my mind. My obsession with them felt like an illness, an addiction I couldn't shake. I'd become a voyeur, watching their lives from afar and never reaching out.

I had stalked their social media like I was a private investigator, digging up every little detail I possibly could. It would have been easier if they shared more, but they were private people and their posts were infrequent.

Lucas and Manson owned an auto shop together, occasionally posting photos of them working in their garage over gleaming engines. There was one photo in particular — God, this was so embarrassing — that I'd found so sexy I had to save it to my phone. The two of them shirtless, hands blackened with grime, wearing only jeans and boots. I'd gotten off to it multiple times.

Out of all the porn I could look at, their simple photos were the ones I returned to.

Jason's account was private, but Vincent frequently posted photos. It was obvious all the boys were devoted to each other, but Jason and Vincent had a romance between them that made me ache. It wasn't jealousy. It was…longing? From the outside looking in, their love seemed exactly like the kind of relationship I wanted but couldn't put into words: freedom coupled with devotion.

But I'd been taught that wasn't possible, and my relationships so far had proved as much.

A relationship was a cage, full of restrictions and misunderstandings, frustrations and jealousy. Dating someone carried the requirement of turning off desire for anyone else, but I often found myself wondering if that was even possible for me.

Was I broken? Sexuality was nothing to be ashamed of, but it was hard to reconcile that when the friends and family I was surrounded by told me otherwise.

I squeezed my eyes shut, imagining them standing over me — Jason and Vincent, Manson and Lucas, too. Surrounding me, making me feel small. A shiver prickled over my skin as I tried to remember exactly how their hands had felt, brushing over my thighs, slipping between my legs.

I was never going to manage to sleep like this. An uncomfortably warm, restless feeling pulsed low in my abdomen.

I was too tired to reach under the bed for my vibrator. I slid my hand into my panties, determined to make it quick. I didn't *need* to fantasize, right? But as the touch of my fingers fed the warmth inside me, building it to a blaze, I couldn't stop my thoughts from wandering.

Manson had once told me that Vincent liked restraints. So when I imagined him touching me, I thought of handcuffs — cold metal clinging to my wrists and ankles. I imagined Vincent laughing at me, teasing me, my degradation making him smile.

I shuddered.

I could think of literally anyone else. A celebrity. Maybe that hot girl I'd seen at the coffee shop the other day, or the guy I'd fucked around with at a club last year. Anyone other than *them*. But no matter who I pictured, their faces morphed, their voices changed, their actions and mannerisms were undeniable.

My brain refused to settle for anyone else as my pleasure deepened and my breaths came a little faster.

I envisioned Vincent chaining me to the bed while Jason circled me. Jason's gaze felt like it could rip me apart, like he saw too much. As if he knew my vulnerabilities and could pluck them all out with expert precision.

He always wore rings. Thick silver rings and black-painted

nails. I imagined those nails disappearing inside me, fingers thrusting into me. I remembered the taste of his cock and the sight of him standing over me.

My fingers tightened on the sheets.

Manson had loved watching them. It had been obvious that being a voyeur turned him on. In my imagination, he was still watching. Circling. Barely visible in the dark around my bed.

"The more you fight, the worse it'll be."

The words slithered around my stomach. Fighting was useless anyway, there was no way I could overcome them. Vincent would bind me too tightly to ever get away.

But I wanted more. More pleasure, more stimulation…more fear. I wanted to feel the thrill of being bound and helpless. I wanted to completely lose control.

"The dirty little slut likes it, doesn't she?" I imagined Lucas's voice saying the words, deep and rough. He'd always been so damn unpredictable. Angry, heartless — he fucking hated my guts, but that made it even better.

I moved my fingers faster, trying to resist holding my breath. I envisioned Manson standing over me, that crooked smile on his face. God, he would love to watch me squirm as the others used me. I was a toy to be used, merely holes to be filled. The thought made me tingle from head to toe.

In my fantasy, Manson grasped my throat and whispered, *"I'm going to watch them fucking destroy you, angel."*

Destroy me. Ruin me. Force me into the corruption I craved.

I wanted to feel like I was being punished. Punished for treating them like shit in high school and then being just as awful when I met them later. Punished for making decisions I regretted but couldn't change.

I pressed my hand over my mouth before a moan could slip out. But I imagined it was Vincent's hand instead, and he was scolding me in that playfully sarcastic voice of his.

"Sshh, don't be too loud now. You wouldn't want Mommy and Daddy to hear, would you?"

My toes curled. Liquid heat rushed through my veins, searing me from the inside out. For a few moments, my mind blanked out, filled only with that perfect explosion of ecstasy. I was left dazed in the afterglow, my tension melting away and my muscles going limp.

Maybe now I could finally get some sleep.

I pulled up the covers, but the fantasies didn't leave me as easily as my satisfied lust. They were still there, lurking in my dreams.

I'd ghosted them, and yet I was the one who felt haunted.

The next few days passed in a blur. By the morning of July 4th, my mom's team of volunteers had completely transformed the empty field alongside the church. There were game booths, bouncy houses, and face painting. The rich greasy smell of burgers and hotdogs filled the air, smoke from the grills wafting through the crowds.

I worked the ring toss game for most of the morning, and wrangling the kids quickly grew tiring. I'd never been particularly good with children, but I also wasn't a very patient person. My mom used to scold me for it constantly.

Luckily, a familiar voice drew my attention in the midst of my boredom. "Stuck with volunteer duty, huh?"

I stood up from collecting the plastic rings strewn in the grass to see one of my old classmates, Danielle, smiling at me from the front of the game booth.

"Hey, girl! Long time, no see!" Danielle and I had been on the cheerleading team together in high school, and we'd kept up casual contact since then. She could be an absolutely ruthless bitch, but we'd always gotten along.

We both had too much dirt on each other to risk *not* getting along.

"My mom generously volunteered my time," I said, rolling my eyes. "At least I didn't get stuck with the face-painting booth."

"You'd be poking kids' eyes out with those claws," she said, eyeing my signature acrylic nails. "So, you're back with your parents, huh? Rough shit. I can't imagine moving back in with my family now that Nate and I are living together. My mom and I would probably murder each other."

Danielle and Nate had gotten engaged last year. They'd been high school sweethearts, so I couldn't say it was a surprise. The only real surprise was that Danielle was settling down at all.

"Oh yeah, you already get it," I said. "If I end up arrested...you'll know why. I need to get myself out of that house again, ASAP."

"You're coming to the bonfire tonight, right?" she said, stepping aside and glaring at the little kid who was eagerly reaching for his turn with the rings.

"Bonfire?" I said. "I didn't know about it."

"Oh, you've got to come!" She pulled out her phone. "Your number is still the same, right? I'll send you the details. We should have a good view of the fireworks, too. *Everyone* is going to be there. It'll be like old times. Plus, Nate and I live really close, so you're totally welcome to crash at our place after." Her phone chimed, and she sighed as she read the message. "Oops, I have to get going. Nate wants another damn twenty-four pack of Coors." She rolled her eyes. "Just what I wanted to be doing — shopping for beer on the 4th."

"See you later, girl." I waved as she left. A night out was exactly what I needed. I could have a few drinks, catch up with everyone, and watch the fireworks. It would be a nice opportunity to get my mind off...other things.

I managed to slip away from the festival after a few more hours when one of the other volunteers took my place. I had just enough time to shower and change before the bonfire. I didn't anticipate it being very cold that night, but a light jacket over my crop top and jeans would be enough. Most of my clothes were still packed and I didn't feel like rummaging through the boxes, but there were only a few choices in my closet.

My hand trailed over a soft black hoodie and I plucked it from its hanger. It was too big for me, but it wasn't mine. The back was emblazoned with a black sheep wearing a wolf's head hood. I glanced at my closed door, as if I was a teen again doing something wrong, before I brought the hoodie to my nose and deeply inhaled.

Maybe it was my imagination, but even after all these years, I swore it still smelled like him.

Manson Reed. He'd put it on me the morning after the Halloween party, the morning after...

I couldn't think about it too much. I slipped it on, grabbed my keys and my bag, and flicked off the light before I left the room.

The sun had set and fireworks lit up the sky as I drove toward the location Danielle had given me. I pulled off onto a narrow dirt road that led back into some clustered trees. It wasn't surprising to see numerous vehicles already parked there.

Some of them sat low to the ground, imported cars with huge exhaust pipes and large spoilers. Others were American classics, built sleek and loud, covered in gleaming chrome. Then there were the lifted trucks, rumbling diesels on thick tires.

If there was anything that could give Wickeston's love of football a fierce competition, it was the love of cars. Classic American muscle was the ideal, but it looked like imports were gathering a strong following, judging by the number of them I saw. I knew next to nothing about engines, but I appreciated the aesthetics of a sleek car.

And I appreciated the speed.

Some of the trucks had been parked in a semi-circle around the massive bonfire, their tailgates open to share coolers of beer. People sat around the fire in folding chairs or milled around in groups, drinking beer, vaping, and smoking their cigarettes. Music was blasting from someone's sound system, and my excitement rose as the sounds of laughter and conversation permeated my car.

I'd always thrived in front of a crowd. Getting people to like me — or fear me — felt like a game I couldn't bear to lose. I already knew a few of the people who would be here, but it was likely that everyone already knew *me*.

That was the funny thing about being the "former popular girl." You were less a person and more an object of fascination, like the latest reality show on TV. People liked you in the same way they liked their favorite celebrity.

Their *idea* of you was what mattered. Reputation was everything.

I parked and flipped down my mirror to do a quick face check. I probably should have put on another coat of concealer; my mom had warned me how bad my dark circles were getting.

Whatever.

The night air was crisp, rich with the scent of wood-smoke. The flames cast dancing shadows across the oak trees, smoke rising in curling tendrils toward the night sky. The pop and crackle of distant fireworks inspired some cheers from those who were able to see the explosion from the edge of the trees.

I spotted Danielle on the other side of the bonfire and headed over.

"Yeeesss, I'm so glad you made it, babe!" She got up from her folding chair to hug me, pressing an ice-cold seltzer into my hands. "Let's get some alcohol in you. It's time for the *real* party."

Nate was seated beside her, and he gave me a friendly nod but said nothing. He wasn't the only one of my ex's friends in attendance. Alex McAllister and Matthew Fink were here too.

"Welcome back to good old Wickeston, Jess," Alex said, pulling me into one of his too-tight hugs. Alex, Matthew, and Nate had all been on the football team with Kyle, and they'd formed a unit that went almost everywhere together.

I knew them well, probably *too* well. Nate was the son of a local police officer and had gotten away with more illegal shit than anyone I knew. Matthew used to get blacked-out drunk before every game because he said it made him "play better." And Alex? He'd been Kyle's best friend, his right-hand man.

Then he tried to make a move on me while Kyle and I were broken up. I turned him down and never mentioned it again, but to judge by his *very* friendly hug, his interest hadn't dwindled.

Ashley used to call him "skeevy," and that was the first word that came to mind as his arms finally loosened from around me.

"City life wasn't doing it for you?" he said.

"Trust me, I'd rather still be in the city," I said. "Would I rather still be paying city prices? Hell no."

I couldn't afford a Nashville apartment, food, and bills off an intern's measly wages; that much was certain. New York felt even further out of reach, but with the right salary, I could make it happen. I just needed to convince my boss I was worth it.

"Sounds like you need a side hustle," he said, reaching into a nearby cooler for another cold can. "I've heard OnlyFans is hiring. I'll be your first subscriber."

His gaze slid over me pointedly, and I rolled my eyes. "Oh, ha ha, very funny. Keep dreaming."

He shrugged, but the way he was looking at me was hardly casual. Alex was hot, no doubt about it. He was exactly the type I usually went for: broad-shouldered with a handsome face, cocky with a massive ego. But I was getting tired of dating the same damn type and getting the same damn results.

Besides, he was my ex's best friend. The idea of dating him felt slimy.

Danielle and I had plenty to chat about and she swiftly

launched into relaying every bit of gossip she knew about our former classmates. Who was married, who was pregnant, and who had ended up in prison. Alex was restless though, and kept glancing up every time another car pulled in.

"Waiting for someone?" Matthew said, crushing his empty can under his shoe.

"He's probably staring at his *baby* again," Danielle teased, rolling her eyes before she explained to me, "Alex did some fancy new thing to his car and now he can't stop talking about it."

"Which one is yours?" I said, and Alex pointed beyond the fire, toward a red Dodge Challenger.

"It's a Hellcat," he said proudly. "Got a new tune on her too. Baby fuckin' hauls ass."

A backfire rang out like a gunshot, and all of us turned our heads toward the road. Whoever had just arrived sounded loud; I could hear their engine long before I could see them. Headlights flashed as they turned into the trees, and Alex slowly got to his feet with folded arms.

"Well, well, well," he said. "The losers decided to show up."

Two cars were approaching, their windows so tinted I couldn't see inside. My breath stilled in my lungs when I spotted the sleek purple Mustang in the lead, violet-colored neon glowing from its undercarriage, the engine rumbling aggressively. I wouldn't have recognized it if I wasn't such a social media stalker, but I knew instantly who it belonged to.

Manson. He'd made a significant upgrade from that old Bronco he used to drive.

A white Nissan 350Z cruised behind him, practically gliding

over the ground, bass bumping loudly from its stereo. That car was Jason's, and if the videos I'd seen Vincent post were any indication, it was a force to be reckoned with in the amateur drift world.

My stomach twisted, and my can crinkled slightly in my hand. If the two of them were here, then all of them were. But I couldn't disappear this time.

My own specters were back to haunt me.

7

JASON

Encased in tinted glass, with the engine rumbling beneath me and bass pumping through my speakers, I felt untouchable. My mind was calm, focused, settled into meditational clarity. My constant racing thoughts and twitching fingers were calmed by the engine's steady drone.

That, and by Vincent's lips wrapped around my cock, gliding his tongue along my shaft.

I slid my fingers through his hair and gripped it, twisting the long brown locks in my fist. He preferred my hands tied, either tight behind my back or raised above my head with me stretched onto my toes. But it was my turn to be in charge.

I needed my hands free to force his head down, fucking into the back of his throat until he choked.

I didn't want to come, not yet. Watching him take me all the way down and feeling his throat clench nearly threw me over the edge into rapture. But I forced myself to wait, hanging dangerously at the precipice of bliss.

I gasped, my entire back going rigid as Vincent hummed and his throat squeezed around me.

"Oh, fuck —" My mind went blank for one precious split second. One moment of pure brain-numbing pleasure, but I surfaced, gasping for air.

"Holy shit..." I went limp against the seat as Vincent slowly lifted his head, giving me a Cheshire cat's wide grin.

"Did you like that?" His voice was husky as he reached across the seat and cupped my face.

"I fucking loved it," I said, chuckling as I came back down to earth. He turned my head toward him for a kiss, my tired body still reacting to that obscenely skilled tongue of his.

I was thankful for the tinted windows and the privacy they gave us. Crowds made me nervous — you could never know who among them would turn on you in a heartbeat. Say the wrong thing, look the wrong way, or kiss the wrong person and you were fucked.

When people saw something that ran contrary to what they held up as *right* and *good*, things could get violent quickly. My mother had never hit me until I told her I wasn't religious. My father had never even raised his voice until a "concerned neighbor" outed me to him, with the damning evidence of having seen Vincent and I fucking around in his Subaru. Words like "bisexual" meant nothing when a father was convinced his son was going down a life of sin.

But fuck all that. I'd embrace sin and launch myself straight into hell if it meant not having to live under someone else's arbitrary rules for my life. I tucked myself away, adjusting my sweatpants back into place.

Yeah, sweatpants at a party. I really couldn't be bothered trying to impress people with my looks. I was 5'7" with a messy head of blue hair that barely hid the ears I'd been told my whole life were *too big*. That shit used to eat me up inside, knowing I'd never be one of those six-foot-something chiseled guys with a perfect amount of facial hair and body mass. It didn't matter to me anymore.

I turned off the engine, the laughter and shouted greetings from outside threatening to intrude on my isolated world. I glanced over at Vincent and found him watching me, a grin still curving his mouth.

"Ready?" he said.

I nodded. "Ready."

Manson and Lucas were leaning against the Mustang and passing a cigarette between each other when we joined them. Lucas looked so serious you'd think he was there for a funeral instead of a party.

"Damn, boys, turn down the smiles," Vincent said. Even when he was sober, Vincent was chill. A by-product of having so much experience being in the wrong place at the wrong time. He slung his arm around my shoulders and held up his THC vape, offering me a hit. I inhaled slowly, held it for a moment, and blew away the vapor into the night sky.

"You got the beer?" Lucas said.

"Yes, sir." I moved to the back of the car and popped the hatch. My car was sitting pretty, slammed low and wide as hell with that Rocket Bunny kit I'd finished installing last weekend. I still had a few weeks before my next competition, so I couldn't resist the opportunity to show it off tonight.

Besides, it was good advertising for Manson and Lucas, considering they'd helped build the engine. Any business we could bring in was good for all of us.

"Let's get it started then, boys," Manson said, holding up a twelve pack of IPAs from his trunk. The box of cheap beer I'd brought was to share, but Manson had the good stuff.

"Why do we come to this shit?" Lucas muttered, puffing at his cigarette as he scanned the faces spread among the trees. "I fucking hate half the people here."

"What about the other half?" Manson said, tossing a beer to me before opening one for himself.

Lucas shook his head. "Don't like them either."

Manson snorted. "Right. Let's get some alcohol in you before you start shit."

"I don't start shit," Lucas grumbled. He was about to pop the top on his can, but the cigarette suddenly went slack in his mouth as he stared toward the bonfire. "Holy fuck. I've just seen a ghost."

We all turned; Vincent a little too quickly because he was probably anticipating an actual paranormal incident. But there was only one ghost who would make Lucas look simultaneously furious and confused. I knew who it was even before I saw her.

Jessica sat on the other side of the fire, her oversized hoodie unzipped and a tight cropped shirt hugging her cleavage. Her long blonde hair was swept over her shoulder, her legs crossed, seated in her folding chair with all the confidence of a queen.

My perfect mental calm instantly shattered.

I'd tried to keep her out of my head, tried to forget the fantasies that Vincent took such pleasure in forcing out of me. Sometimes it disgusted me that I thought about her at all. The woman who used to demand I do her homework for her, who cheated off my tests, and taunted me for everything from my clothes, to my soft voice, to my ears. She shouldn't have come anywhere near my fantasies.

God, but she did. She popped up into my perverted daydreams again and again.

Jessica had never been a woman to back down from a challenge, never one to let anyone know she was afraid. As we stared, her eyes flickered toward us.

The look of absolute horror on her face when she realized we were looking back was priceless. She looked just as flustered as she had when Vincent and I ran into her at the car wash.

"I told you she was back in town," Vincent said. He was holding back a grin, and I could tell he was reading way too much into this situation. We'd now seen Jess twice in a month, which surely meant destiny, fate, or some other grand mysterious power was behind it.

"What are the fucking odds she'd be here?" Lucas said.

"Considering there's fuckall to do in Wickeston except this, pretty good odds actually," I said. I set my thumbnail between my teeth and bit. If I had to stare at her all damn night, I'd have no nails left at all. "Have any of you ever known Jess to miss a party?"

Manson set his beer down on the Mustang's roof, eyes fixated on the blonde woman like a dog that had spotted a fresh cut of meat.

"We should go say hello," he said.

Vincent nodded quickly. "We should."

Lucas shook his head. "We should stop trying to catch a ghost." But his words didn't hide his interest. He kept looking at her.

My common sense wanted to side with Lucas. But the obsessive side of my brain couldn't leave well enough alone. I still wasn't sure what it was about her that had always kept me so fascinated. She was a massive puzzle I couldn't figure out, an unanswered question, a problem without a solution.

She was a challenge, and God, I loved a challenge.

"She gives good head for a ghost," I said, and Vincent nodded his agreement again. The memory of Jess begging for a taste of my cock was one I'd never forget. It was the kind of surreal moment a guy like me could only dream of, the most untouchable girl in school *wanting* to take me in her mouth.

"Be nice, J," Manson said, in that tone of voice that gave me a little chill down my back. Manson had his pills, his therapy, his meditation and all that shit, but there was still something dark in him that would never quite go away. Something born because it had to be, and alive because nothing could kill it.

That thing, that monster inside him, had gotten a taste of Jess and nothing else could satiate it.

I'd known better, but I think Manson had really believed something would come out of that night at the Halloween party. Something more than just a fuck. Maybe he thought Jess would change, that suddenly she'd realize how badly she wanted us. Maybe he thought she would stick around, integrate into our fucked-up family unit as if she didn't already have a perfectly cushy homelife.

Fat fucking chance.

"I guess there's no harm in a little conversation," Lucas finally said. The corner of his mouth twitched in something like a half smile, and I got a sinking feeling in my stomach. Lucas smiling wasn't a good thing; it wasn't because he was thinking happy thoughts.

No, that wasn't a *happy thoughts* smile. It was an *I'm going to start shit* smile.

8

JESSICA

"Ugh, God, I can't believe they showed up here," Danielle said, her voice low with disgust as she took a quick glance at the four men who'd just arrived. "Remember when they used to be *scared* to be at the same parties as us?" She rolled her eyes. "Ever since Mrs. Peters took Manson as her little charity case, now he and his friends show up everywhere."

I nodded along as she kept complaining. The fire was far too warm and my leg wouldn't stop bouncing. I tried to focus on what she was saying, but my stomach was full of butterflies and it was impossible to concentrate.

What the hell was wrong with me?

I kept glancing over at them, those four darkly dressed men with guarded expressions. They knew I was here and they were looking back, watching me with the same caution I was watching them with.

Danielle was right. There had been a time when they never would have set foot at the same party as me or anyone else in the *popular* crowd. But that was the past, and as everyone had gotten older, the lines between "us" and "them" had blurred. The popular kids and the outcasts didn't have such a wall between them anymore, but mingling groups inevitably led to conflict.

Not everything could be forgiven and forgotten, no matter how much time had passed.

I was sitting with three of the men who'd tried to beat Manson to a bloody pulp for making out with me. Honestly, it had been so damn satisfying to see them all knocked down a few pegs when Manson scared the shit out of them with that knife.

But Alex, Nate, and Matthew hardly looked scared now. They looked pissed, tense. It was obvious that with Kyle gone, Alex had slid into his place as some kind of unspoken leader. I'd seen enough brawls in my life to know that his simmering tension would likely result in fists thrown.

Excusing myself, I hurriedly got out of my seat and walked away from the fire to rummage for another drink in one of the coolers.

A shiver went up the back of my neck as I was fishing around in the ice, but it wasn't from the cold.

"Jessica fucking Martin."

The voice behind me was a harsh whisper, rough with bitterness. I knew instantly who it was.

I turned, bottle in hand, a sarcastic smile on my face. "Lucas fucking Bent. Is that how we do greetings now?"

There was a weight to Lucas's deep-set eyes that was suffocating, and it only grew heavier when I spoke. He looked at me like he wanted to peel back my flesh and see the bones beneath. He was wearing a black tank top and ragged denim jeans, his folded arms covered with the bold lines of numerous tattoos.

The happy face inked on his cheek mocked me. So damn cheerful despite the scowl on his face.

"Long time, no see," Jason said as he came to stand by Lucas's side, his eyes moving coldly over every inch of my exposed skin.

We were standing at the back of Nate's white truck, and the cab hid us from those around the fire. But nerves still roiled in my stomach as I looked at Vincent, watching me with slyly narrowed eyes from behind Lucas.

I shouldn't have indulged in those fantasies about them. How the hell was I supposed to act normal around men I'd imagined fucking me until I screamed, tying me up and making me crawl like an obedient little slut?

They were only fantasies, but if given the chance, these men could make them real. I licked my lower lip, drawing it into my mouth and biting down until I risked drawing blood. I desperately needed this drink.

"Bonfire too warm for you?" There was a teasing tone in Vincent's voice. "Or does something else have you feeling hot… and bothered?" He reached over and gave Jason a nudge, the two of them chuckling like it was an inside joke.

It was like they *knew*. As if Jason's bright blue eyes could see straight into my soul.

I curled my lip at their teasing grins. "Oh please, don't flatter yourselves. Move along." I waved my hand at them as if to shoo them out of my way. I doubted I was the only one beating back dirty thoughts, not that I'd ever admit to it.

Lucas didn't move. He stood in front of me like a barricade, his hard expression daring me to step around him.

"We'll take three beers before you go," he said, a cold challenge in his voice.

I laughed at his utterly ludicrous request. He wanted me to fetch beers for *them*?

"Uh, no, you can get your beers yourself." I was trying to get the cap off my bottle, but my hand kept slipping. Were these not twist-offs? The hell?

Lucas snatched the bottle from my hands, set it against his molars, and popped the cap off with his teeth before offering it back to me. Something fiery exploded in me as I stared at his fingers wrapped tight around the cold glass.

That shouldn't have been hot, but…fuck.

"You think I want that now that your mouth has been on it?" I said, unable to muster up my usual venom. It was so embarrassing how uncertain I sounded.

When Lucas laughed, it wasn't pleasant. It wasn't *nice*. It was the kind of laugh you heard before someone died in a horror film.

"I think you'd like my mouth on more than this bottle," he said. Vincent and Jason exchanged another amused glance, and I had the distinct feeling that I was being laughed at.

"Hey now, let's play nice, kids," Vincent said. "Why don't you be a good girl, Jess? The cooler is right there." He glanced behind me, his eyes widening pointedly. "The beers, please."

Good girl. He really dared to say that to me. That phrase had a way of squirming deep into my brain and latching on, its poisonous bite making my knees weak and my palms sweaty.

A traitorous little voice inside me wanted to obey. It wanted to feel the satisfaction of giving in.

With a furious exhale, I tossed each of them a beer with the sourest expression I could muster. Just because I was obeying didn't mean I was going to act happy about it. Lucas looked so damn smug as he took the bottle from my hands.

I wasn't going to give him the satisfaction of another reaction. I avoided his eyes as I squeezed myself past him, trying not to deeply inhale his scent, but I got a whiff of it anyway.

Dark like black pepper, but there was a hint of something soft, like jasmine. It made me hesitate for a moment, my breath catching slightly as he looked down at me.

God, why did he *look* at me like that? Like he was enraged and fascinated at once. Or like he was holding something back…

I turned away from him, only to abruptly encounter another problem. A tall, pale, dark-eyed problem with a grin that ran an icy finger up my spine.

"I told them to be nice," Manson said. I'd already caught my breath; but finding myself so close to him made me forget to breathe entirely.

His arms were bare and, like Lucas, he was far more heavily inked than when I'd last seen him. The twisted body of a snake was tattooed around his shoulders, the lines barely visible above his shirt collar. He plucked the beer from Vincent's hand — who gasped with overexaggerated offense — then popped the top and handed it to me. "No drool on this bottle, I promise. I'll punish these clowns later for their bad behavior."

"Oh *no*, Daddy Manson is *angry*!" Vincent laughed. Jason clutched his heart, adopting a look of abject horror in Manson's direction.

"Please forgive us, Jess," he said, clasping his hands dramatically. "Tell Manson you forgive us."

"No," I deadpanned, rolling my eyes at their antics even though my insides were quivering to have them all so close to me. These men had trampled all over my pride the last time I'd seen them, yet no hook-up since had come close to replicating what I'd experienced with them — complete and total submission, if only for a night.

And Manson...

Manson had opened my eyes to a world I'd never known I so desperately wanted to be a part of.

I couldn't look at his lips without remembering their taste. His eyes were intense; not heavy like Lucas's or sharp like Jason's. They were eerie, like a vague silhouette in the dark, a whisper in an empty house.

"You're in my way," I said softly. I pressed two sharp acrylic nails against his chest, giving him a little push. "Move."

I'd called him Master that night, the last time I'd seen him. I could still remember how it had felt rolling off my tongue. How sweetly natural, how deliciously *right*.

But it wasn't right. Me and him, me and them, could never be right.

Manson didn't move. He spread his arms with a shrug and said, "Looks like there's plenty of ways to walk around me."

Sure, I could have easily stepped around him, but now it was the principle of the thing. He needed to move *because I said so*, and he wasn't going to — for exactly the same reason.

Clearly, we would both just have to stand there glaring at each other until we died.

Manson searched my face as I stared back stubbornly, a small smile playing at the corner of his mouth. "Is it really that hard to give an inch, Jess?"

"Yeah, Jess." Jason meandered closer beside me, sipping his beer. "Can't even give an inch when Manson gave you eight?"

Manson snorted, utterly failing at holding back a laugh as my face tightened with embarrassment. "So you *do* think about it."

"Excuse me?" I sputtered. "I don't think about *anything*. I —" I stopped abruptly at more laughter from Vincent and Jason, realizing exactly what I'd said. I was really doing a fantastic job of appearing calm and collected. "I don't think about it, Manson. Why would I still be dwelling on something that happened years ago?"

He looked so damn pleased with himself. He thought he was so *smart*, didn't he? As if he had it all figured out, as if he had *me* figured out.

"Don't worry, Jess, it's not only you." Vincent shot Manson a mischievous look. "Manson thinks about it too. He still has your panties in his drawer."

Now it was my turn to laugh. The satisfaction of seeing Manson Reed's face turn the slightest shade of pink instantly put me in a better mood. He glanced over at Vincent and said flatly, "I really am going to beat your ass later."

All right, time to get it together.

"Well, as much fun as this has been, you're still in my way," I said, sighing. "Congratulations, yes, you all got a piece. Woooo, I sucked your dicks!" I gave a mocking pom-pom shake with my hands. "I can tell that it was, like, a really big deal for all of you. Sorry about the lack of action in your lives, but..." I shrugged. "A dick is a dick, and you're all just four on the list."

I jumped as Lucas growled in my ear, "Tell me how many of the dicks on your list were pierced, then?"

Of course he had to bring that up. I already couldn't look at him without my brain becoming a giant marquee that flashed: *Pierced Dick, One Night Only, Get Your Fill of Some Prime Pierced Dick!*

Lucas nodded as if my silence proved his point. "Yeah, that's what I thought. Can't forget that so easily, can you?"

I needed all of them to get away from me before I fell down into another orgy rabbit hole. Arguing with them wasn't only making me flustered — it was turning me on. Every biting word they said made me a little more excited.

How far could I push them? How far would they push *me*? I liked a challenge, but these men managed to shake the very foundations of my confidence. Not knowing if I could win made it that much more thrilling.

"Is there a problem here?"

All the boys turned. Alex stood behind Manson, with Nate and Matthew behind him. Their expressions were grim, their stances tense. This party was about to have much bigger problems than some petty teasing.

To say these men had a problem with each other was an understatement. Alex, Nate, and Matthew had all backed up my ex when he'd gone after Manson, but Alex and Lucas had beef of their own too.

Junior year, Lucas had smashed a glass bottle on Alex's head and knocked him out cold in the middle of the cafeteria. Five stitches and a short hospital stay later, Alex came back with a scar and Lucas never returned. Expelled.

I could still see that scar on Alex's forehead, partially covered by his hair. People said Lucas had tried to kill him, but honestly? I didn't believe it.

If Lucas had tried to kill him, Alex would be dead.

I should have walked the hell away from that mess. But my first instinct was to step between Alex and Manson, smile sweetly, and say, "No problems. We're good."

Alex looked like I'd slapped him. Then fury overtook his face, his jaw clenching so tight that a blue vein swelled near his temple. He was wrong if he'd thought he could swoop in and rescue me, as if I was some damsel in distress. This was *my* confrontation. I didn't need him bringing his own grievances into it.

"We're just catching up," Manson said. I was so close to him that when he shifted, he brushed against my back. "How've you been, Alex?"

I didn't understand how he could be so calm talking to the very man who'd been violent toward him on more than one occasion. But this wasn't the first time Manson's self-control had taken me by surprise.

"Can't complain." Alex said. "I saw y'all pull in. Noticed you didn't bring the El Camino tonight." He smiled, but the expression didn't reach his eyes. "Shame about whoever keyed it."

"You still owe me for that," Lucas said darkly. He'd stepped closer so he was right at Manson's side, cold hatred written all over his face.

"Chill out, Bent," Alex said. "I didn't touch your goddamn car. But even if I did, it's only fair. You cut up my head, I cut up your ride." He shrugged. "That would make us almost even."

There was a shuffle and Manson bumped against me. I glanced back to see he had whipped out his arm to stop Lucas from charging forward. He was braced against Lucas's chest, Vincent's hand was gripping Lucas's shoulder, and Jason, from behind him, said softly, "Let it go, bro."

But Lucas looked far beyond simply letting it go. Matthew's fists were clenched and Nate cracked his knuckles, the tension thickening with every audible pop.

"Would you all *quit* it?" I snapped. "Jesus Christ, what are we, sixteen?"

"Never knew you to be such a pacifist, Jess," Alex said. At least he finally dragged his eyes away from Lucas. "You suddenly think they're good guys now that you fucked one of them?"

I swallowed thickly, folding my arms. I hadn't told anyone except my best friend, Ashley, about hooking up with Manson. But apparently, the rumor had still gotten around.

I lifted my chin, knowing confidence was worth more than any petty insults. "Oh my God, Alex, get over it. Seriously, stop being a dick. Do you want to end up with the cops called and this whole thing shut down early?"

"Is that a threat?" Alex took one step toward me, shocking me with how rapidly his anger came to focus on me.

There was a soft sound, the scrape of metal on metal. Alex twitched as he lifted his eyes from my face.

"I'd suggest backing the fuck up," Jason said, his voice low. He'd stepped forward to stand on my left, and Manson nudged closer against my back. Vincent stepped up on my right, still keeping a grip on Lucas's shoulder.

"Chill out, McAllister," Vincent said, his usual jovial tone significantly subdued. "Plenty of room here for all of us, isn't there?"

To judge by Alex's expression, the whole town wasn't big enough for all of them. He sucked his teeth, shaking his head.

"I knew you all were cowards," he said. His mouth twisted with disgust, his eyes aimed right at Lucas. "Good thing you got your friends to make sure you don't start fights you can't win."

Lucas lunged, and this time, not even Manson and Vincent could hold him back. He got in front of me, right in Alex's face, the two of them staring each other down with clenched fists.

"Try me, motherfucker," Lucas hissed. "Come on. Fucking try me."

Alex spread his arms. "I'm right here! Too scared to throw a punch?"

I was certain I was about to see bloodshed. But Manson reached out, grabbed Lucas's shoulder, and jerked him back. For a moment, Lucas looked so livid I thought his fury was going to find a new target, but Manson didn't waver.

"If you've got a score to settle, do it behind the wheel," he said, his eyes moving between Lucas and Alex. "This is bullshit."

"Name the time and place," Alex said.

"Next Friday," Lucas said tightly. "We'll meet at the bridge off

Ellis Street, 10 pm."

Alex smirked. "All right, I'll be there. Better bring your friends." He looked down at me, his eyes lingering long enough to give me an uncomfortable feeling in my stomach. "Gets real dark down those old roads. It isn't safe to wander out there alone." He was speaking to Lucas, but it felt more like a warning for me. "We'll be seeing you."

Alex spat on the ground before he turned and stalked away, his friends moving with him. They rejoined Danielle, who was staring at me with wide eyes as if she couldn't make sense of what was happening. I was left with a pounding heart, nervous energy turning my stomach.

Then I saw the flash of a blade as it was tucked back into Manson's pocket.

"What the hell is wrong with you?" I gasped. Manson's glare was still fixed on Alex, his fingers digging into Lucas's shoulder. "Don't start shit. The knife? Really?"

"Don't start shit, she says." Lucas shook his head as he broke away from Manson's hold, rubbing his hand roughly over his buzzed hair. He tipped back his beer, drained the bottle, and muttered, "I need another fucking drink."

People were staring, murmuring to each other. But I didn't feel vulnerable until the boys stepped away from me, finally doing what I'd demanded all along and getting out of my way. Once they stepped back, the bravery I'd felt when I got between Manson and Alex was gone.

Manson was looking at me strangely, his expression unreadable. I glanced over at Danielle, who mouthed, *What are you doing?*

A great question, and one I couldn't even answer.

I sighed heavily, turning away from Manson and the others. My fingers were freezing from how tightly I was gripping my beer, and I was ready to get back to having a nice normal night out.

I needed this feeling inside me to die. This weird, shameful longing. This feeling that *I'd* done something wrong.

"Do you think you can keep pretending it didn't happen?"

I whirled around. Manson was smirking at me, hands shoved into the pockets of his jeans. The expression I'd found unreadable before was obvious now. It was anger. He was *angry* at me.

I walked back toward him. "What the hell does that mean?"

His smirk widened as I stood toe to toe with him. "Your cheeks got red the second you saw us. You *fantasize* about it." I opened my mouth to protest, but he cut me off. "That wasn't a question. It's obvious. Every time you get on your knees for some handsome airhead, you think it would be a lot more fun if I'd ordered you to do it, don't you? Maybe you even hear my voice in your head, telling you to kneel like a good girl, and it gets you wet enough to actually enjoy that subpar dick you've been fooling yourself with for the past few years."

Rage bubbled up inside me, overflowing as it seared through every limb. "How dare you say that to me —"

"Why? It's true. I can see it in your eyes, Jess, I can *see* it." The boys were watching, but Manson kept his voice low. "I know what it looks like when you lie. You wanted that night to be a fun little experiment. Everyone's wild in college, right? No big deal." He lowered his voice even further, bringing his mouth close to my ear. "But what happens when the experiment is too good? Turns out you're just as perverted as the freaks, but that doesn't fit Jessica Martin's grand life plan, does it?" Venom dripped from his voice, so shockingly angry that I held my breath. "You go chasing dick and realize none of it is quite as good. It's not the same. So you close your eyes and imagine it's one of us instead."

I looked at him in utter disbelief. I was so furious I barely trusted myself to speak. "You're disgusting."

He nodded slowly, as if he'd expected this all along. "Have a good night, Jess."

I scoffed. "What, are you dismissing me?"

"You spent the last five minutes telling me to move," he said, turning back to get a beer of his own. "I moved. You're right. I shouldn't start shit. I made that mistake last time."

Mistake. So it had just been a mistake to him.

All the furious words that wanted to pour out of my mouth wouldn't come. My chest ached, and my hands shook. He was right, but I could never, *ever* admit that to him.

I walked away before any more foolish words spilled out of me. I'd ghosted them. Me. It had been my choice, and I wasn't taking it back now.

9

JESSICA

"Okay, wow, what the hell happened?" Danielle was staring at me as I sat beside her, her expression torn between horror and disbelief. "Were they bothering you, Jess? That looked so creepy, I had to tell the guys to go check on you."

"I'm fine," I said sharply. I was painfully aware of everyone looking at me. Alex was glaring at me from the other side of the fire, Nate and Matthew were giving me major side-eye.

But beyond the fire, on the other side of the clearing between the trees, Manson, Lucas, Vincent, and Jason were staring too.

The subject was dropped, but my brain couldn't let it go, not even after I'd finished my drink and gotten another. My gaze was continually drawn by those four men standing in my peripheral vision. They didn't seem to give a damn I was there anymore, but that only irritated me more.

I kept catching brief pieces of their conversations even from a distance, their voices standing out to me. I desperately wanted to know what they were saying.

Were they talking about me? God, how pathetic was I to even wonder?

I shoved myself up from my chair, cutting Danielle off in the middle of whatever she was saying. "I have to go pee. I'll be right back."

I walked away from the fire, toward my parked car and then beyond it, looking for some privacy in the trees. At least it was quieter out here, save for the boom of the fireworks overhead. It gave me a chance to think.

What the hell did Manson mean, calling what we'd done a "mistake"? It shouldn't have mattered, but what he'd said was getting under my skin. He was mad it hadn't worked out, but so was every other guy I'd ever rejected. Why did I care?

I hurriedly did my business and cleaned up. I didn't feel ready to go back to the bonfire and put on a fake give-no-fucks smile. I couldn't do it. I leaned my back against one of the trees, taking a deep breath.

This was a temporary drama. I was only going to be in Wickeston for a few more months. Once Smith-Davies brought me on full time, I was out of here.

But that didn't make me feel any better. It didn't feel like solving the problem, only running away from it.

I tipped my head back in frustration, arms folded tightly. This was bullshit. Since when was I afraid of facing anyone and telling the truth?

Probably since Manson had made me realize that *my* truth was frightening and confusing.

There was a massive boom overhead as colorful sparks lit up the sky. The party was getting rowdy, people were shouting and there was a sound of breaking glass. Part of me wanted to sneak away and go home.

I peered around the tree as footsteps rapidly approached, gazing into the dark. It was Manson, but he hadn't seen me yet. He stopped about ten yards away with his back to me. He ran his fingers through his hair and sighed heavily as he gripped it.

He looked frustrated. Almost anxious. Apparently, I wasn't the only one bothered by all this.

He took his knife out of his back pocket as he stood there, idly flipping it open and closed. It was an unusual weapon, or at least I thought so. It was a butterfly knife, so the blade tucked into the handles and had to be flipped open. But Manson made it look easy, like it was second nature.

He played with it for a while without much focus, staring off into the trees. But he must have made a mistake, because when he flipped the knife around again, the blade caught his finger and sliced it open.

He hissed, and I gasped, and he immediately turned around. He slowly bent down, picking up the knife from where he'd dropped it. Blood dripped down his finger as he looked at me, his expression guarded.

"What are you doing out here?" he said.

I shrugged. "Same thing as you, I guess. Except I didn't cut myself."

He made a sound that could have been a laugh, but he wasn't smiling. He stroked the pad of his thumb over his bleeding finger thoughtfully. "That's what happens when you play with knives. Eventually you'll get cut."

"Maybe you shouldn't play with them, then."

He nodded. As if to reassure himself he could do it, he flipped the knife again. His fingers were quick and light as the blade swung out. The metal appeared impossibly fluid as he manipulated it through the air and caught it in his opposite hand.

I was suddenly feeling a hell of a lot warmer.

"I'm a bit of a masochist, I suppose," he said quietly, as if to himself more than me. "If there's no risk, where's the fun? It was my own fault. I didn't handle it correctly. The knife did what it's supposed to."

I stepped out from behind the tree and moved closer to him without even realizing what I was doing. He looked down at his bleeding finger curiously, a frown on his face.

"Maybe dull the blade," I said, and he scoffed.

"I knew what I was getting into when I bought it, Jess," he said. "It's supposed to be sharp, it's meant to be dangerous. No matter how much I practice, if I get lax, then I'll get cut."

Why did it feel like he wasn't talking about the knife anymore?

I didn't know what to say. I knew a million things I *should* have said, but I had no idea how to begin.

His face was partially hidden in the shadows. "Are you scared of me?"

I should have been. Him standing there with a knife in his hand and blood on his fingers…perhaps I should have been terrified of him.

But I wasn't. I shook my head.

He stepped closer until he was right in front of me. I fixed my eyes on his throat, saw it bob when he swallowed, traced my eyes over the goosebumps on his skin and the ink etched into his flesh.

"Jess."

I looked up. His eyes were almost black in the night.

"What are you doing out here?" he repeated the question, but it was different this time. He meant something different.

What was I doing out here?

"Playing with things I shouldn't," I said softly.

He lunged forward so quickly I didn't even have time to make a sound. He pressed me back against the tree and jabbed the knife's blade into the trunk high above my head, his arm extended as he clung to the handle. The thud of it hitting the wood left my heart hammering, the thrill of danger leaving tingles all over my body.

He lifted his bloody hand and moved it close to my cheek, but not close enough to touch.

"You might get cut playing like that." His voice was rough, and my stomach quivered. Things felt so different in the dark.

I reached up, carefully, to where his hand hovered near my face. It felt like a magnet locking into place when I put my fingers around his wrist. "I'm not afraid of a little blood."

His hand cupped my cheek, and his lips crashed into mine. I was completely overcome within a split second, all the air snatched out of my lungs, my brain short-circuiting into chaos. He kissed me like he was trying to make a point, like he was punishing me. We parted, and his finger dragged across my mouth...

I licked my lip and tasted iron, and he shuddered as something feral came over his expression.

"God *fucking* damn it, Jessica." His voice was desperately pained. He was so heavy against me, and I liked it too much. I liked the taste of him, how his blood was metallic and sweet on my tongue.

There was something wrong with me. Normal people didn't do this shit, right? But no one could see us. No one had to know...

His next kiss was slow. His entire body moved with it. Surging against me, overtaking me, filling my brain with this vast empty space full of only sensation.

It was as good as I remembered. Better. I'd tried to convince myself that I'd romanticized it all in my mind, but no. He was everything I remembered. His taste, his scent, his body.

He tugged the knife out of the tree and grasped my hand. He held my palm up between the two of us, slowly rubbing his thumb over my fingers.

"You're not afraid?" He watched my face carefully. He'd know if I lied.

I shook my head. "No."

Delicately, he pressed the sharp tip of the blade against the pad of my middle finger. There was a subtle sting as my skin parted, blood welling up. He moved the knife in slow small lines and I was mesmerized by the sight.

What he left behind was a tiny heart, etched into my finger. The pain wasn't even as bad as a papercut, so why did it feel like it sliced so deep?

He took my finger into his mouth and sucked it clean. I could hardly breathe. All I could hear was my own pounding heart in my ears. The feeling of his mouth enclosing me was so damn erotic I wanted to grab him, tear into him, rip that shirt off his body, and —

"You're wearing my jacket," he said. It was an accusation, like I'd done it on purpose.

None of this was on purpose. It just *happened* and then I didn't know what to do.

I looked down at my finger, allowing the blood to well up again before I pressed it against the collar of his shirt. He looked confused until I said, "Now you're wearing me too."

"Uh...Jess? What's going on?"

We both turned. Danielle stood a little ways away, looking between us in utter confusion as her flashlight illuminated us. Manson hurriedly put the knife away, and I hid my bleeding finger behind my back.

"I, um...I was on my way back," I said.

I looked up at Manson. His expression was shuttered again, the desperation I'd seen on his face completely hidden. I had no idea what to say. Whatever had just happened — that moment of chaos, those brief minutes of losing control — seemed like it could have been only a dream.

But that dream left its mark in blood.

He turned away, giving neither of us any acknowledgment at all before he stalked off, hands shoved inside his pockets. I watched him go until he disappeared beyond the parked cars.

Danielle hurried over to me. "Are you okay? What happened?"

I slipped my hand into my back pocket, pressing the cut against the denim. I had no idea how much she'd seen, and the thought made my stomach clench up with worry. "I'm fine. It was...it was nothing."

"Girl, that was not *nothing*. What were you —" She stopped suddenly. "Oh my God, wait. You *did* hook up with him a few years ago, didn't you? Holy shit. I thought that was only a rumor."

"Let's keep it a rumor," I said, my voice tight.

Luckily, she nodded hurriedly.

"Oh, yeah, obviously I wouldn't tell anybody! That would, like...really make a rift in the friend group." She lowered her voice. "Definitely don't let Alex find out. You know he has a thing for you."

I almost groaned. "Yeah. I guessed as much."

"But I won't tell him." She smiled sweetly, looping her arm through mine. "It's our little secret, babe."

I crashed at Danielle and Nate's place that night. She drove me back to pick up my car in the morning, bemoaning that she had to go into the office with a hangover.

She brought up again that she wouldn't tell anyone about seeing me and Manson in the trees. But instead of being reassured, I felt more like she was holding it over my head.

"I'll see you at the race next Friday!" she said, waving to me out her window as she drove away.

I was trying to *avoid* drama, not launch myself straight into the middle of it. Lucas and Alex's grudge race was bound to go badly, regardless of who won. But I couldn't deny how curious I was.

Every time I looked down at my hand and saw the scabbed

heart cut into my finger, a strange feeling of guilt and anger flooded me. Would it scar? Was that moment in the trees going to be a part of me forever, another tie to bind me to the men I wasn't supposed to want?

Another mark of my own indecision?

On Thursday, Danielle called to ask if I wanted to get dinner together before the race, insisting it wasn't an event to miss.

"Alex is going to win, easy," she said. "And you know he'd love for you to be there."

I didn't like the sly tone in her words. I'd told her I wasn't interested in Alex, but she seemed dead set on pushing for it anyway. First my mom, and now Danielle too? Why the hell couldn't people keep their noses out of my dating life?

"You, me, and Candace can sit back, relax, and get tipsy while the guys have their dick measuring contest," she said. I couldn't really think of a good reason to say no to a night out getting tipsy, so I agreed I would be there.

Candace was another friend from high school I hadn't seen in a while. She was a little airheaded, but she loved to have a good time.

That was what I needed, a fun night out proving to myself that I could be around Manson and his friends without turning into a flustered fool.

Friday night, I met up with Danielle and Candace for dinner before we headed toward Ellis Road. It ran along the very edge of a town, a long straight road entirely devoid of streetlights with open farmland on either side. Everyone was meeting at the bridge, and there were about a dozen people already there as I pulled up behind Danielle and parked in the dirt.

The trickle of the creek and chirp of crickets filled the air as we walked together to where Alex, Nate, and Matthew were waiting beside the Hellcat.

"Damn, so you decided to come after all," Alex said as he hugged me. He wore so much cologne that I swear it stuck to me as I pulled away.

"Of course I came," I said, as if it should have been obvious. "Wouldn't want to miss seeing what your baby can do, right?"

He gave me a strange look, one I couldn't quite discern. His competition hadn't arrived yet, so there was nothing else to do besides drink and wait. Danielle had brought wine coolers for us, and the three of us sat on a guardrail beside the bridge as we sipped.

"I've been telling Nate to put in a little tip to his dad that Lucas will be here tonight," Danielle said, laughing as she watched her fiancé throw his glass bottle off the bridge to shatter on the rocks below. "The cops would jump at the chance to arrest him."

"For what?" I said, my fingers tapping rabidly on my drink. "Drag racing? Alex would be screwed too."

Danielle sighed. "Yeah, I think that's why Nate didn't go for it."

"A guy like Lucas will end up in prison eventually anyway," Candace said. "Runs in the family."

I was about to ask what she meant, but a distant rumble caught my attention. As the sound grew closer, the crowd fell silent, staring across the bridge in anticipation. Alex leaned against his car, tipping back a beer as he watched the new arrivals.

Lucas's El Camino sat low to the asphalt, covered in gleaming chrome and midnight black paint. The engine rumbled loudly as he cruised down the road to stop alongside Alex, but when he tapped the gas, the noise roared to an ear-shattering pitch. The familiar blue Subaru behind him parked on the opposite side of the road, and Vincent, Jason, and Manson emerged.

"Don't you think it's weird they're always together?" Candace said. "Like, do they all go on dates together too?" She laughed and so did Danielle, but I couldn't muster up the amusement.

It was smart of them to stick together. Coming here alone would have been asking for trouble, but so was showing up at all.

I guess trouble didn't scare them. Manson had told me as much, hadn't he? If there's no risk, where's the fun?

Lucas got out of the driver's seat, stubbing out a cigarette on the asphalt. It took only a few seconds for his wandering eyes to fall on me. I'd always thought I could give a mean dismissive look, but Lucas proved he was fierce competition in that department. He gave me a once-over, then turned away as if I wasn't even there.

So much for not getting flustered. I was instantly peeved.

"Gross, here comes Miss Drama," Danielle muttered. I hadn't even noticed anyone else arrive, too distracted watching the boys as they gathered on the far side of the El Camino. But I turned my head at Danielle's announcement and groaned when I saw who was walking up, surrounded by a pack of friends.

Veronica Mills. The girl my ex had cheated on me with. Long dark hair, gorgeous curves, a confident smirk. She was the total hot girl package with an ego to match, and by the way she came strutting through the crowd, I knew nothing much had changed since I'd last seen her.

"Can't stand her," Danielle said.

"Total bitch," Candace confirmed.

"If she and the devil were drowning and I could only save one, I'd walk away," I said.

"She's only here to cozy up to her new favorite bad boys," said Danielle, winking as she looked at me.

Wait…she was here to do *what?*

That was when I realized where Veronica was heading. Certainly not toward our side of the road, not toward Alex.

She was here for Lucas.

Oh, hell no. Hell fucking no.

10

LUCAS

I'd shown up for the race that night for one reason and one reason only — to win. I didn't care about giving these lame fucks a night of entertainment. I wasn't going to put on some big dramatic show. That was what these people were hoping for. They wanted to see Lucas Bent, the guy who couldn't control his temper, lose control yet again.

But like Manson had said, we'd settle this behind the wheel.

I raced purely for the rush of it. It was one of the least destructive ways I'd found to release my pent-up energy, an outlet for the anxious electricity that made my limbs shake and my mind go hazy. It was this or fighting, this or drugs, and the other guys had done their damnedest to keep me away from both. Bless their bleeding hearts.

The speed and the power of racing was like nothing else. The adrenaline, the split-second decisions, teetering on the edge of complete destruction — I craved it, all of it.

Alex was glaring at me the second I stepped out of the car, and his face darkened even more when I gave him a simple nod and nothing else. He'd invited all these people out here to witness his own humiliation; he just hadn't realized it yet. He'd even invited...

Fuck. Jessica was here.

I caught myself too late to avoid looking at her. She'd been a goddamn tease since the first time I met her and nothing had changed in the years since. Her short dress left her legs bare, her tits enticingly framed by the bodice. She looked too damn good and it wasn't fair.

One quick look, and all I could think of was throwing her over the back of my car and fucking her until she screamed my name. Proving to every asshole here, once and for all, exactly where she belonged.

Exactly who she belonged *to*.

You fuck with one of us, you fuck with all of us. You're either with us or against us. Maybe the others were fine with her little games, but she made me feel like I was going to lose my mind. She walked the knife's edge of my patience, an edge that had grown so abysmally thin I was shocked she managed to keep her balance.

The headlights illuminated her gaze; her eyes the same dark green color of an oak tree's leaves in the middle of summer. They always looked clever, like she was focusing them slightly, like she had a million things churning behind them. And her mouth, her goddamn *mouth*. It was a sin for a woman to have lips like that.

I could remember perfectly how they'd felt, warm and soft

around my shaft as those eyes looked up at me from the floor. That image of her was branded into my brain — how surprised she'd looked when my pierced cock hit the back of her throat, how her eyes had watered as she worked to take me deep.

The tension that had been building in me all week grew even worse. If Jess wanted to watch Alex race, then she was going to watch him lose. I didn't know why the fuck she considered that bastard her friend. But she'd always surrounded herself with the worst kind of people, like a shield of assholes around her own insecurity.

He probably still thought he had a chance with her. I still remembered the way he used to talk about her, the things he would say when she and her ex couldn't hear.

That was how this whole damn feud had started. When I'd bashed Alex's head open with a bottle, it wasn't just me dealing with some anger issues. It was me dealing with him running his mouth about her, bragging that he'd seen nude photos of her on Kyle's phone. Whether or not it was true didn't matter. I'd wanted to fucking kill him and he was lucky I hadn't.

Jess was a bitch, but Alex was worse. If someone was going to mess with her, it was going to be me or my boys.

I joined Manson, Jason, and Vincent on the far side of the road. Jason didn't look pleased about the amount of people here, surveying the crowd with the hood of his jacket pulled low. I'd told them they didn't all have to show up, but they wouldn't hear of it.

Now that we were out here, I was glad not to be alone. All the people who'd come to watch were friends of Alex. We were on the very edge of town with no one else around. An ideal place for a drag race, but also ideal for an ambush.

"They all look like they came to see blood," Jason said dryly, shoulders hunching even more as he shoved his hands into his pockets. "This is sketchy as hell."

"Stick close to each other," Manson said. "Don't let anyone bait you."

I *wished* someone would bait me. I wanted to hit something, especially as Alex suddenly gunned his engine, yelling out the passenger side window, "Come on, Bent! Let's fucking go!"

Jason and Vincent stayed near the WRX as Manson walked with me to the car. I settled into the driver's seat as Alex burned out his tires, smoke pouring across the asphalt.

"You've got this," Manson said, his voice low as he leaned against the open window. "Remember what he really wants out of this. He'll be looking for an excuse to fight."

"So don't lose my temper," I said, nodding slowly. "One of my strongest qualities."

I could see Jess from here, sitting on the guardrail near the bridge. She was looking at me, at us. Her eyes were wide, the smoke from Alex's tires curling around her feet. Why the hell was she out here, getting involved in something like this? She needed someone to protect her from all this petty shit, from the snakes among her own friends.

I was a fool to even let that thought cross my mind.

"Don't let her distract you," Manson said. I didn't have to give him an explanation for my sudden frustration. He already knew. "Keep your eyes on the road."

"Why did she even come?" I muttered.

Was it Alex? Had she come here to watch *him*? He was her

type, but goddamn it, she was too good for him. The thought pissed me off and my fingers tightened on the wheel.

Focus. That was all I needed to do. Block out the bullshit and see only that long stretch of black asphalt in front of me. I released a heavy breath, rolling the tension out of my shoulders. I imagined the G-force pulling me back in my seat, the engine roaring, the smell of smoke. God, it was better than any high. Nothing could come close, except...

I glanced at her again. Just one look.

She was looking back.

"Ah, fucking hell." Manson's voice snapped my attention back. He was glaring off to the side, a grimace on his face. "Your devoted fangirl is here."

"My fucking *what*?" I hitched myself up in my seat, looking back. A woman with long dark hair was making a beeline for us. I should have expected it, considering she had a habit of showing up to street races. Vincent and Jason were making over-exaggerated motions of disgust and sudden death from the side of the road as Veronica strutted up to the car.

"Good luck in the race, Lucas," she said. "I'll be starting you boys off today." It figured she would be the flagger. It gave her an excuse to stay close. Her tits were pushed up so far they were nearly bursting out of her shirt, not that I was complaining. I liked tits. I didn't think there was fuckall wrong with *showing* tits.

I just didn't like who these tits belonged to.

"Give him space, Veronica," Manson said. I thought he was going to physically recoil when she pouted and brushed her hand against his neck.

"Aw, don't be jealous, Manson." She was tracing the line of the snake tattooed around his neck, her long nails leaving a pink trail on his pale skin. "I can stand on the sidelines with you until Lucas gets back."

"Don't wait for me," I said. She didn't like me, she didn't like any of us. But that hadn't stopped her from trying to convince me to fuck her.

"A kiss for luck?" She leaned down in the window, managing to bump her ass against Manson at the same time. Okay, enough of this shit. I turned in my seat, about to tell her to fuck off —

The passenger door opened.

"Hey, Veronica, babe!" Jessica's voice was dripping with so much fake sweetness it was practically syrup. She leaned over me from the passenger seat, waving her hand at Veronica before she gave Manson's wrist a brief squeeze.

I didn't know what exactly she was doing, but she'd staked her claim like a pro. I didn't let anyone but the boys sit in this car, but fuck, I could make an exception. Jess could sit her ass on my goddamn face if she wanted.

Veronica's lip curled as she took a small step back. "Oh, Jess, how *nice* to see you. Didn't know you were back in town." Her smile had become a grimace. If she were a cat, she would've been hissing. "I think the last time I saw you was…" She paused, with a little giggle. "It was in a video actually. From some Halloween party, I think? You were…well…" She let it hang. I glanced over at Jess, but she wasn't even blushing. Not the slightest hint she was bothered at all.

Damn. That confidence made my jeans tighten.

"Move your ass, Veronica," Manson said. "Unless you want your foot to get run over."

Her eye twitched before she forced a smile back onto her face and turned away with a flick of her long hair over her shoulder. "Fine. Let's get it started, shall we?" She sauntered forward, stopping and turning to face us once she stood even with the front of our cars. She didn't look pleased as she lifted her arms and shouted, "Are we ready?"

There were cheers and shouts from the crowd. Alex revved his engine, and I adjusted my hands on the wheel, glancing over at Jessica right as she plugged in her seatbelt.

"You gonna move your ass too?" I said. I hit play on my phone and turned up the music, letting the heavy beat fill the cab.

"No." She settled a little more comfortably in the seat. "I'm along for the ride."

I shook my head in disbelief. What the hell had this night turned into? "Hear that, Manson? She's along for the ride."

"Better give her a good ride, then," he said. "Turn up your AC. I think she's feeling heated."

"I don't know what you're talking about, Manson. I'm fucking — fucking fine." She hiccupped in the middle of her sentence. Poor girl was blitzed.

"Sure you are," Manson said, giving me a wink. "We're going to have a little talk soon about your drinking habits, Jess."

"My drinking habits?" she sputtered. "The hell do you — Hey!" But Manson stepped back, waving at her with a smirk as he joined Jason and Vincent on the side of the road.

She was in for the ride of her life.

"You're looking a little green, Jess," I said, gripping the shifter.

She laughed forcibly. "You wish. As if I give a fuck where your dick has been. That goes for all of you."

"Are you sure about that?" I slowly let out the clutch as I revved the engine, the handbrake keeping me in place as my back tires spun out. My skin was on fire, my heart was pounding a million miles a minute. That open stretch of road was calling me, the engine rumbling through every nerve. Veronica began the countdown. Five...four...three... "I'm willing to bet you give a fuck about this dick ending up in your mouth again."

"Oh, shut *up*, Lucas, you —"

I didn't get to find out what special name she'd come up with for me. Veronica waved her arms, and I slammed on the gas, the engine roaring as the El Camino's power was finally unleashed.

11

JESSICA

"Oh, shit!"

I grabbed for anything I could get a hold of as Lucas slammed on the gas. The El Camino pulled so hard I was pressed back into the seat as he rapidly shifted through the gears. The veins in his arms were swollen with tension, his eyes fixed straight ahead. The engine was so loud I could no longer hear the music; the vibrations shivering through my limbs.

It was like being on a rollercoaster, my body overwhelmed by the sheer power of the machine I sat in.

The Hellcat hovered right at the edge of my peripheral vision, almost perfectly even with the El Camino, as we flew down the road. Then suddenly, with a shocking metallic pop, it was gone.

Lucas burst out laughing, genuinely something I never thought

I'd hear.

"Fucking money shift, asshole!" he yelled, glancing back in the rearview mirror.

Alex's headlights swerved erratically in the side mirror, growing further and further behind as Lucas took the win. My adrenaline was pumping, my heart was pounding. Caught up in the rush, I let out a cheer before I even realized what I was doing.

The power in this car was shocking, but to see Lucas handle it that well — fuck, that was *hot*.

Lucas kept driving, the fields flying by on either side. When he finally began to slow his speed, I couldn't even see the starting line behind us anymore.

He pulled off the road, the tires crackling on the dirt as he drove onto a narrow path that led back into a field of tall corn stalks. He pulled the hand brake, put the car in neutral, and let the song play out as we sat there in the field.

I tried to keep my eyes straight ahead, staring down the beams of the headlights. But the car felt so small and I couldn't resist glancing over at the man beside me. His fingers were relaxed on the wheel and he was slouched in his seat, head leaned back.

Freshman year was the first time I'd met him. I could remember him picking fights with seniors, how rude he was every time he opened his mouth, how it seemed like he was *trying* to drive everyone away. Even Kyle avoided him.

He'd been dangerous and everyone knew it, including me. Yet, that hadn't kept me away. His tough guy act had only made me more determined to prove I wasn't scared of him. Everyone else may have been intimidated, but me? Lucas didn't scare me.

When I turned to face him, he turned to me too. I had to ask. It was going to drive me mad if I didn't.

"Did you fuck her?" I said, my voice as crisp and disinterested as I could manage.

He reached for a packet of cigarettes on the dash, the joy I'd so briefly glimpsed on his face now stone cold again. He lit up and took a long drag before he hung the cigarette out his open window and said, "Does it matter?"

I folded my arms, turning to face straight ahead again and going rigid in my seat. Of course it didn't *matter*. I didn't care. The leather seat creaked as Lucas shifted his weight, leaning toward me as he took another drag. His face was unreadable, cast in shadow.

"Well? Does it matter, Jess?"

I shook my head. He chuckled softly as I faced him again, shrinking the space between us even further.

"I don't care," I said. "But you have terrible taste."

"Mm, do I?" He rested one arm on the back of the seat, the smoke from his cigarette drifting out the window in a thin stream. He smelled like tobacco and cinnamon gum, dangerous and unbearably sexy. "I guess that's fair. I'll fuck almost anyone as long as I can make them scream."

It was way too hot in here. How the hell did we get so close? My stomach turned with anger, but my thighs squeezed together as I watched his lips close around the cigarette again.

"That's a gross habit," I said, and he lifted an eyebrow at me. He opened his mouth, keeping his dark eyes on me all the while, and stubbed out the cigarette on his tongue. He didn't flinch, his expression didn't even change.

"I think you have terrible taste too," he said, and I don't know what the hell I was thinking, but we were so close I could see the veins in the whites of his eyes and the pulse beating in his throat.

I grabbed his shirt, knotting it in my hands as I tugged him toward me, but he was already lunging forward, pinning me against the door as he kissed me.

I could taste the ash in his mouth, bitter and dark, but it felt so right. A kiss from Lucas Bent was supposed to hurt, it was supposed to drip with venom, and it did. His hand curled around my neck, his body pressing between my legs and spreading them open. My chest was heaving for air, but I couldn't stop, didn't want to stop. My heart was hammering, and I was so furious, so disgusted, so viciously turned on. His hand trailed over my body, rough and hard, when he pulled up my dress and pressed himself against me.

"Terrible taste," he murmured again. "What are you fucking with trash for, huh? Pretty little thing like you." His hand slid over my panties and cupped me, palm rubbing against me, making my breath hitch and a groan burst out of me. "But for your information, I didn't fuck Veronica."

I was ashamed of how relieved I felt. I jerked against his hand, his fingers stroking a teasing circle over my clit. I'd fantasized about this so many times. I'd spent so many months imagining myself with him. Only the tiniest amount of self-control had stood between me and this.

I wanted his fingers inside me. I wanted to shove him back and ride his cock until I came.

He held me pinned against the door, forcing another gasp out of me with his rough fingers.

"Isn't this fucking typical?" he said. "You change your tone the second we've got some privacy."

"Typical…" I could barely get my breath. "Wha-what the hell does that mean?"

He withdrew his hand, leaving me panting against the door in utter confusion as he said, "It means you're a goddamn hypocrite."

Instantly, like flicking a switch, my anger flared. But my legs were splayed around him obscenely, my panties damp with the arousal he'd ignited in me. Humiliation flooded me in a fiery wave.

"*Excuse* me?" My words trembled with adrenaline. "What the fuck are you doing? You can't just…you can't…"

"I can't *what*?" he hissed. "I can't stop? I already did. A taste of your own medicine, little ghost."

I shoved his chest hard, and he laughed as he backed off. "Fuck you," I muttered. "Seriously, fuck you, Lucas. I'm walking back. This is bullshit —"

I reached for the door handle, but he grabbed my arm, pulling me back. "Sorry, sweetheart, but you need to hear this. Don't act shocked that I'm going to speak my mind. What the fuck is your deal? Here you are hanging out with the same assholes that tried to make our lives hell, but then you want to fuck around with us the second you have us alone."

He may as well have slapped me. I blinked rapidly, my conflicting emotions choking my words.

"Do you have any idea how much it wrecked Manson when you ghosted?" he said. "He was so scared that he'd fucked up and hurt you, because you couldn't manage some basic communication."

He shook his head, the disgust evident on his face. "I guess we all thought about it. That we'd pushed you too far."

"You didn't." The words burst out of me so quickly I didn't even think about what I was saying until it was already out. I'd known ghosting was shitty, but I genuinely hadn't thought it would make them worry. "None of you hurt me. That night was weird... and amazing...and..." I shrugged helplessly. "I didn't know what to do, okay? The next morning, I...I don't know. It wasn't supposed to be a long-term thing."

He nodded slowly as he took in my words, staring at my hand as it lay on the seat.

My hand with the tiny heart-shaped cut on my finger.

I made a fist and snatched it back, but it was too late. He scoffed, leaning his head back as he looked at me.

"Those boys are everything to me," he said. "They're the closest damn thing to family I've got. But if I *ever* thought one of them had hurt you, I'd fucking beat their ass myself." His expression left me no room not to believe him. He'd meant it, viciously. "But I know what you're doing. You want to take as much as you can and give nothing back. You wanted us. You still do."

He'd already proven it too. I didn't have a leg to stand on, only anger and my battered pride.

"So what, Lucas?" I snapped. "What exactly was I supposed to do? Start hooking up with all of you? Date one of you? Am I supposed to put on a collar and submit?"

In the deepest, darkest recesses of my mind, I'd imagined what it would be like. No more games, no more one-night stands. What would my life be like if I embraced what felt so right and never looked back?

I'd let Manson fuck me with the knife he'd threatened my ex with. I'd let them cuff my hands and fuck my face, one after the other. I'd crawled, cried, endured, and come out on the other side feeling awakened. It was like nothing else I'd ever experienced. It had fulfilled a need I hadn't known was there.

How could they even expect something like that to work? Why would they *want* it to work? My family would never understand, most of my friends would literally abandon me.

"That's what you want," Lucas said. "You wish you could, but you're so hung up on what everyone else will think that you keep pretending to be someone you're not. Is that really how you want to live?"

I shook my head. "You don't get it. It's not that simple. I don't know why you think it's *simple*."

"Oh, but it is *real* simple, Jess." His drawl got thicker the more irritated he became. "You want us and you don't think you should. That's why you act like this. That's why you're sitting across from me right now. You spent all of high school harassing us so you could be near us, so you'd have an excuse to flirt with what you knew you *shouldn't* have." He was still firmly in my space, crowding me but not touching me. "This isn't high school. This isn't one of your frat parties. We're not kids anymore. Do you get that? It's all in or nothing. Those boys are my brothers. They're my family. They come before everything. You don't get to manipulate us for attention."

We sat there for a moment, silent, our eyes locked.

He was right. Guilt bubbled up in me despite my pride trying to beat it down. The games, the teasing, the constant back and forth — this couldn't go on forever. Something had to give.

My eyes flickered down to his mouth. That hard, nasty mouth that had never been afraid to call me out.

"You know what you need, Miss Martin?" he said, his tone guttural with a promise that sent shivers over my back. "You need someone to take you in hand and put you in your fucking place. You need someone to take control, who won't let you walk all over them."

If he kept talking like that, I was going to end up with my legs splayed around him again in desperation. I squirmed in my seat, trying not to think of the myriad of ways he could take control right here and now.

Something like a smile twisted his mouth, dangerous and mean. "You need someone to punish you properly, fuck you good, and care about you enough not to let you hang out with friends who will stab you in the back the first chance they get."

I was torn in two. On one side, I didn't need that from them or anybody. I was perfectly fine. I had my life under control. I knew what I wanted.

On the other side, I wanted to lose control. I wanted to feel cared about and looked after. I wanted someone who could take command and wasn't afraid to keep it. Someone I could lose myself in, let go, and be vulnerable with.

"Lucas…"

But he didn't want to hear any more excuses.

"We're not your pawns," he said. "And we'll do whatever we damn well please, including fuck who we want."

He put the car in reverse and hooked his arm over the back of the seat as he pulled out of the field. He cranked the radio up, loud enough for it to be obvious he didn't want to hear another word from me.

I grit my teeth. My stomach felt like a raging ocean was inside it, swirling and crashing as I dwelled on his words. He dared accuse me of only wanting their attention, like I was some spoiled child?

I absolutely hated it.

A crowd had gathered around the Hellcat as we approached the starting line. Alex was on the phone, pacing and yelling, his face bright red with fury. A sick feeling of trepidation slithered around inside me when I caught the look on his face — hateful, furious, almost murderous.

Lucas parked, and the moment he got out of the car, Manson was there, excitedly throwing his arms around him. Jason ran up to rub his head with a huge grin on his face as he said, "Fuck yes, dude, that was sick!"

Damn it, I never should have gotten into the car. My panties were damp and my clit was pulsing, the living embodiment of hot and bothered. I was so frustrated, so angry.

And it all was made so much worse by the fact that Lucas was right.

I jumped as the passenger door opened, and Vincent leaned down, a grin on his face. "I hope Lucas wasn't too rough with you."

"Oh, shut up." I got up, squeezing past him. "God, you're all intolerable."

"Yeah, throw a tantrum a little louder, Jess!" Lucas yelled. "Cry about the attention you didn't get!"

I wanted to kill him. I didn't know what I was going to say, but word vomit was coming up and it was going to be messy. But as I turned, I realized someone else wanted to kill him a lot more than I did.

No one was prepared for how fast Alex ran up. Before anyone could react, he'd pulled back his fist and slammed his knuckles against Lucas's face.

12

VINCENT

Alex's punch knocked Lucas back against the El Camino and everything slowed. Lucas's eyes rolled blankly as shouting echoed around me. Jason grabbed Lucas, preventing him from going down —

Then everything came rushing back to full speed.

Manson was in Alex's face and Alex grabbed his collar, fingers knotting in his shirt as he shouted. As Lucas slumped dizzily against the hood, Jason shoved Alex's shoulder hard, pushing him back from Manson and getting in between them, fists clenched, voices rising.

I wasn't a fighter. Never had been. I could talk my way out of most situations and I didn't see the point in escalating shit. Sticks and stones, man. I wasn't built for it anyway; I was just a skinny stoner with a fried egg for a brain.

But I'd been dealing pills and potions since ninth grade, so being able to de-escalate a tense situation was lifesaving. Unfortunately, de-escalation wasn't always an option. Sometimes, things went to shit.

Jason whipped back his fist, the punch landing so hard that Alex's lip split open, blood streaming down his chin. Nate thundered toward them, but Manson watched him approach with a look in his eye that made my blood run cold.

It was high school all over again. Us against them.

Alex grabbed a glass beer bottle from the ground, smashed the end on the asphalt, and held the sharp, pointed glass in Jason's face. "Hit me again, you fucking f—"

I was already reaching under my jacket before the sentence was fully out of his mouth. My fingers brushed against the handle of the pistol tucked into my jeans, cold determination keeping my hand steady as my fingers closed around it.

"Stop! Stop it!"

Jessica ran up and shoved herself between Alex and Jason, a damn foolish move on her part. Alex didn't care who got in his way; she was another obstacle to be removed. His hand snapped out and grabbed her throat, squeezing, with the glass bottle still raised.

The moment his hand touched her, it was like a dark cold shadow settled over my mind.

"Hey. Don't you *fucking* touch her."

It wasn't my voice that made everyone go still. It was the click that accompanied it, the audible sound of a bullet prepared to fire. Everyone stared, wide-eyed and still.

Alex was panting, the glass inches away from Jessica's face. I had the gun aimed for his skull, and Manson had reached his arm around Jess's shoulder to press his knife against Alex's throat. Jason was right behind him and Lucas stepped up on his other side, blood pouring from his nose and staining his bared teeth red.

"You wanna go, motherfucker?" Lucas said, spitting blood in Alex's direction. "Come on. Let's fucking go. But you leave your hand on her another goddamn second and I'm going to break every one of your fucking fingers before Vince puts a bullet in your skull."

Alex's eyes flickered over to me, widening slightly. His big friends couldn't do shit against a gun, but we still needed to get the hell out of here before this situation got any worse. We were in the middle of nowhere, and I certainly wasn't the only one out here who was packing.

Even with Alex's hand squeezing her throat, Jess didn't back down. She didn't even look afraid. She stared at him, eyes narrowed, fists clenched at her sides like she'd fight him herself. I'd pay money to see her punch him in the face, but I needed her out of harm's way. As Alex's hand loosened from around her, she smirked and lifted her chin a little higher.

"Move, Jess," Manson said, his voice low but easy to hear in the shocked silence.

"You need to stop," she said. She turned toward him and her eyes were wide, determined but desperate. "All of you. Please."

When her eyes moved over to me, it was instantly obvious she hadn't already noticed the gun. Her face stiffened in shock, her mouth opening and closing several times without a word.

I put down the firearm, tucking it away under my shirt. But she was still staring at me.

"What the hell, Vincent?" The words were a mere breath as she exhaled.

"Yeah, that's right," Alex said, as if her shock proved a point. He stepped back, closer to Nate and his big friends. The coward probably felt safer with those big bodies around him. "Still think they're good guys, Jess? Only real gentlemen bring guns and knives to a race, huh?"

Murmurs rippled through the crowd. It was our cue to bail out — the quicker, the better. I nodded at Manson, who put his blade away with a quick flash of metal. Lucas spat more blood from his mouth, but luckily, he had the sense to turn away. None of us moved until he'd gotten back into the El Camino and started the engine.

"Let's go." I paused next to Jason, who was standing guard beside Jessica. She looked dazed, as if the true danger of the situation had finally hit home for her. She looked me up and down like she was seeing me for the first time, and jumped when Jason's fingers brushed her shoulder.

"Come with us," he said softly. "Let's get you out of here."

"Jessica!" One of her friends furiously called her name and she looked back. She gulped, and her breath came a little deeper. Her body was practically vibrating with nerves.

For a moment, I thought she'd say yes.

Then she stepped away, shaking her head. "No. I'm...I'm fine. I..." She looked at her friends again, the other girls staring at her as if she'd lost her mind. When she spoke next, she tried to sound confident, "I don't need saving."

But she didn't sound confident at all.

She left to join the crowd on the opposite side of the street. Jason stared after her, his jaw clenched, nostrils flaring with frustration. I clapped my hand on his shoulder. "Let's go. We need to bail."

He nodded. His shoulders were hunched with tension as he got into the Subaru. Manson slipped into the back and I got into the driver's seat, cranking the engine. People were staring, shaking their heads, murmuring. I wondered how tonight would be retold, how they'd spin out the story to make sure we were the villains.

I rolled down my window, watching Jess as we pulled away. Lucas had probably said something to piss her off, and she was trying to keep up appearances, but she was a damn fool to stay here. These people didn't care about her, and her little girlfriends currently giving her questioning looks would betray her in a heartbeat if it suited them.

But what the hell could I do about that?

"Be good now," I said, giving the glaring crowd a friendly grin.

"Y'all fucked up," Alex yelled. "This isn't over!"

No. It was never over.

13

JESSICA

As the El Camino pulled away, the rumbling engine fading into the night, I felt utterly and completely alone. Everything had happened so fast. When I'd rushed between Alex and Jason, it had been impulsive, instinctual. It didn't even register when Alex put his hands on me. I was filled with too much adrenaline to really consider the consequences of what I was doing.

But now that it was over, reality hit me hard. I'd had broken glass shoved in my face and I could still feel the tight grip of Alex's fingers on my throat. He'd dared to put his hands on me, to threaten *me*!

And the people who'd stepped up to defend me weren't even those I called friends. My "friends" had only watched.

But Vincent and Manson, Jason...even Lucas...They'd defended me. Instantly, without hesitation, all of them.

I should have gone with them.

Then I remembered Lucas's words and my anger reared back. He'd made me so damn mad — calling me hypocrite, claiming I only wanted attention. And he'd done it all while proving how desperate I was, how quickly I gave in the moment no one was watching.

It was humiliating, and to make it even worse, he'd been so *smug* about it all. Like he had me all figured out, as if he knew me better than I knew myself.

You need someone to punish you properly, he'd said, as if I was a bratty child. The fucking nerve. I didn't need punishment from him. Or any of them. Or at all. I didn't need anyone looking after me.

I could take care of myself, and that started with me whirling around and marching back toward Alex in a fury.

"How *fucking dare you* put your hands on me!" I yelled, shoving my hands as hard as I could against his chest. He took one stumbling step back, his eyes narrowing into a dangerous glare that would have made a smarter person back down.

But I didn't. All this fury needed somewhere to go, and the more I thought about what had just happened, the more wildly unacceptable it felt.

"It's your own fault," Alex said. "What the hell did you think you were doing? Next time, stay out of my way." He took a step toward me but I didn't back down. If he wanted to get physical, I gladly would. His ridiculous macho act didn't scare me. But my head swam, all the alcohol in my veins reminding me that this was mostly my liquid courage talking. Or liquid foolishness.

People around us were clearly uncomfortable, but no one else said a word. They were trying to watch while keeping their eyes averted, as if they thought that if they didn't look directly at our confrontation, then they weren't responsible for stepping in.

"Jessica!" Danielle called me sharply. As much as I loathed letting Alex feel like he was the victor here, I turned away from him and trudged back toward the girls. Alex could have his tantrum, but I wasn't going to forgive him for this. Drunk or not, there was no excuse.

"Girl, what is going on?" Danielle said as I rejoined her and Candace. "Why would you get in the middle of that? Alex is pissed."

"You should have let them fight it out." Candace shook her head, taking a long drink to finish off her wine cooler.

Danielle's lips were pursed as she looked at me. I could see her mind turning, and I didn't like it one bit.

"Why did you ride with him?" she said, accusation slipping into her voice.

Sipping my drink, I simply shrugged. Okay, it wasn't really a sip — I gulped it greedily, desperately. "Sounded like fun. Is there a problem with that?"

The nastiness in her expression grew as I stared at her. Candace's eyes darted between us, although she didn't dare to say a word. For a moment, I thought Danielle would let it go.

But then her lips twisted into something like a smile and she said, "I just think it's funny how last time you were having a little *fun* with Manson, and this time it's a little fun with Lucas. Which one is next, Jess?"

Out of the corner of my eye, I could see people staring. Alex was pacing as he waited for his tow truck to arrive, swearing up and down that he was going to "make them pay." There was a pool of oil slowly spreading around the Hellcat, and I overheard someone say that he'd shifted into third gear when he'd meant to shift to fifth, blowing his transmission.

It was his own damn fault, but he was still determined to pin the blame elsewhere.

"Shut up, Danielle," I said. "Fucking drop it."

People were departing now that the race was over. But Veronica was still here, and she was talking to Alex now. Her gaze kept darting over to me, as if she was waiting to see what I would do. She nodded sympathetically to Alex's raging, clasping his arm in an overly friendly way. She'd found her next target already.

My face reddened, my skin heating. Is that how Lucas saw me? Hopping from one person to the next in desperate search of attention? Taking a deep breath, I tried to force myself to sober up enough to drive home. But my head was buzzing and I didn't feel comfortable getting behind the wheel yet.

Danielle and Candace were conversing among themselves, and for once, I was glad I couldn't hear what they were saying.

I could feel it from all sides, pricking my skin like sharp fingernails. Judgment. Disapproval. Suspicion.

I didn't belong.

Suddenly, Alex hurled his empty glass bottle against a tree, the sound of shattering glass making me jump.

"God fucking damn them!" he yelled, his voice hitting that ragged volume of sheer unbridled fury. "It didn't use to be like this, man. Those motherfuckers used to know their place."

Nate and Matthew nodded in agreement, their faces set hard as stone.

"We never had problems like this until they started showing up either," Danielle said. She looked at Candace, gasping, "Who whips out a gun like that?"

"That's what happens when people start feeling sorry for them," Veronica said, as if the real problem here was nothing more than misplaced empathy. "They've always been trashy. Kathryn Peters paid for Manson's therapy out of her own pocket, you know. Didn't even do any good. He's still carrying that knife around like he's waiting for the opportunity to stab someone."

"He's never stabbed anyone," I said.

Alex whirled around, jabbing his finger at me. "Why the hell are you still here? Why didn't you bail with your little boyfriends?" His lip curled in disgust. "Or did they not want you either?"

I clenched my fists, glaring at him from my seat.

"You need to learn to fucking control yourself, Alex," I snapped. "*You* did this!" I pointed to his car, my voice rising. "This is *your* fault! People could have gotten seriously hurt. But you couldn't handle losing so instead you're throwing a tantrum like a baby!"

"As if you're one to talk," he said. "You just can't resist making yourself the center of attention, can you? Always so eager to throw yourself into the middle of shit that doesn't even involve you."

He wanted a reaction out of me, and more furious words were rising in my throat. It would feel so good to go off on him, to scream and rage for what he'd done. But I had no safe way to get home, I was stuck here with them.

When I told Jason I didn't need saving, I had been so wrong.

But to my surprise, Danielle spoke up.

"Calm down, Alex," she said, her tone bored. "Jess was only having a little fun with them. She's not *with them*." She glanced over at me, but the look she gave me was strange. "She's on our side."

I didn't know if I was being assured or warned.

"I need water," I muttered, leaving my seat to walk back to my car. The tow truck was arriving, momentarily distracting Alex from his raging as the Hellcat was loaded onto the flatbed. I retrieved one of my water bottles from the backseat and gulped it down, but it didn't settle my churning stomach.

I was still hung up on what Lucas had said. Maybe I owed them an apology. For snapping, for being so rude, for — God, for so many things. But after tonight, there was a good chance I would never even see them again.

Maybe it was for the best. We were too volatile together; emotions were too high. They made me feel like I had no idea what to say or how to act. Everything was so confusing with them and it was probably my fault.

After all, I was the one who couldn't communicate, who'd ghosted them without notice.

Apparently, plans had been made while I was lost in my thoughts. I returned from the car to find everyone looking at me expectantly.

"What about you, Jess?" Alex said. "You coming along or what?"

"Depends where you're going," I said, arms folded.

Candace shrugged. "Anywhere is better than sitting on the side of the road all night, right?"

At this point, I wasn't sure if that was true. Sitting here alone in the dark might be a better idea than going with them.

"Come on, Jess, it'll be fun," Danielle said. "I know tonight has kind of sucked, but the night is young, right? We can turn it around."

Veronica was watching me with narrowed eyes, a smirk on her face. What did she think was so funny? She probably expected me to decline, I bet she would *love* that. It would be a victory for her if I was so uncomfortable that I stayed behind. I'd go to spite them all at this point.

"Sure, whatever," I said. "Let's go then."

"See, Alex?" Danielle said. "I told you, Jess is always down for some fun."

Trepidation prickled up my back, although I wasn't entirely sure why. Everything felt wrong. But I'd be damned if I was going to let them intimidate me.

"All right." Alex nodded. "Let's go have some fun."

The air was cold as it whipped through my hair and it wasn't long until I was shivering. I didn't know where we were going, but we were barreling down a dark road at midnight huddled in the bed of Nate's lifted truck. Danielle and Alex were in the cab with Nate, while Veronica, Candace, and Matthew sat in the back with me. Nate was blasting the radio but otherwise we were silent, tension resting over us like a poisonous cloud.

As Nate took a few more turns, my nervousness rose. I recognized this dirt road, pot-holed and barely wide enough for his truck to pass. Low-hanging branches from massive black walnut trees whipped the truck's cab as we slowed, the suspension creaking with every bump and dip.

I knew where we were going.

The Reed residence was set back from the road with a large dirt yard. The chain-link fence was old and bent in places, but a new gate guarded the driveway, secured with a chain and padlock. Large trees flanked the house, which was a monstrosity built of dark wood with a wraparound porch. It would have been a beautiful home if it had ever been cared for, but Manson's parents had never been capable or willing to do so.

"Doesn't Manson's mom live here alone?" I said, my voice barely a whisper. Last I'd known, Manson had been living with his social worker's family, the Peters, while his mom lived here and his dad went MIA again. Nate turned off the radio and drove slowly along the road, past the front gate toward the far side of the property.

"She died," Matthew said, and the declaration made my heart lurch. I'd never even known the woman, only that she was usually intoxicated and rarely left the house. "She left this place to Manson, and that freak hasn't done shit with it. Whole place should be burned to the ground."

There was a large metal-sided garage on the far side of the property, illuminated by floodlights around its exterior. A mural had been graffitied on the wall that faced the road, depicting the boys' four cars surrounded by swirls of neon colors. That certainly wasn't something Manson's parents would have created. Then who had painted it? One of the boys?

Nate stopped the trunk and turned off the engine. I blinked rapidly in confusion as everyone began to climb out of the truck.

"Uh, what are we doing?"

"Having fun," Danielle said, hanging off of Nate's side, looking as though her drinks had finally caught up with her. Nate was carrying a massive pair of bolt cutters, and Alex had a hammer, along with an unpleasant smile on his face.

"They've actually started calling this place *Losers' Garage*," Mathew said, laughing under his breath. "Like they're fucking proud of it."

Panic drenched me in a cold wave as Nate used the bolt cutters to snip through the fence. This wasn't merely a prank, this was literally breaking and entering.

"Don't they have dogs?" Matthew whispered as he slipped through the fence ahead of me.

"Dogs?" I said. "There are dogs here?" I hung back, but Candace grabbed my arm before she crouched to squeeze through the fence and pulled me with her.

"Shut the hell up," Alex hissed. "I don't give a fuck if they've got trained elephants on the property."

We crept along the interior of the fence, everyone staying low. This was truly unhinged. There was no way in hell we should be here.

I should have turned around. But it was like watching my own train wreck, as if some part of me had already accepted that something awful was going to happen.

We reached the side of the garage. A camera was aimed at the door there, illuminated by an overhead light, and Nate followed its trail of wires to a small gray box. More tangled wires and circuit breakers were within, and Danielle said, "Do you know which ones to cut?"

"Nope," Nate said, before he swung the bolt cutters like a baseball bat and smashed the breakers. The flood lights flickered and went out, plunging us into near total darkness. Nate kept going, cutting through the wires with reckless determination.

"Guys, this is really —"

Alex tapped my arm, cutting me off as he jabbed his finger at a shovel leaned up against the garage. "Grab that," he said, and I lifted it gingerly. "If something comes yapping at you, hit it."

I wasn't going to hit a dog, no way in hell. I'd sooner let them bite me than try to hurt them, but maybe the wooden handle could at least serve as a barricade if I was attacked.

If I was attacked. God, this was fucked. This was so fucked.

Nate slammed his massive foot against the door, busting it open. An alarm screeched and the lights popped on, despite Nate's best efforts to cut off the electricity. I stood rooted in the doorway, the shovel in my hands, as the others rushed inside. It was spacious, with a stairway to my right leading to an upper level, but they were only interested in the cars. The Mustang, the El Camino, the Nissan, the blue Subaru — and against the far wall, a familiar Ford Bronco on massive tires.

The sound of shattering glass fell harshly on my ears as Matthew slammed a brick through the front windshield of the Mustang. Alex whooped excitedly as he brought his hammer down on the El Camino's hood, and Veronica swung a metal pole she'd found into the passenger window. Nate was busting out the Subaru's windows with his bolt cutters and Danielle was laughing as she dragged her keys down the side of the 350Z.

What the hell was I doing here? What was I *doing?*

Distantly, I could hear dogs barking. The alarms were so painfully loud I couldn't think.

Veronica leaned into the broken window of the El Camino and spat on the seat, grinning at me all the while. "Not the first time I've gotten a little drool on these seats."

The alarm was a roar in my ears. I didn't want to think about that. I didn't want to imagine Veronica sitting where I'd sat, her mouth on Lucas. I didn't want to think about the things he'd said to me. I didn't want to feel the disapproval and uncertainty of everyone's gazes on me as they ran through the broken glass and I had only just managed to shuffle inside.

"We gotta bail!" Nate sprinted for the door with Danielle and Veronica right behind him. Alex swung the wrench at the El Camino again as Matthew jabbed a razorblade into the tires.

"Hurry the fuck up, Jess! I thought you were down!"

And what if I wasn't? What then? Rejection. Ostracization. I didn't even know who shouted it, but I guess it didn't matter. It could have been shouted by the universe itself.

All the fingers I'd ever pointed, all the cruel things I'd ever said, could so easily be turned on me. And they would be.

But this was wrong on so many levels, I never should have come here. My heart hammered, panic making me weak. I sucked in my breath and braced myself to turn and face them, to tell them I was leaving this shitshow. But as I turned, I realized they were gone. All of them. The garage was empty and the roar of the truck's engine told me they'd abandoned me here.

They'd left me behind and the barking dogs were coming closer.

14

LUCAS

"Would you stop squirming? Do I need to tie you down?"

I snorted at Manson's suggestion, forcing myself to sit still on the edge of his tub. My adrenaline from the fight had calmed, and I finally felt like I could get some sleep. But Manson wouldn't stop fussing over my busted lip and swelling nose.

It really wasn't a big deal. I doubted my nose was broken, and if it was? It wouldn't be the first time.

But it was a big deal to Manson and this was his effort at apologizing without saying it. If he apologized out loud, I'd reject it because he had nothing to be sorry for. It wasn't his damn responsibility to protect me.

"You better not feel guilty," I said, my movement making him fix me with another glare before he went back to cleaning up my lip. It needed stitches, but I couldn't be bothered with all that. Wounds healed. Maybe they'd scar and be ugly in the end, but I didn't care. "Nothing that happened tonight was your fault, so don't dwell on it."

His eyes narrowed even more. "Yeah, except I had a feeling shit would go south. I should've —"

I grabbed his wrist, yanking his hand down from my face. "Stop. Fucking stop beating yourself up about it. Getting punched in the face is nothing new for me. In the grand scheme of things, this was a damn good evening."

He didn't look convinced. "How do you figure?"

"No one got shot," I said. "No one got stabbed. I'm not in the hospital." I shrugged. "Sure sounds like a successful night to me."

He shook his head, yanking his wrist out of my hold. Jojo and Haribo were barking downstairs, probably needing to go outside again. Manson started dabbing something that smelled nasty on my face, and I tried my best to sit still for him.

"You've still got blood on your teeth," he said.

"You like it. Looks sexy, right?"

That finally got a little grin out of him. Maybe I wasn't ready for sleep yet. Maybe I needed to let off a little pent-up energy first, especially considering things had gotten hot and heavy with Jess before I abruptly cut her off.

"You better be careful looking at me like that," Manson said. He had one hand on the side of my jaw to keep my head steady, and his hold grew a little tighter. "Unless one punch in the face wasn't enough pain for you."

It wasn't enough. It was never enough. That was part of why he and I got along so well, part of why we meshed both at work and in the bedroom. Exploring the edges of what I was capable of enduring was something I trusted him with, but only him.

I ran my tongue over my teeth, glancing down at his obvious bulge. He looked so fucking good, I wanted to sink my teeth into his skin, bite until he bled and let him hurt me in return. I'd let him overtake me because it was the only way I could ever let go, *truly* let go. As terrifying as it was to do that, it was an outlet I desperately needed.

Damn, those dogs were getting loud. Too loud. Manson and I both paused. There was a strange sound I could faintly hear over the music playing in his bedroom, a repetitive screeching. We looked at each other, his frown deepening as he said, "Is that—"

Before he could get his thought out, Vincent burst into his bedroom, tugging a shirt over his head to hide the pistol tucked into his jeans.

"Garage," was all he needed to say before he sprinted down the hall and we both scrambled to our feet.

It was our alarm. Someone was in the garage. We sprinted downstairs, where the dogs were crowded in front of the door, barking frantically. I grabbed the baseball bat in the corner, a weapon we kept close by in case shit like this went down. Jason was carrying a bat too, likely the one we kept near the back door. After the night we'd had, we weren't taking any chances of being caught unarmed.

The dogs burst outside the moment Manson opened the door. A cloud of dust rolled across the yard as a truck sped away down the road, but the dogs weren't interested in the truck. They sprinted toward the trees at the back of the property, their growls and frenzied barking making it clear they weren't only chasing shadows.

Those assholes had left one of their own behind. *Someone* was running around back there, and I had every intention of making an example out of them.

We ran after the dogs, following them into the trees. We were forced to slow down as we spread out, trudging through the overgrown weeds. There was a click and a beam of light came on, the flashlight in Vincent's hand illuminating our way.

"There's no way out back here," I called, raising my voice so it echoed through the trees. "You can't run forever, motherfucker!"

I twirled the bat in my hand, energy vibrating through me. This was it. This was fucking *it*. I hadn't even seen inside the garage yet, but they'd gone too far the second they stepped foot on our property. This was years of harassment coming to a head. It was time for someone to take the fall, a lesson had to be learned here.

They'd be lucky to get their friend back in one piece.

To my left, a few yards away, Manson was flipping his knife in his hands. It caught the moonlight when it flipped open, flashed, then quickly disappeared.

"There's nowhere else to run," Vincent called. His words were punctuated by maniacal laughter as he said, "Come out, buddy! It's just a little beating."

There were some strange noises ahead — grunting and puffing, then a shriek. God, I hoped it was Alex. I couldn't wait to get my hands on that little shit. The coward probably thought he could find a way out back here, but the fence was topped with barbed wire and there was nowhere else to run.

Jojo and Haribo were standing at the base of one of our biggest trees, the hair on their backs standing up in a rigid line as they barked at the branches above. Haribo kept making attempts to leap up, but those squat legs couldn't lift him more than a foot off the ground. I rested my bat against my shoulders, narrowing my eyes. I could barely see a figure clinging to the tree, wedged between the branches.

I frowned. The intruder looked *smaller* than I'd anticipated.

"You're going to be swallowing your own teeth, dumbass," Jason said, his voice low enough that I doubt the intruder even heard him. It was a promise more to himself than anyone else.

But something wasn't right here. There was something familiar about the intruder's desperate panting breaths and the little whimpers of fear that came out with them.

Vincent noticed it too and shone his light up into the branches. "What the hell?"

Wide green eyes stared back at us. Jessica had her arms clung tightly around the branch she was wedged beside, precariously balanced in the narrow V between two tree limbs. Her blonde hair was disheveled and her cheeks were red, her face frozen in an expression that was partially terrified and partially relieved.

"Jessica?" Manson's voice was breathless, heavy with disbelief. "Hey, Jojo! Bo! Heel!" He snapped his fingers and the dogs immediately stood down. Jess's eyes flickered over us, dodging between our shocked expressions and the bats in our hands.

"Why do you have those?" she finally said, and I think something in my brain snapped.

"These?" I said, my voice heightening the closer I got to laughter. I held up the bat, stalking toward the base of the tree to stand alongside Manson. "Why do you think? What the hell do you think these could be for?"

She clenched her jaw, prideful little brat that she was. Her fear was dwindling, replaced with something far more foolish.

"You wouldn't," she said softly. My teeth were clenched so tightly I could imagine them shattering. I glanced over at Manson, but his expression was dark, shuttered as he stared up at her and flipped the knife closed, tucking it back into his pocket.

"Come down from there," he said. His voice was far calmer than I was capable of right then, but there was an edge to it that couldn't be missed. "Now."

Jess quickly shook her head. "Nope, I think I'm safer up here."

"You're perfectly safe," Jason said, tapping his bat repeatedly against the ground. "Come down."

"You guys go back inside," she said. "Take the dogs too. Then I'll leave."

"Leave?" Vincent said. "No, no, no, Jess, you're not leaving. We need to have a little chat."

"No, thanks. I don't think that — Ah, shit!" She'd tried to readjust her position, but her shoe got stuck between the limbs and she slipped, tumbling out of the branches face-first. Lucky for her, Manson was there to catch her. He managed to grab her before she hit the ground, stumbling a bit but keeping his feet. She immediately started wiggling, but Manson was having none of it. He hauled her up over his shoulder, pinning her legs under one arm.

"Let me go!" she shrieked, kicking and bucking, thrashing about like a fish out of water. But he kept walking, marching back toward the garage with the rest of us following. The dogs stayed right at his heels as they tried to get a sniff of Jessica's face. "Let me down! Goddamn it!" She swatted at his ass in a last-ditch effort to escape, but Manson only laughed.

As much as Jessica made me feel like I was losing my damn mind, I also understood her a lot better than she thought I did. She was too much like me, in the worst of ways. Impulsive. Proud. So goddamn stubborn. But because I understood those parts of her, I also understood what she needed.

Attention. Good, focused, four-on-one attention. And she was going to get it now.

15

JESSICA

Manson carried me back to the garage, thrown over his shoulder. My head bobbed up and down, giving me glimpses of the other men's faces. Lucas's expression was fierce, so tense I wouldn't have been surprised if sparks started shooting out of his eyeballs. Jason's was tight and controlled, like he was about to attend the funeral of someone he hated. Vincent was smiling, the eerie expression punctuated by occasional shakes of his head.

"Let's see what you got up to, Jessica," Manson grunted, shifting me slightly as we reached the front of the garage.

"No, no, let's not," I said quickly. All the blood was rushing to my head, and I groaned, my stomach churning with dread. How could I have been so abysmally foolish? When they saw what was inside that garage, my ass was dead.

Vincent squatted down beside us, using a small key to unlock the rolling metal door. He grasped the handle and pulled, and every creak of the metal sounded like another nail being hammered into my coffin.

The collective gasps of shock as the garage was opened made me wish I'd let the dogs eat me out there in the trees.

"Lucas, go put the dogs in the house," Manson said, his voice hollow. "They'll cut their paws in here."

Shattered glass covered the floor, sparkling in the fluorescent light. It crunched under Manson's boots as he carried me inside. The cars were dented, the windows busted, tires slashed. Tools had been ripped off the walls and thrown to the floor, drawers had been flung open and their contents scattered.

"Holy shit," Vincent said. "Holy fucking shit."

Manson set me back on my feet, and for a brief moment, I wasn't captive. Manson stood beside me, surveying the destruction with a slack expression as if he couldn't believe what he was seeing. For nearly a minute, they stared, expressions of stunned disbelief frozen on their faces.

Suddenly arms gripped me from behind, pulling me back against a hard, broad chest.

"We're going to have a nice *long* chat about this, Miss Martin." Lucas had returned, and his voice was so cold that I shivered. Manson and Vincent walked among the ruins, Manson rubbing a hand through his hair as he shook his head. Jason was rapidly typing on his phone, glancing up only occasionally as if taking notes on the damages.

"Thousands of dollars," he said. "Fucking thousands of dollars in damage." He whirled around, glaring at me. "You. *You*…" Any insults that came into his mind clearly weren't good enough. He turned away and slipped out the open side door, which swung crookedly on its hinges. The alarm finally stopped blaring, and Jason was back a few seconds later.

"They cut the wires for the cameras," he said. He swore under his breath, looking at me with disgust. "Looks like they tried to kill the security system completely, but the backup battery took over." He leaned his hands against the trunk of his white Nissan, head bowed over the scratched, dented metal. "Fuck! God fucking damn it!"

"You did it now, Jess," Vincent laughed bitterly. "Fucking hell."

"I didn't do it!" I cried. I jerked against Lucas's hold on me, trying and failing to break it. I didn't even know what to do if I *did* get him to let go of me. Was I going to run all the way back home in the dark? Move out of Wickeston and pretend this night had never happened? Never leave my house again and hope they didn't come knocking on my door?

I'd royally fucked up.

"Keep fighting me and this is going to get a hell of a lot worse for you," Lucas hissed. "You're not running away from this."

"I didn't damage your cars!" I insisted. "It was them. I didn't do it!"

"Oh, right, of course," Vincent said. "As always, it couldn't possibly be *your* fault."

"No, it — I — Please don't call the cops," I said, stumbling over my words. What if I ended up in jail? What the hell would

I tell my parents? What would I tell my boss? "I didn't do it. I fucking swear I didn't."

The words died on my tongue as Manson turned around, glaring at me over the roof of his damaged Mustang.

"Don't call the cops?" he said, his voice dangerously low as he stalked toward me. "No consequences for Jess, right? No fucking responsibility for your own actions?" He was right in my face now, inches away. Behind him, Vincent leaned against a large toolbox with his arms folded.

Manson reached into his pocket and wrenched out a cell phone, several models out of date with a cracked screen. He unlocked it and thrust it toward me. "Call them. Call the police. Believe me, you'd rather have them deal with you than me."

Lucas let go of me as I took the cell in my trembling hands. The glares I was getting from the four of them could have melted steel beams as I opened up the dial pad, my thumb hovering over the 9.

I shook my head, pushing the phone back toward him.

"No." I couldn't meet his eyes, instead staring at the glass-covered floor, chewing the inside of my cheek. "I don't want the cops involved. I'd rather…" I gulped. What the hell was I doing? The turning in my stomach didn't feel like fear. It was something else, something strange. "I want to keep this between us."

Manson's eyes widened, his eyebrows disappearing beneath the hair lying loose over his forehead. Jason rubbed his hands over his face with a groan, saying, "I can't believe it. I can't fucking believe this shit."

Vincent was laughing, a low chuckle that sounded truly maniacal. "So Jess wants to keep it between us. You come here, thrash our shit —"

"Oh, you've got it all wrong, Vince," Jason said, head still bowed over his busted car. "She came here innocently and didn't do a damn thing wrong. Not her fault, as usual."

The guilt flooding through me was heavy, too intense to bear. Even though I hadn't broken anything myself, I was still here. I'd followed Alex and the others, I'd broken in, I'd participated.

Lucas had called it right. I needed to be punished. I knew it, and I dreaded it as much as I desperately wanted it. Anything to make this crushing feeling of guilt and regret go away.

"I fucked up. I...I know this is bad." I gulped. What I was about to ask for felt as difficult as dragging fish hooks through my guts, but I had to do it. "I get it, you're mad. You're angry and..."

"Angry is a fucking understatement," Lucas said, his teeth snapping together near my ear. My heart was pattering like a rabbit facing down wolves — a very foolish rabbit who'd walked right into their den and lingered long enough to be caught.

Although I tried to sound brave, I doubt it worked. I took a deep breath and said, "I can take it."

Manson's mouth twitched as he narrowed his eyes at me. "You can *take it*? What exactly do you think you're *taking* right now? We're pretty damn calm, considering what we're looking at, Jess. If we were to truly show you anger, you'd change your tune."

"Then show me," I said. "Punish me, if that's what you want to do. I'll take it. I deserve it."

Vincent laughed again, but this time, Lucas joined him too. It alarmed me enough that I turned to look at him, standing in the shadows behind me with the lightbulb above him slightly flickering. He was…fuck…

Lucas was smiling.

"Punish you?" he said. "Is that what you want? Does that sound like a fun little game to you? Because this" — he looked around, his smile dangerously tight — "this doesn't look like a game. This looks like you've earned some real fucking consequences."

"Fine," I said. I was blustering my way through every word. "I remember my safeword. You can just —"

Manson whirled toward me like a viper, lean body coiled with fury. His dark eyes appeared almost black as he looked down at me.

"I see what you're doing," he said, his voice a dangerous hiss. "Do you think that because you have a safeword that we won't be properly punishing you? Or have you forgotten what it's like to be over my knee?"

I certainly hadn't forgotten. Finding myself bent over his lap in the middle of a party had been one of the most defining moments of my life, bizarre as that was. I'd accepted his dare to serve him but had never expected him to offer me a safeword, giving me a safety net in case things got to be too much.

That word gave me the freedom to kick and cry over his lap with complete abandon, knowing I had a way out if I needed it. They wouldn't cause me harm, but they also wouldn't make this easy.

I didn't deserve to have it easy. I wanted to erase my shame, get rid of it as quickly as I possibly could. The only way I knew of to do that was to accept the consequences they wanted to give.

Manson was watching my face, eyes narrowed. It was a sharp and accusatory gaze, searching for any crack in my determination.

"You don't know what you're fucking asking for," he said. He brushed a loose strand of hair away from my face, and the brief touch of his fingers against my cheek was electric. "We'll make you cry. We'll make it *hurt*."

Behind him, Jason fixed me with a cold stare. "And we'll enjoy every goddamn second."

Ooh, fuck. My guilt was suddenly crowded by a swell of intense desire.

"Then make it hurt," I said. "I'm telling you that I'm accepting the consequences."

Manson and Lucas exchanged a glance. Then Manson straightened, cracking his wrists. The motion sent a tingle zapping through me. I took a step back, only to flinch when I nudged against Lucas and realized how close he'd been the entire time.

"How is the little slut going to make this up to us?" he said. His breath tingled over my neck, hot and dangerously close. I kept my eyes on Manson, but I could see Lucas in my peripheral vision, leaning around my shoulder as he watched my face. "I think I'd like to see her beg. What do you think, boys?"

God, the fact that this turned me on as much as it shamed me was so confusing. There was probably a psychology student out there who could write their entire thesis studying my horny brain.

Manson nodded along to Lucas's idea as he stepped toward me, his hand cupping the back of my neck to jerk me closer. He was shirtless, every lean muscle defined by a slight sheen of sweat.

"I'd enjoy that," he said, his fingers digging into my neck. "I think I'd like to see her begging for mercy."

"I'll give her one minute until she's wailing like a baby," Jason said. He was still standing against his car, face in shadow from his hood. He lifted his arm and curled his finger at me. "Come here."

Oh, fuck. I instinctually took a step back but bumped into Lucas. He hissed in my ear, "Where do you think you're going? He told you to come, so get your ass over there."

Manson pushed me forward, using his hand on the back of my neck to propel me on my way. I stumbled slightly and Jason grabbed my arm, bending me over the back of the Z. The metal was freezing cold, and I squealed, pressing back against his hand, but it was like fighting a brick wall.

"I should beat your ass black and blue," he said, his words pouring liquid heat into my veins.

"Oh, she'll be getting a spanking," Manson said. "Why don't you start her off?"

Jason was grinning when I turned my face toward him. Shit, I was in for it.

I had a thing for spanking, undeniably. But telling partners I liked to be spanked usually resulted in a few little smacks during sex and nothing more. It was hard to find the words to explain that I didn't want a swat; I wanted a fully-fledged, bent over, legs kicking, doubting-my-own-endurance *spanking*.

Well, congratulations Jessica Martin, you got your wish in the absolute worst way possible. This spanking wasn't for fun, it was for punishment. They intended to make me regret what I'd done, and they had the power to do it.

Vincent rested his hands on the trunk beside me. I had Jason on my right and him on my left.

"Pull your dress up," Vincent said. I hesitated, but he leaned down and said sweetly, "Pull it up or you're taking off everything."

I bit my lip, teeth digging painfully into my flesh. The pain gave me something to focus on besides embarrassment as I reached down, pulling up the hem of my dress. A blush swept over my face, hot and damning. My panties were cheeky little things with scarcely more material than a thong.

Manson and Lucas stepped closer, but it was Jason I kept my eyes on. He passed his baseball bat to Manson, who swung it idly in his hand.

"Look at that cute little ass," Jason mused. "Bubbly. I bet it bounces when you smack it."

I was so nervous I thought I was going to burst. The dread was going to kill me. "Just spank me already!" I blurted. "I don't need to hear your horny monologuing. I —"

Smack!

The force of his swat shocked my pride into a red alert, and it was immediately followed by more. Every slap was sharp and biting, igniting a wildfire against my ass as he swapped between cheeks, making sure each got a stinging introduction to the palm of his hand. I clenched — teeth, fists, thighs, everything. But clenching didn't make it any easier. Jason's pace never faltered.

"Fuck," I growled, bringing up my arm and curling it beneath my face so I could press my mouth against it. But Vincent got his hand beneath my chin and squeezed my face, holding my head up.

"No hiding, Jess," he said. "You wanted consequences, well, here they are. Feels good, doesn't it?"

"Fantastic." I was huffing, holding back my whimpers through sheer force of will. My core was swiftly heating, my pussy clenching despite the pain — not just despite it, but *because* of it.

It had been a few years, but damn, I'd forgotten how impossible it was to maintain any dignity during a spanking.

"Ow!" The yelp burst out of me, hands flying back in a foolish attempt to cover myself. Vincent caught my hands immediately. He held my wrists firmly against my lower back, leaving me without even a moment of reprieve.

"Do. Not. Fuck. With. My. Things." Each of Jason's words had a smack to emphasize it.

The moment Jason stopped, Vincent hauled me upright. He turned me, directing me toward his mangled Subaru. All his windows had been busted out, the glass shimmering around the vehicle like a sad dusting of glitter. He guided me with one hand on the nape of my neck as Manson opened the car's passenger door.

"I believe in making the best of a bad situation," Vincent said, his lips brushing teasingly over my ear as Manson used a rag to brush any remaining shards of glass away from the window frame. "Would I prefer to take you up to my attic and string you up from the ceiling? Absolutely. But I guess that will have to wait until the next time you throw a goddamn tantrum."

Manson smiled at me through the open window, the baseball bat he held tapping on the ground. If it had been Alex or one of the other guys left behind, those bats would have been put to use. They would have made an example of them, a clear warning that they weren't to be fucked with. Instead, it was only me here to take the fall.

My brain was a mess, flooded with confusing hormones, but it didn't need to do me the cruelty of thinking about how hot the four of them wielding bats would be. Bloody beatdowns weren't supposed to be *sexy*.

Vincent bent me over the open window. My feet barely touched the ground, the windowsill digging into my stomach. It put my face level with Manson's hips, with his...

God. He was hard. My mouth gaped open and closed wordlessly as he clutched himself through his jeans.

"How are we doing this, angel?" he said. Vincent shoved up my dress and gripped my stinging flesh before he dragged his nails over me, leaving burning trails behind. "Are you going to show me you're sorry, or am I forcing you?"

I felt like I'd been shrunk down to a minuscule size. Lucas came around the side of Subaru, bat swinging in his hand, to stand behind Manson's shoulder. The two of them looking down at me — armed, dangerous, and furious — was even more fuel for my quivering humiliation.

I sharply sucked in a breath as Vincent smacked my ass. The swat stung as much as Jason's, but Vincent paused before the next smack, allowing the sting to bloom and settle before he ignited it again.

"Answer Daddy Manson, Jess," he said, the tease obvious in his voice.

The expression on my face as I struggled to keep my mouth shut must have been truly comical, because both Manson and Lucas laughed at me. The octaves of their voices in unison made my stomach do a backflip as Lucas reached around Manson's waist and unbuckled his belt. He brought his face close to Manson's neck as he did, his nose tracing along his flesh until he reached Manson's ear and nipped, teeth flashing in a sudden, spontaneous bite.

Manson gave me a cocksure grin as Lucas slid the belt free. The two of them made brief eye contact, something unspoken passing between them as Lucas looped the belt around my throat. It squeezed me, not enough to stifle my breathing but more than enough to lock me into the position.

"Sounds like we're forcing you, then," Lucas said. He gave the belt a tug, keeping my head up as Manson unbuttoned his jeans. He took his time, unhurried. He was too calm, too perfectly in control of this situation, while I was swiftly losing any semblance of calm.

Vincent's spanking forced a cry from my mouth, and I stomped my feet, puffing desperately.

"That fucking hurts!" I choked out the words, which trembled like I was on the verge of tears. God, crying would feel good. It was so hard to hold back. As much as the spanking itself hurt, trying to force myself to be calm and brave hurt too. I was gripped by the constant sense of fighting a losing battle, backsliding into complete debasement with nothing I could do to stop it.

"Aww, it hurts?" Vincent clawed his nails down my ass again as Lucas tightened the belt, holding me in place. "Funny, because it looks to me like you've got a wet spot on your panties, Jess. I can't imagine it hurts *that* bad."

I snapped my legs together, but it was too late. They'd already seen it and shame wrapped around me, searing over my face. It was hardly a secret that pain turned me on; they already knew that. But it didn't make having my reaction pointed out any easier.

Manson pulled down his briefs and his cock sprang free, bouncing in front of my face. Fuck, even in one of the worst positions of my life, he looked so damn good. His head was swollen, his shaft lined with blue veins that were tight against his pale skin.

He leaned down, and for a brief moment, his voice softened. "Still want the consequences, Jess?"

My stomach roiled, but I determinedly nodded my head. "Yes."

"Open up for him," Lucas ordered roughly. I looked up, my eyes locking on to Manson's as he straightened, but I wasn't fast enough to obey. Lucas gripped my face and squeezed my jaw, forcing my mouth open. At the same time, Vincent smacked me again, and the cry that burst out of me was shockingly loud as it echoed around the garage.

"That's what I want to hear," Manson said. "I want to hear you try to scream like that with my cock down your throat."

I'm sure I would. He would claim every scream, every cry, every tear he possibly could.

"You'd better give him what he fucking wants, girl, you hear me?" Lucas said. "I want to see tears." I nodded, although it was difficult while being so restrained. Manson entered my mouth while Lucas held me still, sliding his shaft over my tongue. He nudged against the back of my throat, pressing until it was a struggle not to gag. Restrained bliss flickered over his face as I experimentally stroked my tongue over him.

"If you need to tap out, three knocks on the door," he said. "Understood?"

None of them moved until I nodded. Then Manson thrust hard into my mouth, fucking my throat with a mercilessness that swiftly became overwhelming. Vincent gave me another sharp smack and Manson's cock muffled my cry, choking me with every thrust.

"This is what happens to bad girls," he said, his breath quickening as I tried to use my tongue in unison with his thrusts.

If I could make him feel good, then maybe…

Maybe I'd still get exactly the punishment I deserved.

"Choke on it," Lucas said, and a slight jerk on the belt guaranteed I did. The tears in my eyes overflowed, streaming down my cheeks. Any semblance of composure was completely destroyed.

Manson gasped, lip curling with pleasure as my throat squeezed around him. Vincent and Lucas switched places, and Vincent gripped the belt around my neck. He crouched down, catching a tear as it rolled down my cheek, and licked it from his fingertip.

"Poor little Jess," he said. "Makes your pussy wet, doesn't it?"

Manson buried himself deep in my throat, his breath hitching. God, he tasted good. Sweat and skin, with an intoxicating natural musk as my nose was buried in the dark hair around the base of his shaft. Lucas's big calloused hands gripped my ass, squeezing me roughly. Behind me, Jason said, "Fuck, she turns so red, doesn't she?"

"And she's fucking dripping," Lucas said. He kicked my feet wider apart, throwing me off balance as my toes stretched to remain on the ground. My panties were tugged to the side, the cool air kissing over my skin. "Get your face in there, J. Let's see her shake."

My surprised cry vibrated around Manson's cock as a tongue slid over me, swirling over my clit and dipping into my pussy. Lucas spanked me at the same time, his palm landing in a shockingly heavy smack. My ass was burning, my endurance cracking with every additional spank. But Jason's tongue focused in on my clit, lapping until the muscles in my thighs were twitching, and I groaned. Manson's cock jerked in my mouth, his pre-cum salty and slightly bitter on my tongue.

"You like how that cock tastes?" Vincent said, his green eyes bright and his voice low. "Jason is on his knees between your legs with his face buried in your pussy. It's too bad you won't get to come."

"Oh God, no." The words tried to come out, but they were garbled around Manson's thick cock.

"Fuck…" Manson cursed, jaw clenched. He thrust harder, faster. I knew he was going to come as I lapped my tongue over him, eager to show him I was sorry.

But he gripped my hair and pulled out of my mouth. I was left gasping, then desperately yelping as Lucas spanked me and Jason's lips closed over my clit, sucking until I saw sparks. Manson's cock was right in front of my face, but I couldn't reach it, pre-cum dripping slowly from his slit as he stroked himself.

"Lucas." He snapped the man's name from between clenched teeth. Lucas left me with one last burning swat and knelt before Manson, right in front of me. He took Manson's cock in his hand, unbridled hunger on his face as he looked at the man standing over him and ran his tongue over his lips.

Lucas opened his mouth, taking Manson all the way into his throat. Manson exhaled sharply, lifting his arms and clasping them behind his head. Vincent tugged on the belt around my throat, warning me, "Watch him. Maybe you can learn a thing or two about pleasing your masters."

My clit felt as if it had its own heartbeat, pulsating under Jason's tongue and heating as Lucas locked his eyes on me. The sight of his full lips stroking along Manson's shaft was so unbearably erotic. Manson groaned, long and loud as his hard, shallow thrusts kept him deep in Lucas's throat as he came.

But Lucas didn't swallow. He turned to me and gripped my face again. Vincent pulled up on the belt and said, "Open up. Take it."

I whimpered as I obeyed. Lucas leaned close, and spat Manson's cum into my mouth. It dripped down my chin, too much for me to take. It was disgusting — *God, it was so hot.* It was truly repulsive — *it made me shiver with ecstasy.* I managed to swallow as Lucas watched me, cruel amusement twisting his mouth into a mockery of a grin.

"Take your medicine," he said, using his fingers to catch the drips that had streaked down my chin. He pushed his fingers into my mouth, forcing me to lick them clean. "Every drop." He pressed his fingers so deep into my mouth that I gagged, my chest lurching. My moment of weakness gave him new inspiration. He kept his fingers there, hooked deep into my mouth and pressing on the back of my tongue. "Don't throw up on me now, girl."

"Control yourself, Jessica," Manson ordered, tucking his cock away. Every muscle in my throat demanded I gag again, my muscles convulsing. I was shaking all over as Vincent reached through the open window, gave my ass a smack, and then sunk his fingers inside me.

He thrust into me with a quick steady rhythm, fingers slick with my arousal as Jason kept pleasuring me with his tongue. But the stimulation was far too brief. Vincent pulled his hand back and forced his fingers into my mouth beside Lucas's.

"You like that, don't you?" Vincent said, saliva dripping from my lips. "You like tasting how wet you are?" Jason groaned against me, and my eyes nearly rolled back.

"That's a good girl, keep it down," Manson said.

Finally my mouth was freed, leaving me messy and trembling as Lucas got to his feet and Vincent went back to fingering me.

"Fuck, please..." I keened. The wet sound of his fingers thrusting into me was so humiliatingly loud, as were my gasping breaths. I wanted to curl up at their feet. I wanted to cry, scream, and kick with abandon. "Please, please, please, I'm sorry, I'll be good!"

"I've heard that one before," Manson said, the ghost of a smile tugging at his mouth.

"No, no, please, I mean it, I really mean it, please!" I was certain I wouldn't be sitting down for the rest of the week, but I needed this orgasm so damn badly that I sobbed. "God, Jason, please don't stop, please..."

Manson seized my face. "When you call to your God, you'd better look at him," he said. I shuddered, the heat in my abdomen becoming a throbbing inferno as I realized what he meant. There was only one God before me and it was Manson himself.

"God, please." My voice was tiny, pleading. I was right on the edge. "Please, please, please, let me come, please!"

But Manson's expression was merciless. Vincent was chuckling at my pleading, an utterly sadistic sound that drenched me in shame again. Dignity? What dignity? That was out the window, long gone, an extinct species. My brain was latched on to one thing, and one thing only — somehow managing to orgasm before Manson cut me off.

But I was a fool to think I could win. This was their playground and I was their toy, a desperate horny mess bucking my hips against Jason's mouth to reach my peak faster. Manson was smiling, the expression widening with my every desperate breath.

"Don't," I pleaded, my voice shaking. My pussy throbbed in that blissful, familiar feeling. "Don't stop him. Please, God, don't make him stop, please."

Manson shook his head, as if I were so very silly. "Bad girls don't get rewarded, Jess. And you've been a very bad girl."

He didn't even need to give an order. Jason stopped, the lack of contact making me cry out in protest. He smacked his lips as if he'd just eaten a meal, and instead of pleasure, I got his palm slapping down on my ass again, reigniting my skin with stunning speed.

"This is what happens," Lucas said as I begged with useless abandon. "This is what you earned."

I shook my head frantically, gasping through tears at the stinging pain. My safeword teetered on the tip of my tongue, but I didn't give it voice. I'd told them I could take it and I would. I knew what I deserved, what I needed. And I needed to suffer.

Only when I was wailing, my begging completely incomprehensible, did the spanking stop.

16

MANSON

Jess grimaced as she tugged her underwear up over her reddened ass. She sniffled angrily, looking between the four of us with a pouting lip and watery eyes.

As if she hadn't literally asked for this.

"Don't you give me that look," Vincent said the moment her gaze slid over to him. "I'll bend you back over so fast it'll make you dizzy."

For once, she had the good sense to stay silent. God, she made me feel insane. Every time I looked too long at the Mustang — tires slashed, windows broken, paint keyed, dents in every panel — I wanted to spank her again. I wanted her to *learn*. I would have felt better if I'd thought it would do her any long-term good, but lessons weren't learned in a single day.

Why the hell had she asked for this? And better yet — why had I given in to her? I was fucking infuriated, yes, but I usually avoided shit like this when I was so angry. It felt a little too close to losing control.

But she'd asked for punishment, and who was I to deny her? She'd chosen to face our wrath rather than running off. It was an unspoken show of trust that I hadn't expected, but it left me more confused than anything else.

Why did she have to push me? She knew exactly how to infuriate me. She knew all the right words to prod my temper. It had always been an unending tug of war between hatred and longing with her. She was selfish, spoiled, and completely self-absorbed, but she was also faking it constantly. Faking the confidence, the smiles, faking that she was a good, well-behaved girl.

Good, well-behaved girls didn't get dripping wet when they were punished. Behind that angelic blonde hair and innocent green eyes was a masochist who undeniably craved the pain. I'd already known it and yet it still felt unbelievable.

That was what kept drawing me back in, that was what had intrigued all of us. Jessica went through life wearing a mask, but beyond that mask was a wild, twisted woman, aching for a way out. She hid it, and then she made foolish decisions to avoid admitting what she wanted.

I couldn't make that my problem. I'd made that mistake before.

"I need to get back to my car," Jess groaned, rubbing her hands over her face. Her cheeks were pink, her eyes a little reddened and swollen. If it was up to me, if she were actually mine, this would have been only the beginning of her punishment. If she were mine, she would have been standing in a corner, bare-bottomed, while she waited for her next spanking.

She wanted that — consequences, order, control, someone to pull her out of her attitude and bring her back down to reality. But unless she chose it, unless she chose us, what more was I supposed to do?

"Where are your keys?" I said. She dug around in her dress's front pockets, finally pulling out a small set of keys on a pink lanyard. I snatched them from her hand.

"Hey! You can't —"

"I can smell alcohol on your breath," I said. "You're not driving anywhere. Where's your car?"

She folded her arms, looking off to the side as if that made her defiant stance any better. "Back at the bridge," she said.

I sighed heavily, pinching the bridge of my nose as I looked at the cars again. Flat tires. No windows. At least they'd been scared off before they could start fucking around under the hoods. We had one client's car in there too, but luckily it had been spared.

"I'm too damn tired for this," I said. "I'm not dealing with it tonight. You can sleep here. We'll take you back to your car in the morning."

"What?" Both Jess and Lucas gaped at me in unison. Lucas was trying to keep his anger reined in, but a vein in his neck was throbbing with buried fury as he said, "You want her to stay in our fucking house?"

"I want to get some damn sleep," I snapped, and his mouth shut. "I'm not driving anywhere tonight, and I'm sure as hell not walking her ass home."

Lucas grumbled, turning away from me and pacing to the other side of the garage. I didn't blame him for not wanting her here, but we were all tired. Things probably wouldn't feel any better in the morning, but at least then, I'd have the energy to deal with it.

Jason, who'd been sitting next to Vincent against the back bumper of the Mustang, said, "She can sleep in my room. I'll be in the attic anyway." He took a drag on Vince's vape as he stood, the cloud of vapor curling from his lips as he told Jess threateningly, "If you touch a damn thing in that room besides the bed, I'll spank you again."

Her blush deepened. It drew my attention to the freckles on her nose, and I looked away from her, trying not to stare. How could she make me so angry and then…then make me feel like this? How was it possible to look at someone and feel simultaneously enraged and attracted?

"I won't touch anything," she said.

"Come on, then." I jerked my head toward the house. "I'll show you upstairs."

She followed me quietly, her head down and her arms folded. I snapped my fingers as I opened the door, ordering the dogs to step back. Jojo was already wagging her tail, eager to make friends, but Haribo regarded Jess suspiciously, making small, uncertain barks toward her.

"They won't bite," I said as Jess nervously squeezed behind me through the door. "Unless I tell them."

"That's not very reassuring," she said. The dogs stayed in the entryway as we ascended the stairs, her footsteps soft behind me.

When I took a glance back at her, her eyes were wandering around, taking in everything she could. I would have been so ashamed if she'd seen this place when we first moved in. It had been filthy, damn near condemned. Now it looked like something worth living in.

I abruptly looked away from her, mentally scolding myself. Sigmund Freud could have developed a whole new complex around me being so obsessed with someone so unreachable. Then he could develop another one around the fact that I didn't only want Jessica for me, I wanted her for *us*.

Bringing the woman I wanted into the family we'd built, intermeshing our lives and growing a relationship together, felt natural to me. But to most people, it didn't. Society wanted things to be labeled, to fit into neat and tidy boxes. Sex was meant to be exclusive, romantic, and flawless. Friends were only friends and never lovers, nothing could grow or change. Who you used to be could never be separated from who you'd become.

I hated it, rejected it. I wanted nothing to do with that outlook, that moral posturing. I'd struggled with it like everyone else. The world was sure to always remind me I didn't fit. If I hooked up with a girl, I was straight, but if I dated a guy, I was gay. If I wanted sex to be rough, I was violent. If I wanted to choose my own family and build relationships in my own way, I was perverted. If I wanted to defend myself, to stand up to those who would harm me, I was dangerous.

Reject the boxes you're offered and people will keep trying to shove you into them. They'll put their labels on you and demand you adhere to them, and then if you don't, it becomes your own damn fault that life is difficult.

That was where Jess and I differed. I'd given up on trying to fit in a long time ago and she was still clinging to the dream of societal acceptance.

Jason's room was at the very end of the hallway. I opened the door and motioned her inside, watching as she stepped in and looked around. His bed was small, but he rarely slept in it, shoved into the corner on the right. His desk and computer took up the rest of the space, three wide-screen monitors stretching from one side of his desk all the way to the other. His window was blocked out with a heavy curtain. Blue LED strips in the corners and along the ceiling bathed the room in a neon glow.

Jess turned to face me, her lips pressed tightly together. The neon made her hair appear almost white, glowing ethereally.

"The bathroom is right next door," I said. "The dogs won't bother you. They stay downstairs."

She nodded in understanding, swallowing hard. I couldn't blame her for ghosting, or for letting down her guard with me for one night and then retreating the moment the sun rose. Boxes were safe and easy. Leave the shelter of the box and the world becomes significantly less friendly.

She was probably wiser for trying to fit in. She was following the rules the world had handed her, shitty as they were.

I closed the gap between us. She looked away at first, but slowly her gaze came up to meet mine. I caressed my fingers over her cheek, tucking her blonde hair back over her shoulder. Part of me still felt so angry, fury pulsing in my chest. But it was impossible to look at her without my heart softening. I was weak as hell for this woman. She could stab me in the heart and I'd probably still forgive her.

"So…you and Lucas?" she said, curiosity in her uncertain gaze.

"Are you surprised?" I'd understood her jealousy over Veronica — she had a grudge against that woman going back years. It was a sore subject. But I wasn't sure how she'd react to this. If Lucas and I being intimate with each other was going to make her jealous too, it was a red flag I wouldn't be able to ignore.

But a tiny smile came over her face. She hid it quickly, forcing her expression back to seriousness. "No, not surprised at all. It makes sense."

"Does it? Why's that?"

"You've been best friends for years," she said. "You're calm and he's…not…but I think you help him be. He looks at you like he wants to listen, and I didn't think Lucas wanted to listen to anybody, so…yeah, it makes sense."

The expression on her face when Lucas had taken me into his mouth had been so damn sexy I'd almost come on the spot. She'd looked enraptured, torn between longing and fascination.

The silence stretched between us. She almost turned away but then hesitated, as if there was something more she wanted to say.

"Why'd you do it, Jess?" I said. "Why did you come with them?" I believed her when she said she hadn't caused all that destruction. But she'd still broken in, she'd been right there with them the whole time.

Her eyes darted away, regret making her lips tightly draw together.

"I-I don't know. Everyone else was going. They didn't tell me what exactly…" She shook her head, cutting off the excuse.

I wanted to shake her. I wanted to beg her to *think*, to stop trying so damn hard to please everyone else that she disregarded her own mind.

But I couldn't make it my problem. Not again. I knew better.

I leaned down and kissed her forehead. She leaned into me, eyes closed, a soft sigh escaping her. I hoped she still felt the tension of her ruined orgasm. I hoped it kept her awake, the desperate desire to touch herself overwhelming every other thought until all she could do was fantasize and ride the edge.

"You're not allowed to touch yourself tonight," I said, and she stiffened. "Bad girls don't get to come."

Defiance flared in her expression. For a moment, even exhausted as I was, I almost welcomed the opportunity to bend her over again. But then she sniffed, rubbing her backside tenderly before she said, "Fine."

"I expect a better answer than that."

If she got to push me, then I was going to push her too. Her expression tightened as she struggled with herself, doubtlessly weighing the risks and rewards of any further snappiness.

Finally, she managed to grind out the words, "Yes, sir."

The others were on the porch when I stepped back outside. Jason and Vincent were seated on the bench beneath the window, their faces drawn. Lucas was on the front step, a cigarette between his fingers as he stared toward the garage.

I sat down beside him, nudging against his side. The night air felt good, swiftly cooling me down. But frustration still sat on my chest like a lead weight.

None of us spoke for several long minutes. We'd dealt with this shit almost all our lives, in one way or another. We were accustomed to it. But some days, it all became too exhausting. The pure spiteful energy that had kept me going as a teenager was running out of steam, leaving me bitter and impatient.

I wanted to fucking *live*. Why was that too much to ask for?

"I have a competition in two weeks," Jason said, his voice numb. "Two fucking weeks, man…"

"You'll be ready," I said, turning to look at him over my shoulder. "We'll get the Z fixed in time. I can promise you that."

"We need to get Alex back for this," Lucas said. He held the cigarette toward me, and I took it, relishing the burn as I inhaled. "We need to hit back and hit hard."

"Damn right we do," Jason said. "I should break that motherfucker's fingers for this."

We didn't need to start taking risks when we were so close to getting out of this town. But *not* responding to this was a bigger risk than doing nothing. Alex didn't need retaliation to keep coming for us. He'd come anyway, and he'd keep escalating things if he thought he could get away with it.

We had to make it clear he couldn't. There would be hell to pay.

Vincent sighed, and the bench creaked as he got to his feet. "All right. I think I'll go to bed and have some real nightmares as opposed to this shit. Wake me up early. I'll help get the garage cleaned up."

But I shook my head. "Go ahead and sleep in. Jess can put in some work in the morning to earn that ride back to her car. Just try to get some rest."

His and Jason's footsteps faded away as they went inside and trudged up the stairs. I wondered if Jess was already asleep, or if she was lying awake, disobeying me…

Or if she was awake, adhering to my orders and suffering for it. That was a nice thought.

"Are we really getting wrapped up in this again?" Lucas said. His shoulders were hunched as he stared across the yard. I passed the cigarette, wrapping my arm around his back.

After a moment, I said, "No. We're not getting wrapped up in anything."

He hunched a little more. "Yeah? Why is she sleeping in our house, then?"

"Because I'm not sending her walking home alone in the dark, Lucas. You wouldn't either."

He grumbled something, flicking what remained of the cigarette into the dirt and stubbing it out.

"Look, Jessica likes to pretend her life isn't going to be the dull suburban dream her parents set her up for," I said. "So she riles people up, gets the reaction she wants, and dips. That's how it goes. That's how it's *always* gone."

"Might go differently if we were a little pushier about it."

I looked over at him in surprise, but I'd thought the same thing. None of us had ever *pursued* Jessica — we simply ended up thrown together, clashing like billiard balls knocked aimlessly around a table. It wasn't from lack of desire, it was from simple realism. She wasn't meant for us. She didn't exist in our world; she visited it, had a look around like a tacky tourist, and left the moment it got too real for her.

She was the girl we couldn't have, no matter how close she got. Despite the games we played, the decision was hers in the end. It was her choice.

And the choice was never us. It couldn't be us.

"There's nothing to push for," I said, as if it were really that simple. "She's going to get out of Wickeston and move on to bigger and better things. She'll find some good-looking dumbass who fits her aesthetic, get married in a flashy ceremony, and spend the next twenty years having boring sex and becoming best friends with her vibrator, before she divorces him in a mid-life crisis. She'll be that chick who moves to Vegas for a fresh start and constantly tells everyone about who she was in high school. That's it. No *us* involved."

His chest rumbled slightly, and when I looked over, he was chuckling. "You've got it so bad. You have a whole fantasy life laid out for this woman and you can't even manage a little self-insert? You can't add a little *what-if* in there?"

I was too tired for this conversation. "I thought you didn't want to get involved, so why do you care?"

"Because I can't stand to see you so fucking torn up over it," he said. "You can't let it go. It's been years of this shit, and you still can't stop."

In the illumination from the porch's light, I noticed something on his neck that I hadn't earlier: scratches. Long red scratches, doubtlessly from someone's long pink nails.

I traced my finger over one of them. "You get into a fight with a cat today?" I said, and he scoffed.

"Don't start."

"Hey, I didn't start anything. You're the one who drove her

off in your car and fucked around."

"We didn't fuck around. Much." He added that last word with a sardonic glance in my direction. "At least I didn't carve a damn heart into her finger."

I shoved the back of his head as I got up. "I'm going to bed before I carve you up too. Don't stay out here all night."

"I won't." He waved me away, and I had my hand on the door when he suddenly said, "Hey, Manson?"

"Yeah?"

"What if she wanted to?"

I turned back, my hand still gripping the doorknob. "Wanted to what?"

"What if she wanted to…you know…" He was trying so hard to sound casual. "What if she wanted to get involved? With us?"

I took a deep breath.

"What if she wanted to get involved with us…" I repeated the words slowly, mulling them over as I had so many times. *Too many times.* "What if she admitted she'd been wrong all along and wanted to give this a try? What if she said she'd been hiding her true feelings because she was scared of rejection, but she was ready to throw all that away? What if she woke up tomorrow and changed her whole life to be with us? Damn her mother, fuck her friends, forget her plans. What if?" I shook my head, wrenching open the door. "That's way too many what-ifs for me."

17

JESSICA

I didn't think I would be able to sleep that night. The unfamiliar room was full of strange shapes and smells, the house creaking and settling around me. I'd avoided even going near this house for so many years, and now I was lying in it.

Lying with a sore butt, throbbing clit, and more shame than I knew what to do with.

The door was shut, so unless Jason had cameras under his blankets, there was absolutely nothing to stop me from disobeying Manson's orders and getting off. But I didn't. I wasn't even sure why, only that something stopped me every time my hand got close. I lay there, squirming uncomfortably, replaying what they'd done to me over and over until it became a filthy yet delicious loop in my head. Lucas spitting Manson's cum into my mouth, the warmth of Jason's tongue, the stinging smack of Vincent's hand...

I briefly closed my aching eyes to rest them. The next thing I knew, the heavy curtain over the window was framed with light, and I could hear birdsong drifting in from outside.

It was morning.

I sat up, stretching my arms and rolling out my shoulders. I'd slept better than I had in a long time, but my ass stung every time I moved, like a bad sunburn on both cheeks. Having not showered last night, I surely looked like a mess. I grabbed my phone from the bedside table, surprised it still had any battery left.

There was a text from Danielle. **Hey girl!!! You good? Sorry about bailing, babe, please tell me you're not in jail or something!**

She ended it with a laughing emoji. My fingers tightened around the phone until it was shaking in my hand, and I dropped it on the bed so I wouldn't hurl it across the room. She'd known what they were up to all along and hadn't mentioned a damn thing to me. Had they *planned* to leave me here? To let me take the fall for the whole thing?

I doubted they expected "taking the fall" to be quite like...that.

I shuffled out of bed and fixed it up, trying to leave the pillows and blankets exactly as I'd found them. Everything in here smelled like Jason, his scent saturated into every surface. His massive computer setup occupied more space than his bed, and he had stacks of books piled below his desk. *Fundamentals of Software Architecture*, *Domain-Driven Design*, *Observability Engineering*...and then stacks and stacks of manga and superhero comics.

He'd told me not to touch anything in here, but I couldn't help my curiosity as I cracked open the closet and took a look inside. So *that* was where the mess was; stacks of electronics boxes, loose cables, and clothing were packed inside in a precariously balanced heap. I decided it was better to shut the door again than risk it all tumbling down.

It didn't sound like anyone else in the house was awake yet, or if they were, they certainly weren't making any noise. I put on my shoes and opened the bedroom door, but almost slammed it again when I found their massive gray pit bull sitting in the hallway, waiting for me.

I stared at her, she stared at me. Last night, she'd sounded like she wanted to bite my ankles off, but this morning, she gave me one long look with her big brown eyes and then her tail began to thump on the floor.

"Aw, you're not so vicious, are you?" I said, crouching down to scratch under her chin. She was definitely a cuddler and immediately moved closer, almost knocking me on my ass. "Oh, honey, you are not a lapdog, but you are so cute."

Glancing down the hall as I gave her belly rubs, I spotted their other dog at the top of the stairway. He regarded me suspiciously, giving me an uncertain bark before he waddled back downstairs.

Oh, well. At least one of them wanted to be my friend — probably one of the only friends I had left after last night.

Slipping into the bathroom, I took one look at myself in the mirror and groaned. I gave my face a thorough wash with warm water, working some of the tangles out of my hair with my fingers. I still looked like a gremlin who'd crawled out of the woods, but whatever.

Before I left the bathroom, I tugged up my dress to get a look at my backside in the mirror. It didn't only feel like a bad sunburn; it looked like it too. My skin was bright red and my fingers left pale imprints when I pressed them against my cheek. Damn, that stung. It also brought back memories of exactly what it felt like to bend through that window with my mouth full and my ass getting smacked, and a shiver ran over my entire body.

I wasn't eager to take a spanking like that again. But the other parts, the parts that had me gasping with pleasure, I would gladly experience again.

I took a deep breath and slowly exhaled. I needed to find Manson so I could get back to my car. The pit bull — was her name Jojo? — was still waiting for me in the hall when I came out and walked along with me as I wandered toward the stairs. There were two more rooms, one of which was right next to the bathroom.

The door was wide open, the room within coldly utilitarian. There was a bed, dresser, and clothes hamper in the corner, but nothing else. Perhaps a guest bedroom? There were a few things on top of the dresser, but as tempting as it was, maybe it was better not to push my luck with the snooping.

The next room, closest to the stairway, also had the door cracked open. I could only see a sliver of an open closet through the crack, but nothing more.

I stood outside the door, listening carefully. There were no voices or footsteps — either the boys were outside, or still asleep. I glanced down at Jojo and found her looking back, licking her chops excitedly.

"It's not snooping if you open the door," I whispered and pointed to the crack. "Wanna go in, girl?"

To my surprise, she nudged her nose against the door and trotted inside without any hesitation, hopping up on the bed. With one glance, I knew this room had to be Manson's. I recognized the bull's skull hanging on the wall above the bed, painted black with an intricate gold design. Everything was meticulously clean — from the shelves beside the closet covered in vinyl records, to the desk in the corner that held a laptop and an oil diffuser. It was switched on, filling the room with a citrusy floral scent.

So much for not snooping.

A record player sat on a table below the shelves, and I squinted my eyes to read the record sitting on it. *Bauhaus.* I'd never heard of them, but it was probably because the album had come out in 1980.

"Didn't you get enough of going through our shit last night?"

I whirled around, clutching my hand to my heart before it could leap out of my chest. Manson leaned against the door frame, arms folded as he watched me. Oh God, why did he have to look like *that?* All broody and irritated, regarding me through narrowed eyes as he tried to figure out what I was up to. He was wearing a shirt this morning, but the black fabric clinging to his frame didn't make it any easier not to stare.

"I, um…the dog, she…I was trying to get her…" I waved my hand vaguely in the direction of Jojo, who thumped her tail happily as she lay curled up on Manson's bed.

"Right," Manson said. "It was Jojo. I guess you two have decided to get along?"

"I'm just glad she didn't eat me," I said. I was suddenly *far* too aware of the fabric of my dress brushing against my well-spanked backside. It made my skin prickle.

"Her bark is way worse than her bite," he said, jerking his head toward the hall in an indication that I should follow him. "I don't think Jojo is capable of biting anybody. Haribo is the one you have to watch out for."

Following him down the stairs, past the kitchen on my right and the living room to my left, we reached the front porch. The day was warm and humid, but it felt like someone dropped a rock into my stomach as Manson hopped off the porch and trudged across the yard toward the garage.

"Um, I need to go get my stuff…" I said as Manson walked inside, his shoes crunching on glass. God, it looked even worse in daylight. The dents, the broken glass, the ruined paint…I must have looked sick because when he turned around to answer me, he looked alarmed for a moment.

"Are you good?" he said, and I nodded, motioning at the destruction around us.

"It's just…it looks really…shocking. In daylight."

He grimaced as he nodded. "Yeah. It's bad. Which is why you don't need your stuff yet." He grabbed a push broom from the corner, holding it out toward me. "You're going to get to work cleaning up all this glass. Then I'll take you to pick up your car."

Grasping the broom's smooth plastic handle, I sighed. At least it wasn't another spanking. I got to work, carefully sweeping glass from around the cars and underneath them. Manson watched me for a while, his intent gaze flustering me. It was easier once he finally stepped away, taking the stairs to the upper level. The garage was spacious, and the area at the back seemed to be where they did most of their work. There were all kinds of machines I didn't know the purpose of, toolboxes, stacks of tires, and a grease pit that an old car was parked atop of. Lucas was in the pit, his forehead creased with concentration as he worked.

He hadn't even looked at me.

Manson was on the phone upstairs, pacing as he spoke. I only caught snippets of the conversation, enough to put together that he was talking to his auto insurance company. I put my head down and swept a little faster.

By the time I was done, I was sweating through my clothes and my head was pounding with the need for a coffee. Lucas was still ignoring me, but once Manson was off the phone, he came downstairs to check my work.

"Not bad," he said, inspecting the area around the cars. "You got underneath too?"

I nodded, wiping the sweat off my forehead. He watched me do it, his lips parted as if he had something more to say but had completely forgotten. I glanced behind him and caught Lucas's eye for a split second before he turned his back to me again.

"All right," Manson said. "Go get your stuff, I'll drive you to your car."

The Bronco was particularly bouncy as Manson drove down the road, the massive tires rumbling over every dip and pothole. He had the radio turned up and the AC blasting, but kept the window rolled down so he could hang his arm out in the breeze.

I couldn't bear to sit there the whole time in silence. The longer I sat, the more I thought about all the perverted things he could do to me now that we were alone and my thighs squeezed together. The long soak I was planning to take in the tub once I got home was going to have to involve my vibrator too.

Surely his "no touching" rule didn't apply *today*. I'd been a good girl for him.

I closed my eyes, mentally scolding myself. He didn't get to tell me what to do. None of them did.

I glanced over at him out of the corner of my eye. He was different than he'd been in high school. He was far more confident now, his measured speech and careful movements showing an obsessive control over how he presented himself.

"So…when did you start doing the whole mechanic thing?" I said when I couldn't bear to stay quiet any longer. He sat up a little straighter, as if he'd been deep in thought and I'd snapped him out of it.

"The *mechanic thing*." He chuckled. "We're an auto tuning shop, first and foremost. We build cars for competition, speed, and power; we can bolt on parts, swap an engine, fabricate custom pieces, and advise clients on how to get the best performance out of their vehicle. Once we get a bigger space, and the funds, hopefully we'll be adding a Dynamometer to the shop too."

I had no idea what that was, so I smiled and nodded.

He continued, "But uh…it wasn't exactly a childhood dream. I guess I fell into it naturally, though. When I got this beast…" He patted the wheel affectionately. "It was my way out. Freedom. I could get in a vehicle that was entirely my own and drive away from that fucking house. But as I'm sure you remember, the beast was a piece of shit back then."

I giggled, memories coming back to me. "Oh, trust me, I remember. Like that time you were trying to fix it in the school parking lot in the pouring rain?"

"Yeah, that shit happened way too often. But since I didn't have the money to pay someone to fix it, I had to figure it out myself. So I learned."

"And you kept it running all this time?" He nodded, and I shook my head in surprise. "That's really impressive."

His lips twitched into a smile he tried to hide behind his hand. "Honestly, we never would have been able to start the shop without the money my mom left me. I had no idea she even had anything left, but I guess she managed to keep it hidden from my dad even when she was…" He trailed off. "Anyway, we opened the shop once we moved into the house so we haven't been here very long. Our first builds were our own cars, so the more we raced and were able to show off what we could do, the more clients we found. We're only just getting started." He nodded to himself, his speed slowing as we neared Ellis Road and the bridge. "Once we get out of Wickeston, we're going to keep getting bigger and better."

He said it determinedly, as if he were commanding the universe to give him what he wanted instead of merely hoping for it.

Luckily my car was still there, sitting right where I'd left it on the side of the road. I doubted it would get towed sitting overnight, but after the night I had, I wasn't going to assume the best of anything.

Manson pulled into the dirt beside it and parked. "Well, Jess, I can't say it's been fun, but it's been…something."

We looked at each other. He readjusted himself in his seat multiple times, as if he couldn't figure out a comfortable position, before he said, "I guess this could be the last time we see each other, so...have a great life and stay the hell out of my garage."

The last time. Oh, I did *not* like how that sounded. Not one bit.

"Yeah." I nodded, my hand hovering on the door handle. "Okay, um...bye."

God, I could gag from how awkward I felt. That was a *terrible* goodbye, that was...Shit, it didn't matter. I couldn't let it matter.

I hurriedly hopped out of the Bronco, digging for my keys in my bag and unlocking my car, trying all the while not to look back at him. The weather had grown disgustingly muggy, and getting into the car felt like crawling inside a hot tin can. I turned on the engine, frowning as it sputtered. I turned the AC on full blast and leaned my head back as I waited for the cool air to fill the cabin.

But as I sat there, my eyes wandered. Manson hadn't left yet. In fact, he was staring at me, his hand slightly raised as if to get my attention.

I rolled down my window.

"What's wrong with your car?" he said. He sounded as if the answer had already exasperated him and he hadn't even heard it yet.

"Nothing," I said. It was a little louder than usual, but that was normal. Maybe. It had sounded like this for months, so whatever it was probably wasn't serious.

He sighed so hard I could hear it even over the noise. "Your engine is fucked up."

I shook my head. "No, it's not, it's totally —"

The check engine light popped on. The rattling under the

hood increased in volume, with a persistent knocking sound that only grew worse as I let the car idle. It sounded like someone was banging a hammer repeatedly against a steel pipe.

Manson was watching me with his mouth pressed into a thin line.

"Okay, that's not good," I said as the RPMs began to randomly fluctuate without my foot touching the gas. The knocking sound became alarmingly loud. "All right, let's —"

There was a loud bang and the engine abruptly shut off. All the lights on my dash popped on and I was left staring in shock as I tried to figure out what had happened. I opened my door, the fumes of burned oil making me cough as Manson shoved open his door and got out.

"God, I do not need this today." I groaned, staring at the stream of smoke trickling from beneath my hood. Without a word, Manson popped the hood and lifted it, taking a look around before he suddenly dropped to his knees and looked underneath the car.

When he got to his feet, he was shaking his head as if the underside of the car had personally insulted him. He held up a ragged chunk of something covered in oil, looking at me as if I should have known what it was.

I didn't.

"Is that…bad?" I said.

His mouth twitched. "This is part of your engine block, Jess. Trust me, it's bad."

18

JASON

I'd decided to work on the couch for the day, my pajama-clad legs propped up on the coffee table as I stared at endless lines of code that blurred in front of my tired eyeballs. Haribo was squished against my side, snorting in his sleep, but he jerked awake when my phone rang.

It was Manson.

"What's up?" I put the call on speakerphone and set it on the armrest beside me. Usually I took the weekends off, but after last night, I had way too much restless energy and needed to put it into something substantial. Doing any work on the car was useless until we heard back from insurance, so getting this client's website work finished up was my goal for the day.

"Jess's car broke down," he said. His voice was low, and I

could hear the tension in it. "Her fucking engine blew the minute she turned the damn thing on."

I couldn't help but laugh. "I do love to see karma at work. You leave her there to figure it out?"

A long silence followed my question.

"Shit, Manson." I leaned back on the couch, now fully invested as I picked up the phone. "What the hell are you doing?"

"Waiting with her for Ted to get here," he said. Ted was also known as Mr. Teddy Tow, owner and operator of Wickeston's resident towing business. Most of our clients arrived on the back of his truck. "We'll haul her beamer back to the shop and..."

"And *what?*"

I turned, looking toward the hall. Lucas was standing there, wiping his greasy hands on a towel. He was frowning so deep it looked permanently etched into his face.

"What the hell are you towing her back here for?" he said, talking loudly so Manson could hear him.

"Don't give me shit for this," Manson said. "You know you'd do the exact same thing if you were in my position."

"I fucking would not," Lucas said. "I'd laugh at some well-deserved justice and flip her off as I drove away. So why the hell aren't you doing that?"

"I have to say I'm with Lucas on this one," I said. "Not that I'd be the one working on her car, but...shit, man, after last night? I'm still hung up on revenge fantasies, not being her fucking white knight."

"Who's having a revenge fantasy?" Vincent shuffled into the room, looking exhausted as he edged past Lucas. He plopped down on the couch beside me, nudging Haribo out of the way, and dropped his head sleepily on my shoulder.

"Me," I said. "But it won't come true because apparently Manson thinks Jess is a damsel in distress. She broke down."

Vincent snickered, saying to Manson, "Don't worry, man, I get it. Jess breaks down, stranded on the side of the road, desperately needs help, you come to the rescue, bing, bang, boom, orgy. Sounds like a plan."

Lucas groaned. "You're all going to drive me to an early grave."

"I think Jess will do that first," Manson said, and he was probably right.

In my opinion, Jessica could fuck off. I'd given her half the spanking she deserved and seeing her again was only going to make me want to continue. Sure, I'd had a fucked-up crush on her since sophomore year and those feelings hadn't dissipated, but they'd gotten a hell of a lot more complicated. How was it possible to detest someone and yet want them so damn badly?

Insurance was likely going to cover the damage to the vehicles, but it was still a pain in the ass. What was going to be far more difficult, if not impossible, was pressing any charges against the guys who had done it. Our cameras had captured only brief footage of Alex and the others before being disconnected, and considering one of the perpetrators was the son of a local officer, it was likely more trouble than it was worth to try to go after them.

But Lucas and I had already begun discussing our own methods of getting back at those fucks. If you wanted something done right, you had to do it yourself.

Maybe that was Manson's thought process too. But whether he was more focused on fixing her car or fixing *her*, I couldn't guess.

Something told me it was the latter.

"Look, just bear with me here, okay?" Manson said, and Lucas and I exchanged a look. "I don't think she can afford this repair."

"All the more reason to drive the fuck away," Lucas said.

"I thought her parents were pretty loaded," I said. "I don't think she's strapped for cash."

"You know it's not always that easy." I could tell Manson was trying to keep his volume down, as if he didn't want her to hear. "I don't think she wants to ask her parents for the money."

"Well, boo-fucking-hoo," Lucas retorted. "Sounds like you play shitty games and win shitty prizes. Jess can deal with her shit prize alone."

"Ahh, come on," Vincent said, stretching comfortably. "I'm sure she can find a way to pay us."

Something clicked in my head. An idea, a memory, something that rushed through me like adrenaline and sparked my energy.

"We'll figure something out for her," I said, and Lucas threw up his hands.

"I fucking give up. You're all hopeless. Fucking…horny-ass… desperate…" He kept grumbling all the way down the hall and up the stairs. A door slammed, and the old pipes groaned as the shower turned on.

Manson sighed. "He's pissed off, isn't he?"

"I mean…yeah. He's pissed," I said. "But if Jess needs a way to pay, I think I have an idea."

———

Vincent was asleep again by the time the tow truck, Manson,

and Jess arrived. I jogged out to the gate with Haribo at my heels to unlock it for Ted, allowing the big flatbed to drive into the yard with Manson and Jess in the Bronco behind him.

Jess hung back in the yard as Manson and I helped Ted get the BMW unloaded into the garage. I kept glancing over to see how she'd react to having Haribo sniffing around her shoes. Slowly, she squatted down and offered the little dog her hand, scratching his chin when he finally gave her a friendly lick.

There were rarely hard feelings with dogs, even a moody little creature like Bo. I almost felt betrayed that he didn't try to snap her fingers off.

"Thanks, Ted." Manson knuckle-bumped the driver as he prepared to leave. "I owe you one."

"See you for the next one," I said, giving Teddy a wave as he hopped back up into the truck. He was a grizzled guy, pock-marked and gray-haired, but had the biggest heart. He and Vincent could talk for hours, the two of them never running out of stories and cringy jokes to tell each other.

Ted gave us a salute and a smile that was missing a few teeth. "I'll be seeing ya', Mr. Reed! Over and out, Zero Cool." The engine rumbled as he pulled away, dust from his tires drifting through the yard as Manson went to shut the gate behind him.

"What did he call you? Zero Cool?"

I turned. Jess had Haribo cradled in her arms like a baby. The smug mutt was lying there with his tongue lolling out, happy as could be. Little traitor.

"It's from a movie," I said, heading back into the garage. "There was this film called *Hackers* that came out back in the

90s. Zero Cool is an alias for one of the characters. Ted loves his movies almost as much as he loves to tell old stories he only partially remembers."

"He was very talkative," she said, a surprisingly gentle assessment. She popped her lips, swaying slightly as she waited for Manson to return. Her lips were pink, glittery, juicy-looking — probably sticky with gloss. I bet they tasted sweet as candy, almost as good as her pussy.

Fuck. I didn't need to remember that right now, feet away from where it had happened. I'd had my mouth between her legs, I'd listened to her every little cry of pleasure and pain, I'd relished the trembling *I* was causing in her. It made me mad how much I'd enjoyed it, how the sight of her perfect ass bent over my car made my cock start to harden the moment I thought about it.

She obviously still spent time working out, judging by her toned muscles. I wondered what gym she went to, because it certainly wasn't mine. It was probably that nice one near the new movie theater, the gym that had a sauna and a tanning bed. I'd been meaning to check that place out. Not because of her, obviously; she had nothing to do with it.

"What did you do to your car?" I said, and she groaned.

"I don't know," she said, setting Haribo down. "It's been making weird noises for a while. Like someone was banging pieces of metal together in my engine. But it still drove fine so I figured it wasn't serious."

I burst out laughing. "It's been making weird noises for a *while*? What's a while, Jess?"

She shrugged. "I don't know. A year? Maybe?"

I opened her driver door and popped her hood. I may not have been a mechanic, but I knew my way around a vehicle. Jess came around to peer at the engine beside me, eyes narrowed.

"See that?" I said, removing the oil cap and giving her a good look at the black gunk collected inside. "Motor oil isn't supposed to be a paste. If oil can't get through your engine, it's going to overheat and break. When did you last get your oil changed?"

"Six months after I got it, I think."

I stared at her in disbelief. "Six months after...you mean in high school? You haven't had an oil change in over *four years*?"

Manson came back just in time to hear my outburst. He paused for a moment, looking as stunned as if I'd said she fueled the damn thing with hair spray.

"I was busy, okay?" she said. "I didn't drive that much in college unless I was coming back home."

"Right, yeah, of course," I said. "Did you cheat in all your classes there too?"

It was a low blow, but Jess had been aiming low ever since I'd met her and she obviously hadn't changed. I was looking for a fight though; I'd admit that. Seeing her face right next to my thrashed Z didn't exactly make me feel warm and fuzzy.

"Okay, okay, let's be nice," Manson said, getting between us. I innocently put up my hands and stepped back, letting him do his job. It was his shop so if he wanted Jess as a client, he could fucking have her.

But having her as a client still meant we *all* had to deal with her. Hence the brilliant payment idea I'd told to Manson earlier. If Jess was going to be coming here as our customer, we needed to make it worth our while. And if she didn't have cash, then we needed something else.

Lucas finally joined us, stalking into the garage, looking like he wanted to kill something. He was wearing a short-sleeved button-up shirt and his good jeans — the ones that didn't have massive holes and grease stains all over them. When the hell was the last time he wore something with *buttons*?

I sniffed as he stood near me, arms tightly folded across his chest. "You're wearing cologne," I said.

His expression didn't change. "Maybe you should consider doing the same thing. I can smell you from here."

I glared at the side of his head but still gave myself a quick sniff when he walked away. Lucas went over to Jess, wedging her between himself and Manson in front of the car.

"You guys can fix this thing, right?" she said, her tone eager as she looked between the two of them. I rolled my eyes, perching myself on a stool to watch the show. I already knew what they were going to tell her and she wasn't going to be happy about it.

"You're going to need a new engine," Lucas said, his face contorting with disgust when he peeked inside the oil cap. "And there will be labor costs." He whipped a small towel out of his pocket, cracking it repeatedly in the air as he stared her down. "There's a lot of labor involved."

She sighed heavily. "Okay. Great. How much is this going to cost?"

The laptop we kept in the garage was looking a bit worse for wear since the night of the break-in, but at least it still worked. Manson brought up the spreadsheet I'd made to simplify pricing for the shop, plugging in numbers and estimated working hours. I noticed him input far more labor hours than would likely be necessary, but I didn't say a word.

He printed the quote, and I grabbed the paper, presenting the estimate to Jess with a flourish. She sharply sucked in her breath.

"Are you kidding me? No way. There is no way." Her eyes darted across the paper, widening with every line. "Why is labor so expensive?"

"There's a surcharge," Manson said. "For having to deal with you."

I grinned at the appalled expression on her face. This was even more fun than I'd thought it would be. She sputtered, and her eyes looked like they were going to pop out of her head.

"This isn't fair," she said. "This has to violate, like, a law or something. You can't charge more for just one person!"

Lucas snapped the towel again. "Do you really want to start a discussion about breaking laws? Because we can have that conversation, but I don't think you're going to like it."

Jess closed her eyes for a moment, taking several long, deep breaths. When she opened her eyes again, it was obvious she was forcing herself to remain calm. "Look, I can't afford this."

"Go to another shop, then," Manson said simply. "There's Autosphere downtown. Cheap work and cheap parts. They're usually booked up for a few weeks, but it's better than dealing with us, right?"

"Or ask Mommy and Daddy for help," I said. "I'm sure they'll fork out the cash."

I could clearly remember when she'd shown up senior year with this car, still shiny and new, a birthday present from her parents. My parents had bought me a car too. But once they found out I was using it to "sodomize strangers" in the back seat, they'd sold it along with nearly every other gift they'd ever bought me.

It hadn't had the effect on me they'd hoped for though. Sodomy didn't require a car.

She glared at me. "I'm not a child, Jason. My parents don't pay for everything."

"Oh, well, excuse me," I said. I leaned back and pulled out my phone, as if the entire thing didn't interest me anymore. "You've never had a problem figuring out how to pay for shit, Jess. I'm sure you'll think of something."

She'd figured out how to pay me years ago when I finally started demanding compensation for her cheating off my tests and harassing me into writing her essays. I still had the photos she'd sent me on my laptop, saved into an encrypted folder.

It was fucking shameful how many times I'd jacked off to them.

"How long will it take to fix the car?" she said. She actually sounded like she was trying to be reasonable.

Lucas shrugged. "How long will it take you to pay us?"

"I don't have —" Her voice had gotten louder again. She stopped, paused, and lowered it. "I don't have the money to pay you right now."

"We also take alternative payment methods," Manson said, and a grin spread over my face.

"Alternative payment?" she said, frowning in confusion. "What, like, Bitcoin?"

"If you don't want to pay with cash, maybe you have something else of value," I said.

Jess looked utterly lost. "Are you trying to get me to sell my organs or something?"

Lucas, who'd been in the shower when I'd told my idea to Manson earlier, also looked lost — only he appeared significantly more murderous about it.

"One moment, Miss Martin," he said roughly. "We need to have a little meeting with our accountant."

We gathered together at the far side of the garage as I explained. We discussed it in sharp whispers, Manson and I teaming up to get Lucas on our side. I'd expected him to put up more of a fight but once I'd explained — and after a long minute of him grumbling about how "it had better be worth it" — he agreed pretty quickly.

We turned in unison to face Jess again, catching her off guard.

"So, who's buying my kidney?" she said, a very nervous smile on her face. She had no idea how close she was to the truth. But it wasn't random organs we were interested in.

It was the whole package.

19

JESSICA

"Y"ou're serious? You want me to pay you by…what…having sex with you?"

The completely serious expressions I received in response told me I'd gotten it right. We were seated in their kitchen at a round wooden table with mismatched chairs. Glasses of cold water were placed between us. They'd left the back and front doors propped open, allowing the dogs to wander in and out while a blessedly cool breeze swept through the house.

Vincent had joined us, or rather, we'd joined him. He'd already been at the table when we came in, groggily consuming a bowl of Fruity Pebbles cereal.

He looked significantly more awake once I asked my question.

"It's not *all* about sex," Manson said. He was looking at me with single-minded focus, as if no one else in the room existed. "It's about submitting. No more running, no more teasing, no more bullshit. You give us what we want, we give you what you need. You're ours until your debt is paid, simple as that."

I shook my head in disbelief. "I'm *yours*? Please. This sounds like the plot for a bad porno. Which one of you is playing my stepbrother and where's a washing machine I can get stuck in?"

"You can call me big bro," Vincent said, winking at me as Jason rolled his eyes. Jason was sitting closest to me, and in my peripheral vision, I could see him watching me, bright blue eyes unnervingly focused.

What was he looking for when he stared like that? Weakness, fear, excitement? He was too observant, and it made me feel like I was under a microscope.

"We're not made of money, Miss Martin," Lucas said. He was sprawled in his chair, one arm slung over the back. His body language said "boredom", but his expression was far too hard for that to be true. "Frankly, it's pretty damn generous of us to offer this. These special funds of yours can't pay the rent."

"Obviously there will be boundaries." Manson was having none of the banter. He was all business, elbows on the table as he leaned toward me, my outrageous invoice sitting in front of him. But there was a gleam in his eyes, tension in his stance. He was thoroughly enjoying this. "Your safeword ends anything and everything. If you agree to the deal, we can start working on the car. We have to wait for parts to come in, shipping an engine takes time. I'd say we'll have it fixed in five, maybe six weeks. In the meantime, you'll be paying off your debt."

"By doing what exactly?" I said. "Being your on-call Fleshlight?"

"If that's how you would prefer to think of it." Manson wasn't giving an inch and I hated it. This calm, perfectly controlled side of him made me irrationally frustrated.

"You'll be doing whatever pops into our sick heads," Jason said. "We can't give you a schedule ahead of time, princess. We're busy, you know. But if you're walking around town and one of us happens to snatch you up, you'd better be ready for it."

"Free use," Lucas said. "Whenever and wherever we want."

My insides tightened, squeezing like there was a band low in my belly. It was a scenario that sounded good in fantasy — so damn good. But actually following through with it? Submitting myself to them, using sex as payment? Letting them fuck me whenever and wherever they wanted? That wasn't exactly subtle. It wasn't easy to hide.

If I'd thought one night as Manson's slave was wild, then I couldn't even imagine what something like this would mean for me.

My palms were sweating. My mouth was too dry, and I paused to take a long drink of the water. It seared a cold trail down my throat, and I shivered as I set the glass down.

"It's your choice, Jess," Manson said. "You have options here."

Yeah. He kept reminding me of that, dangling it in front of my face like he *hoped* I'd choose something else. But I knew better than that. Manson wanted me to agree just as much as the rest of them, but he wanted me to *choose*. He didn't want me to relent out of desperation.

He wanted me to acknowledge that I wanted it too, even if I

didn't fully understand why.

I could go somewhere else. Another shop, another mechanic. I could ask my parents for money and they'd give it — but I also didn't want to deal with my mom holding it over my head, and I knew she would.

In a few months, I didn't plan on being in Wickeston anymore. I planned to have a career, to move somewhere better than this. Somewhere nobody knew me, where there were no expectations and no grudges. Somewhere I could start over.

Until then, maybe…maybe I could indulge myself.

"Fine," I said. I folded my arms, smiling smugly when they all looked at me in surprise. "What? Did you think I'd chicken out?"

"I knew you'd agree," Jason said. "You never could back down from a challenge."

"Damn right," I said proudly, shoving myself back from the table. "So when do we —"

"Sit back down." Manson's tone brooked no argument. The words felt like a physical force pulling me back, and I plopped myself into the chair instantly. "We're not done here. We need to go over your limits."

I blinked rapidly as I stared at him. I'd spent enough time watching BDSM-flavored porn and reading kinky erotica that I'd encountered the idea of hard limits — boundaries around what one was willing to do in a scene. There were soft limits too, things one was cautious about trying, but was willing to do under the right circumstances.

But I'd thought my one and only real-life encounter with all this had come and gone. Messing around for one night had led to the establishment of a safeword, but beyond that, there had been no further discussion.

The fact that we were having one now felt strangely serious.

It felt intimate. *Too* intimate.

"Is that really necessary?" I tried and failed not to squirm in my seat. "Let's just keep it open for discussion."

"It's always open for discussion," Manson said. He was sitting directly across from me, and I was finding it impossible to look away from him, despite the uncomfortable intensity of his gaze. "But if one of us wants to throw you in a trunk or tape up your mouth, we need to know ahead of time if that's something you can handle."

"Do you have any health problems? Or blood circulation issues?" Vincent said.

"What about allergies?" Jason added. "Do you have any problems with silicone? Vinyl? Latex?"

"Are you on birth control?" Manson said, his eyes boring into me like he could extract the answer from my soul.

"I...uh..." This shouldn't have been difficult, but I was stumbling over every word I tried to get out. I was a big girl. There was nothing wrong with what I liked. So why the hell did it feel like there was? "I'm not...against...the trunk thing."

Lucas's mouth twitched. Vincent muttered something that sounded very much like, "Thank you, Satan, I've finally been blessed."

"I don't have any allergies and I don't have any other health issues either. And of course I'm on birth control. I have an IUD," I finished. Manson nodded.

"Okay, those are the basics," he said. "Now we need limitations."

Everything that came immediately to mind sounded like a good idea to me, but I tried to tamp down on my excitement. "Is there such a thing as no limits?"

"No." Vincent's response was blunt. "That's not something we do. Everyone has a limit, and knowing what they are keeps all of us safe."

"It keeps Lucas from catching a murder charge." Jason chuckled, despite Lucas's glower.

I nodded, but I still was unsure of what to say. Where could I even begin? "I mean, I...I don't want any broken limbs. In case that wasn't already obvious."

Vincent snorted. "Damn, there goes my torture scene idea. I'm kidding!" He laughed harder when he saw my expression. "We're not *that* intense, Jess, relax."

"I know it can be intimidating to start," Manson said. He sounded surprisingly understanding, sympathetic even. He got up from his seat. "Hang on, I have something that will help."

He left the room, going up the stairs. The four of us sat in silence, staring at each other like we'd begrudgingly negotiated the end of a war. Lucas wasn't looking at me, instead staring at the tabletop in front of him as if it held the answers he was looking for on its worn surface.

"Whose idea was this?" I said, looking between the three of them. Jason raised his hand with a cocky grin.

"That would be me," he said. "I'm admittedly a hard ass when it comes to being paid for my work, and you have certainly caused us a *lot* of work. Seems like fair compensation."

"Being your plaything is fair compensation?" I tried and failed to sound skeptical. Instead, my voice hitched and Jason's grin turned cruel.

"Honestly, Jess? Last night wasn't enough." He leaned closer toward my seat, one hand spread on the table beside him. I looked at his black-painted fingernails and thick rings and imagined that hand wrapping around my throat. Despite the brightness of his smile, his voice was dark. "I have plans for you, just you wait."

"We," Vincent clarified. "*We* have plans for you. And we've had plenty of time to think of them."

They'd had years of time. Years of arguments, bullying, lust, close-encounters…plenty of fuel for whatever sadistic fantasies they had involving me.

When Manson returned, he had several pieces of paper in his hands that he slid across the table toward me.

"This should get you on the right track," he said. A quick glance told me that it was a list of fetishes, each with a series of questions next to them: my interest level on a scale of 1-5, whether or not I'd done it before, and whether or not it was a soft or hard limit. The questions repeated twice, both for my interest in experiencing the activity myself or inflicting it on someone else.

Blindfolds…caning…fisting…orgasm control…oooh boy, I needed to rein in my thoughts. Looking at this list while they all sat right in front of me was a recipe for embarrassment.

I folded the paper and slipped it into my bag. "I'll look it over. I can't guarantee I'll be done by tomorrow though."

"If you can't finish it in time, then you need to give us a timeframe of when you will," Vincent said. "It's all about communication. Give me your phone."

I handed over my cell. It made me nervous to have Vincent poking around on my phone, especially since Lucas was leaning over and very obviously watching the screen.

"Is there something on here you don't want me to see, Miss Martin?" Lucas eyed me like he could read my mind. "Should we check out your photo gallery?"

"Or how about your search history?" Jason suggested.

"No!" I said quickly. "That's a hard limit. No going through my search history."

"All right." Vincent held up his hands innocently. "No snooping, I promise."

The last thing I needed was them realizing the accounts I looked at most often were their own.

"I added you to a group chat with the four of us," Vincent said as he handed back my phone. "All our numbers are saved, so if one of us contacts you, you'll know who it is."

"He fixed my contact name for you," Jason deadpanned, and my cheeks heated. His name in my phone was still set to "Homework Dispenser," a remnant of one of my more shameful moments in high school. I could have done without him finding out about that, especially with the way he cracked his knuckles. Something told me my ass would be paying for that later.

"There's one more thing," Manson said, leaning back in his seat. "We need to go over the rules."

I narrowed my eyes. "What rules?"

"If you're submitting to us, then you follow our rules," Vincent said. "Don't worry, they're not hard."

"But the consequences for disobeying will be." Lucas

sounded far too excited about the consequences part, and I shifted uncomfortably on the hard wooden chair. Any time they mentioned punishing me, I felt the same odd amalgamation of terror and excitement — like I was about to jump out of an airplane and parachute to the ground. I both wanted it and dreaded it.

"Okay," I said. "And the rules are?"

"If you want to get off, you need our permission," Manson said, smiling as if he knew how frustrating that would be for me. "No touching yourself, no using toys, and no allowing anyone else to get you off either, unless one of us explicitly says you can."

I grit my teeth. There was no way they could enforce that. They couldn't watch me twenty-four hours a day. But *I* would know if I disobeyed, and the thought of blatantly defying them wasn't very appealing even if they would never know I did.

"Jessica." Manson's firm tone snapped me out of my thoughts. "Do you understand the rule?"

I took a deep breath. "Yes, I understand."

"That leads us to rule number two," he said. "And that's how you address us. In this house, when you answer, you say *yes, sir* and *no, sir*. Is that understood?"

"Yes," I said, then caught myself and quickly added, "Yes, sir."

Goddamn it, my pride was taking a beating. I was struggling against it, trying to keep my head high and humble myself at the same time. Maybe this was going to be harder than I thought. I'd never done well with rules — pretending to follow them was far easier than actually doing it.

But I couldn't pretend here. I couldn't fake obedience to them.

"And the final rule…" Manson's fingers tapped on the back of his chair. "You will always communicate with us openly, honestly, and respectfully. Regardless of what it is. If we tell you to do something and you don't think you can, tell us. If something frightens you or hurts you, say something. If you don't want to continue…"

"Say something," I repeated. "No ghosting." They all nodded. "Okay. I can do that."

I had no idea if I actually could. How could I be completely honest if I wasn't sure of my own truth?

Lucas was looking at me strangely, and I wondered if the uncertainty was obvious on my face. I tried to keep my expression neutral.

"All right then. Get the questionnaire filled out," Manson said. "Then we'll be in touch."

He made it sound like this was a shady deal we'd agreed to in a dark alley, instead of in broad daylight sitting in their kitchen. My hands were shaking as I shoved my phone into my pocket.

"What happens after my car is fixed?" I said. "What then?"

"You go back to pretending we don't exist," Vincent said, staring up at the ceiling almost wistfully. Then, with a dismissive shrug, he added, "Or keep playing."

I wanted to tell him we couldn't play forever, but that was far too scary a declaration to make. Part of me wanted to dive in head-first and forget all the *shoulds* and *should-nots* that I'd spent so long hung up on. Part of me wanted to cling to this, hold this dirty little secret close.

Another part of me wanted to run away again, because running was easier than introspection. It was easier than acknowledging that maybe I'd spent years forming and adhering to my own lies about myself and who I was.

"Okay," I finally said. "I'll pay my debt. I'll play the game. Until the car is fixed, I'm yours."

20

JASON

High School - Senior Year

Jessica Martin was a dirty rotten cheater.

Wickeston High School's resident princess didn't sit next to me in every class because she liked me, althoughI'd been foolish enough at first to think she did. There I was, fifteen years old and awkward as hell, sitting next to the prettiest girl in school. She couldn't keep her eyes off me either. Every time I glanced up, she was looking back, those big green eyes with her long lashes mesmerizing me.

It turned out she wasn't looking at me at all; she was looking at my tests. Every single one of them.

I got the hint when Kyle cornered me in the hallway one day and "convinced" me to start writing his essays. Jessica was tucked under his arm the entire time, smirking at me like she thought it was funny that her caveman boyfriend could shove me around. I was fresh out of a tiny private Christian school, accustomed to uniforms, tight schedules, and a stringently merciless disciplinary policy. Wickeston wasn't like that. To a shy, quiet kid like me, that place was the wild west.

Kyle had about six inches of height on me and fists the size of bricks, so I went from being the quiet AP kid to the popular crowd's personal homework dispenser. I tried to make a game out of it, convincing myself that I was getting more studying done by doing their work for them.

I cringed when I thought back on it. God, I'd been naïve.

Then I met Vincent, Manson, and Lucas. We were all a bunch of outcasts, but together, we were stronger, accepted by one another. It made me bolder to fight back, to branch out, to explore.

It made me fall in love, too, with this goofy clown of a guy who talked about concepts like free love and sexual acceptance. He gave me words to describe how I felt; he didn't lose his shit when I told him I was so damn confused because I *liked* girls, but shit, guys could get it too. Vincent Volkov turned my world on its head.

By the time senior year came around, everything changed.

My parents kicked me out over the summer and Vincent's family took me in. Adulthood hit me like a ton of bricks and suddenly I was free. Free to act, talk, and dress however I damn well pleased. Free to love who I wanted, free to have sex how I wanted.

I was free to stand up for myself.

I had to be clever. I had to play to my own strengths. I couldn't best these assholes physically, most of them anyway. But blackmail became my favorite pastime. I learned how to gain access to social media accounts, collecting private information as if it was a sport. It helped that Vincent supplied most of the jocks who bullied me with their party drugs. He got his money, and I got life-ruining information I could hold over their heads.

But there was one person I was *particularly* looking forward to getting back at — Jessica Martin.

I probably took a little too much joy in planning how it would go down, but really, there wasn't much to plan. I considered getting her account passwords; a quick phishing email from a spoofed address would do the trick. I imagined going through her DMs, finding the nudes she sent to her boyfriend, threatening to leak them. I imagined it…but I didn't do it. I couldn't. It felt too personal, like something I wouldn't be able to forgive myself for doing. I wanted to get back at her, but I couldn't bring myself to do something that could very well ruin her.

I couldn't bring myself to hurt her.

So I was going to keep it simple. If she wanted to use me to cheat, she was going to pay me one way or another.

I waited until after cheer practice, when she was the last one to file into the showers after nearly everyone else had gone home. I had to give her props — she worked hard when she wanted to. She hadn't become cheerleading captain without reason. She'd practice for hours, long after everyone else was done. The weather was cold, but she was red-faced and sweating when she finally trudged into the showers.

I followed.

"Don't take the shower at the end, it's mine!" she called. The door swung shut behind me, a row of lockers separating me from the shower stalls on the other side. My heart was pounding with every step. The girls' locker room smelled different than the boys'. Not necessarily better, but different.

She froze when I came around the lockers. She was bent over her gym bag, wearing her uniform, a change of clothes clutched in her arm.

"Uh, hello?" She straightened up, staring at me. "You can't be in here."

"I don't see anyone else around to get offended about it," I said. "I figured you'd want our conversation to be private."

She folded her arms. "Our conversation? Hmm, yeah, no, I don't remember putting *waste time conversing with a random loser* on my schedule today." She scoffed, brushing past me toward the mirrors. I watched her face in the reflection, keeping my distance.

"You used my answers for your test," I said. She swiped her finger over her lower lip as if touching up her lipstick, but the motion seemed fabricated. She was nervous. Trying to look disinterested. "I expect to be compensated."

"Compensated?" She laughed, glancing back at me over her shoulder. "Compensated for what? For me sitting next to you? A lot of people would pay *me* for that privilege."

I had no doubt they would. But lucky me, I had something she wanted, something she *needed*.

Feeling this much confidence was such a head rush. I just wanted to see her squirm. "Sorry to break it to you, Jess. Things are going to operate a little differently now. If I do the work, I'm getting paid. That goes for your boyfriend too."

I had plans for Kyle. The amount of blackmail I had on him

could probably put that bastard in prison, but I considered myself a pretty nice dude. Nothing had to happen as long as he backed off.

"Is this part of your whole new thing?" she said, narrowing her eyes at me in the mirror. "The dark clothes, dyed hair, piercings. You shouldn't let Manson and Lucas influence you like that, you're better off staying a nerd."

I'd changed my look, it was true. After a lifetime of wearing uniforms to school, polo shirts and khakis had been all I knew. But without my parents breathing down my neck, I let loose. Lucas helped me buzz my hair short and dye it. Manson pierced my ears and I'd stretched the holes. I was envious of Lucas's tattoos, but stick-n-poke wasn't my style, so Vincent and I were both saving up to get pieces done.

Maybe to Jess it looked like I was trying too hard, but it didn't stop her from staring.

She looked at me differently this year. It was like something surprised her every time she saw me. I wasn't going to fool myself into thinking it was an attraction, but it was something.

It was a crack in her armor.

"I'm not joking." I stepped closer until my reflection filled the mirror behind her. She smelled so good. Strawberry and vanilla, sweet cream and sugar. I wasn't sure if it was shampoo, perfume, or that gloss she put on her mouth, but it practically made me salivate. "Either you start paying up every time you use me to cheat or I'm telling the principal."

There it was, nice and simple. No real blackmail other than the simple threat that I would tell someone exactly what she'd been doing.

Her eye twitched. "Fucking snitch."

I grinned as I reached around her, bracing my hands on the edges of the sink and caging her in. I'd never been that close to her, close enough that I could see the freckles on her shoulders and a tiny scar on her arm. The iridescent pink glitter from her lip gloss shimmered on her mouth, and it made me want to bite her. I wanted to take her lip between my teeth and hear her groan, feel her shudder. But it was enough to see the way she looked at me as I brought my lips close to her ear.

There was uncertainty, yes. But there was excitement too, a sudden light in her eyes that I hadn't expected. It caught me off guard, and I lowered my tone as I spoke.

"A hundred bucks," I said. "Every time."

"Wow. Overpricing yourself a little, aren't you?" Her voice had grown softer but her gaze hadn't. "I think the principal will be a little more concerned about you following me into the girls' locker room than me *maybe* taking a little peek at your test."

"Let's try it," I said. "We'll go talk to him together."

Her eyes left my face, skating down my arm beside her. She seemed to stare at my hand for a long time, focusing on my knuckles wrapped tight around the edge of the sink.

"Fine. Back off so I can get my purse. Oh, *wait…*" She turned around. Chest to chest, toe to toe. Her tits were right there and I couldn't stop myself from looking down at them. She looked so soft, her skin so smooth. When I forced my eyes back up to her face, she was smirking. "I don't have any cash today. Oopsie. Too bad."

But I wasn't the only one whose eyes wandered. She looked at my neck, a flicker of confusion going over her face as she focused on the hickey my t-shirt didn't cover. I used to be so paranoid about those marks, and with good reason. It was part of what tipped my parents off in the end, what made them start asking questions.

But without them to worry about, I loved the bruises. I loved looking at them in the morning and remembering how they came to be. Like last night, while Vincent's teeth and hands left marks all over me, he'd made me talk about Jess. He'd made me say aloud all the ways I dreamed of fucking her — by myself, with him, with Manson and Lucas, everywhere and anywhere.

I had to stay focused. I backed away from her, shrugging like none of it mattered. "That's too bad. So are you sitting in on this conversation or what?"

I turned and walked away, rounding the lockers but keeping my pace slow the closer I got to the door, giving her the opportunity to change her mind.

"Wait!"

I stopped, allowing myself a self-indulgent smile. It was a good thing she couldn't see me, because what she said next almost made me choke on my own saliva.

"What if I gave you a nude?"

I poked my head back around the lockers so fast I almost got whiplash. "Nudes? Of you?" Thank God, Satan, and any other deity out there that my voice didn't crack. I had to keep it cool. "Overpricing yourself a little, aren't you?"

She didn't look happy about me throwing her own words back in her face. "Frankly, sending you a nude is overpaying," she said, waving her hand. "But whatever. Give me your number."

"Hey, woah now. I'll take your nude as payment, Jess, but I

have conditions." She glared at me, but since she'd suggested it, I was going to milk this for all it was worth. "I don't want some old pic Kyle has jacked off to. I want you to take a new one, just for me."

She rolled her eyes. "Yeah, sure, fine."

Holy shit, holy shit, *holy shit*. She was serious. She was actually going to do it. "Take one and send it, now," I said. "Not later."

She laid her hand over her heart, an expression of mock offense on her face. "Jason, don't you *trust* me? I think you'd show a little more appreciation. It's not like I send nudes to just anyone."

"I really don't give a fuck how many people have seen you naked." I leaned back against the lockers, trying to figure out a way to keep myself calm. "All I care about is that *this* photo is meant for me."

She shifted slightly. There it was again, that spark of excitement in her eyes. Like this was thrilling for her. Like it was a game.

"Fine, it'll be a brand-new shiny nude just for you," she said. "Bye. Leave. I'd like to shower before they start locking up the campus."

My entire body tingled. "Go ahead. Do your thing."

"You have *got* to be kidding," she growled in frustration. "Ugh, at least face the other way. I'll scratch your fucking eyes out if you turn around."

"Easy, kitty." I turned around, arms folded. I didn't need to stare at her naked and I wasn't going to push for it. But I didn't want her sneaking out of paying me either. I did the work, I deserved something in return. If this was what she wanted to give, fuck, she could pay me with nudes anytime she wanted. "I'm not here to be a creep, just to make sure I get paid."

"Yeah, sure, this isn't creepy at *all*." There was a shuffle, then the soft sound of fabric hitting the floor. My cock jumped. She was getting worse at trying to keep up this "bored and irritated" act. There was tension in her voice but it wasn't anger.

I took a risk and spoke my mind. "Personally, Jess, I think you like it when you get a taste of your own medicine."

"What's that supposed to mean?"

"It means you like it when someone is an asshole back to you."

There was a long pause, and I knew I was right even when she finally said, "I'm going to pretend you didn't say that."

Her camera clicked multiple times, a pause between each. Damn, was she doing a whole photoshoot back there?

"What do you prefer?" she said. "Tits or ass?"

Christ. Was both a good answer? Because it was both. "Surprise me."

"Something tells me you're an ass man," she said breezily.

"What makes you say that?"

"Vincent has a nice ass."

I stiffened, my muscles snapping into high alert in an instant. Regardless of whatever strides of equality and acceptance the rest of the country made, Wickeston remained homophobic as fuck. Vincent and I kept things subtle, but it wasn't exactly a secret. So I braced myself. I got ready for a snide comment, a poke at my masculinity, maybe worse.

"Don't tell him I said that," she said quickly. "Or I'm retracting all future nude payments."

That…wasn't what I'd expected.

"Won't say a word," I grunted, nerves making my voice hoarse. "Vince doesn't need the ego boost anyway."

I'd definitely be telling him. Absolutely, no doubt about it, I was blabbing the second I got the chance. He was going to completely lose his shit. I wasn't the only one who was perving out over this girl.

After another minute of her snapping photos, she finally said, "Alright. Give me your phone number."

I rattled them off, my heart rate skyrocketing. I waited with my back still turned to her until my screen lit up when her text came through. I opened the image attachments, keeping my breathing steady. My cock was so hard now there was no hiding it, the tent in my pants was almost cartoonish.

But God, she was…perfect.

"Jesus fucking Christ." The words slipped out in a whisper, reverent and disbelieving. I quickly tucked my phone away. She was still naked behind me, so I didn't look back even though the temptation was there, simply waving at her over my shoulder. "See ya'. Nice doing business with you."

"Are you going to show anyone?"

Her sudden question made me pause. She didn't sound worried. She sounded…curious? Intrigued?

Did I dare to think she sounded hopeful?

"Do you *want* me to show someone?" The question hung in the air, a long pause without an answer. But her silence was an answer in itself.

I prodded experimentally, "Who do you think I should show it to first? Vincent? He'll be jealous as hell to know I have it. Or how about Manson? Every time he stands next to your locker, he'd be thinking about it. What about Lucas?"

Her gulp was audible. Her voice didn't carry as much of her usual confidence as she said, "Very funny, Jason. Now, would you get lost?"

I left the girls' locker room that day with a lot more than vindication for all the work I'd been doing without pay. There was more to her than I'd thought. Beneath that perfect exterior lurked a masochistic little creature longing for someone to take control. It was a side of her I could actually understand, something I could relate to.

Something I could play with.

21

JESSICA

I made up a story to tell my parents once I got home. Mom thought I'd spent the night at Danielle's again, and I didn't correct her, but trying to explain my car breaking down and my ensuing bargain was significantly more difficult.

In the end, I settled for telling them I'd gone to a local shop and knew the mechanics from high school, so they were able to give me a discount. Dad wanted to know the hard numbers to make sure he couldn't get me a better deal elsewhere, but I was able to deflect by focusing on Mom's questions instead.

"Who are these boys again?" she said, narrowing her eyes at me from the end of the table. We were seated for dinner, the first full meal I'd had all day.

"Lucas and Manson," I said, trying to keep my mouth stuffed

with as much food as I could to delay the questions. But Mom reached over and smacked my hand as I reached for another roll.

"Stop stuffing your face, Jessica Marie, slow down." She sighed heavily in disgust. Across the table, my little sister, Steph, snickered, pleased to see someone else getting scolded. "Lucas and...Manson, you said? Those better not be the same boys that got expelled for assaulting other students."

Damn it, of course she remembered that. Both incidents had resulted in the school sending letters to parents explaining the situations and the action that had been taken. Mom had lost it both times, convinced that Wickeston was going to hell in a handbasket and my high school was growing more dangerous by the day.

"Well, I mean...yes?" I winced, and Mom threw up her hands in exasperation, glaring at my dad as if this was all his fault.

"Roger, are you really not going to say anything about this?" she demanded. "About our daughter going to a shop run by *criminals*?"

My father responded in his usual slow, measured voice, "Now, Charlene, calm down. I don't think we need to worry much about it —"

"Not worry? *Not worry?!*" Mom's voice had reached that ear-splitting pitch that usually sent me running out the door. "You want her dealing with these men? Who knows what they could do? They could be traffickers, Roger!"

"Mom, they're not traffickers —"

"You never know, Jessica. That's the thing, you never know." She jabbed her finger at me in warning. "Just the other day, Jeanie's daughter said that some couple was following her around the Walmart, probably trying to snatch her up. People have been talking about it all over Facebook."

"Ah, yes, Facebook, the epicenter of breaking news," I muttered, and Mom's fork clattered on her plate. "Listen, Mom, I swear they're fine. They're not dangerous."

That wasn't exactly true. Those men were extremely dangerous, but not in the way she thought. They were a danger to my pride, my reputation, and my panties.

"One of them threatened your boyfriend with a knife," Mom snapped. "I swear, how did I raise a daughter with no damn sense?"

I dropped the subject because there was truly no point in arguing with her, and the rest of dinner passed in strained silence.

But her words still bothered me once I'd retreated upstairs. She knew only the barest details about those men, but that hadn't stopped her from making wild assumptions about them. Just like most of the people I'd gone to high school with, Mom was more interested in gossip than in the actual truth.

I paused to take another sip of coffee. I'd gotten through almost the entire list Manson had given me and the questions had become pretty obscure. I had to Google the definition of "katoptronophilia," only to realize it meant getting turned on by having sex in front of a mirror.

That was a five out of five on the interest scale for me, along with dozens of other fetishes that had never even crossed my mind.

Extreme bondage. Impact play. Whips, chains, domestic discipline, marking, scarification, degradation; the list went on and on. In a weird way, it was reassuring to see things I was interested in on a list like this. It was a reassurance that someone else out there — more than a few someone's — had the same desires I did. But it also made me feel like I was in over my head.

Spanking and handcuffs felt acceptably kinky, even a little trendy. But there were fetishes for stalking, kidnapping, and captivity, all of which had me practically shivering with desire. They fell under the umbrella of "consensual non-consent," which involved the submissive person roleplaying that they weren't willing. All of it got a five out of five from me.

By 1 am, I'd completed the entire sheet and was squirming in my seat from the fantasies it inspired. At least it was finished and I could have a little date with my vibrator before bed. Except...

Damn it. Their stupid rules. I wasn't supposed to masturbate without permission, and again the question sprang to my mind: how would they even know?

I saved the pages to my phone and attached them in the group chat Vincent had set up, along with the message: **If this list ever gets in front of anyone else's eyes besides you four, I WILL KILL YOU.**

I left my phone on my desk, locked my door, and rummaged under my bed for the box I hid my sex toys in. It wasn't a particularly large collection, but well-used. Usually, I didn't feel such a thrill when I opened the box, but knowing I was doing this against their orders made it feel particularly naughty.

My ass was still sore from the last spanking I'd gotten, yet I was prepared to break a rule already. I should have warned them that rules and I didn't get along.

My phone buzzed again, and I sighed. I should have guessed at least one of the boys would be awake. I snagged my vibrator from the box and tossed it on the bed, flopping down among my pillows before I checked the text. It was from Manson.

Our customer's proprietary information is of the utmost importance to us. Your dirty little secret is safe.

Staring at the screen, I imagined him looking over the list. I'd been brutally honest, even for the kinks I never thought I'd admit to liking. I'd felt wildly brave while filling it out, but now that it was out of my hands, I was nervous.

When do I get to see your lists? I feel like it's only fair I get some blackmail material on you too. I responded.

A text from Lucas came through. **It isn't blackmail if we're not afraid of it getting out. If the public wants to know how I fuck, that's fine with me.**

I shook my head, smiling despite myself. It was easy to imagine Lucas loudly declaring exactly what he liked to anyone who would listen.

To my surprise, Manson responded with an attachment. Then Lucas, then Jason. Then Jason again, with the message: **This one is Vince's. He's at work.**

I vaguely recalled that Vincent worked as a bartender, but I wasn't sure where. I opened up Manson's attachment first, unable to resist skimming through the list. My thighs squeezed a little tighter together as my eyes widened, and I found myself pinching my lower lip as I read. Every time I found our interests to be similarly aligned, there was a little throb in my chest as if my heart had jumped in excitement.

Reading through his answers was far more of a turn-on than I'd expected. I reached for my vibrator, flicking it on and slowly trailing it over my inner thighs. He'd rated scarification as a five on his interest scale, and immediately I thought of the tiny heart etched into my finger. There was something so unbearably erotic about him slicing into my flesh, watching my blood well up and consuming it right in front of me.

What would it be like to let him cut into me deep enough to scar? To beg him not to hurt me and have him smile at me in response, knowing that he wasn't going to stop —

Are you about to get yourself off, Jessica?

My phone almost slipped through my fingers. The text was from Lucas.

I messaged back hurriedly. **You told me I wasn't allowed to without permission.**

So you DO remember the rules, Manson responded. **Why are you already breaking them, brat? Trying to get spanked again already?**

Put the vibrator down, and start begging for permission instead, Lucas's next message read.

Shit, I'd already fucked up. But how did they *know* this? What was going on?

I frowned, switching off the vibrator and setting it aside. My curtains were open, and I leaned toward the glass, peering down into the yard. Nothing but darkness was out there, but...

I snatched up my phone again. **Where are you? How did you know I was using a vibrator?**

Lucas's next message was quick to arrive. **It doesn't matter where I am. But if you pick up that toy again and start using it without permission, I'll know.**

Lucas's text had a photo attached, and I had to wait for it to load. But once it did, it stuttered my breath to a halt.

It was a photo of my bedroom window. The curtains were open, and the light was on. The angle was taken from somewhere below. I scrambled toward the glass again, taking a much more thorough look at the yard. The bushes, the trees, the wooden fence, behind the garbage cans…nothing.

Does it scare you? Knowing I'm watching you?

I stared at his message, then back out into the dark. It didn't scare me, not exactly. This feeling was different.

How long have you been watching me? I wrote.

Doesn't matter. Just consider yourself lucky that I'm willing to give you permission to orgasm.

Vincent responded for the first time, but it was just a laughing emoji and a confetti effect. That fucking clown. My fingers flew over the keys.

What do I need to do?

My fingers tapped rapidly on the mattress as I waited for his response. I kept glancing at the window. Even being on the second floor, I had the irrational fear that I was going to look over and see Lucas outside, staring at me from the dark.

Kneel on your bed in front of the window and give me a show.

I stared at the text for a long time, chewing my lower lip. I could refuse and go to sleep, but I was hot and uncomfortable already. Sleep wouldn't come easily unless I found some way to get this tension out.

It was the middle of the night and all the other houses on our street were dark. But what if someone saw me?

Yes or no. Before I get bored.

With my heart pounding, I crawled across the bed to kneel right in front of the window. Somewhere out there, Lucas was watching me. That smoldering heat in my belly flared with a vengeance. I tugged down the waistband of my pajama pants until they pooled around my knees, nervously licking my lips as I gazed out into the dark. But unless my face was closer to the glass, the only thing I could see was my own expression staring back at me.

There's a good girl. Give me something sexy to show the boys when I get home. I'll be recording.

I picked up the vibrator and turned it on, taking a deep breath. I started slowly at first, touching it lightly to my abdomen and caressing it over my pubic mound. They were all going to see me do this. Lucas would go home, show them this video…

Would they jack off to it? Stroke themselves to the sight of me, spill their cum when I wasn't even there to taste it? The thought made my breath catch.

I had set my phone aside, but I could still see the screen.

You'd better have that thing on its highest setting.

I paused, flicking the button on my toy in the other direction. The vibrations grew stronger, reverberating through my hand. I rarely used this setting; it took me from zero to one hundred so fast it was almost painful. I moved it between my legs, adjusting to the power of it before I grazed it over my clit.

Don't be pussyfooting around. I want to see you shake.

At least he couldn't hear me whimper as I pressed the vibrator against my clit.

"Oooh, shit," I whispered, exhaling heavily as I moved the vibrator again. This wasn't the type of speed that would slowly ease me up to an orgasm. It would rip my orgasm out of me and beat me with it.

If you keep moving that vibrator away, I'm going to come up, tie you to the bed, and make you lie there with it between your legs all night. You wanted to break the fucking rules, this is what happens.

I moaned, my hand shaking as I held the vibrator in place again. I struggled to stay upright in front of the window, my legs rapidly beginning to ache. My clit wanted to retreat from the vicious vibrations, but my body was still responding. The tension built brutally.

How does it feel, fucktoy? Is it a little bit too much for you?

I nodded mindlessly, rocking my hips against the vibrations. There was something deliciously degrading about being referred to as nothing more than a toy.

Every inch of me was tense, rising so quickly toward an orgasm that I couldn't manage to relax a single muscle. I held my breath in an effort not to make a sound, but even that fragile self-control was going to break.

Don't stop. Make yourself come for me. Keep the vibrator there until I give you permission to stop.

"Fuck…" My voice cracked. My toes curled. I doubled over as I came, clapping my free hand over my mouth to muffle the groan that came with it.

Jesus Christ, it was too much. It hurt — it felt so good, but it *hurt.*

Sit up. Don't you dare hide your face from me.

I barely managed it. I was shaking my head, whispering "please" over and over again as if he could hear me. As if Lucas gave a fuck about mercy.

She looks like she's gonna cry, boys. Should I let her stop?

Another confetti message came through from Vincent. I would have been mad if I hadn't felt like my clit was about to break.

Let her cry. Goddamn it, Manson.

Make her go for another minute. Sixty seconds. Jason's idea at least put an end in sight. I leaned my hand against the window, the reflection of my own face too much to bear. My hair was disheveled, my cheeks were pink, my mouth hung open because I was panting so hard. God, my clit was so sensitive even a feather would have made me flinch. But this? This was torture. I wasn't building toward another orgasm; I was still lingering at the end of the last one. Trapped, suspended in pleasure limbo.

That's sixty seconds. Stop.

I almost sobbed with relief. I switched off the vibrator and tossed it down, collapsing onto the bed as I tried to catch my breath. My legs were twitching, my clit felt as if I'd hooked electrodes up to it. They hadn't even touched me and they'd reduced me to this. My phone kept buzzing as I stared at the screen, bleary-eyed.

I think I killed her, boys.

Rest in peace, angel.

Vincent switched it up this time and sent some fireworks.

I was too tired to drag myself out of bed and into the shower. I was too tired to even send them a snarky response. I crawled under the blankets, and my exhausted body melted into sleep within minutes.

22

LUCAS

As a kid, I'd always been a climber. I'd clamber up into the branches of the massive oak trees that grew around my childhood home, getting as high as I could. Sometimes it would be to hide from my parents, since I was always getting into trouble back then, but mostly I liked the feeling of looking down on the world.

From up high, everything that scared me was so far away. I was untouchable up there, my calloused bare feet balancing me amid the thick foliage. I could hide for hours, sometimes even falling asleep. Although my brother hated when I did that, because he thought I was going to roll out of my perch during a nap and break my neck.

It had been a long time since I'd climbed a tree, but it felt as natural as ever when I pulled myself up into the limbs of the big poplar outside Jessica's window. It was thick with leaves, shielding me from her sight but leaving her entirely visible to me. She kept her curtains open, sitting at her desk as she filled out the sheet Manson had given her. Her bed was right next to the window, covered in numerous pillows and a couple fluffy stuffed animals.

Did she like toys like that? Fluffy things with big eyes, intentionally designed to be as painfully cute as possible? She'd never struck me as a cutesy girl, but what did I know? There was a lot of pink in her room, soft pastels and delicate glass figurines. She had multiple shelves of trophies and medals — from cheerleading competitions, I guessed.

Could she still do the splits like she could back then? I had avoided football games and anything that put me remotely in the territory of the jocks, but I'd seen her at practice many times. I'd always been secretive about watching her, but I'd had hiding spots all around campus. I'd usually sneak up to the gymnasium roof, have a few cigarettes and watch her flip around the field, shouting directions at the other girls on her team.

We hadn't gotten along back then either. I'd come to Wickeston as a transfer student, making my second attempt at getting through ninth grade and she'd turned up her nose at me right away. I was used to that, though. My previous school hadn't been any better. At least in Wickeston, people didn't know anything about me. They didn't know about my brother; they hadn't seen Benji Bent's name all over the local news.

I wasn't entirely sure why I was there outside her window in the first place, but I chalked it up to merely curiosity. What made this woman want to make a deal like this with us? Why was she bothering when she had a dozen other choices she could have gone with?

It was a game to her; another dare she couldn't refuse. But if she thought she could play this game better than us, better than me, she was sorely mistaken.

Although I was impressed at how seriously she seemed to be taking this task of writing out her limits. She kept her laptop open, occasionally typing something and scrolling through search results. She remained focused for hours until she finally finished and sent the end result to the group chat.

I opened the list, swiftly scrolling through. I'd have to take the time to study it properly, but not here, not when Jess had just gotten out her vibrator and clearly intended to put it to use.

Such a naughty girl, thinking she could hide her pleasure from us.

I would have paid cold hard cash to hear the noises she made when she came, one hand pressed against the windowpane as she obeyed my instructions. The way her lips kept parting, gasping for air, her entire body shaking from the intensity — I was rock hard the entire time. I wanted to *feel* her shake like that. I wanted to pin her down in that pretty pink bedroom, cover her mouth so her parents couldn't hear her moan my name, and pound her into the mattress.

That night was the appetizer. I was starving for the main course.

I usually started my day far earlier than the rest of the house, but we were all on slightly different schedules. Vincent worked night shifts on Thursdays, Fridays, and the weekend, so he was usually asleep during daylight hours. Jason's sleep was always fucked up, so there was no telling when he'd be awake, and Manson would gladly sleep until noon if we let him. But I was awake at the first crack of dawn, which gave me enough time to sit out on the porch with a cigarette and black coffee.

I liked those predawn hours, when the eastern sky was slowly growing brighter and mist lay in a soft white blanket over the ground. Sound was muted, the air was still crisp and slightly cool. The world felt like it was sleeping, leaving me alone with my thoughts.

However, I wasn't the only early riser that morning. The garage door was open, and I glimpsed Jason's blue hair as he moved around the cars. He'd probably been awake all night.

The past few days had flown by faster than a blink, but that's what working from dawn until dusk will do to you. Since Manson had been preoccupied dealing with insurance to get the cars fixed, I'd picked up the slack in the shop, with Vincent taking his days off to help too. We were all on edge, but it wasn't only because our day-to-day stressors had piled up.

We had a new toy we were eager to play with, and responsibilities were getting in our way. Jessica occupied my thoughts far too often, drifting in when I should have been concentrating on more pertinent tasks. But I wasn't the only one.

Manson had fucked me so damn hard the night before that I was walking stiff this morning. I liked it as rough as I could get it so I wasn't complaining, but he was particularly vicious when he was restless — and Jess made him restless as hell. She was too unpredictable, too damn confusing, and all that tension built up in him until he was practically bursting at the seams.

It was a relief to end a long day by letting my exhausted mind rest while Manson took control. But Manson didn't bottom and I liked to switch. While he was fucking me, I was thinking about fucking Jess at the same time.

She was ours to play with now, but when we were collapsing into bed after midnight and rising early, it didn't make much sense to try to drag her out of sleep in the middle of the night. This wasn't high school anymore; we had jobs and responsibilities to take care of. Instead, Manson made her edge in the morning and record the deed, sending videos of her gasping on the verge of orgasm to the group chat. It probably wasn't as torturous for us as it was for her, but it certainly didn't make self-control any easier.

Watching a video of her grasping a vibrator in one trembling hand, while covering her whimpering mouth with the other to be sure her parents didn't hear her, had me starting every day with a hard-on that wouldn't quit.

We just needed the right opportunity to break in our new fucktoy, a chance to have her to ourselves.

I stood up from the porch and stretched my aching back before I discarded what was left of the cigarette. I took my coffee with me as I trudged across the yard to join Jason in the garage.

"Did you wake up early or not sleep at all?" I said, finding Jason holding a hand vacuum with all the doors of his Z wide open. He was cleaning up the remaining bits of broken glass from his seats and floors, carefully getting into every nook and cranny. Haribo was lying close by and he gave me the stink-eye as I walked in. That little dog had the biggest attitude I'd ever seen. He technically belonged to Vincent, but he was always following

Jason around as if that dude needed protection.

Not unlike Vincent himself.

"Didn't sleep," he said, turning off the vacuum. "Vince and I are driving out to the body shop today, so I figured I should clean up. We're gonna stay at Dante's over the weekend so Vincent doesn't have to make the commute to work."

Dante was a close friend of ours and had been one of our first clients; we'd built his T-Bird into a beast that consistently ran low 10s at the track. He lived far closer to Vincent's job than we did, so instead of commuting to the club four days out of the week, Vince would sometimes stay at Dante's place instead.

I sipped my coffee, watching as Jason slammed the doors. It was a good thing he was going with Vincent — Jason turned into a grumpy little shit when he didn't sleep, but he'd stay up for days at a time regardless and it would only get worse if he was left to his own devices. He'd fixate on a project, and once his brain got going, he wouldn't stop until he collapsed or until Vincent made him.

"I thought you were driving over this afternoon," I said. "It's six-fifteen in the morning."

He sighed, pausing to lean down and pick up Haribo. "Yeah, well, like I said, I couldn't sleep. Going on forty-eight hours awake, so I may as well try for seventy-two now."

"Does Vince know you're doing that? He's gonna be pissed."

Jason grunted again in response. I was going to have to convince Vincent to put some sleeping pills in his cereal or something. He slouched down on a stool, rubbing the little dog's belly.

"Have you looked at Jess's list yet?" he said. It had been easy to guess that she was the current fixation making him so irritable.

"Yeah." I'd studied it thoroughly, multiple nights in a row. Sometimes I revisited my favorite sections, just to remind myself that her interest in being "stalked" and "kidnapped" really was a five out of five. "Have you?"

He nodded. "I don't think she knows what some of those things mean, dude. That chick is not into golden showers. I don't believe it."

"I guess you'll have to try it and find out," I said, and he laughed as he shook his head. "We all know she's a freak. She's trying to keep up appearances and please her parents."

He rolled his eyes. "What a waste of time." He paused, birdsong filling the silence as streams of sunlight peeked in through the trees. "Speaking of which…her parents are going out of town today."

That caught my attention. "Oh, yeah? How did you find that out?"

"Facebook," he said. "They're flying to Cabo for their anniversary, and will be gone for a week. Her little sister is staying at a friend's."

"You already got her family's passwords?"

"No, there was no shady shit involved," he said. "Her mom posts personal information like she's writing her own memoirs in real time. I didn't even have to try."

"Who's doing shady shit?"

Manson wandered into the garage, stretching his arms.

"Well, well, look who dragged themselves out of bed at the ass-crack of dawn," I said. I let him take my coffee, and he gulped it like his life depended on it. "You look like a zombie. Also, Jessica's parents are going out of town today. She'll be all alone in that house, waiting for company."

That quickly woke him up. "Damn, looks like I've got an opening in my schedule tonight. We should pay her a surprise visit. Wouldn't want her to be lonely."

"One little problem, though," I said. "Her house has a security system."

Jason was shaking his head at us. "I'm guessing it wouldn't be any fun to just knock on the door?"

"Just *knock*?" Manson said. "Then it wouldn't be a surprise. Where's your imagination?"

"Don't listen to him," I said. "He's pissy because he hasn't slept in three days."

"Jesus, man, you're still not sleeping?" Manson's brow furrowed with concern. "You're going to lose your damn mind."

"Okay, okay, I get it, I need to sleep." He set Haribo down, waving his hand as if to brush away the topic. "But if you're going to stage a break-in at Jessica's place, you're going to need help." He spread his arms with a little grin. "And I'm exactly the genius to do it."

Manson groaned, "Genius, huh?"

"Hold off on any insults until I've taken care of your security system problem," he said. "After all, I'm doing this solely out of the goodness of my heart. It's not like I get to participate in your game, considering I have to go get this mess taken care of." He jerked his thumb at the Z.

Manson innocently put up his hands. "Oh, sure, sure. You are clearly the genius to do this."

"Smartest guy in the house," I said. "What would we do

without you?"

"That's better. Now what time did you want to break into Jess's place?"

I glanced over at Manson. "Sundown?"

He nodded. "Sundown."

"Creepy," Jason said. "I'll work a little magic before Vincent and I have to take off. I'm sure Jess will just love the thought y'all are putting into your first date."

23

JESSICA

I couldn't remember the last time I'd had a house all to myself. When I lived in the dorms at the university, I had three other roommates, so someone else was always bound to be there. But this morning, my parents had left early to catch their flight to Cabo, having dropped off Stephanie last night to stay with a friend. I had complete free rein of the house to do whatever I pleased.

A few years ago, I would have used this opportunity to throw the loudest and most outrageous party I possibly could. I'd managed to have a handful of truly wild parties at my parents' house over the years, and they still didn't have a clue.

But now, all I really wanted was a day to relax, especially after a difficult morning at work. My boss had assigned me to work with one of her pickiest – and wealthiest – clients, leaving me the responsibility of answering his daily long, rambling emails. The man had so many questions I often felt like I was repeating myself, but I was excited that my boss wanted me to personally engage with one of her most important customers.

The moment I finished work, I stripped out of my presentable clothes and put on an oversized t-shirt — no pants required. I ate snacks on the couch and played music as loudly as I wanted. I had skipped the gym for the past few days, and told myself this was my last day of being lazy so I needed to take full advantage. After this, I had to get back into my routine.

Although, my routine was going to be different now that I had four men ordering me around.

Every morning that week, I'd woken up to a text from Manson ordering me to edge myself. It was torture, lying there first thing in the morning with my vibrator between my legs, only allowed to bring myself to the very edge of orgasm before I had to stop.

I'd tried to avoid looking at the kink lists they'd sent me, purely because I knew it would work me up, and there would be nothing I could do about it. But that evening, I couldn't resist. I settled on the couch, scrolling slowly through their lists with my bottom lip clenched between my teeth.

I wasn't remotely surprised to see that orgasm control was a five out of five for Manson. I was already painfully well aware of how much he enjoyed that. All of them claimed an interest in consensual non-consent, with Lucas and Jason not only ranking it high as a giver, but as a receiver.

I'd always had a feeling they all fucked around with each other, they had a comradery that went beyond friendship. Vincent and

Jason had been not-so-secretly dating for years, and I'd known Manson was bisexual. Lucas had always been a mystery, but he was far less of one now that I'd seen him and Manson together in the garage.

They weren't monogamous; that much was clear.

This was a new territory for me. I was used to being in relationships where monogamy was an unbreakable rule. Even looking at someone else too long had led me into fights with previous partners. I felt as if I was *supposed* to be jealous and possessive, but it frankly didn't make sense in this situation.

I'd been furious about Veronica potentially getting with them; but the thought of them spending time with a manipulative, conniving, evil asshole like her was upsetting. I had too much history with Veronica to not get pissed off.

I still felt a little silly caring about it at all; it felt too serious. But I was in the thick of it now. I'd agreed to have sex with them, submit to them, be their toy to do with as they pleased. I think that was a big enough investment to be allowed to care about who else they had sex with.

Besides, they were way too good for Veronica. They deserved better.

I kept reading, sipping iced tea as I lounged on the couch. Vincent ranked high in nearly every aspect of bondage, which wasn't surprising. Any type of restraint was five for him, as were most types of impact: whipping, spanking, slapping. Jason had all the weird kinks I had to Google the definitions of, but at least it expanded my vocabulary. I didn't know what the hell "omorashi" was until I'd filled out my own list.

Now that I knew, I was even more horrified at myself. Why the hell did I have to like the weird shit?

I was working myself up far too much. Continuing to peruse those lists for any longer would qualify as sexual torture, especially when I had no hope of relief. Manson seemed determined to punish me with edging for as long as possible.

Instead, I got out my sketchbook and pencils and began to draw. I may not have been hired on as a designer yet, but I still needed to practice and ensure I was developing my skills. It helped refocus my energy, all my concentration going into each careful stroke of graphite across paper. I'd never considered myself much of an artist, but designing a structure required more than just artistic vision. The dimensions had to be right, the shape and layout had to draw the eye and appeal to the senses.

I wasn't entirely sure where I was going with it at first, but before long, Manson's house began to take shape on my paper. I drew it with a new front porch, focusing in on little details in the wood and framing around the windows.

It wasn't true to life, but that was the point. A big part of my job was being able to envision what could be, the potential within a building or plot of land. That possibility needed to be captured, put on paper and perfected before it could be made real.

Before I knew it, time had gotten away from me. When I lifted my head from my sketchbook, stretching the ache out of my neck, it was already dark outside. I set my drawing aside and picked up my phone, finding another text from Danielle.

Hey girl! Are you down to hit up Billy's? It's karaoke night!

I sighed, tossing my phone aside on the couch. No, I wasn't

down to spend the night at a dive bar with Danielle, Nate, and whoever else they brought along. I knew exactly what Danielle was doing too. She thought they'd taught me a lesson, knocked me down a few pegs so I'd keep my head down and fit back in with the group.

We'd done the same damn thing to new girls on the team. If anyone came into the team a little too cocky, we'd find a way to break them, then keep them close, making them earn back our good graces.

It was fucked. There was a reason Wickeston's cheerleading team had been considered so vicious — I'd helped make sure it stayed that way.

Besides, why go to a dive bar when I finally had the opportunity to watch whatever documentaries I wanted without my mom or sister complaining they were boring? I put a bag of popcorn in the microwave and sat on the kitchen island as I waited for it to cook, mindlessly scrolling my phone.

Click.

I paused. That had sounded exactly like the latch on the storage room under the stairs. It *couldn't* have been, obviously. But then…what *had* that sound been?

I slid down from the island and peered into the hallway. The storage room door was closed. The only sound was the decorative wooden clock on the shelf next to the stairs, slowly *tick-tick-ticking* toward the next hour. The house was so quiet I could have heard a pin drop.

The first of the popcorn kernels burst and the sound made me jump so hard I laughed. It had been so long since I was home alone; I was actually getting freaked out. I shuffled back into the kitchen, and after browsing through my mom's wine collection, I poured myself a glass of Moscato. That would help me chill out.

I returned to the living room with my popcorn and wine, but I was feeling too chilly now to keep going around without pants. I was on my way to the stairs to get my sweatpants when I walked into the entry hall again and realized something had changed.

The screen and keypad for the security system were blinking as if they'd been reset. I typed in the code to arm the system, but the pad beeped, and ERROR flashed across its screen.

I sighed heavily, but it wasn't worth messing with. Our neighborhood was hardly dangerous. As long as the deadbolt was locked, then —

The front door was cracked open.

I stood very still as I stared, the slightest whisper of wind squeaking in through the crack. I couldn't remember stepping outside even once today. Did my parents forget to lock up this morning? I could have sworn it was closed only minutes ago.

I closed the door, turning the lock and the deadbolt. Goosebumps prickled over my arms, and I waited, listening intently. I *knew* the door had been closed. I'd walked through the hall multiple times that day and had never noticed an error on the security system.

A thump made me whip around toward the stairs, my heart pounding. A footstep? I started for the stairway but abruptly stopped myself. This was not a horror film and I was *not* about to become the first to die by running to investigate a mysterious noise. I hurried back into the living room and grabbed my phone.

A text from Lucas was waiting for me. **Are your doors locked, fucktoy?**

Cold realization dawned on me, and I cursed, the frightened tension easing out of my chest. I should have known they had something to do with this.

I texted back. **Yeah, my door is locked. Why wouldn't it be?**

They thought it was funny to break-in and scare me? Oh, I'd show them something funny.

I snatched one of my mom's magazines off the coffee table and rolled it up. I kept my phone in my hand as I crept back into the hall, all my senses on high alert. Which one of them was it? Or was it all of them? My stomach quivered with excitement, like I was playing a twisted game of hide and seek.

A message from Vincent popped up next. **If a cheap lock pick kit from the joke store can get through your deadbolt, I wouldn't trust it to still be locked, Jess.**

Jason's text followed right after. **Tell your parents to replace your security system. The company hasn't even patched a three-year-old security exploit, they can't keep you safe.**

Another soft sound came from the second floor as I started up the stairs. I tucked my phone away and gripped the rolled-up magazine a little tighter.

"I know you're up here!" I called, my loud voice sounding strange in the empty house. It was so silent.

My trepidation only grew as I reached the landing, and my gaze flickered to the doorways before me. All other rooms were closed, but the bathroom and my bedroom were open.

"Come on, guys," I said, my voice trembling despite myself.

"Stop hiding! Do whatever it is you came here for and…" I fell silent as I peered into my room. Something had been written on my vanity mirror in red lipstick, the words unreadable until I got closer.

Time to pay up.

I laughed slightly, nervously. "Okay, really creepy! That better not be my fucking Mac lipstick." I checked under my desk, then crouched down and checked under my bed.

The only place left was the closet. I stared at the closed door, my heart thumping in my ears. It was a game, just roleplay. But I still hesitated as I reached for the louvered door, trying to see into the darkness between the slats.

Slowly, I lowered myself to the ground. I pressed my cheek against the carpet, peering through the small gap under the door. It was so dark. I pulled out my phone and turned on the flashlight, aiming it underneath.

Two pairs of boots stood on the other side.

I stood slowly, moving as if I had a grizzly bear standing directly in front of me. The door was pushed open, clattering slightly as it hit the wall. Manson and Lucas stood side by side, the tiny closet making them appear larger than life. Manson was wearing tight dark jeans and a black t-shirt, his arms folded as he watched me. Lucas's tattooed chest was bare beneath his denim vest, his lean muscles tensing as he stepped forward.

Manson gripped his arm, fingers digging into his bicep. My eyes darted between them as Manson's grin widened.

"You have three seconds before I let Lucas go," he said. "How much ground can you cover in three seconds?"

Lucas's eyes narrowed, locked on me. He was breathing fast,

his stance eager.

"One." Manson started the countdown.

How far could I go in three seconds? Not far enough.

"Two."

Fight-or-flight kicked in despite my bravado with the magazine. My brain said *run*, so I ran, sprinting toward my door. Heart pounding, thoughts focused on only one goal — escape. But I still heard what Manson said next.

"Three. Get her."

24

JESSICA

I sprinted down the hall, their footsteps pounding right behind me. A hand brushed against my back as I ran down the stairs, but I was too quick. I grabbed the banister at the bottom and used it to swing myself toward the living room, but my feet slipped on the wooden floor and that mere second of hesitation gave Lucas the opportunity he needed.

He grabbed me from behind, one arm around my waist and the other seizing my throat and squeezing as I shrieked.

"Mm, little fighter, aren't you?" His voice was a harsh whisper, dripping with eagerness. His lips brushed against my ear, his chest hard against my back. "I knew you would be."

I slammed my elbow back, jabbing it into his side hard enough to loosen his hold. But my attempt at escape didn't get me far.

Manson was right there to grab my arm, and I twisted, pulling so hard that I slipped and sent us both sprawling to the floor.

Manson landed on top. He straddled me and wrapped his hand around my jaw, pinning my head down as he leaned over me and *laughed*. The sound sent a shiver all the way up my spine as Lucas walked into my field of vision, standing behind Manson's shoulder.

"Now that wasn't very nice," Manson scolded. "Feisty little thing."

"No getting away this time," Lucas said. There was an energy to his voice that I hadn't heard before — higher and faster than his usual tone, strained with hunger.

I scratched at Manson's arms as his fingers dug into my face, leaving rivulets of blood blooming across his skin as he taunted me.

"You should be more careful about closing your curtains, Jess," Manson said. "Waltzing around here with your ass hanging out, windows open…" Lucas crouched beside him and leaned over me, bringing his face close to mine. "It's almost like you're asking for it. Any old creep off the street could have come in here."

"Poor little fucktoy," Lucas murmured.

I bucked my hips, throwing Manson off balance for a moment and nearly slamming my arm into Lucas's face. I twisted to my stomach and crawled, but one of them grabbed my ankles and dragged me back, screaming as I went.

"Where ya' going, sweetheart?" Lucas had me now and his body pressed heavily against my back. "You look so goddamn angry. Do you know how fucking hard that gets me? I wonder how long you can keep looking at me like that while I tear open that tight little cunt."

"I. Hate. You," I growled, each word clipped and short,

thrown at him like mere pebbles at a bear. Manson circled me as I lay pinned to the floor, then lifted his foot and pressed my skull down with his boot. Lucas was grinding against my ass, his weight squeezing the breath out of me.

"Fuck yeah, keep squirming," he said, his voice tight. "Such a little tease, isn't she, Manson?"

"Always has been," he said, pressing my head down a little harder. "Always will be."

Lucas's hard cock pressed against me through his jeans. Liquid fire rushed through my veins, igniting every nerve, fear and excitement overtaking me. I kicked and struggled as if my life depended on it, as if I actually hoped for an escape.

But there was no escape. I really had asked for this.

Good girls didn't get railed on the kitchen floor while they screamed how much they hated the men fucking them, but there I was.

"You sick bastards!" God, it felt good to scream, but I was already so out of breath. They were stronger than me, controlling me like I was nothing. Lucas tugged at my oversized shirt, rough fingers brushing over the nape of my neck before the fabric tore. He ripped through my t-shirt with his bare hands, then traced his fingers along my spine before he unclasped my bra.

"Stop!" I kicked my feet, hands scrambling against the floor. "Get the fuck off me!"

But I knew he wouldn't. I didn't want him to.

He tossed my clothes away, leaving only my panties, then he roughly squeezed my ass, fingernails digging into my skin.

"Cut them off her," Manson said. There was a familiar

sound, a click of metal. I sharply sucked in a breath, stiffening when something cold and hard tapped against my leg. It slid under the side of my panties, and Lucas tugged, slicing the knife easily through my underwear. He did the same thing on the other side and pulled the ruined fabric off me, leaving me entirely naked.

For a moment, one that seemed suspended in another reality, Lucas leaned down close to my ear. "Are we doing this, Jess? Still think you're ready to play?"

I let my muscles relax for those brief few seconds as I said, "We're doing it. Don't fucking stop."

Then the moment shattered, and Lucas chuckled low and dark in my ear. Manson removed his foot from my head, but it came with a command. "Get her up."

Lucas hauled me to my feet, his fingers gripping my hair. Manson pulled a chair out from the table, scraping it harshly across the floor, and Lucas shoved me into it.

The moment my ass hit the chair, Manson caught me by the throat. I gripped his wrist, digging my nails into the scratches I'd given him. But my grip loosened as Lucas handed the knife back to him, and Manson brought the weapon close to my face.

"I can scratch too, angel," he said. "But my scratches will hurt a lot more than yours."

He traced the very tip of the blade across my cheek, and I didn't dare move. I remained completely rigid, gulping hard against his hand. Lucas stripped off his vest, the numerous pins affixed to it clicking when he tossed it down on the table. He whipped his belt out of his jeans and they sagged low on his hips, showing off the muscular V that led down from his abs. He came closer, doubling over the belt and snapping it together.

"Put your arms down," Manson said, his voice low in warning. "Or I make you bleed."

I lowered my arms to my sides. My heart pulsed against my ribs and my stomach felt hollow as Lucas wrapped the belt around my waist and arms, then secured it behind the chair, pinning my elbows to my sides. Only then did Manson release my throat and took a step back, regarding me thoughtfully.

The butterfly knife flipped open and closed in his fingers, the weapon spinning like a toy. Lucas was behind me, lurking just out of my sight. I could hear his boots pacing slowly across the wood floor.

"Don't feel like you should give up the fight," he said, suddenly pulling my head back by my hair so I was forced to look up at him. He gave my cheek a few sharp, stinging pats before he released me. "I like my toys interactive. It's so much more fun when they scream."

"You do have the prettiest screams," Manson said, his voice frighteningly sweet. He came closer, and a whimper of alarm burst out of me as he traced the blade over my breast and tapped the flat of it against one of my pierced nipples.

"Sensitive, aren't they?" He moved the knife away and pinched the hardened bud between his thumb and forefinger, forcing a shocked gasp from my mouth. "Does that hurt?"

"No." I grit my teeth, inhaling sharply. "Not sensitive...I don't...I don't care..."

The fridge's ice dispenser turned on behind me, followed by the familiar sound of cubes clinking into a glass. I jumped when Lucas's fingers brushed the back of my neck, shockingly cold as he swept my hair to the side.

"This ain't some Mr. Darcy courtship, sweetheart." Lucas reached over my shoulder, clutching an ice cube in his fingers as Manson stepped back. He trailed it over my skin, cold water dripping onto my thighs. "This is payback."

He swirled the ice around my nipple and at the same moment his lips pressed against my neck. I jolted, the burning cold almost as shocking as the tenderness of his mouth. Lips and tongue explored my neck, warm and sparking with pain when he nipped me.

Then that initial tenderness vanished. He bit me hard, drawing my flesh into his mouth, teeth digging in. I screamed in shock, but Manson was quick, pressing his hand over my mouth to muffle the cry. Lucas suckled the bruised skin as he swirled the ice over my nipples, first one and then the other.

"Are you still going to lie to us?" Lucas hissed. "Or are you ready to admit how sensitive you are?"

Manson uncovered my mouth but kept a grip on my face. I choked down the desperate, needy sounds that kept trying to escape from my mouth as he said expectantly, "Well? What do you have to say now?"

"No!" I snapped, even though the word nearly broke as Lucas used one hand to roll my nipple between his fingers, tugging lightly at the jeweled bar pierced through it.

"No," Lucas repeated slowly. He clicked his tongue in disapproval. "What do you think of that, Manson? She says no."

"Good girls don't say no," Manson said, smiling like he pitied me.

"Fuck you." I managed to get the words out without groaning, but my self-control was short-lived.

Lucas's hand dipped down, cold water dripping over my

stomach as the ice melted. I caged my scream behind clenched teeth as he pressed the ice against my clit. It was so cold, jolting my nerves with all the finesse of a car slamming through a brick wall. He swirled the cube around, over my labia, and then down —

He pressed it inside me. The sensation was different than anything I'd ever experienced, so unexpected that for a moment my mind was an utter blank. I strained against the belt, my thighs squeezing his hand, and a desperate high-pitched moan escaped me.

Lucas withdrew his fingers and the ice with it. I was left shaking, gasping with my head hung down. It hurt, but God, it was good. My pussy ached for something warm and my eyes fell on the bulge in Manson's jeans.

"What's wrong, girl?" Lucas said, the ice clinking as he went for another cube.

"Please not again, fuck, please!"

Lucas looped his arm around my neck, and his muscles flexed, bicep and forearm squeezing my throat.

"Nervous?" Manson said. He placed his palms on my knees and it was shockingly easy for him to force my legs apart, spreading them wide. "A sensitive little slut like you *should* be nervous."

"Please, please, please, oh my God." The words burst out of me as I strained against their grips.

Ice dripped on my chest as Lucas held up another cube in front of my face. "No? You don't want it?" I shook my head, begging still, my words running together. "Oh, but I think you do."

I bucked and squealed, "Lucas, *please*! No, no, no —"

"Aw, why are you fussin' now?" he murmured, trailing the ice over my thighs and leaving goosebumps in its wake. Manson followed the ice with his tongue, the sensation of cold ice and hot mouth throwing my nerves into a frenzy. "You said you're not sensitive. But by the sound of that scream, I know that's not true."

Scream? But I hadn't —

Lucas pressed the ice against my clit and got exactly the sound he wanted out of me. God, could the neighbors hear this? Did they think I was being murdered?

"I lied, okay? I lied!" I babbled, my voice trembling as he mercilessly circled the ice over me. Manson rested his cheek against my thigh, chuckling softly every time a pained sound burst out of me. "I'm sensitive, yes, you were right, you were so right, I'm sorry I lied, I'm sorry!"

Lucas propped his chin on my shoulder. "Are you now? You think I should take this ice away and we'll fill you with something better?"

"Oh *God*, yes." I sounded pathetic, but I didn't care. I would've begged them on my knees if they'd given me the option.

"Suddenly so eager," Manson said, his dark eyes peering up at me. "Does a thick cock sound better than ice?" I nodded, still murmuring my pleas.

"It's too bad I like the way you squirm when it's inside you," Lucas said. "The way you *squeal.*" He pressed the ice inside again, pumping it barely in and out of me. "Music to our ears, isn't it?"

Manson held my trembling legs apart, mocking my desperate gasps before he said, "Sweetest sound in the world."

"Here's your choice, Jess," Lucas said, so damn conversational while I was a gasping wreck. "One hole gets our cocks, the other gets the ice. What'll it be?"

Oh God, no. How was I supposed to handle that? I'd be a

screaming, shaking mess. I'd…I'd be exactly how they wanted me to be. Unraveling in their hands while they used me like a toy.

"Both of you? At the same time?" I looked at Manson as I said it, wide-eyed, imagining the girth of their cocks side by side. I wouldn't survive it; of that much, I was certain. Death via destroyed pussy was impending.

"I don't think you're ready for that," Lucas growled in frustration, as if my lack of readiness was a personal insult. "We have to break you in first."

Manson nodded in agreement. "As fun as it would be to rip that little pussy open and make you bleed, we won't do that to you. Yet."

The anticipation in that word made my heart throb painfully. Not yet? *Yet?*

Lucas grabbed my hair and gave it a tug. "What'll it be? Pick which hole gets it."

Quietly, as softly as I possibly could, I gave him my answer.

"What was that? Speak up, girl."

"My ass," I said, still barely above a whisper. "I want you to fuck my pussy and put the ice in my ass."

If it was possible to die from embarrassment, I would have dropped dead from saying that.

Lucas loosened the belt and Manson tugged me to my feet, kicking the chair out of his way. With one hand around my throat, he walked me backwards until my butt hit the kitchen table, his body crowding close to mine.

"Are you ready to be a good girl for us?" he said as Lucas's arms wrapped around his chest. Lucas rested his chin on Manson's shoulder, tenderly kissing his neck. He tugged at the neckline of

Manson's shirt, pulling it aside so he could bite. Manson didn't wince at the pain; he smiled.

I nodded quickly, shivering at the touch of the table's cool wooden surface on my naked skin. "I'll be good. I promise I'll be good."

He smirked, regarding me as Lucas's nails dragged down his chest. "Should I let Lucas fuck you?"

The other man stiffened at the sound of his name, growling softly as he popped the button on Manson's jeans. It was like he couldn't stop touching, as if he craved the contact so much that he was on the verge of ripping Manson's clothes off.

Watching them had my insides clenching with need. "Please," I said. "Yes, please, let him fuck me."

Lucas slipped his hand into Manson's jeans, stroking him. Manson closed his eyes for a few seconds, his breath deepening as he savored Lucas's touch. All my desire that had been torturously building throughout the morning hit its peak. I wanted them, both of them, in whatever way they wanted to take me. I dared to reach out, cupping my hand over the bulge in Manson's jeans so my hand moved in unison with Lucas's.

Softly, darkly, Manson said, "Lucas, do you want to fuck her?"

The other man's eyes were black as night when he looked at me. "Yes. I want to make her scream."

"Ask nicely."

Lucas bared his teeth for a moment and buried his mouth against Manson's neck as if to keep the words inside.

"Please let me fuck her." He said it like it was a curse. He sounded so desperate, like it physically pained him to ask, as if the longing was unbearable.

The desire in his voice was one of the sexiest things I'd ever heard.

Manson's fingers dug into my throat as he kissed me. His kiss was deep, possessive, consuming the breath right out of my lungs. I was wound so tight I was shaking, hot and cold clashing inside me, creating a storm I couldn't escape.

When Manson pulled back, my eyes fluttered open to see him drawing Lucas closer. Lucas caught me, hands gripping my hips as Manson kept a hold on my throat. Then he was kissing me, ravenously, making my legs go weak.

Lucas wanted to hurt me. I could feel it in the way he pressed himself against me, hard and heavy. When his teeth caught my lip and bit down, I returned his viciousness, raking my nails down his back. It was a war of who could be harder, whose breath would catch first.

Then both of their mouths were on me at once, our tongues twining. It was messy, ravenous, their tastes mingling together as I moaned.

"Please fuck me," I said. I wanted them out of their clothes, and I tugged at the hem on Manson's shirt. He hurriedly whipped it off, tossing it to the floor. Lucas lifted me, setting me down so I was sitting atop the kitchen table. He pressed me back until I was lying flat, and Manson helped him, drawing my legs up toward my chest.

"Hold your legs up," Manson said. "Grip your thighs, keep them spread." I obeyed, holding my legs and spreading them until I was completely exposed. Manson stood on my left side with Lucas between my spread legs, hands tracing my inner thighs as I shivered.

"God, I've waited so fucking long to have you like this," Lucas said. He reached back, grabbed the sweating cup of ice from the island and set it on the table. He hurriedly unzipped his jeans before he gripped my ass, spreading me open even more.

"What a sexy little fucktoy you are," Lucas said. He stroked my clit, my body twitching at the pleasure he drew out of me. He kept rubbing me and then his mouth was on me, tongue moving over my puckered asshole. I gasped, panting as Manson leaned over.

His mouth replaced Lucas's fingers on my clit, and I saw stars.

"Oh, you like that, don't you?" Lucas growled. He paused to grab one of the ice cubes and pop it into his mouth, then he was back between my cheeks. I shuddered as his tongue probed my ass, his mouth cold as he rimmed me. He pushed the ice forward, pressing it against me before sucking it back. All the while, Manson's tongue flicked over my clit with merciless focus.

"God, that feels so good," I gasped. "Please...please don't stop."

The table creaked beneath me, my muscles shaking violently. All thoughts emptied from my head as I shook with pleasure.

"Fuck, Manson! Lucas, please!" I cried out their names as my back arched, convulsing with ecstasy as I came. They didn't stop until I was spent, until my cries grew frantic from overstimulation.

I lifted my head in time to see them kiss, Lucas licking my arousal from Manson's chin.

"I'll fuck her throat," Manson said, his voice rushed, shaking. "And you make her scream." Lucas nodded hurriedly, chest heaving. He stripped out of his clothes, and Manson came to my side, angling my upper body closer to the edge of the table.

He tugged down his briefs enough to allow his cock to spring free, inches from my lips. Pre-cum glistened on his head, and I opened my mouth eagerly, longing to taste him.

He gripped his shaft, stroking himself slowly.

"Do you want it?" he said, bringing himself teasingly close. "Want me to fuck your throat?"

"Yes, sir." I nodded, gripping my legs even tighter as Lucas's finger began to tease my ass.

Manson gripped the back of my head, pressing into my open mouth. He paused when he hit my throat, giving me a moment to adjust before he was fucking me in earnest, hard and fast. Every jerk of his hips hit deep, activating my gag reflex embarrassingly easily. Over the sounds of my own choking gasps, my body alight with the burning afterglow, I heard Lucas spit and his finger swirled the saliva over my hole.

Then the ice pressed against me again.

"Ahh, fuck!" My words were garbled, indiscernible, as Lucas pushed the cube inside. It wasn't very big and was melted smooth, but it wasn't the size that made it difficult. I squealed at the shocking ache, and then the unbearable cold as it settled inside me.

"God, that feels good," Manson groaned. He gave a few more hard thrusts into my mouth before he eased out of me, wincing as if it pained him. His reddened head was swollen, his balls drawn up tight. He was edging, holding himself back. He gripped my hair tight as he bowed his head for a moment, breathing deeply to steady himself.

Lucas stood between my legs, his pupils dilated as he stared down at me, stroking himself. His naked body was covered in tattoos, from his shoulders to his thighs. A curved metal bar was pierced through his cock, one silver ball positioned low on his slit and the other nestled behind his head.

"I want you to watch Lucas fuck you," Manson said, looking down at me. "Beg him for it, go on, let him hear you."

I did, babbling my pleas. Lucas's cock jumped as my voice broke in anticipation, a primal growl ripping from his mouth.

"Fuck yes, scream for me," he said, pressing inside. My swollen pussy took him greedily, slick as he sunk in deep. The smooth ball on his piercing stroked me, strange and foreign, but so damn good. He was warm, blazing inside me in comparison to the cold of the ice cube in my ass.

He pounded into me, the slap of our skin loud as it echoed through the kitchen. Manson watched with rapt attention, encouraging me, "That's it, angel, take his cock. Fucking take it all."

"Lucas!" His name fell broken from my lips, punctuated with a sob. The table groaned at his pace, squeaking on the tile. He gripped my legs, his hands closing over my own as he jerked me toward him with every thrust.

"This is what you needed, isn't it?" he said. "A good, hard fuck to teach you your place, remind you whose pussy this is." I groaned, clenching around him. "I don't care how many cocks you've had. I don't give a single fuck how many bodies you've been with. This pussy is ours and it has *always been ours*."

The pleasure tightened low inside me, pulsating, reverberating through my limbs. "It-it hurts…so good…"

"Say it," Manson ordered, keeping a grip on my hair as Lucas pounded me. "Whose pussy is this, Jessica?"

"Yours!" I cried out as Lucas's brutal pace wrenched animalistic sounds from me. My legs were twitching, every stroke drawing out my ecstasy until I couldn't think.

"That's right," Lucas growled. "That's fucking right. And we're going to wreck this cunt for anyone else, you hear me?

I nodded mindlessly. Lucas fucked me like he hated me, my cries spurring him on until he was throbbing inside me. He clenched his teeth as he slowed, pressing himself so deep that it ached.

Manson's voice cut through the blanket of pleasure smothering my brain. "I think we should leave her with a reminder of who owns her, pup."

"Damn right." Lucas's voice was ragged as he leaned over me, his face looming before my tear-filled eyes. "You're going to get on your knees and take our cum on your face, little fucktoy."

I gasped as he pulled out of me. I was pulled up from the table, dizzy and stumbling, and Manson shoved me to my knees. They both stood over me, shoulder to shoulder. Lucas jerked his cock inches from my face, his expression caught somewhere between agony and ecstasy as he groaned. He was rough with himself, body coiled like a spring. Manson stroked himself rapidly, breath shuddering, teeth bared.

"Please," I said. "Please come on my face."

"Fucking...Christ..." Lucas's cock twitched as he came, hot semen spurting over my skin. Manson followed almost immediately after, hard stuttering breaths accompanying every pulse of his cock. Their seed dripped over my cheeks, my lips, my chin. Marking me, claiming me.

Reinforcing what I already knew — they owned me.

25

LUCAS

I brought the cigarette to my lips again, savoring a slow drag. Menthol and tobacco hit my throat with a pleasant burn, the nicotine steadying my shaking hands as I looked out on the Martins' picture-perfect backyard. The grass was trimmed, and the bushes were tightly manicured. Everything was neat and tidy. Maintained. *Controlled.*

Tension knotted through my neck and shoulders when the glass door behind me slid open. But it was just Manson. His hair was still disheveled with a sheen of sweat across his bare chest. Jess had left long scratches on his arms, and the sight made my cock twitch again, but I was too tired for round two.

"How is she?" I said.

"I think we fucked the sarcasm out of her, for now," he said, grinning as he held up his hand. I passed him the cigarette, reading what he wanted easily. "She's getting cleaned up in the bathroom, changing into something comfortable."

"I can walk back to the house. You can take the car when you're ready."

"Come on, man." He gave me a *look* before he brought the cigarette to his mouth and inhaled. "You're dropping. You shouldn't be by yourself."

Dominant drop was what he meant. That intense feeling of guilt and exhaustion that could hit you after an intense encounter like the one we'd had. But it wasn't just the dopamine suddenly leaving my system that made me want to take off.

I didn't stay after a fuck. Ever. My policy was to hit it and bail. I wasn't a gentle guy, so sitting and talking, "decompressing," all that soft shit? It wasn't for me. Putting space between Jess and I was for the best. We had our arrangement and her *debt* to us didn't involve getting any warm and fuzzy feelings about each other.

"You know how it goes," I said, taking the cigarette back as he offered it. "I'm not the guy you want around when everyone is feeling vulnerable. You can take care of her."

Manson made a disapproving noise, but I was being honest. What the hell did I know about this shit? The closest I'd ever come to a *normal* romantic relationship was with him — and even that I knew I wasn't great at. I could swing from hot to cold and back again within the space of a week, but he knew me too well to be bothered by it.

At least, I didn't think it bothered him. He'd never said anything about it. When I needed space, he gave it easily. When I needed to give up control, I trusted him to take it.

But I didn't need softness. I didn't need intimate, quiet moments.

That was what I told myself anyway.

My dad had been a man-up-and-take-it type, who would rather beat his sons into toughness than offer a shred of compassion, and Mama hadn't been much better. Gentleness wasn't just a foreign concept; it was fucking uncomfortable, like trying to have a conversation in a language I only had an elementary knowledge of.

But Manson had told me even before we showed up here that I needed to stay. For her. To look after her. Care for her. Do all the nice, compassionate, *gentle* things I was supposed to be able to do but couldn't.

"Look, I'm fine," I said, stubbing out my cigarette against the sole of my shoe and looking around aimlessly for an ashtray. Apparently no one in this household smoked.

Manson plucked the cigarette out of my fingers, nodding his head back toward the house. "Come on. I wanna show you something."

It was a trap to get me to come back inside, but whatever. If he wanted me to sit around like a baboon with his thumb up his ass, sure, I'd stay.

Jess was showering, the sound of running water coming from the closed bathroom door. Our cum had been all over her face, her chest, her hair. She could wash it away, but I hoped the scent of us would linger. I wanted to leave her with something tangible, something she couldn't easily forget and others couldn't deny.

Fuck, if I was a dog, I probably would have pissed on her to stake my claim. Maybe I really would, eventually, if she stuck around that long.

Manson was sitting on the edge of the couch when I came to his side, staring down at a piece of paper in his hands. It was a half-completed sketch showing the front of a house with a wraparound porch. I wasn't sure what I was looking at until I realized how familiar the house was.

"Is that our place?" I said.

"Pretty sure it is. She's taken some aesthetic liberties." He traced his finger lightly along the intricate woodwork designs she'd drawn along the windows.

"Did you know she could draw?" I said as he carefully put the paper back down on the coffee table. The water in the bathroom had turned off, and it made my heart speed up a little.

"Not until now," he said. "She must have drawn all this from memory."

She had even drawn flowers and bushes along the front porch. The new features were small, but the effect was drastic. It made the house look more like a home, like someone had put love and care into it.

"Should we plant flowers?" I blurted out. The dirt yard was so damn barren.

"It does look nice...I guess we could." He didn't sound entirely pleased about the idea, but I couldn't blame him. Living in that house at all was a challenge for him, even with all the changes we'd made.

We'd done a lot of work since we moved in, but it was always with a single-minded focus. We needed to get the house ready to sell. As fortunate as we'd been to get the place after Manson's mom passed away, his childhood home carried far too many memories for him.

He was braver than me. I hadn't been back home to see Mama even once since Dad and I left. Even now, years later, I didn't think I'd have the courage to walk into the house I'd spent the first fourteen years of my life in.

Jess walked into the living room, squeezing a towel on her damp hair. She looked between us, her eyes narrowing as she tried to figure out what we'd been up to. Then she looked down and spotted the drawing on the coffee table.

"I swear I'm not just drawing your house for fun," she said quickly, as if that would be so awful. "It's for work. I need to present a project to my boss at my six-month review and your house has a lot of..." Her lips pursed as she pondered. The way her face scrunched up made me feel...hell, it made me feel *something*. Like an aggressive need to squish her cheeks. "It has a lot of potential. Great character."

"Why are you drawing a house for work?" I said, wincing when my voice came out far gruffer than I intended. She was dressed in a big t-shirt and leggings, her smeared mascara washed away. She had so many freckles on her cheeks that I hadn't noticed before, and her eyelashes were almost as light as her hair.

"I work in architectural design," she said. "I've been interning with this big company in New York City. If I prove myself, the boss says she'll take me on full time. Then I'm out of Wickeston for good." She smiled, draping her towel across the back of one of the kitchen chairs before she headed for the fridge. "We have wine if you guys want some. Mom doesn't keep beer in the house though."

Damn, we really had fucked the sarcasm out of her. Was this all she needed? A hard fight followed by a harder fuck and suddenly she was looking a lot more worthy of Manson's little pet name for her. Manson, of course, jerked his head toward the kitchen to get me to follow her. I swallowed down my groan, but went along. Hell, if I was here, I could at least try.

Besides, maybe he was right about the drop. The more time went on, the more I felt it — a tightness in my chest that quivered like anxiety but swayed with exhaustion, raw and uncertain. I wanted to settle down somewhere quiet and chill.

Jess was in the pantry, stretching up on her tiptoes as she tried to reach a box of Girl Scout cookies on the top shelf. Her shirt was hitched up enough to give me a damn fine view of her ass wrapped in those skintight leggings, and I paused for a moment to admire her.

I thought I'd come the second I sunk into her. Years of fantasizing about her had nearly culminated in one goddamn thrust. Having her suck my cock all those years ago had nothing on being inside her, hearing her, watching her fall apart. It was the hate-fuck I'd needed for years, even better than my fantasies. No wonder Manson was so hopelessly fucked for her.

As much as I thought she was spoiled, prideful, selfish...I was fucked too. We all were, really; it just manifested in different ways.

I reached over her head, easily plucking the cookies off the shelf and handing them to her. She hurriedly dug into the box, popping one into her mouth and groaning as if it was orgasmic.

"God, these are my favorite," she said, sighing contentedly before she held out the box. "Want one?"

"Thin Mints? Fuck yes." I didn't want just one; I took a whole sleeve for myself before she went back to browsing for snacks.

One of Vincent's sisters used to be a Girl Scout, and every time they had a sale, we'd stock up with as many cookies as we could afford. Frozen Thin Mints and coffee were basically my breakfast of champions for a while.

I stuffed two cookies into my mouth right as Jess turned back around. She giggled when I coughed, the mouthful not going down quite as quickly or easily as I'd hoped. She held out the box again, saying, "Here, you and Manson can have at it. I shouldn't have anymore."

"Shouldn't?" I stared back at her incredulously. She'd had *one* cookie. "Says who?" She shrugged, muttering something about sugar and carbs, but I shoved the box back against her chest. "Girl, we broke into your house, shoved ice up your ass, and fucked you over your mother's kitchen table. Eat some goddamn cookies."

"Ugh, fine," she groaned, but her tone was teasing as she snatched the cookies back.

Teasing or not, I still lunged for her, forcing her back until she was pressed against the crowded shelves.

"Are you forgetting the rules?" I said softly. Her eyes were wide in the dim light as she looked up at me, her chest swelling as she drew in her breath. She laid her hand against my chest, curiously tracing the gap where my denim vest left my skin bare.

Her touch left goosebumps on my skin.

"I did forget, sir," she said, just above a whisper. She leaned a little closer. "I'm sorry. I should've said fine, *sir*."

The way she smiled at me was both wicked and sweet, challenging me as she placated me. Most people would never dare. Most would be running scared.

Not her. Why the hell wasn't she scared of me?

Better yet, why didn't I want her to be?

I sighed, straightening up and stepping back. "Watch yourself, fucktoy. Manson will get really pissed if I spank you right now."

"Mm, well, we wouldn't want that, would we?" The tone of her voice said she absolutely fucking would, the little brat. She slipped out of the pantry, snatching a box of crackers as she went, and I turned my attention to the bottles of wine on her counter. I eventually chose something dark with an interesting label — I wasn't a wine guy, but Manson liked reds.

"Glasses are in the cabinet to your right," she said. I didn't know why she was watching me fumble around with this when she could have been comfortably cuddling with Manson on the couch. I grabbed a couple coffee mugs since they were the first things I saw in the cabinet, filling them to the brim and taking a heavy sip of mine.

As I lowered the mug, Jess looked like she was holding back laughter.

"What?" I snapped without meaning to, but it didn't faze her.

"You're not used to this, are you?" she said, and my pride bristled.

"I've had sex before, Jess," I said. "Plenty of times."

"I don't mean sex." She laughed. "I mean *this*. Like, being with someone."

Oh. Right. I guess it was that obvious. I didn't belong here, in this nice house, surrounded by photos of Jessica's family and her mom's *Live Laugh Love* decor.

I hadn't felt that way when I'd broken in. Getting Jason to disarm the security system, borrowing Vincent's lock pick kit, creeping through the house with Manson and texting some creepy messages had just been part of the game. But I'd played my round and the fact that I was still lingering felt far more invasive than having broken in in the first place.

"I'm not the sit-and-talk type. I'm not usually stuck with someone for this long." She froze for a moment, and I winced. "I didn't mean it like that. I'm not *stuck*. We broke into your fucking house." I sighed heavily, rubbing a hand over my head. "Do you want me to leave?"

Me, not we. I was the odd one out here with my fucked-up hang-ups. Besides, Jess had never liked me. She'd liked the idea of me, sure, that much was obvious. But me? As a person? That was laughable.

But she shook her head, looking at me like I'd suggested something ludicrous.

"How about you pour a little more wine in that mug and come to the couch," she said. She laid her hand on my arm, squeezing my bicep slightly before she walked back to the living room. Okay, fine, she'd convinced me. I was going to do this aftercare thing even if it killed me.

I returned to the living room, where Manson was lounging on the couch and Jess had flopped down beside him, munching on her cookies. I gave him his wine and took the remaining side of the couch, sitting stiffly on the pristine white cushions. How could someone live with this much white furniture? I'd dirty it up just by looking at it.

"How much was today worth?" Jess said, taking a sip from her glass as she glanced between us. "That was at least a $1500 fuck, right?"

My post-nut clarity must have been broken, because I almost told her it was worth the cost of our cars and more. I had to gulp down a little more wine to drown those words before I said something I'd regret.

"What do you think, Lucas?" Manson asked. "Maybe four or five?"

I shrugged. "I'd say five. I'm feeling generous."

"Five hundred?" she said excitedly.

"*Five* dollars," I said, then quickly held my wine out of the way as she launched across the couch, swatting her hand at my head. I caught her wrists and pulled them down, hauling her onto my lap. "Hey, hey, watch it! I was *joking*, girl."

"Almost made me spill wine on your couch," Manson said, staring down at the crisp white cushions beneath him with a horrified expression. "I feel like if I get a stain on something in here, I'll be cursed."

"Oh, you will be," she said. "My mom can detect a crumb buried in the carpet from ten yards away. I've seen her do it." She sipped her wine, wiggling her feet slightly. She was a tense little ball on my lap, and now that she was there, I wasn't sure what to do with her.

"Can your mom detect semen on a kitchen table?" I said, and Jess swatted my chest.

"You'll both get the curse of a lifetime for that," she said. To my surprise, she leaned across the couch to grab her cookies and the TV remote, then promptly settled back down on my lap. "I hope you like 15th century Gothic cathedrals because that's what we're watching."

She could have told me we were watching a documentary on the bowel movements of elephants and I still wouldn't have moved a muscle. Manson moved closer from the far side of the couch, and

Jess stretched her legs to rest them on his lap. Her back was against my arm and shoulder as she munched on her cookies and stared at the TV. But as the minutes passed, her shoulders slumped and so did the cookies. Then her head sunk down and rested against my shoulder, a soft sigh melting her body against mine.

I glanced over at Manson for help, but damn it, he'd knocked out too. I hadn't been able to relax a single muscle, but as Jess's breathing steadied, I dared to wrap my arm around her.

She fit perfectly. Like a puzzle piece tucked against my side, soft and warm. Her hair smelled sweet and slightly fruity, like strawberries.

But my scent was there too.

26

JESSICA

Morning greeted me with the sun warming my bare legs and the twittering of birds. I lay there for a while and watched them flutter through the tree outside my window, eyes half-lidded with comfortable sleepiness, warm and drowsy in my blankets.

I had a vague memory of being carried to bed last night. Lucas cradled me up the stairs, and Manson's hand cupped the back of my head so it wouldn't get knocked on the wall in our narrow hallway. I wasn't sure how late it had been. I'd tried to stay awake, but the moment I settled on Lucas's lap, my eyes grew so heavy that no amount of willpower could have kept them open.

I'd had more sexual partners in my life than I could count, but I'd never had two men at the same time. Out of all those partners, no one had ever gotten it quite right when they fucked me. Some had come close, sure. But my casual flings and one-night stands still left me with an unscratched itch. A need for something more intense.

But Manson and Lucas played with my mind as much as my body. They wound me up, building the tension, taking their time to set a scene. Breaking into my house, hacking the security system, hiding in my closet...and the way Lucas had begged for Manson's permission to fuck me, looking at me like he wanted to rip me apart...

God, why was that so hot? The way Manson exercised control made it feel like the most natural thing in the world to submit to him — natural, except for the fact that everyone I knew would judge me for it if they found out.

Normal people didn't do that.

Maybe normal people were boring.

But as I sat up in bed, sighing contentedly at the sunny day outside my window, my satisfaction was shaken. I'd felt this perfect sense of fulfillment before, after that Halloween party almost three years ago. But I'd thrown it all away. I'd decided it wasn't worth taking risks for.

Was it any different now? The only reason I'd agreed to do this was to get my car fixed, or at least, that had been the most readily available excuse. And that was what I needed, an excuse, something I could point to and blame. Something I could hold up in front of nay-sayers and say, *See? There's not really anything wrong with me! It was only because...*

I shoved back the blankets and got up. I wasn't going to ruin a perfectly fine day with an existential crisis over a good fuck. I was heading for the bathroom when I noticed the creepy lipstick message had been cleaned off my mirror, a sticky note left in its place.

I'll buy you a new lipstick.

Manson's handwriting was sharp and precise, but this note was written much smaller, messier. It had to be Lucas.

I folded the note and set it down beside the aforementioned tube of lipstick. I'd seen a side to Lucas last night I hadn't known existed, a side of him that crept out after the viciousness had dissipated. He'd looked so out of place, nervous and uncertain. As if being in a normal suburban home was too much.

Maybe it was. No one had ever known much about Lucas's home life except vague bits and pieces. He'd moved to Wickeston with his dad — a hulk of a man with the same permanent scowl as his son — after his parents separated. They'd lived in the trailer park on the west side of town, keeping to themselves until they had an explosive public brawl at a local diner.

I don't think Lucas lived with his father after that, but I wasn't sure. I could only imagine that once you got to the point of fighting your own dad, things probably weren't going well at home.

I hopped in the shower, taking my time to wash my hair, exfoliate, and shave. When I got out and wiped away the steam from the mirror, I couldn't help staring at the marks all over my body. Brushing my fingers across my neck, I pressed my skin here and there to feel the subtle pain of the bruises they'd given me.

I liked how they looked, how they felt dirty and beautiful at the same time.

By the time I left the bathroom, I only had ten minutes before I had to hop on a video call for work. Dressing up quickly, I got in front of my computer just in time, only to realize I'd been in such a rush I'd failed to do *anything* to cover the hickeys on my neck.

I spent the entirety of my meeting with my shoulders scrunched up like a turtle, hoping the marks weren't obvious. If anyone noticed, at least they didn't say anything. Thank God it was almost Friday. Hopefully they would fade over the weekend.

A text from Lucas was waiting for me when I finally closed my laptop. **Send us a photo. I want to see our handiwork.**

I stripped down to get a good photo for them. I wasn't ashamed that I loved being a tease; who *wouldn't* want to feel desired, to flex your own power to seduce? I sent the photo I took to the group chat and wasn't disappointed by their response.

Fuck, you look sexy covered in bruises, Manson said.

Damn it, one sec, I dropped my jaw on the floor, Vincent wrote. **Shit, I knew should have called out of work and gone with you fucks.**

Jason's text came next. **God, Jess, how am I supposed to work with a hard-on?**

I hope you know I'll be getting the locks and security system replaced, I responded. I did need to do something about that, unless I wanted to feign ignorance to my parents about why the system had stopped working. **So good luck catching me again. I'm a faster runner on open ground.**

Are you? Manson said. **We'll have to test that out.**

Lucas was far less subtle. **A goddamn lock won't stop me, fucktoy. I'll have you whenever I want.**

Maybe we should let her run, was Jason's suggestion. **I think it would be fun to go for a hunt. We could use our paintball guns and bag ourselves a fucktoy.**

Thank God they couldn't see my face. I was red as hell as I imagined being hunted like an animal, shot down and gutted. What the hell was wrong with me? This was hopelessly perverted.

The group chat didn't stop their teasing, but when another text came through from Lucas, it didn't come through the group.

I've got a task for you. What's your work schedule like during the week?

I lounged on my bed, feet up as I replied. **A task? How exciting. Better make the instructions clear so I can't fuck it up.**

I couldn't resist pushing their buttons; it was too fun to see them getting worked up. I gave him my schedule; I worked only until noon during the week, except on Mondays when I had a full day.

Fuck this up and your ass will feel the consequences, Lucas wrote. **Although I'm sending a chaperone with you to make sure you don't. Last night wouldn't have been possible if Jason hadn't disarmed your security system. We owe him, and obviously, so do you.**

So it was Jason who'd gotten past the security system. I wasn't surprised; he'd always been absurdly smart.

Lucas went on. **Vincent will pick you up on Tuesday after work. You'd better behave yourself unless you want him to bring a paddle along with him.**

I'll skip the paddle, thanks, I said, even though the thought gave me that twisty feeling in my stomach again. **I'll be perfectly behaved, so tell him to bring something to reward me with instead.**

Oh, he will. Don't you worry about that, fucktoy.

The next few days were spent trying to get back into my routine. I woke up early and took my mom's car to the gym — thankfully, she didn't mind me borrowing it while she and Dad were gone. I warmed up on the treadmill before I moved to weights, and by the time I was done, I was dripping sweat. The burn felt good. There was something about the pain that made me feel alive.

Unfortunately, while in the middle of my workout Sunday morning, a familiar face approached me in the middle of a set.

"Oh…hey, Alex." I took my earbuds out as he stood beside me, regarding him cautiously. What the hell did he want? I hadn't seen him at this gym before, but maybe he usually came at a different time. He had his shirt off, showing off muscles that were chiseled to perfection worthy of a Greek god.

But those muscles didn't do shit for me when they were attached to his backstabbing face.

"We missed you at Billy's the other night," he said, almost too casually. "I wanted to check in. Make sure we're good."

"Good?" I stared at him in surprise, then lowered my voice as I said, "You broke into a private garage and fucking abandoned me. Why the hell would we be *good*, Alex?"

"Things got a little out of hand; I'll admit. I thought you were gunning for those losers, Jess. The same guy who busted my head open…" The look he fixed me with left me no doubt this was a warning. "I'm just saying I'd hate to see you get mixed up with the wrong people."

I smiled tightly. "Thanks for your concern. Now if you don't mind…" I put my earbuds back in, dismissing him without a word.

He gave me a forced smile before he walked away, and I felt his eyes on me until I finally walked out the door thirty minutes later.

I had no idea if my relationship with my old friends was repairable; frankly, I didn't want it to be. Maybe it was better to be a loner.

My nerves were high as Tuesday rolled around, and I distractedly got through work, knowing Vincent would be showing up soon. I still had no idea what this 'task' was, but I'm sure Vince had something unexpected up his sleeve.

It was just after noon when his blue WRX pulled up in front of my house. I'd been pacing around, trying to convince myself I wasn't nervous — why the hell would I be nervous? It was Vincent Volkov, the guy who'd always been a class clown, who used to get invited to the popular kids' parties because they knew he'd have drugs to sell. He didn't have the same dark, vicious aura that the others did, but there was something about him that severely disarmed me. His teasing nature meant people usually underestimated him, including me.

I had a better idea of what he was capable of now, but I still didn't know what to expect. As I watched him step out of the car through the kitchen window, my heart sped up and I rubbed my sweating palms on my jeans.

God, he was hot. Way sexier than he had any damn right to be. He strode up to the front door with Ray-Bans on, his long hair loose and wavy around his face, wearing tight acid-wash jeans and an oversized tie-dye shirt with a flaming skull on it. The colors clashed, but it weirdly worked for him.

Anything weird worked with Vincent.

I was already on my way to the door before he rang the bell. When I answered it, he was lighting up a joint dangling from his lips.

Had he lost his mind? He was smoking here, in the middle of the day, in *this* neighborhood?

"Are you really smoking weed on my front porch?" I said, completely incredulous.

He pulled the joint from his lips, blowing the smoke away over his shoulder. "Damn right, baby. Want a hit?"

I wasn't going to think too deeply about the way him calling me *baby* made me feel. I was going to ignore the fact that it brought my heart stuttering to a stop before it flew off again at a gallop.

I shook my head at his offer, and grabbed my bag from its hook, locking the door behind me as I stepped outside. "Nope, thanks, but I'm not trying to go through the rest of my day paranoid."

"Paranoid?" He blew a loud raspberry, wrapping his arm around my waist after I'd locked the front door. "What do you have to be paranoid about? I'm with you. I'll make sure you don't go running off naked into the woods." He lifted his eyebrows suggestively. "At least not without me."

I laughed despite myself as we walked down the driveway. "I'm not afraid of a spiritual awakening, Vincent. More like paranoia about the fact that it's illegal."

He stopped on the opposite side of the WRX, staring at the joint clasped between his fingers. "Weird how a little rolled up herb can get you locked behind bars," he said. "Legality is just a bunch of old dead folks telling you what to do."

I shook my head at him as I slid into the car, huffing in surprise when I sank into the strangely deep passenger seat. The seatbelt was weird too, a three-point harness that I had to slip my arms through and then clip into place between my legs.

"I'm surprised you don't have cuffs in here," I said, squirming around as I adjusted the harness.

"Right there." He pointed, and I looked overhead, finding a cage of metal bars installed around the interior of the cab. It reminded me of the dune buggies I'd ridden in when I went out to Nevada for a bachelorette party. Sure enough, a pair of leather cuffs dangled from the bar above my head.

"Perfect for wrists or ankles," he said, his grin widening. "But I think that harness will be enough to keep your ass in the seat for now. My rides can get a little rough."

I had no doubt he was right, in more ways than one. The WRX shuddered as he started it; the rumble of its engine not as deep as Manson's Mustang or the El Camino. It purred low and steady, and Vincent turned the music up loud as we pulled away from the curb. He sang along to the lyrics about choking and sodomy as we picked up speed, flying past my neighbors' houses. He earned us more than a few odd looks from folks out watering their lawns and trimming their rose bushes.

"What are we listening to?" I shouted, praying all the while that no one was going to mention to my mother that they'd seen me drive away in a loud car with a long-haired stoner.

"You've never heard System of a Down?" He practically gaped at me. "Oh, we need to get you to expand your musical horizons, Jess. What do you usually listen to?"

It didn't take long to realize that Vincent's musical knowledge went significantly deeper than mine. But he wasn't restricted to one genre. His playlist changed wildly as we drove, from screaming metal to melodic electronic and classical orchestra.

"I'll make you a playlist," he finally insisted. "We'll start with more approachable shit and then work our way deeper."

For as long as I'd known Vincent, he'd always managed to put other people at ease and now was no different. We drove through town with the windows down, and I dangled my arm out in the breeze.

I'd known him longer than the other boys. I'd met him in first grade, if *he threw dirt at me* could qualify as a "meeting." He'd gotten quieter as he got older, going from the loud class clown in elementary school to an extremely introverted kid in middle school.

But in high school, he was known as the guy who always had drugs to sell. Marijuana, prescription drugs, Molly — unless people were looking for really hard shit, Vincent was their guy. Even if they thought he was a freak, a Satanist, or whatever else people whispered behind his back, he was simply hard to hate.

"Your car looks...better," I said, carefully broaching the subject.

"Jason and I took care of that over the weekend. Got the windows replaced and the dents repaired. We still need to do something about the paint, but I might hold off on getting mine touched up." He chuckled softly. "With the way I drive, my paint doesn't stay in good shape for long anyway."

"Is that your way of telling me you're the worst driver in the house?" I teased. "Should I strap in a little tighter?"

"I said my driving was rough, not bad." He shot me a sly smile and reached across, his hand sliding along my leg to tightly grip my thigh. The touch of his fingers was like dropping a lit match on kerosene. "Before I take you home today, I'll show you. We'll take the long way home."

"Dirt roads? In this car?" I looked at him skeptically.

"You'll see," he said. "Not all fast cars are built to stay on asphalt."

"What are we doing today anyway?" I said, trying not to let my flaming arousal affect my voice. The effect these men had on me wasn't fair. "And why did Lucas send you as my chaperone?"

"Because I'm the only man for the job, obviously," he said. "Mr. Grumpy Face wants to give Jason a thank-you for helping out, and I happen to know exactly what Jason likes."

I burst out laughing. "Mr. Grumpy Face? Oh my God, I'm calling him that next time I see him."

"Please do, I'll be right there to watch him spank you for it."

We pulled into a parking lot, apparently having reached our destination. I narrowed my eyes at the buildings nearby as Vincent parked, trying to figure out where we were headed.

"Wait a minute…is that Satin Novelties? There's a sex shop in Wickeston now?" I stared at the shop in disbelief. The windows were covered with black paper, and the door had a big red sign on it that read, *No One Under 18 Permitted Entry*.

"Yep, they replaced the old tire shop when it went out of business," he said, taking his keys from the ignition as he opened his door. "Pretty sure there were protests when the place opened up. It really got some panties in a twist around here."

We met at the back end of the car. We couldn't have looked more like polar opposites — his tie-dye and long hair in comparison to my carefully preened ponytail, heels, and a white blouse. I hadn't been sure what to wear, but my rule was always to overdress, just in case.

To judge from the way his eyes were roaming over me, he liked what I'd chosen. I couldn't see his eyes beneath those sunglasses, but I noticed as he licked his lips and subtly adjusted himself.

He held out his hand, nodding toward the shop. "Shall we, fucktoy?"

27

VINCENT

Satin Novelties made me feel like a kid in a candy store. Sure, everything was online now and I could easily order whatever items I wanted to be delivered, but there was something so enjoyable about wandering around the physical shelves, stumbling upon an unexpected item and letting your imagination run wild. Especially when I had the source of so much inspiration right in front of me; her hand in mine.

I led Jess inside, the bell on the door jingling as we entered. Almost instantly, a hand shot up from the front of the store, near the register.

"Welcome in!" a cheerful voice called. "My name is Julia. Let me know if you need any help!"

"Wow, that's a lot of enthusiasm," Jess said softly, and I smiled to myself as we wound between the shelves of lube and erotic novels toward the front counter. A young woman with long bright red hair was sitting behind the register on a stool, a wide smile spreading across her face when we walked into view.

"Who let this clown in here?" she said. She hopped off her stool, coming to rest her elbows on the counter. "Oooh, but you brought a cutie along with you! Did he kidnap you? Blink twice if you need help."

"I mean, it wasn't *exactly* a kidnapping," Jess said, glancing over at me mischievously as she played along. "I got in the car willingly."

"Well, considering this weirdo hasn't tied you up yet, you're in a better spot than most victims that end up in his deathtrap of a car." She held out her hand, and Jess took it with a smile. "I'm Julia, by the way. You must be Jessica. Lucas mentioned you'd be coming by."

"My car is not a death trap," I said. "Just because my driving scares you doesn't make it deadly."

"Mm, nope, I think it's pretty deadly." She pursed her lips, waving me away. "Go shop or something, would you? Give me and Jess a chance to get to know each other."

I innocently held up my hands as I backed away. If there was one thing Julia couldn't resist, it was a hot girl. She kept talking as I roamed among the shelves, explaining how we all knew each other. She and Lucas used to work together when this place was still a tire shop; she was the only coworker of his that he hadn't completely hated. She'd been a student at Wickeston High, but a grade above the rest of us, although she ran in some of the same circles. We ended up at a lot of the same parties as a result, including the club I bartend for.

"I remember you from the cheerleading team!" Julia exclaimed, practically squealing in her excitement. "I always saw you at the football games. Girl, you were *amazing*. Like holy shit, I could never be that flexible."

I got a quick glimpse of Jess's face as I passed by and was pleased to see her smiling. Most of our friends weren't people that Jess was familiar with, but they were people she could trust.

She needed people like that. People who weren't going to tear her down behind her back, who didn't make adhering to a strict mold one of the caveats of friendship. As much as it pissed me off, finding Jess abandoned in our garage by her so-called friends had made me sad more than anything. She clung to those people because they were familiar, not because they actually did anything for her life.

I used to try to make everyone I met into a friend, regardless of who they were or how they'd treated me. I'd convinced myself that enough kindness could turn anything around, but not everyone was — or deserved to be — a friend. Learning that lesson hadn't been easy, but painfully necessary.

I smirked as I picked up a pair of nipple clamps and tucked them under my arm. Jason didn't know exactly how Lucas was planning to thank him, and I was glad Julia was keeping Jess busy. I planned to have her arrive at our house with a whole box of goodies, like a doll that came with accessories. It tickled my humor to imagine not only Jason being surprised by Jess, but Jess being surprised by what exactly she was in for.

Jason had certain kinks he didn't often get to indulge and I was eager to give him the opportunity. But I grabbed a few items for myself too; I wasn't going to miss the chance to play when I finally had Jess all to myself.

"I think that's everything," I said, setting my basket down on the counter for Julia to ring up. I slid myself in front of it before Jess could get much of a look. "No peeking now. That would ruin the surprise."

Jess scowled at me, screwing up her mouth to protest, but Julia howled excitedly, "Ooh, yes, girl, keep it a surprise!" She leaned around me, lifting her eyebrows in a cartoonishly pervy way. "Trust me, you're going to have fun."

"Hm, we'll see about that," Jess said, although the skepticism in her tone softened jokingly. Julia rang us up and was handing my card back when the jingle of the doorbell caught her attention.

"Sorry, guys. Duty calls." She lifted her hand and gave the same enthusiastic greeting to the overwhelmed-looking couple who'd walked in, then lowered her voice and said, "Ooh, I think I've got some first-timers. They'll either freak out and bail or buy the whole shop. Time to work some magic! I'll see you around!"

Jess's stomach was rumbling as we left the shop, although she tried to deny it. But there was a fast-food place right across the street, and the smell of grilled onions and greasy burgers drew me. We took a table outside to eat, the striped umbrella overhead shielding us from the sun.

Jess inhaled her burger before I'd eaten even half of mine.

"I had a hard workout this morning," she said, when she noticed me eyeing her empty tray. "And I had a small breakfast —"

"Chill, girl." I chuckled as I poked a handful of fries at her. "Who the hell taught you that you need to justify what you eat?"

She stared at me for a moment before she stammered out, "Oh, uh, my mom, I guess. She's always been picky about food."

"That's not being picky, it's being invasive. It's no one's damn business what you eat, as long as you're eating." She smiled, reaching across the table and grabbing some of my fries. "There you go. Steal as much as you want."

Her smile widened and she pulled her legs up to sit cross-legged on the red plastic seat. There was such a difference between the way she smiled in public — at parties, with her friends, her peers — than she did here, with me. This smile was far more open. It was honest rather than a carefully formulated expression. I liked that. I wanted to see it more.

I wanted to see every expression she had, as raw as I could get it.

I had a view of the parking lot from my seat, so I saw the old red Chevy as soon as it pulled in. It was loud, puttering as if it had an exhaust leak, and my eyes followed it, although I didn't think much of it. It parked crooked and the engine cut off, but I was already looking at Jess again when the driver stepped out.

I didn't see him clearly until he was passing by our table. Then I glanced up, and nearly fucking choked on a mouthful of burger.

"Woah, are you okay?" Jess reached across the table for me as I coughed, managing to choke the food down despite my sputtering. I paused as I caught my breath. Jess's eyes were wide as she looked at me. But then her gaze flickered up, over my shoulder, and she gave an awkward smile as she said to someone, "He's okay."

Shit. Fucking shit.

I glanced back in time to make brief eye contact with the man who'd stepped out of the truck. He was old, with a long lean frame and gray stubble on his cheeks. His hair was greasy and grown out to his shoulders, but beyond his haggard appearance was a stunning familiarity that made the food in my stomach turn sour.

His mouth twitched in a crooked smile before he turned away and kept walking. He recognized me; I'd seen it in his eyes.

I hurriedly gathered what remained of my food, setting my tray on top of Jess's empty one. "Come on. We need to go."

Jess blinked at me in surprise but followed me as I threw our trash away. I grasped her hand before we ran back across the street, looking over my shoulder with paranoia all the while.

He wasn't supposed to be back. Fuck, he wasn't even supposed to be *alive*.

"Okay, what the hell is going on?" Jess said the moment we were both back in the car. I felt better with the AC blasting on us and all the doors closed, the tinted glass hiding us from the world.

Maybe I'd been wrong. Maybe it wasn't him.

But that truck...it was the same one he'd driven for so damn long. And the way he smiled, the sharp angles of his face, his dark eyes...so much like his son.

"You saw that old man?" I said, shoving my wallet in the center console. She nodded. "That was Manson's dad. Reagan Reed."

Her eyes widened as she turned in her seat, looking back across the street. "Shit. I take it he hasn't been in town for a while?"

"Not since the funeral," I said, pulling out of the lot and back onto the road. "We thought he was dead. *Hoped* he was dead, I guess. Don't mention this around Manson, okay? I'll tell him, but don't bring it up."

"I won't." Her eyes were on me as I drove, studying me. Clever girl. She'd figure me out if she kept trying. "He scares you too, doesn't he?"

I sighed, my fingers flexing on the wheel. She'd never gotten the whole story — she'd heard some of the surface-level things Reagan was capable of, enough to know what kind of man he was, but nothing more. It wasn't my story to tell, and besides, I didn't want to scare her.

Manson had rarely brought anyone over to his parents' place in high school, but I'd gone over twice myself. Both times I'd been eager to leave. Reagan's presence in the house was like a poison in the air. I'd watched his wife and son cringe around him; heads down, eyes lowered, voices kept evenly cautious.

It was nothing like how it was in my own home. My sisters and I had never been afraid of our parents. We respected them, certainly. As the oldest, I'd always been expected to be the one to set an example, to look after my little sisters and help support the family. But I was happy to do those things out of love, not fear.

I'd be lost without my old man, and my mom was one of the kindest, wisest people I knew. They'd taken in my boys when no one else would, fed them, loved them. They'd accepted Jason under their roof without a second of hesitation when his own family kicked him out. If Manson and Lucas hadn't been so damn ashamed of accepting help, my parents would have brought them into the house too.

"Reagan freaks me the fuck out," I answered honestly, but smiled at the end to try to reassure her. "But don't worry about it. He'll probably bail out of town again in a few days; he never sticks around very long."

She settled back in her seat, but a crease of concern remained on her forehead, pinching her eyebrows together. Reagan hadn't been back in Wickeston since his estranged wife died. He didn't attend the funeral, but he sure as hell was pissed about the will. Apparently, Manson's mom had been well-off when she married Reagan, including having inherited the house from her own parents. But years of an abusive marriage and alcohol addiction sapped everything they had — *almost* everything.

Every penny she had left, she gave to Manson. It wasn't a fortune, but between that inheritance and the house, it had completely changed the tides of our lives. It had given us all a place to live, a haven where we could be together. It allowed us to dream of bigger and better things.

I'd be damned if Reagan tried to ruin that now.

But I didn't want to dwell on that old man or the trouble he could cause. It was a beautiful day and I had an even more beautiful woman sitting in my passenger seat, probably wondering if I was going to take her home or snatch her away for my own nefarious plans.

It was definitely the latter.

Instead of taking Route 15 all the way back to her house, I took a turn and wound through narrow backroads, keeping my eyes out for any lurking cops. I kept driving until the asphalt ended. The road ahead of me went winding through farmland, fields of corn on one side and overgrown trees on the other.

Jess glanced over at me. "Why did you stop?"

I tightened my grip on the shifter. I knew this road like the back of my hand. I probably could have driven it with my eyes closed. But she didn't know that. "Just giving you a chance to prepare yourself," I said.

Her eyes widened, darting between me and the road ahead. "Wait, prepare myself for what —"

I slammed into gear and punched on the gas pedal. She sucked in a breath as the car surged forward, backfires popping off like gunshots as my tires caught traction and dug into the earth. We launched over the first bump in the road, dust kicking up behind us in a cloud.

She was grateful for that harness now — she was clinging to it for dear life.

28

JESSICA

Vincent was hurtling down narrow curving roads, tires skidding in the dirt, flying over bumps and dips without a care. I could have sworn the car *flew* over one particularly large bump, and all four tires left the ground as the engine buzzed like an overgrown honeybee. I had one hand in a death grip on the grab handle above the door and the other locked around his thigh.

But it was clear he knew what he was doing. With one glance, I saw the joy on his face, the excitement and concentration. Every turn was tight, the variations in the rutted road requiring him to constantly adjust his speed. Every dip gave me the brief sensation of flying, my stomach rising and falling with the road.

It was like being on a roller coaster. I shrieked as he sped through a tight curve, and the back end of the car slid around the turn before we launched forward again. I giggled, then laughed, unable to stop myself from smiling.

"Holy shit, this is fun!" I screamed as we flew over a bump again, sailing past a herd of cows that fled in surprise.

"Welcome to rally racing, Jess!" He raised his voice over the engine, laughing along with me. "Scared?"

"No!" My heart was racing, my limbs were tingling, high on adrenaline. "This is amazing!"

We came out of a long stretch of trees to find open fields on either side. There were more cows grazing in the distance, and on the opposite side of the road was an old barn, its dark wooden roof leaning slightly to one side. Vincent slowed and turned, pulling into the unfenced field and driving toward the barn.

Now that he'd slowed down and I could actually catch my breath, I said, "So Manson and Lucas drag race...and you do this? Rally?"

"That's right. Rally is pretty varied as a motorsport, but the main difference is that if I compete, I'm not running directly against other competitors on the same circuit. It's still focused on reaching a destination as fast as you can, but there's more to it than your typical drag race. Like going off road." He smiled, taking his sunglasses off as we neared the barn. "That's my favorite. Remind me to show you the rally competition they hold in the Isle of Man sometime. It'll blow your mind."

The barn doors were wide open, allowing him enough space to drive the WRX inside. Sunlight fell in pale beams through the old boards, dust motes swirling in the light as Vincent cut the engine but let the music keep playing.

He settled back in his seat, looking at me with a smile that spoke of wicked things. "I thought you were going to piss yourself by the way you were screaming back there," he teased, and I shoved his shoulder.

"I wasn't scared," I said confidently. "I'm braver than you think."

He caught my wrist and held it, keeping me drawn close toward him. "You've got me there. I should have known you were brave with those nipple piercings of yours. Not even Lucas is brave enough to get that done."

"Considering Lucas shoved a needle through his dick, I doubt he'd have a problem getting his nipples pierced," I said. Vincent leaned toward me; his smirking mouth hovering dangerously close to mine as he held my wrist captive.

"I wouldn't be so sure of that," he said. His thumb was rubbing slow circles on the back of my hand. "You didn't see him when he got it pierced. He's actually terrified of needles."

"Did he freak out?" I laughed. "Come on, you're messing with me."

But he shook his head. "Nope, I'm not even exaggerating. He was a mess and I got it all on video."

Oh. I needed that.

"You have to show me." I leaned closer and let my exhale touch his lips. Arousal was coiled in my abdomen like a serpent in the sun. Tight, warm, ready to strike.

"Oh, I can," he said. His fingers brushed my arm and his green eyes fixated on my lips. "For the right price."

"Price…" I echoed. I brushed his hair back, intentionally

keeping the touch of my nails as light as possible on his skin. He shivered, and it made me smile. "I feel like I already owe you such a debt…"

"Trying to play sweet with me now, are you?" He grasped my chin, giving my face a little shake. "You'll have to try harder than that, baby. Jason is a brat too. I know how you work."

I tweaked an eyebrow at him in surprise, irritated that he'd seen through me so easily. "Jason? A brat? Mister Straight-A's with a nice Christian upbringing? I doubt that."

"When he ate your pussy in the garage, did it feel like the way a good boy would eat it?" he said. The way his lips curved around those words had no business being so erotic. Thinking about Jason eating me out as the rest of them spanked me and fucked my mouth made me throb, my pussy getting far too greedy for her own good.

Every word he said was winding me up, and he smelled so good. I wanted to press my nose against him and inhale him into my lungs, run my tongue over his skin, taste the sweat and salt…

Damn it all, what was wrong with me? For the sake of my pride, I needed to put up at least a little resistance, but when he was looking at me like that…

What the hell was there to resist?

He laughed again as he laid his hand against my cheek. His humor came easily, and I liked the way he laughed — it sounded innocent and wicked all at once.

"Come on," he said. "I want to show you something."

He got out of the car, and the distance between us felt like a cruel effort to remind me who was in charge. Damn it, most people would have taken immediate, full advantage in that situation. I was practically fucking him with my eyes, yet he was *still* making me wait.

I came to join him in front of the car. The barn creaked softly around us; the rustle of the breeze through the grass and sweet birdsong creating a relaxing ambience. But as soon as I settled beside him, leaning against the car's warm hood, I spotted something partially hidden in the shadows.

A massive painting covered the barn's inner wall. I narrowed my eyes and stepped closer, surprised to find a mural of a dark, smiling clown. The character's eyes bulged from their head, their mouth stretched into a wide, sharp-toothed grin as it stared down at me with one icy blue eye and one bright green.

"Wow…" I stepped even closer, brushing my fingers across the rough, weather-worn boards. Up close, I could see the varying shades of paint used to create depth, shine, and shadow. It was stunningly detailed. I glanced back at Vincent. "Did you paint this?"

He nodded, coming to stand beside me. "I started it when I was seventeen. That was when I first found this old barn. It's been abandoned for years. The family who owns the property doesn't even live in the state, so no one bothers to poke around. I used to drive out here when I needed time to myself."

"Why a clown?" I said. The face paint was almost identical to what he'd worn that night at the Halloween party; dark shapes around his eyes and the lips painted black.

"I've always been into the clown motif," he said. "Clowns are performers, meant to entertain you. But some people find them terrifying and others find them funny. Some think they're sexy." He waggled his eyebrows at me, and I laughed, shaking my head.

"Don't lie. You've got a little bit of coulrophilia yourself." At my skeptical look, he explained, "You're aroused by clowns."

"I think not," I said. He slipped his arms around me from behind, his chin easily resting on top of my head. "Maybe only if those clowns happen to be you, Lucas, and Jason."

"Oh? You admit it then: you're into the men behind makeup." His grip tightened, prodding that burning arousal inside me. I was starkly aware of how wet my panties had become. "A clown is just a human being with a painted face and some weird clothes. It's about perception. Whether they're considered funny, scary, sexy — it all comes down to who's watching you. The audience gets to define what they see. It's all one big performance."

I understood that. Sometimes no matter what you did, you couldn't change the way people perceived you.

"I didn't know you liked to paint," I said. I felt so small tucked under his chin like that. I wasn't particularly short, but he was so tall and lanky that I seemed tiny in comparison anyway.

"My family is pretty artsy. One of my little sisters, Mary, is a way better painter than me. She should be in galleries, and she's only fourteen. But we all got the itch to create things. My parents encouraged us to express ourselves. I've got boxes full of beaded bracelets from the twins. And the littlest, Kristina, she loves to draw."

"Such a big family. I guess that makes it easier, living with the other guys. You're already used to a crowded house."

"It's a real circus," he said. "In both instances. But I like that. It's a good feeling to have a bunch of people you love close by. Makes you feel safe, like you're never alone."

Longing split my chest. I had no idea what it felt like to be surrounded by people I didn't need to perform for. If I was alone, at least I couldn't be judged.

"Does your family know?" I said. "I mean, do you tell them about…"

"About being a polyamorous bisexual who believes in sexual freedom? Absolutely." He smiled. "Makes it easier that my parents are total hippies, and kids don't have the same hang-ups adults do. My sisters know that their big brother has a lot of love to give, and love is beautiful."

"So *you're* the romantic one," I said. "I should have known."

"I've had the most practice. Jason is a sucker for romantic shit, even though he denies it."

I looked at him over my shoulder. "You really love him, don't you?"

"Absolutely. I love all those bastards, obviously, but love is a little different with every person you share it with. Sometimes it's passionate and romantic, or deep and platonic, or any combination in between. A lot of people don't understand it, but I don't need anyone's understanding. I accepted that a long time ago."

Half the time, I felt the same way. No one needed to understand me or my reasons. I didn't have to justify myself. But the other half of the time, insecurity reared its ugly head and reminded me that when people moved too far outside what society understood, you'd swiftly find yourself rejected.

"Do you have any other hidden talents?" I said, turning to face him. He kept his arms around me, as if we'd been touching for years instead of mostly avoiding each other. That was the thing with Vincent; things felt comfortable. They felt intimate without any effort.

He smiled down at me in that wicked way of his again, before he held up one finger in a just-you-wait motion. He walked back to the car and opened the trunk, where he'd stored the mysterious box of toys he'd bought in the sex shop. I'd only got a glimpse — there was something that looked like a blue alien dick in there — but seeing him rummage through it sent a zing of excitement down my spine.

When he straightened up again, he had a coiled length of braided black rope in his hands.

"Ooh, let me guess," I said. "You were a really enthusiastic Boy Scout?"

"Very." He stood in front of me, slowly running the rope through his fingers. "I always had a thing for knots. I wanted to know the most, and I wanted to be the fastest at tying them. There was a game we used to play...silly kid games, you know? Some of us would be pirates and some of us would be sailors, and my favorite part was capturing as many sailors as I could and tying them up."

He *looked* like a pirate. Long-haired, mischievous, dangerous. "That doesn't sound like a game kids should play."

He shook his head. "Absolutely not. Luckily, as I've grown up, I haven't lost my love for games. I still like capturing my victims and tying them up — except now, I know what to do with them once I've got them tied."

I was practically bursting with need. I held out my wrists, keeping my expression cautiously skeptical, while inside, I was screaming for his touch.

"What exactly do you plan to do with me, pirate?" I said. His smile was restrained, as was the brush of his fingers over my throat.

"Be patient," he said. "And do as I say unless you want to get hurt." My throat bobbed against his hand as I swallowed, and he ordered, "Strip down. Take everything off."

I thought about resisting, pushing back so I could find out what this pirate could do with his bratty victim. But I liked the way he looked at me when I teased, so as I stripped off my shirt, I said, "Please don't hurt me, sir. I'll do whatever you say."

He smiled, swinging a length of rope around in a quick circle as I took off my shoes, then unbuttoned my jeans and peeled them down. When I lifted my head after tossing them aside, his carefully concocted expression was gone, leaving something that looked like amazement in its place.

"What?" I said, hating that I sounded more vulnerable now that most of my clothes were off. It was inevitable, I guess. Confidence and insecurity ran hand in hand inside me.

"It's funny how life works," he said, eyes roaming over me like he was trying to learn every curve. "A few years ago, I thought the closest I'd ever get to something like this was when I danced with you at prom."

"Prom…" I hadn't thought of that night in so long. It had been a shitty day all around, but there had been that moment outside, in the pouring rain. "Yeah. Wild how things end up."

Wild, senseless, chaotic. I wasn't sure if anything made sense anymore, but maybe it wasn't supposed to.

"I've thought about this for a long time, Jess," he said. His fingers traced along the edge of my bra, lightly touching the pale blue satin fabric. "What are you waiting for? I said, *everything* off."

The authority in his voice was different from the other guys. It hovered on the edge of merely being playful, put with a sharp warning beneath the surface. I had a feeling he could switch from jovial to serious in a split second, so I obeyed.

The air was warm and slightly humid as I stood there naked, my clothes dumped aside in a pile. Shafts of sunlight fell over Vincent's face as he smiled.

"You are too fucking beautiful," he said, looping the rope around my wrist. "Do you know what I like to do with beautiful things?" He pulled me closer and caught me around my throat, maneuvering me until the back of my legs was pressed against the grill of his car. "I like to break them. I like to watch them crack into pieces as I destroy them."

"Don't..." My protest was soft, and he cut it off with a quick squeeze of his hand. He maintained that pressure on the sides of my throat just long enough that a light-headed rush came over me.

"Shut up." Again, he said it like it was a joke, but the joke carried sinister weight. "That's exactly what's going to happen, baby. I'm going to break you, and you're going to cry and beg me to stop even though you love it. Then, a couple days from now, Jason is going to have his turn with you and do the same damn thing. We'll break you again, and again, and again. As many times as necessary."

My heart was hammering as he eased me back, pushing me until I was lying against the hood of the car. My toes barely touched the ground and the hood was still slightly warm. He roped my other wrist and then pulled them taut, securing the rope to the bars inside his car. His every movement was so careful and practiced, you'd think he tied people to the hood of his car all the time.

Maybe he did.

Soon, both my arms were bound and spread. I was lying flat enough that it wasn't too much of a strain on my shoulders, but I certainly couldn't move much.

"You make a sexy hood ornament," he said, arms folded as he stood over me. "It would be fun to drive you around Wickeston like this. I could stuff your ass with a vibrating toy and have you dripping the entire time."

"Don't you dare," I said, torn between being aroused by the idea and horrified as I tugged at the rope. It didn't move, not one bit.

"Nah. I wouldn't be able to get away with it. If people see some poor woman tied to the hood of a car, they'll get concerned. Can't expect the general public to know a little brat like you enjoys being treated like you're nothing more than a toy. Besides, my ride runs hot." He patted the hood affectionately. "I'd hate for your ass to get burned."

He reached out, his fingers between my legs. I held my breath, so tense as I waited for him to make contact. There was a slight squeak — the sound of his fingers swiping across the hood. He didn't touch me at all, but lifted his hand so I could see the shine on his fingertips. "You see, filthy girl? That's all you. Already dripping on the hood you've been tied to." He brought his finger to my mouth, tapping lightly against my lower lip. "Open up."

I pressed my lips tightly together, shaking my head.

"Well, Jess," he said, his tone mockingly disappointed. "If you're going to insist on keeping your mouth closed, I may as well give you a good reason."

He disappeared from my side as he went back to the trunk. After a brief moment, he returned carrying a tall white candle. It was slim and looked like the type of thing my mom loved to put around the house at Christmas.

"What's that for?" I said.

His answer was to nudge the base of the candle against my clit, rubbing the wax over me for several moments before he pressed it inside. I bit my tongue, striving to keep myself silent as he pumped the candle in and out.

When he used his opposite hand to rub my clit, I broke almost immediately. I gasped, my mouth opening, and his hand snapped out to catch my jaw, fingers hooked into my mouth. I couldn't close without biting him, which I gladly would have done.

It was like he read my mind because he leaned close to my face and hissed, "If you bite me, I'll bite you back." The viciousness in his tone sent a clear warning, so different from his usual joking attitude. He slipped the candle out of me, setting it between my teeth before he withdrew his finger from my mouth. He pulled a lighter from his pocket, holding the candle in place as he lit it.

"Better not let it drop," he said. I had my teeth clenched into it, but if I dared to open my mouth, I'd drop the burning candle on my bare chest. I could taste myself on the wax, and I groaned, wriggling in protest. "Since your mouth is occupied, tap your hand three times on the hood if you need to call red. But I don't think you'll be stopping me."

My eyes widened as I realized the candle was already beginning to drip, wax streaking down the side as another bead quickly formed at the tip. Vincent ran his hands up my inner thighs, igniting a ticklish shiver. But that shiver betrayed me. The bead of wax trembled and fell, landing right between my breasts.

It wasn't the first time I'd had wax dripped on me, but it was no less shocking. The split second of pain, the whisper of a burn that quickly faded…I wanted to cry out, desperately, but I somehow managed to keep my teeth clenched.

Another drip fell as I shook. I squealed around the candle, exercising every bit of self-control I had not to squirm again.

"What an unfortunate predicament you've gotten yourself into," Vincent said as he sunk two fingers into my pussy, drawing out another desperate moan. "Whether you struggle or not, it's still going to drip. How fun. Oh, *but…*" He held up his finger, reaching for something in his back pocket. What he held up was a red-tipped wand that I assumed to be some kind of tool. "I have something that'll make it even *more* fun."

Then he brought it down and tapped it against my thigh.

It *shocked* me, electricity bursting through every nerve ending. My entire body tensed, and I thrashed against the ropes. There was no escape from him bringing it down again, tapping it against my other leg with the same effect. I screamed, teeth still clenched, more wax dripping onto my chest in tiny, wicked bites of heat.

Vincent laughed, giving the wand a little spin in his hand. "Aww, does that hurt? Was that a *I'm-having-so-much-fun* scream or *I'm-in-agony* scream? I couldn't really tell, let's hear it again." Another tap, another shock, another scream. I couldn't manage to hold it back. "Well, what do you know! It sounds like both, Jess." He brought the wand higher, hovering right over one of my hard nipples. "It sounds like you're enjoying the pain. How fortunate for you."

He lowered the wand. I tried to shake my head, but it only caused a few more drops of wax to fall. He grinned right before he tapped it down, and my back arched as I screamed at the shock.

But he was far from done with me, and moved the wand between my legs. I was whimpering even before it touched me, anticipating the pain, building it up in my head until it was a monster hovering over me. Vincent paused with the wand *so painfully close*, watching my face.

"I love seeing you work yourself up," he said. He clicked the button on the wand, igniting a spark of electricity at the tip that was accompanied by a crackle. The sound alone made me jump, and more wax dotted my skin.

How had Jason survived him all these years? Maybe they balanced each other somehow, sadist versus sadist, feeding off the bliss of torturing one other.

Better yet, how could four sadists live in one house and not completely destroy each other with their sick games? How could *I* survive them, when my mind and body were betraying me at every turn, making me ache for their cruelty? All my fake struggles didn't change reality — I wanted this, I *longed* for it.

"Sshh, sshh, Jess." He kept the wand terrifyingly close to my clit as he leaned forward, bracing himself on the hood with one hand beside me. "You deserve this, you know. For being a bad girl. Bad girls need to be punished, don't they?" He nodded as he said it, and I managed a tiny nod in return. My tongue kept forming the word "please," over and over, but it didn't come out right with my mouth full. "I'm going to count to three and then I'm going to do it. Ready?" I shook my head, and he laughed. "I think you are. As ready as you'll ever be. One…"

I almost tapped. *Almost.* But I was curious. I wanted to push myself. Wanted *more*. My legs were shaking, and I whimpered as two more drops of wax fell onto me.

"Two."

My entire body clenched. I didn't know whether to look away or watch him do it.

"Three."

He tapped the wand against my clit. I screamed, dissolving into sobs as I struggled to hold the candle in place. A cocktail of adrenaline and dopamine rushed through me in response to the pain — the perfect high.

"Good girl." He leaned over to kiss my forehead, and I absolutely melted. I wanted him inside me; I wanted his body on mine.

Why did the pain make me feel so *alive*? It was the same kind of thrill I'd felt strapped into the passenger seat as he sped down the road, skirting the edge of danger. My hips bucked up eagerly, thoughtlessly. They were met with the wand again.

Vincent gave my face a little slap as I whined through the sting. "Such a slut, moving your hips around like that. You just want to get fucked, don't you?" He pouted at me mockingly as I tried my best to keep still. No wiggling, no struggling, no frantically grinding my hips in search of any stimulation for my swollen, stinging clit.

He straightened up as he regarded me, twirling the wand in his hand. "Tell you what. I'll fuck you. I'll even take the candle out of your mouth. But I'm still going to use the wand the whole time." He ran the wand up my leg, but he didn't press the button. I shivered under its metallic touch, expecting a shock at any second. "So, are you going to keep yourself quiet, or are you going to be screaming your lungs out the entire time?"

I shook my head. Slowly, regretfully. But I couldn't do it. I wouldn't be able to keep quiet. I was too overwhelmed, too on edge. I needed to scream, and inevitably, I'd fail and disobey if he ordered me to be quiet.

"No? At least you're honest." Nevertheless, he grasped the candle and eased it from my teeth.

"I won't...won't be able to...to keep quiet," I managed to get out. My skin felt so hot, and I was vibrating with energy. "I can't do it, Vincent, please..."

"Please? Please what?"

I wiggled on the hood. "Please fuck me. Please. I'll try to be quiet. I really will try."

"You'll *try*." He held the candle over me, moving it slowly, keeping it tipped so drips of wax spattered across my thighs. I bit my lip, but I couldn't hold back the whimpers. "Noisy little thing, aren't you? Never could shut the fuck up. Next time, I'll get one of the boys to keep your mouth occupied. But lucky for you, I like the way you scream."

He pulled open his belt, unbuttoning his jeans to set his cock free. He spat in his hand and stroked it along his shaft, before nudging his swollen head against me. I tried to press onto him, desperate to feel him, but he shook his head at me and tapped the wand against my clit again — and again — both shocks tearing ragged screams out of me. As I screamed, his cock jerked, and he grabbed one of my legs and pushed it up, spreading me open for him.

"You're so wet," he murmured, looking down at me as I panted for breath.

With a soft groan, he thrust inside me. He didn't start out slow, he didn't take his time. He fucked me hard and fast, pounding into me with a brutality that was a punishment all on its own.

"Filthy little slut," he hissed and then tapped the wand on my side. "Shit, you clench so tight every time I shock you. It feels so fucking good." He shuddered along with me as he shocked me again, humming with pleasure as if my screams were music to his ears. "Scream all you want. No one can hear you out here."

Why had I ever thought that Vincent would be the *nice* one out of the four? He was relishing every cry, his eyes wide with excitement, groaning with pleasure every time I tensed from the shocking pain. God, and he felt so good. The angle of his cock pounding into me hit that sweet spot that had my toes curling.

I was going to come and the pain was only edging me closer. The more I squealed and uselessly struggled, the more pleasure I felt. I was stunningly aware of every kiss of the breeze over my skin, the goosebumps on my chest, the biting crackle of electricity, the aching depth of Vincent fucking me. Those physical sensations were the only thing left in my mind. Nothing else mattered in that moment.

"Do you want to come?" He hovered the wand over my clit again. "It's going to cost you."

"Please!" I strained against the ropes, wide-eyed, as the wand came close. "Please, Vincent, no, no, no, no."

"I know you already owe us *such* a debt," he said, mocking my earlier words. "But I'm sure you don't mind paying up when it feels so good."

"Oh, God...fuck...please..." I knew the price was pain, and the pleasure I'd get in return would be so worth it, but the anticipation of it might kill me.

"Fear turns you on," he said. "I can feel the way you squeeze around me when you beg. It's going to happen, Jess."

"God, Vincent, please don't. I can't...I-I can't—"

He waited until my gasping fell silent. His expression had sobered, and his words were sincere as he said, "Remember your safeword, baby. Don't forget where you are."

I nodded. I was getting lost in the fantasy, but that didn't mean my grasp on reality had left me. I was still grounded, still aware of where my boundaries lay.

"I remember," I said. "I'm okay."

Electricity crackled, sparking through my clit and tingling through my nerves. He laughed at my screaming, and that laugh was my breaking point. I squeezed around his cock as I came, desperately crying his name. My head went limp against the hood as I stared at the old beams high above me, utterly dazed. Vincent moaned, fucking me with a new urgency that made his hips jerk erratically.

"Fuck, Jess," he growled. "Do you have any idea how many times I've thought about this? How badly I've wanted to make you scream?" He grabbed my face, forcing me to look at him. "Have you fantasized about it? Tell the truth, right fucking now. Tell me if you've thought about this happening."

"Yes!" My voice sounded so broken, thick with pleasure, mindless with pain. "I've thought about it…I've fantasized… about you…about all of you…"

"Naughty girl, aren't you?" he snarled. His cock was swelling, twitching as he came closer to his orgasm. "You're not supposed to do that, are you, baby? You're not supposed to think about how the dirty freaks get your cunt wet. But you can't help it, can you?"

Mind and body bent to his will as I shook my head. I couldn't help thinking about them, wanting them, longing for things I wasn't supposed to want.

He pressed in deep, baring his teeth with a guttural curse as he came inside me.

29

JESSICA

High School - Senior Year

I didn't feel joy as they set the crown on my head. It tangled in my hair and scratched on my scalp. The lights were too bright as they focused on me, the excited cheers of my peers deafening me from the mass of shadows beyond the lights. Faceless applause to drown out the snickers and murmurs.

"All right, big smiles!" One of the yearbook staff, I couldn't remember her name, popped in front of us with her camera at the ready. With Prom King and Queen announced, the music was turned up and pounding again, hammering along with my heart. I turned toward Kyle, laid my hand on his chest and plastered a smile on my face. I made sure to cock my hip at just the right angle and extend my leg forward, white stilettos balancing me precariously on the sleek wood floor of the gymnasium.

"You'd better smile, Kyle," I muttered through my clenched, smiling teeth. "Don't fucking ruin these pictures."

His hand encircled my waist, revolting me. "Always got a fake smile at the ready, don't you, Jessica?" The words were returned through his own plastic smile. "That's why no one likes you. You're fake as fuck."

Smile. Just smile. The camera flashed. If I was going to have to look at these photos hung proudly on my mother's wall for the next who-knows-how-many years, I was going to make sure I looked good in them. It didn't matter who I was standing next to. It had never mattered.

It didn't matter if everyone hated me. It didn't matter that right before the announcement, Kyle had let it slip that he wanted to break up again. It didn't matter that he'd blurted out he was dumping me. Again.

It didn't matter. God, it didn't matter. Just smile.

People were cheering for a dance. With every step down from the stage, I fixed that smile a little tighter on my face. I held Kyle's hand, damp and moist around my own. He was sweating through his tux, his eyes wandering the crowd. Always wandering. It didn't matter what I looked like, or how I dressed, or what I did in bed. It didn't matter.

It was never enough.

We danced. The camera flashed. *Make it look like you're having a good time.*

But the moment the song stopped, a lull in the music and the crowd's dwindling attention allowed me to slip away. I hugged the wall near the back of the gym, dipping under streamers and metallic ribbons, running away from the unwanted conversations and hypocritical congratulations.

No one was surprised I'd won. This was how it was supposed to be. This was the world nicely fitting into the same old routine.

The Cheerleading Captain and the Quarterback. How cute. How convenient. What a fucking cliche.

I shoved hard against the first door I found and finally slipped outside.

Standing on the concrete steps behind the gym, I looked out at the overflowing dumpsters. A single light illuminated the steps and rain poured around me, cold as it mercilessly drenched me. My dress's layers of pink satin were swiftly soaked, too tight and heavy as it clung to me.

The rain ruined my makeup fast enough. It didn't matter if I cried.

I tried to hold it back. I sat on the step, stifling the hiccupping sobs in my chest.

No one likes you. You're fake as fuck.

I felt hot and cold at the same time. My stomach twisted with the alcohol I'd been sneaking all night. It didn't matter what Kyle said. He was an asshole anyway, and I deserved better.

I wrapped my hands around my bare arms, covered with goosebumps from the cold. I was just as much of an asshole as Kyle. It was the only reason we'd ever really worked together. We'd deserved each other.

Two absolutely awful people deserved each other.

I jerked up my head at the sound of a footstep. Vincent stood to the right of the stairs, wearing a leather jacket, button-up black shirt and trousers, dry beneath an umbrella.

I sighed heavily, looking away from him. "Oh, God, it's you."

"Damn, people are usually way more excited to see me at parties." He came up the steps and sat beside me, moving the umbrella so we could share it. I was used to him wearing oversized joke t-shirts and tight jeans. The sight of him in black, fitted clothes, was...nice. It was actually nice.

"Well, I'm not looking for any party favors," I said, trying to subtly wipe my sniffly nose on the back of my hand. "Unless you've got Xanax."

"I might. I've got whatever the people need." I could feel his eyes on me, probing at me, like a doctor's fingers looking for an injury. "You've never wanted downers before."

"I don't want to feel anything," I said. I stared straight ahead at the soaked bags of trash. "Not anything at all."

"I don't usually comment on how people get their high, Jess. But something tells me I shouldn't sell you xannies. Not like this."

I shook my head bitterly. "Oh, great. A dealer with a conscience. Won't even take advantage of a damsel in distress?"

He snickered. "You're no distressed damsel. You're a very dangerous queen bee." He looked pleased when that got a little laugh out of me. We were silent for a few moments, before he said, "So...you got Prom Queen."

"Yeah." I reached up, brushing my fingers lightly across the plastic crown tangled in my soaked hair. "You'll probably hear my mom scream clear across town when I tell her."

"And the uh...the King is absent?"

I swallowed hard. *Don't cry again. Don't cry. Don't be weak over a guy.*

"The King has found conquests in another kingdom," I said, trying to sound as haughty and careless as I could. Like it was a funny little game that couldn't really hurt.

Vincent didn't say anything, but his silence was better than empty words of comfort. I would have known he was lying anyway. His relationship with Kyle was tolerant only because he supplied him with Adderall at a discount. But then he laid his jacket across my shoulders, holding the umbrella between his knees. "You must be freezing in that dress."

I was. My entire body was covered in goosebumps and I'd been struggling not to let him see me shiver. The warmth of the jacket made my shoulders sag as the tension went out of them.

"This jacket smells like weed," I said.

He nodded. "Probably because there's weed in it."

"If a cop finds me wearing this, am I going to get arrested?"

He smiled mischievously. "Only if they search you."

We sat in silence for a few more moments, surrounded by the patter of rain and the upbeat dance music pounding through the door. Then the music changed, the melody slowing to become "Holy" by Justin Bieber.

"People are going to wonder where I am," I said softly.

"Fuck 'em."

I looked at him in surprise, and he shrugged. "Fuck 'em, Jess. They don't need any more entertainment from you. Did Cinderella care about anyone wondering where she was when she ran away from the ball?"

I shook my head in disbelief. "You've seen *Cinderella*?"

"I have four little sisters," he said. "Of course I've seen it —

the animation is a classic! When that glass slipper shattered…" He laid his hand dramatically over his chest. "My heart shattered with it."

I giggled, despite the festering pain still gripping my chest. "Who knew you were such a romantic?"

He stood suddenly, tucking the umbrella against his shoulder before he extended his hand to me. I stared at his open palm, blinking rapidly in confusion. "What?"

"Doesn't feel right for the Prom Queen to not get her slow dance," he said, a slight smile playing around his lips.

"Dance?" I said. "Out here? With you? In the rain?"

He shrugged. "Yeah. Why not?"

A thousand reasons, a thousand excuses, prickled over my tongue. But I took his hand and let him pull me up from the step. I let him wrap his arm around my waist, beneath his leather jacket, still warm around my shoulders.

"I'm going to get you all wet," I said as I pressed my soaked dress against him. I glared when he laughed. "Don't you dare make a dirty joke out of that."

"I wouldn't even think of it," he said. "I don't mind if you get me a little wet, Jess." He winked, and I rolled my eyes. But as we swayed in the rain to the muted sounds of the music, the pain in my chest loosened its grip. The fearful clench of insecurity around my lungs stopped swelling, and I took a slow breath before I dared to rest my head against his chest.

"You're really tall," I said, because I didn't know what else to say.

"That's why the ladies call me Daddy Longlegs," he said, and I smacked his chest even though the joke made me laugh.

"Kyle will kill you if he sees us out here," I said. Behind us, the slight movement of the doorknob made me tense, and Vincent's hand tightened on my waist. But no one came out.

"And waste his supplier?" he said. "I doubt it." He paused for a moment, swaying with me. "I don't care anyway. These are supposed to be the best nights of our lives, right?"

"Are they?" It was weird to feel this way. Melancholy and sad, confused and angry, but…there was something else crawling its way through all the muck of my emotions. Something warm, tender, and small.

Desire. Longing. A wish that everything was different.

"You know I never wanted Manson to get hurt," I said, so softly it was almost imperceptible over the rain.

"I know. The road to Hell is paved with good intentions, right?"

"Right." I closed my eyes. Senior year was coming to its end, and I'd messed up everything. My road was well-paved indeed, with intentions both good and bad. I'd been so certain it was the road I wanted, but now only a dead end lay ahead.

Things would change after high school. They had to.

The song ended, and I pulled away first. I cleared my throat and straightened my shoulders, sniffling back the last of my sadness. I was better than this. I had to get back in there. I took off his jacket and held it out to him.

But Vincent was staring at me with a look I couldn't fully understand. "What?" I said as he finally took the jacket.

He shook his head, slowly, with a sigh that felt so heavy. "Damn. You got me too."

I was about to ask what the hell he meant, but the door behind us opened and someone exclaimed loudly, "Oh, thank God! Jess, what the *hell?*"

Ashley hurried out to me, holding an umbrella that she quickly brought me beneath. Vincent stepped back as she fretted over me. "Was it worth getting soaked for some weed? Oh my God, your lashes are falling off. Here, let's get you to the bathroom." She gave Vincent a disapproving glare. "Maybe next time, do your deals someplace a little less shady?"

"But where else can I find conveniently placed dumpsters to throw my clients' bodies in?" Vincent said right before we slipped inside, and Ashley groaned in disgust.

"He's such a creep," she said. "Take me with you next time, girl! Don't trust that weirdo. You know Mark Ringwald told me that Sarah Everdeen told him that her cousin found out Vincent is into some really fucked up shit. He's, like, a devil worshiper or something."

"I think devil worshippers only sacrifice virgins, so I'm pretty sure I'm safe." I was joking, but Ashley nodded as her mouth formed into an 'O,' as if I'd told her incredibly important information.

We cleaned up my makeup and Ashley called a friend who had an emergency wardrobe change. I could go back out on the floor and dance with my friends, sneak more vodka from Ashley's flask, and pretend I was having the best night of my life.

And maybe there had been something good that night. Something small and uncertain, but warm despite the rain. Maybe I didn't know it yet. Maybe I wouldn't know it for years. But that small thing stayed, even unnurtured, and waited for its opportunity to grow.

30

JESSICA

I was still walking funny when Vincent dropped me off at home. He even walked me to the door, back to being a gentleman now that he was done torturing me until I screamed.

We stopped at the door, and he leaned over me as he gripped my face in his hands, squeezing my cheeks as he made me look up at him. "You're going to be a good girl until Friday, right?"

Friday was when I would be going over to their house to complete my task for Lucas. I would be showing up as an accessorized toy for Jason to play with as he pleased. I still didn't know what exactly Vincent had in that box, but come Friday, I was sure I'd be getting intimately acquainted.

"It might be easier to be good if you send me that video you mentioned," I said, daring to push my luck.

"Video? Of Lucas's piercing?" Vincent laughed. "If I'm going to risk him murdering me for you to get a laugh, you're going to need to do a little more than take a few little shocks." I gaped at him in offense, about to protest his assessment of what he'd done to me as being *a few little shocks*, but he cut me off before I could. "Show Jason a good time, and I'll consider it more seriously."

I groaned, but he wasn't going to budge. Still, I was willing to try to behave if it meant getting to see Lucas at his most vulnerable. Part of me didn't even believe a man like that had any fears at all.

Vincent left me with a ravenous kiss, pressing me back against the door as his tongue dipped past my lips.

"I'll see you soon," he said. He'd promised to pick me up on Friday, even though I told him I could drive my mom's car over. "Oh, and one more thing…"

He walked back to the car, returning with something in a black plastic bag. "I'll take the rest of your new toys to the house, but you'll need to be wearing this when I pick you up."

"What is it?" I said cautiously.

"So suspicious." He patted my cheek like I was a silly little thing, asking silly little questions. "Don't worry. You'll look sexy. Jason will lose his mind."

The fact that he wouldn't simply tell me it was lingerie was concerning. Almost as if it…wasn't…lingerie. The moment his back was turned, I snuck a look in the bag, but all I could see was black lace fabric. Maybe it wasn't so bad, then.

It was bad. Oh, God, it was so embarrassingly *bad*.

My reflection stared back at me from my bedroom mirror, my furious glare making me look even more ridiculous. I'd just gotten off work, and Vincent would be here to pick me up soon, so I'd put on the "uniform" he'd given me. After struggling for several minutes to squeeze it over my ass, I was now wearing a black frilly maid costume.

The dress barely covered me. Bending over slightly would show my panties. My tits were pushed up tightly together in the bodice. But it wasn't just a tiny sexy dress, oh no. That wouldn't have been mean enough.

There was also a collar with a silver bell. Every time I moved, it made a tiny tinkling sound.

But even *that* wasn't all. Nope.

There were also ears. Fluffy black and white ears attached to a headband. When I put them on, nestled in my hair, it made me look like some kind of cat girl.

I snatched my phone off my bedside table and messaged the bastards responsible. **What the hell is wrong with you?**

Three bouncing dots appeared almost instantly.

Too many things to count, Lucas replied. **Or were you referring to something in particular?**

You know exactly what I'm talking about. I'm not wearing cat ears.

As I waited for a response, I glanced at myself in the mirror again. The dress looked good from the back; I'd admit that. I looked ridiculous, but strangely cute? Maybe even sexy?

I think we need a visual reference, Manson wrote.

Yeah, Miss Kitty. I read the text in Vincent's voice, thick with humor. **Let's see how you look.**

Huffing in frustration, I wrote back, **Ridiculous. I look completely ridiculous.**

I pulled up my camera and looked at myself. Okay, it *did* look a little sexy. The dress was silly but flattering. Another text from Lucas popped up right as my finger hovered over the button to snap the photo.

Don't make us come over there, girl. Picture. Now.

My stomach did that ridiculous twisty thing. I snapped a picture, then took a few more to be sure I got a good one.

I sent the photo, and Lucas responded, **Fuck, I'm tempted to have another round with you myself.**

You need a leash to go with that collar, Manson said.

And a few chores to keep you on your hands and knees, Vincent added.

Aw, too bad for you, I wrote. **I'm only serving Jason today.**

Time to get out of this dress and put on something normal before Vincent got here. No way was I going to risk someone seeing me publicly in this, even if it was only a short drive between our houses.

The dress was a bit too small for me, squeezing in all the right places. The tight fit meant that getting my arms out of the sleeves was nearly impossible without ripping the dress.

After a few minutes of increasingly desperate struggling, I picked up my phone and texted furiously. **I'M STUCK IN THE DRESS, WHAT AM I SUPPOSED TO DO?** Then I quickly added, **If you laugh at me, I'll never speak to you again.**

You'd better keep your mouth shut then, because that

shit is hilarious, Vincent wrote. Damn him, damn all of them! **I think you killed Manson. He can't stop laughing.**

I groaned. At least I could take off the ears and collar. The dress by itself wasn't too bad. A little *too much* for a regular Friday, but whatever. My reputation around here was already far from sparkling clean. Considering there were videos online of me crawling on my hands and knees dressed like a sexy angel, I doubted someone getting a glimpse of me like this would do much damage.

I'm sure Jason will help you get the dress off, Vincent's next text read. **I'll be there in fifteen minutes.**

It had been years since I'd found myself waiting so nervously for a date. Not that this was a date, exactly. I didn't know what the hell to call these rendezvous because the five of us certainly weren't together, but what the hell was I doing, then? It was strange to be waiting for one man to pick me, with the intention of delivering me to his boyfriend for sexual favors, on the behalf of his other friends who were also fucking me...

If I hadn't been a slut before, I sure as hell was now.

Vincent arrived, his bass bumping loud enough to carry into the house. I came outside before he even got out of the car, hurriedly locking up the house. I still hadn't thought of a good story to tell my parents about the security system. Maybe they'd accept it if I feigned ignorance.

Vincent rolled down the passenger window as I traipsed across the lawn toward him, cat-calling loudly, "Damn, baby, look at you! Owwww!" He howled so loud that our next-door neighbor, Carol, poked her head up above her rose bushes.

We made very awkward eye contact, and I waved. "Hi, Mrs.

Fischer. Nice day out."

"Oh, yes. Lovely." She tried to smile, but she couldn't fake it as she looked at me. "I take it you're…enjoying the sunshine?"

I managed a painfully embarrassed smile before I hurriedly fled. I sunk into the passenger seat and scooched down low after I'd strapped in, trying to avoid being spotted by any more neighbors.

"I've sold weed to that lady before," Vincent said. "I used to meet her and her husband after Sunday service so they could pick up their order. They tried to rope me into a threesome once."

My eyes practically bulged out of my head. "Mr. and Mrs. Fischer tried to — What? No fucking way."

"There's more freaks out there than you think, Jess," he said as he pulled out of my neighborhood. "People act all high and mighty publicly, but behind closed doors? Everybody has their thing."

"And I take it *this* is Jason's thing?" I said, pulling the cat ears out of my purse. "I didn't see anything about this on his list. Pet play was only a two on his interest scale! And it wasn't any higher on mine. If he expects me to start meowing like a cat…"

"First of all, you look sexy as hell, so chill out." He reached over, giving my chin a little nudge with his knuckle. "Second, I'll give you some advice about Jason from someone who knows him even better than he knows himself."

I fixed him with a mild look, lips pressed into a thin line. "So it's *your* advice, right? Considering —"

"Considering I've been single-handedly blowing his mind since junior year?" He gave me a wide smile. "Considering I broke him out of his shell and helped introduce him to an entire world of sinful deviancy? My advice is exactly what you should be listening to."

"All right then," I said, folding my arms and crossing my legs. "Teach me what you know, Mr. Volkov."

He gave a slow exhale, shaking his head. "Oh, sorry, you got me thinking of how fun a dirty teacher roleplay would be…"

"Come on, focus, weed-for-brains! Tell me!"

He slammed on the brakes so abruptly that I gasped. Luckily, there was no one else on the long country road ahead of us as Vincent leaned over to my seat, his long fingers gripping my jaw.

"I think you're forgetting some rules," he said, his tone so different from his usual jovial one that fear tickled my stomach. "It's all fun and games, Jess, but don't make me remind you to show the proper respect for me. If you think that just because I smoke, I'm going to let you get away with that smartass shit, you're in for a very uncomfortable awakening. Unless you want to spend some time hanging by your ankles and getting acquainted with a snake whip, I suggest you change your tone."

"Ooooh, shit." I barely realized I said it out loud until he grinned. "Yes, sir, I'll change my tone."

"That's better." He kissed my mouth before he let me go, driving on like nothing at all had happened. Except now my heart had quickened, and I was sweating even more, my bare thighs awkwardly clenched together.

"Here's the thing, Jess," he said. "It's not about the ears. It's not even about the costume. It's about subservience."

"Subservience? What, like he wants me to serve him? Be his slave? That's familiar." I stopped myself short of saying something sarcastic. I desperately needed to get my tongue under control.

"Trust me on this, because I know it's not something you're good at." He gave me a sly glance as he turned onto the dirt road toward his house. "Be a good girl for him. Okay?"

"That's it?" I said. "Just be good? Don't be a *brat*, you're saying?" He nodded, and I sighed softly. "You're right. I'm not good at that."

"He'd still enjoy you even if you were your regular sassy self," he said. Their front gate was already open, so he was able to pull straight into the yard. "But I'm telling you this for your sake. Jason has a paddle in his room that I'm not sure you want an intimate meeting with, but he'd gladly introduce you."

"I thought you said Jason was a brat," I said, slipping out of the harness as Vincent parked in the garage. The white Z was parked right next to us, and the damage that had been done to it was now repaired. The Mustang and the El Camino, on the other hand, were still sporting some large dents, but their windows and tires had been replaced. "Honestly, who uses that paddle more: you, or him?"

"I do, but that means he's eager for a turn on the other end of it," Vincent said. "Make sure you put on those ears and collar before we go inside. They're going to expect you to be fully dressed."

I did as he said, the collar jingling with every step across the yard. I was greeted by a blast of blessedly cool air and some very excited dogs as we stepped into the house. I expected Manson and Lucas to be in the garage, but Manson called to me from the living room as I knelt down to give some love to Jojo and Haribo.

"Let's see that little dress you're stuck in, Jess!"

I pursed my lips at how amused he sounded. I walked into

the living room with Vincent right behind me, to find Manson and Lucas sprawled out on the sectional sofa. Lucas had one leg thrown on top of Manson's, game controllers clutched in both their hands. The TV showed a game menu for something involving bright characters and big guns.

"Well, goddamn..." Manson got to his feet, circling me slowly. "I didn't understand the appeal of the ears before, but I think I get it now."

"Have I unlocked a new kink, Manson?" I said. He was dressed casually today in black joggers and a ribbed white undershirt, but not even his relaxed clothes could stop me from staring. He hooked his finger on my collar, tugging me closer.

"Unlocked a new one...maybe," he said. "You've definitely catered to an old one. I like this collar on you. I should put you in collars more often."

Lucas hadn't gotten up from the couch, but he leaned forward as he said, "Give me a little twirl, let's see the back."

I obeyed, unable to resist a cheeky smirk as I turned and slightly bent forward, giving him the best view of my ass beneath the tiny skirt. He exhaled aggressively, like a bull snorting before he charged.

"Someone is going to have to rip that thing off you," he said, his gravel tone telling me he'd prefer to be the one to do it.

"And that someone is right upstairs," Vincent reminded him. "Jason's never going to get her in one piece if you pervs keep drooling." He steered me out of the room and back into the hall as Lucas threw up his hands in protest.

"I'll decide when I'm done drooling, asshole!" he called, but

334 | HARLEY LAROUX

Vincent ignored him. He opened a door in the hall, rummaging around in the storage closet, before he pulled out a large bag. "Here are the toys from Satin. You remember where his room is, right?"

I nodded as I grabbed the bag. Jittery nerves had my stomach feeling like a shaken can of soda — but what did I have to be nervous for? It was just Jason...sharp-eyed, unassuming Jason, who looked at me like he could see under my skin, who'd eaten me out until my legs shook. Who was rather ridiculously well-endowed...

Yeah. Nothing to be nervous about at all.

I marched up the stairs, aware of Vincent's eyes on my back the entire time. I didn't look back, but I did hear him say to Manson and Lucas, "Hurry up and get on Discord. Jason's going to have his headset on."

31

JASON

Only thirty seconds remained, and I'd just planted the bomb. DumpTruckKiller and I were the last two alive, and the enemy team was moving in. I crouched behind a wall as the bomb ticked, wincing when DumpTruck cursed sharply over the headset and said, "Shit, I'm down." It was just me, then. One versus five. The clock ticked down.

Ten…nine…eight…

A helmet popped out in an alley, and I fired, killing him instantly. If one was here, the others wouldn't be far behind.

Six…five…four…

Two more. I took out another enemy with a headshot, but the second one dodged me, crouching behind barriers as they made their way closer to my location. Footsteps pounded behind me and my screen flashed red as gunfire popped, my health bar rapidly declining with only two seconds remaining.

The round ended, VICTORY popping up on the screen. There were several cheers through the headset as I leaned back, stretching my arms over the back of my chair. "And that's how it's done, boys. Good game."

Echoes of the same answered me, along with the high-pitched shrieking of some obnoxious kid on the other team, who I quickly muted. Someone in chat was raging too, typing furiously, **CampBloodCouncilor is hacking. WTF was that headshot? Reported.** I laughed, setting the headset aside for a moment. They could report all they wanted, but I wasn't cheating.

"Wow, that was pretty exciting."

I banged my knee on the desk from turning so fast. Jessica stood in my open doorway, a black plastic bag in her hand. She was wearing — *holy fuck* — a tiny maid costume, a collar with a bell, and cat ears.

My mouth hung open for a moment. Had I passed out? Was I dreaming? Had Vincent put magic mushrooms in my breakfast again?

"Are you fucking with me?" I said. "How did you get in here?" Vince had to be behind this. He was the only one who'd seen "cat girls" in my search history, and he hadn't given me a break about it since.

I'd been joking when I'd looked it up anyway. Half joking. You could get off to something and still consider it a joke.

"The others wanted to surprise you," she said, walking into the room and casually dumping the bag on the floor. "They thought this costume was *hilarious*."

Thank God I'd cleaned in here. I wasn't a messy person; I was disorganized. I'd gotten the smallest bedroom in the house, but I only spent time here to work and nap, or if it was too hot to tolerate sleeping next to Vincent. Mostly, this room was just a place to keep my computer setup since it took up so much space.

I'd put off washing my sheets since she'd slept in my bed, finally throwing them in the laundry only yesterday. Usually I was pretty good about that, but when I smelled her scent on the blankets, the last thing I'd wanted to do was make it go away.

Her pale blonde hair was glowing in the light from my blue LEDs as she sat on the edge of my bed. It made her look psychedelic, like something out of a perverted fever dream. The tiny dress hitched up on her thighs and I was salivating already.

"So, you're the one responsible for breaking the security system?" she said.

"I didn't break it. I found and utilized an exploit that allowed me to control it."

She nodded slowly. "Meaning…?"

"I hacked it. It wasn't even that hard. Your parents seriously have to replace that shit. I'll install it myself if I have to."

Jess hummed as she nodded again. If I didn't know better, I would have said she looked impressed. "The rumors in high school were true, weren't they? People would complain about you getting their passwords and messing with their accounts, but I honestly didn't believe it. You were always so quiet."

"That's how I got away with it," I said. "People don't suspect the quiet ones."

Being underestimated allowed me to slide under the radar. She gave me a long look, regarding me as if she was trying to discover some secret. I worked from home, so I wasn't dressed to impress. I wasn't even wearing a shirt, and these sweatpants doubled as pajamas. But her eyes lingered as they got lower, probably because these thin pants didn't hide shit.

That little dress she was wearing didn't hide much either.

I'd come up with this entire idea of sex-as-payment. I'd sat there and watched her agree to this deal, but that didn't mean I really believed it. I'd thought she would back out by now. I'd thought she would start ignoring our texts the day after Manson and Lucas had their fun with her. So I'd kept my distance, because why should I get my hopes up for something that wasn't going to happen?

But to see her sitting there, dressed like that...

"Uh, Jason?" She snapped her fingers, and I shook my head, blinking rapidly. I had a tendency to zone out into my thoughts, but I'd been staring at her blankly the entire time. Shit.

"Sorry, sorry, I..." I licked my lips, uncertain of what to say. "Why are you...I mean...okay, fuck it, I'll just say. Why are you here?"

"To serve you," she said, with a teasing sigh. "Lucas and Manson said they owed you, so apparently, I'm your interactive *thank you* present. I think they're calling you, actually." She frowned in the direction of my desk.

Voices were calling my name from the headset, and I picked it back up, placing it over one ear. The boys had finally joined the Discord group, which was how we talked to each other during multiplayer games without yelling across the house.

"What's the holdup, J?" Lucas said. Vincent and Manson were both snickering. "Everything good for the next round?"

"Sorry to keep you waiting, buddy," Manson said. "We had a few things to take care of first."

"I got a little distracted," I said dryly, and Vincent meowed before laughing even harder.

"Do you like the accessories she came with?" Lucas said, and I suddenly remembered the bag Jess had come in with.

"You brought along some goodies, huh?" I said as I put down the headset.

"I haven't even looked," she said, innocently putting up her hands. "Vincent was really determined to keep things a surprise, except for this dress. Which I am stuck in, by the way."

I paused. "Wait…you can't get the dress off?"

"Nope." She popped her lips and sighed again, crossing her legs. "I guess you'll have to help me."

Oh, I'd certainly be helping her. That dress was going to be in pieces by the time I was done.

Squatting down, I had a look in the bag. Her foot was tapping nervously on the rug as I withdrew the first toy, still sealed in plastic. I held it up so she could get a good look. "Do you know what this is?"

"I don't know. A rose with a tale?" Her eyes widened and she leaned forward for a closer look. "Don't tell me that goes *inside* me?"

"The tail does," I said, pointing to the bulbous tail attached to the larger part of the toy. "The top is supposed to simulate oral stimulation." Her mouth opened in a silent 'O' as I delved in for the next toy, my brain buzzing with options.

I didn't understand why some people felt intimidated by using toys in the bedroom. Why *wouldn't* you want to use every item at your disposal to blow your partner's mind? If Jess wasn't reduced to a trembling, empty-headed, orgasm-drunk puddle by the end of this, then I hadn't done my job.

I'd fantasized about this — about *her* — for way too long. The beautiful, untouchable girl. The woman who was supposed to be off-limits. I wouldn't settle for anything less than blowing her mind.

Her eyes followed me as I stood up. "Do you want to play a game?" I said, motioning toward my chair.

She dragged her lip through her teeth with uncertainty. "It's been a long time since I played a video game," she said. "Is it competitive?"

"Very. It's simple, I promise. Only a few buttons to learn."

She sat up a little straighter. "Okay. Teach me."

Damn, there was something about hearing those words out of her mouth that gave me tingles all over. She got up from the bed, smoothing down her skirt as her bell jingled. I imagined the noise it would make while I fucked her, and I wondered if it would be possible to train her to get turned on by the sound of a bell.

I guess I was going to find out.

I held up my hand before she could sit down at the desk. "Wait, first things first. Take your panties off."

She pursed her lips, turning to face me. Her green eyes appeared ethereal in the blue glow, like cut jewels glittering in the light. She held my gaze as she reached under her skirt and tugged her panties down, a simple black pair with lacy edges. I held out my hand and she gave them over, placing them in my palm a little more roughly than necessary.

"Finally got my own trophy," I said. I brought the fabric to my nose, inhaling as she watched. Her lips parted slightly when I said, "Christ, you smell good."

Her cheeks darkened and she shuffled her feet. I held up two of the other toys I'd found in the bag — an anal plug and a pair of metal nipple clamps. They had even remembered to include a new bottle of lube. "I know how much you like a challenge, princess. So today, you're going to learn to play on hard mode."

"Is that how you play?" she quipped. It was an obvious attempt at a dig, but if she thought she was going to get to be a brat with me, she had another thing coming.

"Sometimes I do," I said, and her expression faltered. "Depends on my mood. What doesn't depend on my mood is that if you start talking back to me, you'll pay the consequences."

I pointed behind her, and she turned. A slim wooden paddle was leaned up against the side of my desk, its surface covered with holes for better aerodynamics.

I grabbed her collar and tugged her toward me. Her chest pressed against mine, her eyes wide as I pulled up on the collar and forced her to her tippy-toes. "If you give me any attitude, if you disobey, I'll bend you over and make you thank me for every swat until your ass is black and blue. Is that understood?"

She nodded quickly, voice slightly squeaky from the pressure of the collar. "I…Yes, sir." She worked her jaw, as if the words were thick and uncomfortable to get out.

"Now bend over. The boys are waiting, and I need you plugged before you play."

32

JESSICA

The paddle remained directly within my sight as I bent over. I rested my hands on Jason's desk, gnawing my lower lip, trying my hardest not to let my nerves overtake my mouth as I remembered Vincent's warning.

I thought of what it would be like to bend over for the paddle, to hear the swish of air before the sharp cracking contact. To have to hold myself in place and thank him while enduring a punishment like that…I shivered.

"Excited, princess? You're wet already."

Taking a deep breath, I looked back at him. It wasn't fair of him to be wearing those thin joggers and nothing else. I could clearly see his dick imprint on them. His bare chest was covered in colorful tattoos, a neon canvas that I couldn't tear my eyes away from.

"Yes, sir," I said.

He put the metal nipple clamps and anal plug aside on the seat of his chair. His fingers were warm as they probed between my legs, pushing and spreading me. Slowly, experimentally, he buried a finger inside my pussy. The cold metal of his ring pushing inside made my breath catch, and I moaned, unable to formulate words as a second finger joined the first. He curled them inside, pumping them slowly in and out.

"That feels so good," I said. Then I added quickly, "Sir."

"So you *can* learn. Good girl."

Good girl. Oooh, fuck, that made me weak. My insides clenched and his fingers paused before withdrawing completely. A moment of unbearable anticipation passed, then something firm and strangely textured stroked over me.

"Keep being obedient for me, and I'll make you feel so good you won't be able to think straight."

It was the alien dildo he was rubbing over me, coating the silicone in my arousal before he pressed it inside. It was narrow at the tip but quickly widened, its curved shape feeling entirely foreign. One side was smooth, but the other side was textured with little raised bumps, like suckers on a tentacle. It crawled over my nerves, the strange sensation making me squirm as he pressed it deeper.

"How does that feel? Have you ever used a dildo like this?"

"It feels weird. It feels…ah…" I caught my breath as he pumped it in and out, taking his time, letting me feel every unnatural inch. "It feels good, sir…the bumps…"

"You'll be riding this while you play the game," he said. A few more deep thrusts and he withdrew it, leaving me shifting back and forth with the need for more. There was a soft click, then a drip of something slick and cold landed between my cheeks.

"You'll have this plug inside your ass too," he said, reaching for the anal toy on the chair. He spread more lubricant around it, using his finger to coat the surface. "Don't worry, I'll take it slow. But I'll need you to be a good girl and open yourself up for me. You can kneel down and bend over the bed if that will be easier for you."

Easier, he said. Yes, certainly easier to die from humiliation in that position. But I was trying to be obedient, and it wasn't as if he hadn't seen me naked before…

But not like this.

I sank to my knees so I could crawl to the edge of his bed and bend over it. His blankets smelled fresh, like they'd just come out of the laundry. But his scent was still there too — sweet, subtle, and musky. I hadn't realized I missed that scent until it was flooding my nose again.

"Hold your ass open for me."

My face was on fire as I reached back and held my cheeks apart. I buried my face against the blanket, internally cringing at how exposed I felt. But Jason reached up and gave my collar another tug. "Keep your face up. Don't hide yourself. I know it's hard, but you can do it for me, can't you?"

My feet kicked lightly in protest before I managed to say, "I can do it, sir."

His finger swirled over my puckered entrance, spreading around the lubricant before pressing inside. I resisted the urge to muffle my groan in the blankets, pressing my lips tightly together. But as his finger kept probing me, the sounds came out — whimpers and barely restrained gasps.

"There you go. Loosen up for me." His voice was soft and calm, soothing as his finger was replaced with smooth metal. He took his time, the fullness building slowly, my body stretching to accommodate the intrusion. "That's my good girl. Almost there."

The plug settled in to sit tightly inside me, and I groaned, my muscles clenched around it to keep it in place. Jason pushed my hands aside as he gripped my ass, inspecting his handiwork.

"God, that looks so sexy," he said. "How does it feel?"

"So full," I whispered. "I don't think I can fit the dildo inside me too."

"Sure you can," he chided me gently. "You're going to have to get used to having both holes stuffed anyway, Jess. You won't always be taking us one at a time." The bed creaked as he leaned against it, blue eyes locking me in an icy stare as he tugged my collar to turn my face toward his. "One of these days, Vincent and I are going to take you together. Think of this as practice."

My eyes must have gone absurdly wide at the suggestion, because his mouth spread into a grin. "Oh, you like that idea, don't you? I wonder how many times you'd come with both our cocks fucking into you, stretching out these little holes. And speaking of orgasms…" He pulled me upright, holding me tight against his chest as my bell jingled. "I wonder how many of them it takes to make you cry? I guess I'll have to find out for myself." His hand traced the neckline of my dress, teasing over my cleavage. "You're stuck in this?"

I nodded, then gasped in shock when he took the frilly bodice in his grip and *ripped*. The cloth was thin and tore easily, leaving my breasts laid bare. I wasn't wearing a bra, and he tugged lightly at my nipple piercings before he carefully began to remove the jewelry.

"Jason...Jason, please..." I wiggled against him as he set aside the jewelry and reached back for those vicious metal nipple clamps. I didn't know what exactly I was begging for, only that I desperately wanted to. "I'll be good. I promise I'll be good..."

"I know," he said, widening the clamps. "But you like a challenge, don't you? You're going to sit at my desk, with your nipples clamped, your ass plugged, and that greedy pussy of yours riding a dildo, and you're going to try your best to win. You're not going to let this distract you, are you?" I shook my head, a whimper bursting out of me as he attached the first clamp.

The pinch was so tight, sharply painful, igniting the trail of nerves that seemed to lead straight from my nipples to my clit.

"I won't let it distract me, sir," I said, taking slow deep breaths as I adjusted to the new stimulation.

"Good girl." His lips brushed against my neck right below my ear, and I leaned into his touch. His lips were soft, but his hands were hard, the juxtaposition of sensations making me tremble as he attached the second clamp.

"Fuck, Jason...it hurts, it fucking hurts." I cringed against him, sucking in quick breaths in an effort to steady myself. My brain was jumbled already. I'd come in here thinking it would be a struggle to be obedient, but now, that was all I wanted to do — be a good girl, please him, make him proud so I could hear more sweet words.

He left me kneeling there, struggling not to tug the clamps off to relieve myself from the pain. He sat the flat base of the dildo on his chair and curled his finger at me. "Come here. Time to play."

Jason adjusted the seat for me, but the sheer length and girth of the dildo had me staring at it with wide eyes. I was supposed to somehow bury the entire thing inside me?

"We'll go slow," Jason said, his voice thick with sadistic excitement. He held my arms for balance as I lowered myself down, the dildo filling me inch by inch. By the time it was fully sheathed inside me, I was shaking. My legs felt weak. It ached somewhere deep inside, and the sensation was as much pleasure as pain.

God, I was so full.

"Let's see what you can do, princess." He stood behind me and leaned down, caressing his fingers over my arms. His hands came to rest on mine, moving my left hand to the keyboard and my right to the mouse. "The W, A, S, and D keys move you around." He pressed my fingers on the keys, his hand fully engulfing my own. "Look around with the mouse. Right-click shoots, the R key reloads." I shivered as his lips touched my ear, his breath hot on my neck. "You'll figure out the rest as you go. Oh, and one more thing…"

He grabbed the headset and put it on me, adjusting my headband so both fit comfortably. He left one ear uncovered so I could hear him, but through the other, I heard, "Jason needs to hurry the fuck up or I'm starting the round without him."

My thighs clenched together. It was Lucas, and Vincent's laughter followed right after. "You gave him all those goodies and you expect him to rush?"

"It's *Jason*, come on. We all know he takes his sweet time," Manson said.

There was a microphone in front of my mouth, attached to the headset. Jason remained bent over my back, close enough to hear their conversation come through the speakers and snicker at it.

"Sorry for the wait, boys," he said. "I had to get Jess ready to play."

"And I'll be playing to win," I said, getting a gasp and a chuckle out of the men listening. Trying to speak without allowing the desperation to taint my voice was nearly impossible, but I tried.

"I hope the fucktoy can carry her weight on a team," Lucas said.

"Of course she can," Vincent said. "You like to win, don't you, Jess?"

"Damn right." A notification popped up on the screen and I clicked the button to "join match." As I stared at the loading screen, I rocked slightly in my seat, plunging the dildo a little deeper. It felt good now that I was beginning to adjust to the size, so firm and thick.

"That's right, chase the pleasure," Jason said. The round started, dropping my character into the middle of a futuristic city. My objective showed up at the top of the screen: destroy the enemy base. I shivered as Jason's fingers traced back up my arms. "Don't lose focus."

I hadn't played any video games since middle school, but Manson, Lucas, and Vincent were clearly experienced. They gave instructions over the headset, alerting each other to enemies, gunfire popping off. The very first glimpse I got of the enemy team, I was dead within a few seconds. I huffed, growling in irritation as I waited for my character to spawn back into the game.

"Getting pissed already?" Jason laughed.

"Well, he didn't even give me a chance to aim," I said. It was so hard to focus. I shifted again, the dildo and the plug both moving inside me. Suddenly, right before I spawned, Jason knelt beside my chair and reached around my waist.

"Spread your legs," he said. I obeyed, my eyes darting down to see what he was doing. He had the rose toy in his hands, and the bulbous tail was vibrating. He pressed the bulb against my clit, and instantly I groaned, my entire body coiling at the sudden stimulation.

"Eyes on the game," Jason hissed.

"You good, Jess?" I could hear the grin in Manson's voice. "Tell me what he's doing to you."

"I'll tell you when we win," I said, exhaling hard as Jason moved the vibrator in a small circle over me.

"If we win, I'll come and see what he's doing for myself," Manson said, his tone darkening.

Despite trying my best, I was terrible at the game. Jason teased me every time I died, saying, "Aw, again? Come on, you can do better than that." The more irritated I got, the more he worked the vibrator on me. I was trying not to make any loud noises, but I couldn't stop another moan.

"Damn, groaning like a desperate little whore, aren't you?" Lucas said.

Growling, I responded, "Shut up."

Instantly, Jason smacked his palm against my inner thigh. I jolted, too shocked to cry out as I looked at him. But he smacked me again, saying, "Eyes on the game. Remember your fucking manners."

Damn it, the *rules*. I gnawed my lower lip, squirming as my skin stung. "I'm sorry, sir."

"Are you?" Manson said. "Then maybe you'd like to try that again. Lucas said you're groaning like a…?"

"Like a desperate little whore," I said, spilling out the words as quickly as possible. My pussy clenched, and it was a good thing the game was about to end because I was incapable of playing any further. I couldn't even make myself sit up straight as everything tightened and familiar waves of ecstasy built higher…higher…

"Fuck, Jason," I was panting, about to orgasm, and the way he kept moving the vibrator gave me no choice. I came, eyes squeezed shut, body locked in pleasure's vice-like grip. Jason forced my legs to stay spread apart, the vibrator pressed to my clit, his eyes on my face.

"Tell them how good it feels," he said.

I babbled, half of it not even making sense. "So good, fuck… oh my God, I'm so full, please —" A curse came through the headset, followed by a heavy exhale. "Oh, God, please, please, please, it's too much!"

Right when I thought I might combust, Jason pulled me up. I gasped at the sudden loss of fullness inside me, my face heating when I noticed the wet spot I'd left on his chair. He took my headset off and set it aside, his hand disappearing beneath my short dress as I was pressed back against the desk.

"God, you're so wet," he said. He brought his fingers to his mouth, licking off my arousal as he stared down at me. "I want to taste you. All of you."

He tipped my chin up and brought his lips to mine. He was tender at first, leaving a dozen soft kisses on my mouth before delving in, lips parting, tongue probing. I finally had my chance to drag my nails down his neck, his chest, grabbing his arms as I pulled him closer. His hard cock nudged against my belly, and I reached for it, grasping him through the thin fabric.

He smiled against my mouth. "What are you trying to do to me, hm? You want more?" His fingers spread over my throat, and I nodded, moving eagerly against him. "You'll get more. You're going to take it all, princess, even when you're begging me to stop."

He moved me back and laid me on the bed. He spread my limbs and cuffed them, binding my wrists and ankles with restraints connected to the bed's four posts. All the while he kissed me, sometimes quickly, sometimes slow and deep. He straddled my hips, praising me as he removed the clamps from my breasts but left the plug in my ass, taking his time to rub and suck my aching nipples into his mouth in between kisses.

"Touch me, please," I begged, arching my hips toward him. One orgasm was simply not enough, not when he kept teasing me like this.

He got off the bed, grabbing the rose toy and his headset. He laid the headset beside me and said, "Yeah? Want me to make you come again?" I nodded with a moan. "I'm going to make you come so many times there won't be a single thought left in your pretty little head."

I wasn't entirely sure whose curse came from the headset, but it sounded like Manson's. I squirmed as I thought of the other three men listening in on all this, hearing every gasp, every breath, every plea.

Jason slipped the bulbous tail of the toy inside me. He pressed a button, and it came to life again, the tail vibrating within me while a soft hum emanated from the rose itself.

"God, you're beautiful," he said, fingers spreading me open. He dipped his head down, mouth closing over my clit, tongue lapping at me.

A little cry burst out of my mouth. I jerked against the cuffs but could barely move. I could only gasp, "Oh my God, Jason, that feels so good!"

His mouth left me, but the toy swiftly replaced it. This time, he used the larger part of the rose, and I flinched at its touch, the suction on my sensitive clit almost too much to bear.

"We're just getting started, Jess," he said, smiling at me wickedly as I panted. "We're not stopping until that slutty little brain of yours is completely empty. The only thing I want you thinking about is chasing the next orgasm."

If my body had a steam pressure meter, mine would be in the red. I was writhing beneath him, both trying to get away and trying to get more. I was going to come again; I could already feel it. But this orgasm didn't build gently. It slammed into me, cracked open my raw brain, and wrenched out a shuddering cry.

"Jason, please." My voice broke. "Please, I'm going to come —"

"You're going to keep coming until I've said you had enough," he said. "Be a good girl and don't try to keep yourself quiet, understand? I think the boys deserve to be able to hear you."

Oh, they heard me. It was impossible not to. I yelled as I came, muscles so stiff they ached. I was shuddering, then desperately twitching when the stimulation didn't stop. When he moved the toy, he used his mouth instead, alternating the sensations. I wanted to reach for him, tangle my fingers in his blue hair and clutch his head between my thighs. I wanted a reprieve from the pleasure, but I also didn't want him to stop.

"You taste so fucking good," he growled, lifting his head. He pressed the rose against me again, moving it in a slow rocking motion as he tugged and probed with the vibrating bulb inside me. I couldn't even be sure if my last orgasm had truly ended, or if he'd drawn it out so long that it was peaking again. But it felt so amazing that my toes curled, my thighs trying in vain to squeeze together.

"Scream for him, Jess."

"Such a good girl."

"That's it, no fucking mercy, J."

The voices coming through the headset broke me almost as much as the overstimulation. My vision blurred as my body convulsed. "Fuck, Jason, please!"

Heat gushed between my legs, my pussy clenching so hard I squeezed the bulb out. The sheets were soaked beneath my trembling thighs, and when I managed to look down, Jason was staring at me with shock and awe in his wide eyes. His face was damp, wetness dripping from his cheek.

"Holy shit, did you just squirt for me?" he said. I nodded in exhaustion, nearly sobbing from the rush of ecstasy. He ravenously buried his head between my legs again, pressing the bulb back inside me and holding it there. I could only gasp as his tongue lapped hungrily at my overstimulated clit and probed around my entrance.

When he lifted his head again, he looked half wild. He

hurriedly tugged off his pants, and his thick cock sprang free to stand rigidly at attention. I wanted to touch him, claw at him, bite, fight, and cry out my ecstasy.

"I like vibrations too," he said, teasing against my slick opening with the rose's tail still inside me. "I think I'll keep this inside while I fuck you."

"You're already so big, Jason," I said. "How...how..."

He chuckled at me, pausing to pick up the headset. "Hear that, boys? Jess doesn't think I'll fit."

"Not all of us are blessed with horse cocks, J." I recognized Vincent's teasing voice, even faint as it was.

"Oh, it'll fit," Lucas said huskily. "She might scream, but it'll fit."

"Tell her yourselves."

Jason fit the headset on me again. I tried to steady myself, but it was useless. There was no way I was going to maintain my pride through this.

"Are you being a good girl?" Manson's voice was low in my ear, and I whimpered immediately, longing to know if he had his cock in his hand, if he was enjoying my sounds, if he was getting off to this.

"I'm being good," I said, then gasped as Jason pressed against my entrance again. He pushed a finger inside, then a second one, getting me used to the stretch. "Oh my God, it's so tight...fuck..."

"You're okay, sshh, there's my brave girl," he said gently. "I know you're scared, princess, I know. It's going to hurt, but you want to be good, don't you?" I nodded, as his words soothed me and his fingers pumped inside me. I *did* want to be good. I wanted to please him. I wanted to see the pleasure on his face when he buried his cock inside me. He kissed my mouth once, twice, and then again as he drew his fingers out of me. "Such a good girl. I knew you could do it. Deep breaths now, you'll be okay."

I recognized the slick sounds of one of them jerking off on the headset. Jason entered me, taking his time, opening me slowly. He twitched inside me as he encountered the vibrator, inhaling deeply and then letting it out with a groan.

"Please, aah..." I strained against my bindings as he shoved himself all the way in. He brought the rose back, pressing it against my clit as he thrust into me, and my brain utterly shattered. The noises I made, keening like an animal, only served to make the men listening in more excited.

"That's it, take it, Jess." Vincent's voice was rushed and tight. I wished he was there, in the room with us, shoving his cock into my mouth so I had something to muffle my sounds.

"Let me hear those pretty screams." Manson's voice made me shiver, so thick with pleasure as he listened to me that I whimpered his name.

"Mm, do you like when Manson talks to you?" Jason said. He released my ankles from the cuffs and pressed my legs up to angle his cock even deeper inside me. Every thrust made me cry out, and I nodded brokenly at his question. "Do you like that he's getting off on how pathetic you sound right now? Tell him how it feels, Jess."

"It's so tight," I whimpered. "It hurts and feels so good and... and...fuck...Jason, please..."

Lucas's voice was harsh as he demanded, "Come for us, girl."

Jason groaned as I locked around him, reaching up to pin

me by the throat. His hips jerked in short, rapid thrusts, slapping against my skin.

My voice was weak as his hand squeezed, baring his teeth the harder he fucked me. "Please, I can't come again…"

"Sorry, princess, but you have to take it," he grunted, jaw tight. "Come for me again. Cry if you need to. I want to see you break."

The look of sheer possessive pleasure on his face sent me over one more explosive edge. His grip on my throat tightened, enough to give me a light-headed rush as I sobbed my release. Praise came over the headset, the words flowing together, and I drank it up like the god's ambrosia.

Still dazed, I barely understood Jason when he leaned close to the headset and demanded, "Get up here before she fucking passes out."

33

MANSON

Jason's demand came just in time, because I was already on the edge of losing control. I liked to share. I loved to watch. But listening without seeing, hearing without touching, was fucking unbearable. I wanted to see her face, touch her soft skin. I wanted her to open her mouth for my cum and take it all.

Jessica was ours until her debt was paid. *Ours*. I wanted to savor every second of that before it was all taken away again.

The three of us practically tripped over each other getting upstairs. Vincent made it to the door first and shoved it open, groaning with pleasure as he took in the scene. Lucas was right behind me, and he cursed, pressing close against my back as I paused in the doorway.

Jess was straddling Jason's lap on the bed, her back against his chest, her legs hooked around his thighs and spread wide. He'd unchained her and removed the plug and vibrator from inside her. Her head was limp against his shoulder, her eyes glazed as she looked at me and her lips moved to silently form my name. She was impaled on his cock and my gaze fixated on the mesmerizing rhythm of his shaft pumping in and out of her.

Vincent knelt between her legs, gripping her thighs as he pushed them wider. He tongued her clit, and her entire body writhed. Jason leaned back, his chest heaving as Vincent grasped his balls and fondled them, his mouth buried right at their point of union.

I was already on the edge, far too worked up to draw this out. My pants were already off since Lucas had been stroking my cock and his own as we listened downstairs, and I would have come in his hand if Jason hadn't called us up. Jess reached a trembling arm for me as I came closer, tugging down my briefs so she could touch me. She reached for Lucas on her other side, stroking both of us in unison.

"God…fuck…" Jason moaned, fingers digging tightly into her hips as he came. He pumped into her with short, punching thrusts. Seeing his eyes roll back, hearing Jess whimper as he filled her, pushed me to my peak. Cum spurted over her hand, onto her face, her breasts. Lucas followed, reaching down to viciously grip her hair as he came on her face.

But Vincent wasn't done. The moment Lucas finished, Vincent pushed Jess back, shoving her and Jason down against the mattress. Neither of them looked like they had any energy left — Jess lying utterly limp and cum-drunk as Jason slipped out of her, his eyes half-lidded. His cum seeped out of her as Vincent lifted her leg and entered her.

I caught my breath at the sight. Vincent gripped her thigh with one hand while the other was tangled in Jason's hair, holding him down as Vincent fucked her on top of him. My legs couldn't hold me anymore, and I collapsed heavily on the bed, leaning back against the wall as I watched. Lucas crawled up onto the mattress beside me, dropping his head against my chest as he caught his breath.

Jess was limp as a doll, face flushed, covered in our seed. Vincent used her hard, the bell on her collar jingling with every thrust, her soft cries almost too sweet to bear. God, I loved to watch them with her. How they pleasured her, used her, cared for her. There was something beautiful in trusting them so damn much that we could share this. Our lives were twined for better or worse, and despite all the bullshit, I wouldn't have it any other way.

Vincent came inside her, pressing deep, her ruffled skirt bunched up around her hips as her eyes fluttered closed. He leaned down and kissed her, then Jason right after, who was lying on the bed like a man half-dead.

Lucas sat up, and I leaned forward when Vince pulled out of her. She was dripping with our essence, and when Vincent pressed a finger inside her, she squirmed weakly, barely able to keep her eyes open.

"Fuck, that's a beautiful sight," I said, pushing my finger inside with his, feeling the warmth and the thick wetness. She was shaking, and Jason wrapped his arms around her, nuzzling his face against her messy cheek. He licked my cum off her skin and a smile broke out on her exhausted face.

"Do you like how he tastes on me?" she said softly, and I almost lost my mind. I nudged Vincent aside so I could close my mouth over her, my touch causing her entire tired body to jolt. She begged as soon as my tongue was on her, twitching with every stroke.

"Ah, Manson! Please, I'm so sensitive, please!" But I took my sweet time, probing my tongue inside her, savoring the taste of her. Of us.

But she was worn out. She'd reached her limit and needed rest. I left her with kisses on her thighs before I pulled her off of Jason and laid her head on the pillows. She still had the dress on, although it was torn. Jason crawled up and collapsed beside her, murmuring gently as he kissed her cheek, "We'll take care of you, princess, just relax. You were so good. I'm so fucking proud of you."

I smirked as I reached for his bedside drawer and the pocket knife inside it. I flipped it open, using the blade to cut through the last bits of fabric that were clinging to her. She watched me do it with half-lidded eyes, not even flinching when I brought the knife close to her skin.

What an honor to be trusted like that. It almost scared me as I looked at her, her serene face smiling back at me with a tired expression that could only be described as cum-drunk. It scared me because of how it made me feel, how instantly my entire chest clenched.

I knew better than to get attached to things I couldn't have. Situations, objects, people — I had to keep myself at a distance. But I looked at her and knew I was fucked. The way Jason looked at her, after spending all week withdrawn and feigning disinterest, told me he was feeling the same thing.

We were already sinking in too deep; and I, for one, knew I couldn't stop.

34

JASON

N ow that I finally felt like I could sleep, I didn't even
want to.

The bed really wasn't big enough for all of us. Jess
lay naked on her back with my arm around her, our deep breathing
in unison. She felt so warm, her skin sticky with sweat, her muscles
still quivering. Vincent had wedged himself into the corner of the
bed behind me, slowly scratching my back as he hummed some little
tune. Lucas sat at the end of the mattress, leaning against the wall
with his legs sprawled out in front of him, and Manson sat right
beside him, his knees pulled up as his arms rested limply on them.

I couldn't bring myself to close my eyes. I liked this sight
too much — this beautiful woman laid out beside me and all the
people I loved most around me. If I closed my eyes, if I fell asleep,

I feared it might all wind up as a dream.

I used to have terrible nightmares like that, imagining that I'd gone back in time and the family I'd found was gone, Vincent was gone, all my freedom — gone. I would wake up in the middle of the night, gasping and shaking with my parents' words echoing in my head.

I will not have my son living in sin, not under my roof!

I took a deep breath. I didn't want to think about that right now. I was safe. The nightmares were memories, not predictions of the future.

The mattress creaked, and Lucas grunted, "Gonna go downstairs and get a drink." He eased off the bed, stretching his arms over his head. Vincent sighed, and when he shifted, I reached back and grabbed his wrist.

"Sorry, babe," he said softly. He leaned down and kissed my head, squeezing my shoulder. "I really do need to get ready for work though."

He got off the bed, and I groaned as I sat up, running my fingers through my mussed hair. Jess had opened her eyes and was staring up at me, her makeup streaked, her face and chest still messy with our cum. I pushed her hair back, chuckling softly at the state of her.

"I'm a mess, aren't I?" she said, a little smile on her face.

I nodded. Her cat ears had fallen off and were lying on the floor; the only thing she still wore was her collar.

It was only a silly accessory, but I didn't want to take it off her.

She sat up, easing her arms around my neck. She rested her head on my shoulder, her arm reaching back for Manson. He moved closer and took her hand, twining his fingers through hers.

"My legs feel so weak," she said. "You fucked me until I can't even walk."

"Mission accomplished," I said. It was a point of pride for me to see her looking dazed and thoroughly pleasured. It felt like a long-awaited victory.

I'd thought finally having sex with Jessica would leave me bitterly vindicated, but I felt no bitterness at all. I felt like I'd finally sucked in a breath after holding it for far too long, like all the tension had gone out of me.

"Come on," I said. "Let's get you cleaned up. You look like a toaster strudel."

She laughed so hard she snorted, and it was possibly one of the cutest things I'd ever heard. I helped her off the bed on her wobbly legs, leaving Manson to sprawl out on the mattress with a satisfied grin on his face.

Vincent emerged from the bathroom right as I was leading Jess toward it, his hair brushed and tied back. He caught her face as he passed us, giving her a lingering kiss.

"I'll see you next time, baby," he said, giving her a wink before he went on toward the attic to get dressed. I usually slept far worse when he was away for work, but maybe tonight I'd manage a solid six hours.

She went into the bathroom first to use the toilet, and I joined her once she'd finished up and opened the door again. She sat on the edge of the tub as I turned on the hot water in the sink. I took a washcloth from the cabinet and dampened it, before I sat beside her. "Relax, I've got you."

She closed her eyes as I wiped her face, taking my time to clean her smudged makeup from her cheeks.

"How do you feel?" I wiped down her neck, taking care to be gentle. I cleaned around the collar, prolonging taking it off her for as long as I could.

She gave a heavy sigh, her mouth twitching slightly as she said, "I guess I have a kink for cat maids now. Thanks for that, Jason."

"There's more new kinks where that came from," I said. "Just wait. They get weirder."

"Oh, I know. Your list gave me a lot of new words to learn," she said. When she spoke again, her teasing tone was gone. "I feel really good. Relaxed...tired." She opened her eyes, those green irises searing into me. "I feel happy."

My heart skipped a beat. Being here with us, taking part in this, made her happy? She took the washcloth from my hands, rising from the edge of the tub.

"Your turn," she said, grabbing a clean cloth from the cabinet and leaving the used one beside the sink. She dampened it as I stared, admiring her naked body. When she returned and sat down again, she pushed my hair out of my face with one hand and used the other to wipe the cloth over my skin.

"And how do you feel?" she said. She was going to put me to sleep doing this. The soft touch of the cloth was so relaxing.

I closed my eyes, savoring the moment. "I feel like this is surreal. Like Vincent and I saw you at that car wash and fell into some kind of fever dream."

"I know the feeling," she said. "Almost like it's not supposed to be happening. Like we broke the rules."

I caught her wrist as she wiped the cloth along my throat, drawing her a little closer. "We always break the rules, Jess."

Her lips were pliant as I kissed her. It felt too good to pull her close, to cup her face and stroke my thumb over her cheek. And when her breath hitched, shuddering slightly as she inhaled, that soft feeling in my chest got even fucking softer.

"Tell me the truth," I said, barely parting from her to speak. "How long have you wanted this?"

When she lifted her eyes to mine, they looked uncertain, almost afraid, as if someone was pounding on the door that protected her most tightly kept secret.

She took a breath and then whispered, "Always."

A soft knock at the door made us both jump. "It's unlocked," I said, and Manson opened the door to lean against the frame. His hair looked wild, sticking up at odd angles, and he was wearing only his briefs.

"I'll admit, I listened out here for a little bit to see if you two were fucking again." He trudged over, grasped Jess's chin, and tipped her face up to claim a kiss of his own. "How are you doing, angel?"

"Really good," she said. She paused, muffling a yawn behind her hand. "Exhausted, honestly."

"I can drive you home," he said, and pointed his finger at me in warning before I could volunteer myself. "You need to stay here and rest. No more excuses. You're going to get yourself in an accident driving so tired, J."

I sighed, but I didn't have the energy to argue. He was right; I was exhausted and the lack of sleep was hitting me hard. It wasn't the best idea to drive when I could barely keep my eyes open.

I didn't want to take her home at all. I wanted to drag her back into bed and fall asleep between her and Vincent again.

"As much as I love to see you naked, we have to get you some clothes too," Manson said as Jess got to her feet and stretched. I couldn't help but grasp her hips, pulling her toward me and kissing her stomach before I let her go.

"You can borrow some of mine," I said. I was just a few inches taller than her, unlike the other giants in the house, so hopefully she could find something that wasn't too big.

Manson went to get his own clothes as Jess and I shuffled back down the hallway to the bedroom. I pulled a few things out of the closet for her as she put the jewelry back in her piercings.

"Your parents come back the day after tomorrow, right?" She nodded, and I continued, "I'll drop by your house tomorrow and see what I can do about the security system. They still need to replace the damn thing, but you at least need something that works in the meantime."

There was a clever look in her narrowed eyes as she watched me. "You only decided I need security *after* you fucked me?"

I brought over some clothes for her, dumping them on the bed before I grabbed her ass and pulled her against me. "That pussy absolutely needs its own security detail. But I can't follow you around twenty-four-seven, so…"

The way she was looking up at me brought her face close to mine, her entire body pressed against me. "Careful, Jason. If you keep talking about protecting me, I might end up thinking you care."

A dismissive sound left me. "Yeah, yeah, I'm just protecting my property. Don't read into it."

"Wouldn't dream of it," she said. It all sounded like a tease, but was there any truth in it? Did she want us to care? Or did she already know that we did and thought we were foolish for it?

She dressed, yawning again as she pulled my t-shirt over her head. It did something to me to see her standing there in my clothes. The sweatpants were pooling a bit around her ankles and the shirt was too big, but as she pulled it over her head, I swore I saw her pause for a moment and sniff.

She still hadn't taken the collar off, and it jingled every time she moved, so she couldn't have forgotten it.

Manson poked his head into the room. "Ready?"

Jess nodded before she turned back to me. "Thanks for the clothes. And for a really fun time." She kissed me, the touch of her lips too quick. "I'll see you tomorrow."

I almost asked her to stay. I nearly dragged her back and told her she'd be coming to bed with me.

But then she was gone; Manson wrapping his arms around her shoulders and walking her down the hall.

I collapsed onto the bed, scrubbing my hands over my face before I stared up at the ceiling. This was exactly what *wasn't* supposed to happen. This feeling, this…longing. The reawakening of a high school crush that had somehow intensified despite time and distance.

When I'd transferred to Wickeston High, Jess and Vincent had been my first true temptations to sin. A seductress and a jester, challenging my carefully guarded thoughts. I was used to being surrounded by rules, to living with the guilt of being a sinner who must repent, repent, repent. Do not give into temptation.

Worship. Pray. Beg for forgiveness.

But then the floodgates opened. Jess was untouchable, beautiful, proud. Vincent was tempting, seductive, too damn charming to resist. Back then, the reality of what I was facing hit me hard. I couldn't choose one or the other. I couldn't settle.

I couldn't live as anything less than fully myself, unless I wanted to remain in an endless cycle of praying for forgiveness of my own nature.

The Jessica I'd known back then had surrounded herself with all the right people. She'd presented herself as picture-perfect. That's what you did when you were pretending, when you were trying to prove that you belonged. The "right" people had been her armor and the "perfect" life was her own grand production. Her peers were her audience.

Now, the curtain was drawn and the costumes were gone. Jessica was just Jess, a woman trying to figure out who the hell she was like the rest of us.

I didn't know what it meant — for her, or for us. Time and distance hadn't kept us from being pulled back together again, but for what? This was the woman we weren't meant to have, whose life plans were going to take her away from us again.

Vincent claimed her showing up again was a "sign," but a sign of *what,* I truly didn't know.

35

JESSICA

The Mustang's interior was pristine as I slid onto the leather passenger seat. It smelled like Manson inside — that distinctly dark, spiced chocolate scent I'd come to know as his.

"Any preference on music?" he said. He cranked the engine and the Mustang roared to life, the entire car trembling before it settled. Almost everything inside looked original, except for the speakers, radio, and the thick purple bars that extended around the interior like a cage. I recognized them as similar to the ones in Vincent's car, and I wondered if Manson had cuffs dangling from his too.

"Surprise me," I said, watching as he flicked through a playlist on his phone while the car idled. He picked a song and adjusted the volume, a hauntingly ethereal voice coming from the speakers.

"I have to let the car warm up before we leave," he said. "It'll be a few minutes."

We sat in silence, the engine quieting slightly as we waited. I was so tired; my muscles were weak with exhaustion. But the clothing Jason had put me in was warm and cozy, swaddling me in his scent.

Part of me didn't want to leave. Up in Jason's bedroom, I'd been tempted to collapse back into bed, pull Jason and Manson close and demand Lucas snuggle up too. Lying there with them had felt so comfortable, so normal. Like I was meant to be there.

I cleared my throat, unable to bear the silence any longer. "When did you get the Mustang?"

"About a year ago," he said. "She'd been sitting on someone's property for years and needed a lot of work." He glanced over at me. "But she was worth the effort."

"She's beautiful," I said. He looked down and away, but not quick enough to hide his smile. I didn't know shit about cars, but I knew a nice one when I saw it. "Does she have a name?"

"Name?" His brow furrowed for a moment. "No, I...I've never been into naming inanimate objects. It's not good to get attached to possessions."

He put the car into gear, backing out of the garage. He pulled out of the yard onto the dirt road, parking for a moment while he closed and locked the gate. We bumped slowly along the dirt before we turned onto Route 15, the engine growling aggressively as Manson picked up speed.

The streetlights flashed overhead as I watched him out of the corner of my eye, trying not to make it obvious. The muscles in his arm were taut as he moved the gearshift, eyes focused on the road.

"Do you wanna see how fast she can go?" he said, his expression turned mischievous.

I pulled my seatbelt tighter, bracing myself. "Oh, hell yes."

He accelerated, the force of it pressing me back into my seat. The engine roared so loud it drowned out my laughter as he sped down the road. The wind whipped through the open windows, and we passed the turn for my house in the blink of an eye. Our speed reached 90...100...110. I braced my hands against the metal bars encircling the cab, my heart in my throat as we flew down the open road.

"Holy shit, Manson!" I shrieked as he downshifted, wrenching the wheel as the tires squealed. The back end of the car slid out in a half-circle before he straightened out, our speed climbing again as he took the narrow twisting road that led up into the hills behind the gated community of Wickeston Heights.

He was smiling wide as he whipped through the road's curves. It was no wonder he'd fallen in love with this: the speed, the power, the freedom. He brought us to the crest of the hill and pulled off to the side, the tires crackling in the dirt. There was a lookout here with a view of the town, and he parked right next to the large boulders guarding the edge of the hillside.

"You know, coming up to the lookout with someone usually means you're trying to get lucky," I said. People had been coming up here for years with the sole intent to have sex, hotbox their vehicles, drink, or generally be degenerates.

"I think having you in my car at all is pretty lucky," he said. The sincerity of his words caught me off guard, and I shifted in my seat, staring at the distant lights. This feeling was almost sad, but too full of desire to be melancholy.

Was I just tired and overthinking? There was something about the way he was looking at me that made me feel like I couldn't get enough air despite the open windows. I wasn't supposed to feel like this. This soft vulnerability. This *need* that had nothing to do with sex. This was *only* supposed to be about sex, nothing more.

Why did it feel like there was more?

He spoke before I could. "Let's go see the view."

We got out and joined each other at the front of the car. He leaned against the hood, hands inside the pockets of his hoodie as he looked out at the twinkling lights below. I leaned beside him, the metal warm through Jason's oversized pants. Wickeston looked a lot prettier from up here — all glittering lights spread out in the darkness. The breeze picked up and made me shiver a bit, and I glanced over as Manson unzipped his jacket.

"Here, you must be cold," he said, ushering me closer. He pulled me to his chest, and I leaned against the hood between his legs as he pulled the jacket around both of us. His chin rested on my shoulder, his hands finding mine beneath the jacket.

He pressed lightly on the pad of my middle finger, and I said, "The heart healed. No scar."

"You sound disappointed," he said.

"I guess I hoped it would scar," I admitted. "I liked looking at it. It made me feel like…I don't know." I shrugged sheepishly. "It made me feel like maybe I'd been forgiven. At least before I went and fucked things up again."

It wasn't easy to admit; I hated to say I was wrong. People

would take advantage of that. If you gave them even an inch, one single moment of weakness, they'd find a way to wield it over you. Pride kept me safe. It was a barrier I'd thought no one could breach.

Oh, how incorrect I'd been.

"I know that probably sounds really hypocritical of me," I said, as his silence drew out. I needed him to say something, anything. It felt like such a silly thing to admit that a little cut on my finger made me feel so much. If I'd tried to tell that to anyone else in my life, they would have laughed or been disgusted, horrified, maybe even concerned.

"I think we're all hypocrites, in one way or another," he said, and his arms tightened around me. "As we grow up and figure out who we are, sometimes our thoughts change before our behavior does. It's not pretty, and it can be fucked up, but we're not perfect. We've all done it."

"Yeah?" My voice sounded far more timid than I wanted. "You've done it too?"

"I…well, fuck…" He cleared his throat uncomfortably. "Once I met this girl, and I thought she was the most beautiful woman I'd ever seen. But I wasn't good enough for her, you know…I was a mess and didn't know how to talk to anyone. I was always in my own head just trying to get through another day."

I swallowed hard, thankful for the jacket's warmth. I knew this story and it wasn't easy to hear, but I needed to.

"I think I should have hated that girl," he said, but he didn't sound hateful at all. "Because she was always with the same people who hurt me, and she stood for everything I didn't. Perfection, popularity, beauty…she was part of the system that rejected me.

She was what we all were supposed to aspire to be, or to have." He turned his head, so his cheek rested on my shoulder and he was facing away from me. "But I didn't hate her, Jess. Never. Not even once. I don't think I could, even if I tried, even if I wanted to."

There were parts of myself that only existed because people wanted them, parts of me designed entirely to please people who didn't even care in the end. I'd thought it would be easier that way, but it didn't feel easy at all. It felt like I'd ripped myself in two pieces and couldn't make any of the edges match up again.

"You should probably hate her," I said. "Because it sounds like she deserves it."

"Nah, that's not true." He kissed my neck, making me smile despite myself. "I'm not good at hating people, Jess. Hate is too heavy, it's too much. I'd rather find the good in people, when I can. I'd rather give some grace to others who are figuring it all out, because I'm trying to do the same thing."

"Do you ever feel like you're running out of time? I know we're young, but sometimes I feel like life is rushing by me so much faster that I can't keep up with it. Like I missed a lesson everyone else already figured out, or like I'm starting over…"

"I get it." He lifted his head from my shoulder, smoothing my hair back from my face even though the breeze whipped it right back again. "Seeing you in Wickeston again was like seeing you come back from the dead. I thought you were done with this place."

"I thought so too," I said. "Things didn't exactly go according to plan. I made the mistake of thinking I'd land a big career straight out of college, as if money, a house, and a job would all fall into my lap." I rolled my eyes at myself, at my own naivety. "Now my mom gets to rub it in my face that college was a terrible choice after all." I put on my best imitation of my mother's disapproving drawl as I said, "I should have been looking for a *husband* all this time instead. How will she ever see any grandbabies if I'm too busy chasing a job?"

Manson shook his head. "I've never met your mom, but I have a feeling I know where you get your stubbornness from."

I looked over my shoulder at him, narrowing my eyes. "Oh, you have no idea. That woman could argue with a brick wall and win."

We both laughed — a moment passing in comfortable silence.

"You're trying to get to New York," Manson finally said. "You want to live in the city?"

"I think it would be exciting to live downtown," I said. "I used to think that all I wanted was a cute little apartment in Manhattan. But…maybe not. Maybe living outside the city would be nice. Close enough to visit when I want, but still far enough away that there's some peace and quiet." I sighed. "I'm still undecided on so much. All I know is that I want to get the hell out of this town and go where no one knows my name."

"You want to escape who you were," he said.

"I've fucked up a lot of things. I drove people away. I was selfish." I was glad my back was to him, because I didn't think I could meet his eyes. "I was awful toward you. I treated you all like shit."

"Why did you do it?" His voice was soft, gentle. My eyes began to sting, surprising me, and I hurriedly coughed to make the tears go away.

I'd asked myself that same question many times and I still didn't feel like I had a good answer.

"I couldn't stay away from you," I finally said. "It seemed like you didn't care what anybody thought, and that…it irritated me. It made me mad that I didn't feel that way, that I cared too much. I couldn't stand how I had *everything* I was supposed to want, except…"

"Except?" he coaxed me. I turned to face him, and his arms adjusted to accommodate me.

"Except I wasn't happy," I said. "Everyone kept telling me I was supposed to be, so I kept pretending that I was. I thought eventually it would click, that I would feel okay. But the harder I tried to pretend, the worse I felt. I hated who I was, but I didn't know how to be anyone else. I thought a few years in college would turn it all around. I made so many friends, I drank way too much. I said yes to everyone because I thought maybe it would make me a better person, but it…it didn't work." I sighed, my shoulders feeling so heavy. "All those friends? They don't call. They don't care. Just like the friends I had here, they only want me if I'm Jess the Party Girl, or Jess the Stuck-Up Bitch. Even now…I don't know who I'm supposed to be."

That was the truth, as messy, ugly, and hypocritical as it was. I tried not to meet his eyes as I said it, afraid of what I'd find there. It made me feel pathetic, and not in that fun, sexy way like when I was begging them for more. In a gross, weak, shameful way.

"I'm sorry," I said. "I don't expect you to forgive me. Any of you. But I know I really messed up so many times."

He clicked his tongue, nudging my chin up until I met his eyes. I braced myself for judgment but didn't find any on his face.

"I can't forgive on behalf of anyone else," he said. "But I

forgave you back then. I've forgiven you every day since. I'll always forgive you. And if you talk to the boys like you just talked to me, I know they'll forgive you too."

It made me feel like crying. I held it back, swallowing hard and inhaling sharply. I was certain I didn't deserve forgiveness like that. That was part of why I wanted so desperately to leave. I'd burned too many bridges, hurt too many people.

But maybe I hadn't destroyed *everything*. Maybe there was still something good to be found here.

"What are you smiling for?" I said, a tremble in my voice as I looked at him.

He didn't respond with words. His answer was his lips pressed against mine.

He cupped his hand around the back of my head, holding me close. His tongue probed my lips and they parted for him easily, our breath mingling as I knotted my hands into his shirt. I wanted to pull him closer, hold him impossibly tighter. As if I could live in this moment, this feeling, forever.

By the time we pulled up in front of my house, I knew I didn't want to spend the night alone. Manson walked me to the door, but as I unlocked it, I turned to him and said, "Will you stay?"

His face was in shadow, but I still saw his eyes widen. He hesitated as I stood there, the door halfway open, the cool air seeping out from inside.

"You want me to…?" he said. "To sleep here?"

"Yes. I do." I wasn't used to being the one to ask, opening

myself up for rejection. I wouldn't blame him if he said no. He'd be right to keep his distance.

But he took my hand. "Yeah. Of course I'll stay."

It was like I was a teenager again, sneaking a boy into my house when my parents weren't home. I didn't want to imagine how pissed off my mother would be if she ever found out about this, but she wouldn't. What she didn't know couldn't anger her.

He let me lead him upstairs, quiet as he looked around. When we reached the hallway on the second floor, he paused, staring up at the wall. My mom's numerous framed photos smiled down at us, chronicling my life from infancy until now. The majority of the pictures were from beauty pageants, including glamor shots spanning throughout the first twelve years of my life.

"Yeah, I was one of *those* kids," I said, as he inspected them. The photos looked silly; I'd been as young as two for some of those pageants, dressed in sequins and glitter with a full face of makeup. Perfectly straight false teeth hid the gaps left by losing my baby teeth, and poofy wigs covered my soft wispy hair. I'd been a toddler, wearing dangling earrings and lipstick, smiling big and bright.

Manson looked at the photos one by one, and I wished I could see into his brain. I wanted to know what he was thinking when he lingered over the family portraits or traced his finger along the frames.

"Did you enjoy it?" he said, his question catching me off guard. "The pageants?"

No one, not even my mom, had ever asked me that. I wasn't even sure how to answer.

"It made my mom happy," I finally said. "She thought it taught me social skills, and she was right. I was never afraid to be in front of a crowd, even when I was really little."

I'd learned to drown out my nerves with floods of false confidence, to look at every other little girl I encountered as a challenge. I learned to always strive to be the best, to harden my emotions, to view the world as my stage. I'd even had a coach. I could still remember her and my mom making me walk back and forth as I hit all my "points" as I would have to in competition.

"Pretty feet, Jessica, remember? Pretty feet!"

"Give them a nice big smile, come on, nice pretty smile!"

"Don't clench your fingers like that. Let the judges see pretty hands!"

Be pretty so you'll win. Be pretty so they'll like you.

"That's not what I asked."

His tone wasn't demanding, but my first instinct was to lie. Of course I enjoyed it! Why wouldn't I like dressing up nice, getting attention, feeling like I was the prettiest little girl in the world? What else could I have wanted than to make my mom proud, to have others look at me in envy, to feel like I was the best?

"When I won, I enjoyed it," I said. "But there was only one winner. And sometimes…many times…that wasn't me."

Someone else was prettier, smarter, more graceful, more skilled. It hurt to lose, but it also pushed me to win. To try harder, to perform better. No matter what it took, no matter how many times I won first place, it was never enough. The competition didn't end once the sequins came off and the glitter was washed away.

Manson stepped closer. Before I even realized what was happening, he'd scooped me up, my feet leaving the ground as he easily carried me the rest of the way down the hall.

"What are you doing?" I said, as he shoved open my bedroom

door with his foot.

"Getting that sad look off your face," he said, smiling at me crookedly as he stopped next to my bed. He dumped me on the mattress but followed me down, crawling on top of me. He buried his face against my neck, the combination of his mouth and warm breath trailing over my skin making me erupt in a fit of laughter.

"Fuck, no, no, no, I'm too ticklish there!" But he already knew my weakness, as he swooped in right for that sensitive spot behind my ear. I shrieked and struggled as he easily held me down, laughing at my helpless thrashing.

"That's better," he said, flopping down on the pillows, and I finally had a chance to catch my breath. We lay there, side by side, staring at the ceiling as our gasps slowed. When I sighed, still shivering with leftover giggles, I turned my face toward him.

He was staring back.

"You're beautiful," he said. "How other people look couldn't ever change that."

I smiled, then stared at the ceiling as if that would hide how deeply I was blushing. Plenty of people called me beautiful — but it was different when he said it.

We stripped off our clothes until I was wearing only panties and Jason's t-shirt, and he was in nothing more than black briefs. I pulled him onto the bed and my hands roamed over him slowly, exploring him in a way I'd never allowed myself to do before. I followed the lines of his tattoos, finding scars and freckles in the moonlight streaming in my window. He let me do it, lying there with his arms folded beneath his head as I touched him.

We shifted around, finally settling as he pulled me close, with my back to his chest. His arm wrapped around my waist, heavy but not clinging, like a weighted blanket that immediately relaxed me.

"Are you comfortable?" he said. His mouth was so close against my neck, and he was so warm.

"Yeah. Really comfortable."

His steady breathing lulled me into a dreamless sleep within minutes.

36

MANSON

When I woke up and saw long blonde hair splayed across my chest, I thought I was still dreaming.

Jess was nestled under my arm, with her back against my side and her hand resting on my bicep. She was wearing Jason's shirt, her bare legs curled up slightly so her feet were pressed against my calf. The sun had just risen, a reddish orange glow peeking through her curtains.

I didn't usually wake up this early, but I didn't usually sleep away from home either. That familiar ache of anxiety bloomed in my chest, growing like a mass that pressed on my lungs.

I'd made a mistake. I wasn't supposed to sleep here.

The last time I'd slept by her side, we'd been in my old bedroom in the Peters' family home. I'd laid awake for hours that night just looking at her, at how soft her face was while she slept, how her lips twitched and her nose wrinkled as she dreamed. A simple dare had brought her into my arms, and it had seemed too good to be true.

Because it was. She left in the morning with one of the sweetest goodbyes I'd ever heard and then — nothing. Gone. Ghosted.

I was left feeling like I'd made the biggest mistake of my life and had no idea how to remedy it other than to simply let her go. That was the choice she'd made, and I had to respect it.

But now, if she made that decision again...*when* she did...

I didn't know if I could respect it this time.

I was able to get a better look at her room in daylight. I hadn't been paying much attention when Lucas and I broke in here, too distracted with the game to bother examining my surroundings. Her walls were painted crisp white, and there were still a few cardboard boxes stacked in the corner, taped shut and labeled with a sharpie. She hadn't finished unpacking yet; maybe she didn't intend to, especially if she planned to move in a few months anyway.

Her blankets were covered in a sunflower print. Glass figurines lined one of her shelves, and they caught the light and refracted it in prisms across the wall. The three shelves below were covered in trophies, medals, and sparkling crowns.

There was a stack of books on her desk, open notebooks and sticky notes spread across its messy surface. I tipped my head so I could read the spines, my eyes feeling too dry after having slept in my contacts. A book titled *Form, Space, and Order* had numerous multi-colored tabs sticking out from its pages, and most of the other titles looked like similar non-fiction. She had jars full of pencils and pens, and a small potted plant that looked like it was struggling to survive.

She sighed softly, squirming into a more comfortable position that pushed her closer against me. I curled around her, nuzzling my face against the back of her neck. She moved with me, her body shifting to twine with mine. She stretched her legs, her butt moving back to press right against me. My cock predictably twitched, swelling as she moved and slowly blinked her eyes.

"Good morning," she said, her voice husky with sleep. She sounded so sexy like that.

Kissing her neck, I moved slowly along her skin. She made little sounds, soft whimpers and gentle sighs, her body utterly limp as I turned her onto her back and slid under the covers.

I moved between her thighs and slid her panties down, tossing them out from under the blankets. She giggled sleepily as they flew across the room, then gasped when I trailed kisses up her thigh.

I loved the smell of her, the warmth, the softness of her skin as I closed my mouth over her. Her thighs tensed, squeezing around my head as I sucked on her clit. I took my time, savoring her, stroking my tongue over every fold. My cock was achingly hard, and I knew she was sore, but I also knew she liked the pain.

"Ah, Manson…" She fisted the sheets and shuddered as I focused on her clit. I pressed two fingers inside her, humming in appreciation when she cried out. I curled my fingers, her muscles contracting around me, throbbing as her sounds grew more desperate.

When she came, it was with a groan that made my entire body tingle. I lifted my head from her, pushing back the covers to kneel over her.

Her pupils were swollen, her eyes half-lidded. I reached down and grasped her beautiful face in my hands, relishing how pliant she felt. I was used to her fighting back, passionately resisting, relishing being overcome. But having her like this — soft and submissive, quiet and accepting — was an instant head rush.

"Are you sore?" I said, leaning over her to bring my mouth temptingly close. Her lips were parted, and I couldn't help myself — I stroked my fingers over her lower lip, then pressed two fingers into her mouth. She opened for me, lips and tongue so tender as I explored her.

When I withdrew my fingers and rubbed her clit, her back arched up off the mattress.

"I'm sore," she gasped. "But I don't care." She grasped my hips, tugging at the elastic band on my underwear. "Fuck me. Please."

Those words stunned me into silence for a moment. Goddamn it all, I was done for. If she tried to ghost again, I was certain I'd become one myself. I hurriedly tugged my briefs off, discarding them on the floor and crawling closer to her mouth.

"Get it wet for me," I said. My cock was rigidly hard as she opened her mouth, gazing up at me as her tongue stroked over me. I pressed into her throat, knotting my hand in her hair, holding myself there until she gagged, her eyes watering.

"Fuck, that's right. Choke on it." She didn't pull away, despite struggling to keep me so deep in her throat. I released her head after several long seconds, the tight pulsations of her throat feeling so damn good. But I repositioned myself between her thighs, knowing that her pussy would feel even better. "You sure you want it, angel? You must be aching."

Jason had been merciless, and I loved the thought of sinking into that sore cunt, fucking her until she came again despite the pain. But I needed her to want it. I needed her to crave suffering for me just as much as I craved her in return.

She lifted her hips, pressing toward me as she whispered, "Fuck me like you hate me, Manson. Make it hurt."

I had to pause, closing my eyes and inhaling slowly. When I opened them again, she was looking at me like she was on the verge of begging, nudging herself against me, her wide eyes pleading.

"Tell me that again, angel," I growled. "Tell me what you want."

"Fuck me." God, she was begging for it, her voice heavy with need. "Please, Manson. Fuck me hard. I want to struggle to take it."

"Yeah?" My brain was going to snap if she kept looking at me like that, drawing me in with her eyes. She reached for me, gripping her fingers around me and stroking me.

"Please," she said, like the anticipation alone was painful. "Fuck me, sir, please, please, please —"

I entered her hard, gripping her thighs and pressing them up so I could get a deeper angle. Her eyes went wide, grasping my arms as she cried out. Her nails dug in — I fucking loved those long, sharp nails — and I grinned at the sting, hunching over her as I fucked her.

"Is this what you want? Hm? You want it to hurt?" She nodded rapidly, her sleepiness now replaced with fierce endurance. It was impossible to look at her face without my balls tightening, warning me that my stamina was going to be short-lived.

"Fuck yes, hurt me…" Her voice broke on the words, and I nearly did too. "Harder…I want it harder…"

My mind was entirely engulfed by her, the feeling of her, the sounds. Her voice was contorted between pleasure and pain, and she cried out with every punishing thrust.

"Are you going to take whatever I give you?" She nodded again, whimpering as she did. "Then open your mouth."

She obeyed immediately, without even a moment of bratty hesitation. I spat, hitting her outstretched tongue, and she swallowed it down with a smile. I rubbed her clit, knowing I'd be lucky to last another sixty seconds, but I wanted to see that perfect ecstasy on her face one more time. She writhed beneath me as I crushed her into the mattress, her breath coming in tight gasps.

"That's it, angel. Come for me. Right now."

"Ah, fuck...Manson. Please —"

I cursed, my body shuddering and clenching as she throbbed on my cock. I came, pumping every last drop deep inside her as her eyes fluttered closed and she went limp.

I was barely able to hold myself up, but I didn't want to pull out yet. I liked that feeling of my dick plugging her, holding my cum inside her. With her pussy clenched around me and that smile on her face, all I could think about was how I couldn't let her go.

Ever.

I couldn't watch her walk away again. I couldn't see her disappear into a future that didn't have us in it. I couldn't handle her choosing to leave behind what she obviously craved.

I tried to catch my breath, mentally scolding myself for such completely ludicrous thoughts. I had to be able to live with this, *just* this. She was a temporary fixture in my life and I had to accept it. I'd have to let go, eventually. We'd have to say goodbye.

No. Fuck that. I couldn't live with it and I goddamn wouldn't.

I reached for her bedside table, grabbing some tissues for her before I pulled out so she wouldn't drip on the bed. She hissed softly as I slipped out of her before wiggling in contentment, pressing the tissues between her legs.

"Mm, it really is a good morning," she said. She looked over at me as I sat on the edge of the bed, tiredly running my fingers through my hair. "Thank you, sir." She giggled slightly after she said it. "Or should I say Master?"

"You better be careful about using that title," I said, unable to stop the smile on my face. "Otherwise I'm going to end up never letting you go."

What I didn't say was that title made me goddamn feral. As in, throw-her-over-my-shoulder, steal-her-away, and keep-her-locked-up-just-for-us *feral*.

"Maybe I wouldn't mind that," she said, and my heart felt like it glitched for a moment.

"I think you would." I curled my arm around her and dragged her closer, kissing her neck. "I think you'd mind if we stole you away and kept you as our little fucktoy forever. We'd fuck you like you want, punish you as you need, and have in you in our beds whenever we damn well please."

She shyly looked down. "I mean, that's kind of my ultimate fantasy."

"Wait…really?" She had to be joking with me. It was one of my deepest desires to relish complete and total control over a willing submissive, although maintaining a twenty-four-seven lifestyle of dominance and submission wasn't something I was quite ready for yet. I was only twenty-two and something like that was no joke; it required responsibility, patience, and far more time than I was currently able to give.

For now, the idea of a weekend getaway where the boys and I "kidnapped" our toy to have our way with her was a particularly tempting prospect.

"Tell me," I said, lying back down beside her. "I want the details."

"Oh, God," she groaned, covering her face with her hands. "I want you to take me away, Manson. Snatch me up, kidnap me, drive me out somewhere, and use me. Put me on my knees, make me serve you. Make me obey." She sighed as she lowered her hands, but the spark in her eyes was bright and eager. "Make me your slave again for a few nights. I don't want to think, I don't want to worry, I just want to let go."

Did she have any idea what those words did to me? How much they fueled me to make this happen? I leaned down, chastely kissing her mouth before I whispered, "I won't tell you when, or how, but we'll do it. We're going to fulfill that fantasy of yours, angel."

She got in the shower as I was leaving, lamenting that her parents were going to be back the next day.

"Knowing my mom, she'll probably smell that I had boys in the house," she said, with her arms around my neck after she'd kissed me goodbye. "Maybe it'll make her finally stop harassing me about getting a boyfriend."

Boyfriend. I wondered what it would take for her to call one of us by that word, if it was even a possibility or if I was truly a fool.

I pulled out my phone on the way downstairs and saw a text from Jason, asking if I could leave Jess's front door unlocked when I left.

I have some free time today so I'm going to do what I can about that security system, he wrote. **Her parents will probably be pissed if they come back and it's still broken.**

I left the door unlocked as he'd asked. It was already getting warm and sticky outside, but for once, I didn't mind. I felt good, better than I had in a long time. I started up the Mustang and sat for a moment while she warmed up, smiling at nothing as I hummed a tune.

Damn it. What the hell had she done to me?

I pulled out of her neighborhood with the windows down, playing Siouxsie and the Banshees loud as I headed toward home. Maybe I'd take the day off and insist Lucas do too. We'd been working too damn hard these past few weeks.

Then, just a little ahead of me on the side of the road, I spotted an old red Chevrolet truck.

My eyes locked on it as I passed. The windows were down; the cab was empty — I passed far too quickly and jerked my head back, swerving on the road as I tried to get a better look.

Fucking hell, that wasn't…that couldn't be…

I wrenched the wheel around; the tires squealing as I flipped a U-turn. I turned down the music as I pulled up behind the truck, staring at the license plate with a sickening feeling in my gut.

I recognized the plate. The dent in the rusted back bumper. The crack in the glass on the back windshield.

I stepped out of the car but left the engine running. My hands were suddenly cold, but sweat was dripping down my back. Every step felt slow and robotic as I walked toward the Chevy's driver side door. There was a roaring in my ears like a distant ocean, pulsing with the beat of my heart as I peered through the open window into the cab.

Ripped seats, ash all over the dash and a distinct odor of menthol cigarettes. I swallowed down my rising nausea as I realized the door was only partially closed, so I eased it open. The keys were gone, but there were black plastic bags on the passenger seat and in the bed of the truck, clothing and trash littering the floor.

And there, barely visible beneath the front seat, was a shotgun with the initials R.R. carved into the wooden stock.

Reagan Reed. My father was back.

I'd smoked through the last of my pack of cigarettes by the time Jason pulled up in front of Jess's house. I'd parked a little way down the road, so she wouldn't see me out the windows and come ask what I was doing.

Jason had already spotted me as he stepped out of the Z, walking over to tap on my window curiously.

"What's up?" he said as I cranked the glass down. "I thought you were going back home. Did you decide to go for round two?"

His jovial smile faded as I said, "My dad is back in town. I saw his fucking truck."

He didn't look nearly as surprised as he should have. He swore softly, awkwardly running his fingers through his hair as he said, "Where'd you see him?"

"The Chevy was parked along Route 15," I said, automatically reaching for my cigarette pack. I scoffed in disgust as I remembered it was empty, crumpling the pack in my hand before I threw it to the floor. "He wasn't there, and his keys were gone too. But all his stuff was in there. What the hell are you looking at me like that for?"

"Vincent was supposed to tell you," he said. "But he thought you might…"

"He thought I might *what*?" I snapped without meaning to, and Jason gripped my open window, leaning down as he looked at me.

"He wasn't trying to stress you out, okay?" he said. "He saw your dad when he and Jess went to Satin —"

"My father saw Vincent with Jess?"

I wrenched open my door and Jason stepped back. I was trying the best I could to keep myself calm, but fucking hell, Vince had known about this for *days* and hadn't said anything? Jason tried to start again, but I was speaking too fast as I paced.

"So the man who threatened to kill me, who swore he'd put me six feet under for taking *everything* from him, saw Vincent with Jess in public, and Vince decided to tell me fucking nothing?" I lowered my voice, anxiety gripping me so tight it was difficult to breathe. "Did he think Reagan wouldn't recognize him? After Vince came with me to every funeral arrangement, when he was right there in court with me? He knows exactly who Vincent is!"

My dad had challenged Mom's will before she was even in the ground. He hadn't bothered to come to the funeral or help with the planning. No, that was all me. Vincent had come to every awkward meeting, whether it was with the funeral director or the probate litigation attorney. He was the calm, optimistic presence

I'd needed when I was working through so much turmoil.

Dad didn't have the funds to pursue challenging the will in court. He'd shown up for one hearing and then vanished again, but not before making it clear to me that if he couldn't get what he wanted legally, he was willing to try other methods.

Namely, putting a bullet in my skull.

"Manson." Jason gripped my shoulders, the strength of his hold finally making me pause. "Deep breaths, man. It's okay. You're okay. Vincent was going to tell you, I know he was. He was just trying to figure out the right way to do it. Then with work, and Jess, and everything…he must have forgotten. I know he'll feel like shit that you found out like this."

I finally took a deep breath. I had to think logically here.

"Jess isn't going to mean anything to him," Jason said, his tone perfectly even. Reasonable. Calm. At least one of us was. "In his eyes, she's just some girl. He's not going to bother with her."

"We don't know that," I said, staring at her house. Her unlocked front door, her fucked-up security system…

As if he read my mind, Jason said quickly, "I'm going to go get her alarm fixed. You should head back to the house. Take the day off, relax…" I gave him a look, and he rolled his eyes. "Yeah, yeah, I know, you don't relax. But *try*. Get into Vincent's stash. He'll have something to calm you down."

I nodded, clasping his arm for a moment in thanks. I hadn't meant to get so upset, but it was hard to think clearly where my father was concerned. I hadn't heard a thing from him or seen any sign of him since Mom's funeral, and I would have preferred to keep it that way.

Hopefully, this was just a temporary thing. There was nothing left for him in Wickeston, and if he had any sense left in that rotten head, he'd move on again sooner rather than later.

His truck was gone when I drove past again, but it didn't make me feel any better.

37

JESSICA

I took an extra long shower that morning, savoring every drop of hot water on my aching body. I'd likely be walking stiffly for days, but the discomfort was weirdly satisfying.

It usually felt strange to have someone sleep by my side. I hadn't had anything that qualified as a "steady" relationship since sophomore year of college — and even that only lasted three months. I preferred to keep it short and sweet. The longer I was with someone, the more annoying they became.

But this was different. Sleeping next to Manson hadn't felt strange. It felt like coming home at the end of a long day and sinking into your favorite pillow, like a warm blanket on a cold night. I slept like a rock, and when I woke up and saw his hair all messy, his face soft with sleep…God, how could I resist him?

It made no sense that a man who was so unlike me made me feel so heard. So *seen*. The messy, uncertain side of me that he brought out felt more like the real me than anything else. It was the side of me that craved scary, unusual, vulnerable things. Things that felt too close for comfort, too real, too raw.

This little game of ours was far harder to play when my heart was determined not to follow my own rules.

The number one rule was to not get attached. The moment that happened, I'd be in trouble. I could already feel it and it was starting to freak me out, the little ways in which I found myself trying to get more time with them. Even when I wasn't fulfilling my "duties" as their toy, I still felt this pull to be around them.

I had to be careful. I had my own plans and I couldn't allow them to be spoiled now.

Jason hadn't told me what time he would be arriving, but when I stepped out of the bathroom, I could hear someone downstairs. My bedroom door was wide up and I walked out to peer over the railing into the entryway.

"Y'all really don't like to knock, do you?"

Jason looked up at me. He was seated in the open doorway with a laptop on his outstretched legs, his shaggy blue hair contained under a black baseball cap.

"Knocking feels like asking permission," he said. "And I wasn't asking."

Rolling my eyes, I turned away before he could see me smile. After hurriedly getting dressed, I came downstairs to find he was still sitting in the same spot, forehead creased with concentration as he stared at long lines of text on his screen.

"Do you want some coffee?" I said, peering at him through the doorway from the kitchen.

"I'm good," he said, holding up a neon green and black energy drink can.

"Ah, I see, you prefer to fuel yourself with straight battery acid." The coffee machine groaned and that delicious bitter bean juice began to drip. I added some sweet cream to my mug before I walked back to the entryway and sat down beside him. He was so focused on his screen it wasn't until I bumped against his shoulder that he flinched in surprise and looked over at me.

"I thought your screen would look like *The Matrix* or something," I said.

He chuckled, shaking his head. "There's a lot less floating neon symbols and a lot more math."

A minute in silence as I watched him, sipping my coffee. Math was one of my strongest subjects, but whatever he was doing didn't look like the math I was used to. He was speaking an entirely different language in those long lines of code.

"I'm almost done here. I just need to test one more time…"

He hit the Enter key and looked up at the alarm's control panel. The screen blinked, its message changing from ERROR to READY TO ARM.

"Damn, that was fast," I said. "What did you do?"

He cleared his throat awkwardly, getting to his feet. "I may have overengineered it a little."

"Meaning…?"

"I made a few changes," he said. "Made it a little more difficult for anyone else who decides to try to get in here." He shut the front door, went to the keypad, and typed in our code. The system chimed and the screen switched to ARMED.

"And how exactly do you know our pin?" I said. "I guess I shouldn't be surprised."

"You can change it after I leave," he said, glancing back at me. "Or don't."

"I'll change it," I said, pushing up to my feet. "Don't want to make things too easy for you."

"Brat." He scoffed as he disarmed the system again and disconnected his laptop. "Your parents shouldn't notice anything, although you may need to have them reconnect any key fobs they had for it. That's how I did it, by the way. Your key fob."

"You stole my key fob?"

"Nope, I intercepted the radio signal it sent to the security system," he said. "Most of these systems don't encrypt anything, so all the data I need is right there. Easy."

"Most people don't think that's very easy."

"I'm not most people." I was standing by his side, and when he turned toward me, he brushed his fingers over my neck, over the slight red line the collar had left on my skin. "Your parents come back tomorrow, yeah?"

"Unfortunately." The touch of his fingers gave me goosebumps over my arms, and I quickly rubbed them. "I'm sure my mom will find something to complain about the second she's in the door."

"She just got back from vacation," he said incredulously. "What could she have to complain about?"

"Anything and everything." He followed me into the kitchen,

leaning against the island when I took a seat on one of the stools. "Let's see. She'll complain that there's dishes in the sink, I ate all the cookies in the pantry, my nails need to be filled…"

He snorted. "Your mom gives a fuck about your nails?" Then he paused, looking off in thought. "Then again, my mom was always scolding me over wrinkles in my shirts."

I'd seen his mom a few times when she'd drop him off at school. Where my mom did everything she could to be the glamorous center of attention, Mrs. Roth had seemed more like she was trying to blend in with the local retirement community. *Uptight* had been her entire vibe and that had reflected in her son — at least, it used to.

Uptight was far from how I'd describe him now. *Intense* was a far more accurate word.

"It sounds to me like you need to get out of the house tomorrow," he said, finishing off his energy drink and tossing the can into the trash. "I have a competition at the Fairgrounds Speedway. You should come."

"Competition? Like drag racing?"

"Drifting," he said, meandering around the kitchen as he talked. "You've probably seen some videos Vincent posted."

I hurriedly sipped my coffee so he wouldn't see my guilty face. He couldn't possibly know how hard I used to stalk their social media, could he? But he was smirking at me as I lowered the mug, and I said, "Is this an invitation, or an order?"

"Let's say…an invitation you can't refuse," he said. "We'll pick you up in the morning."

I *did* want to get out of the house. But holy shit, having them show up here to pick me up meant having my mom see them. If she didn't already have plenty to complain about, she definitely would then.

But I couldn't always cater my life to my mother.

"All right," I said, bracing my elbows on the island and leaning forward toward him. "As long as I don't have to dress as a cat again."

Despite my misgivings, my mom was in a good mood when she and my dad got back the next morning. She was sunburned as a lobster, but that only made her cheerier as she gushed about how tan she was going to be.

But of course, all that cheeriness flew straight out the window when she spotted my ride arrive.

I'd warned my parents I was going to be spending the day with friends, but I hadn't specified *which* friends.

"Jessica!" Mom hissed my name as she marched into my room. I was in front of the mirror, blending out my eyeshadow as she came over to me and perched one hand on her hip. "Who did you invite over here?"

"It's just my ride," I said, putting away my palette and brushes. Loud music was thumping from outside, and I wondered whose car it was, my stomach light with excitement. I didn't know what to expect from today, but I was looking forward to seeing something new.

But mostly, I was excited to spend all day with the four men who'd been consistently blowing my mind for the last couple of weeks. The Fairgrounds were about an hour's drive away from us, which meant I didn't even have to worry about bumping into anyone who knew me.

It would be the first time I was going out in public with all four of them. The idea was as intimidating as it was thrilling.

I had to deal with Mom's judgment first though, and she was not pleased.

"No, absolutely not." Mom shook her head, her lips pursed as she turned on her heel. Her feet pounded down the hallway as she called back to me, "I wasn't born yesterday, Jessica."

The doorbell rang, and I hurriedly grabbed my bag, going down the stairs two at a time. "I'll get it!"

"No, no, I think your father should get it," Mom said sharply. She was standing in the entryway between me and the door, glaring into the kitchen where my dad sat at the table with his e-reader and a coffee. "Roger. Roger!" She snapped her fingers, and my dad turned his head, tipping down his glasses as he looked at her. "There's a strange man at the door. Answer it!"

"Oh my God, he's not a strange man," I said. "Everything is fine, Dad. You don't need to get the door."

"Mm-hm, I thought so," he said, turning back to his book with an exhausted sigh. Mom looked absolutely exasperated. I headed for the door, but right as I reached for the knob, she barreled ahead of me and opened it.

If Lucas was surprised to see my mom, he certainly didn't show it. He was standing back from the door, his hands shoved into his pockets as Mom stared him down. He was wearing ragged denim jeans and boots laced up to his knees, his tattoo-covered arms bare. He was the furthest thing from "parent friendly" possible.

It was strangely satisfying knowing Mom was horrified and

there was really nothing she could do about it.

"Can I help you?" she said in the kind of icy tone that usually sent people running for the hills. I tried to mouth, *Sorry!* to Lucas from over her shoulder, but I don't think he caught it. The Bronco, El Camino, and the Z were all parked along the curb, making quite an entourage for them merely being "my ride."

Mom wasn't buying it; I could see it on her face.

"Morning, ma'am. I don't think we've formally met. I'm Lucas Bent, a friend of Jessica's."

My mouth dropped open. Holy shit, what version of Lucas was this? He sounded *polite*. If it weren't for the massive boots and tattoos, Mom may have actually thought his soft drawl was charming. Apparently he could clean up that dirty mouth of his after all.

But Mom regarded him like he was a bag of flaming dog shit discarded on her doorstep. "I know who you are. What exactly are your intentions with my daughter?"

Okay, now was the time to intervene. I gently grabbed her arm, ushering her back from the door so I could squeeze past her.

"Mom, that's enough, seriously, I'll take it from here," I said. If she hadn't cared so much about what the neighbors would think, she probably would have yelled at me right there on the front porch. I was shocked that fire didn't shoot out of her eyeballs as I slipped out the door, waving to her as I said, "I'll be fine. I'll text you on the way home."

Her mouth was pressed into a thin line of fury. "We are not done with this discussion," she said, jabbing her finger at me as I grabbed Lucas's wrist and hauled him down the sidewalk.

"Pleasure to meet you," he said, and the door abruptly slammed.

"Sorry," I said, grimacing up at him. "She's uh...protective."

"I don't blame her," he said, his voice returning to its usual gruffness. He yanked me back to him, obviously not pleased that I was currently the one dragging him along, and put his arm around my waist to keep me close. "She has good instincts for trouble."

The Bronco was parked in front of the El Camino along the curb, with Vincent in the driver's seat and Jason beside him. A flatbed trailer was hooked up to the Bronco with the Z secured on top of it, its wheels strapped into place. Music was playing loudly from inside the cab as Jason rolled down the window and whistled at me.

"Damn, look at those legs," he said, leering out the window at me in my tiny denim shorts. Manson was leaning against the back bumper of the El Camino, and he stubbed out his cigarette as Lucas and I came down the driveway.

"Hey, Jess." His smile made my stomach flutter as he came to greet me. I anticipated a kiss, and was caught by surprise when he hugged me and nothing more. But he was thinking clearer than I was. My mom was undoubtedly watching us from one of the windows, and if she saw a kiss, I was never going to hear the end of it.

But I didn't *like* that he felt as if he had to hold back from kissing me. I didn't like it at all.

"Have you ever seen this guy try so hard to be polite?" I said, giving Lucas a teasing poke as Manson and I separated. "I had no idea there was such a good boy in there."

Manson laughed, and to my surprise, Lucas stopped me before I could open the passenger door. He made a face as he opened it himself, waiting expectantly as I stared.

"Well? Sit your ass down," he said, when I didn't move. I certainly hadn't thought he'd opened that door *for* me. I blinked rapidly in surprise, lowering myself into the passenger seat as I narrowed my eyes at him.

"Are you...are you *blushing*, Lucas?" I couldn't believe it. It had to be a trick of the light or something because there was no way his face was red right now. He scowled deeply, waiting for Manson to sit down in the passenger seat before he slammed the door and stomped around to the driver's side.

"He was blushing, right?" I whispered quickly. "Don't tell me I imagined that."

Manson laughed again. "Careful, Jess. Getting Lucas flustered is risky business."

"I don't even know how I flustered him!" I said, but then it was too late to discuss any further, as Lucas wrenched open his door and got into the driver's seat.

He cranked the engine to life, shaking his head as I kept staring at him. "It's a hot day out, fucktoy, so you can stop gaping at my face being a little red. Here." He handed me the auxiliary cord connected to his radio. "You pick the music."

38

LUCAS

Wretched biological mechanisms giving me away. I would have rather bled out than have my face go red, but there I was, hot and bothered, as Jess's clever little brain tried to work out what she'd done to cause it.

I'd be damned if she figured this one out. Manson would be too, because it was all his fault.

We had about an hour of driving ahead of us, and since we were towing the Z, we couldn't simply haul ass to get there. Still, I couldn't resist pushing the El Camino a bit. I raced ahead of the Bronco, swerving around the slower cars in my path. Every time I picked up speed, Jess's smile widened. I had a radar detector on the dash so I wasn't worried about cops, and pushed my speed even more to see what she would do.

The sudden acceleration caught her by surprise, and her hand darted out to clench around my thigh. She had a new color on those pointy claws of hers, the same deep purple as Manson's Mustang. I had to wonder if she'd done it on purpose.

I slowed down, and Jess sighed softly as she settled back into her seat, staring out the window at the open fields. She moved her hand away from me, but I reached over and brought it back, leaving my hand on top of hers as it rested on my leg.

"You haven't run away from us yet," I said, glancing at her to try to gauge the reaction on her face. "Enjoying yourself a little too much?"

"Of course I haven't run away. I still need my ride back," she said, as if that was the only reason in the world. "Maybe I should have you guys give me a little speed boost too."

"That sounds like trouble," Manson said. "We need to work on getting you to change your oil on time before we move on to giving you any extra acceleration."

"Ugh, boring," she groaned. "I want a fast car too."

I barked out a harsh laugh. "Already trying to add on more to your debt? That would *definitely* cost more than you can afford."

Her fingers squeezed slightly around my thigh. "Are you sure about that?"

If this little vixen wasn't careful, we were never going to make it to the damn speedway, because I'd be pulled over on some back road, fucking her silly. I glanced over at Manson, but he was too busy staring at Jess's ass nudged against his side to be paying attention.

"What do you need more speed for?" I said, my cock rising to the occasion far too eagerly. "You trying to start racing too?"

"No. I just like going fast," she said. "Although I wouldn't mind getting to beat you in a race."

"Not a chance of that. Not with that BMW, no fucking way."

She gave me a saucy smile. "Sounds to me like you're scared of me winning. Don't you think he sounds scared, Manson?"

This time, Manson caught my eye. Our little toy was feeling feisty today, and I could see from his face how much he enjoyed it. He leaned closer to her, warning her, "I think he sounds like he's about to spank your ass if you don't start behaving."

"You need to occupy that bratty mouth of yours before it gets you in trouble," I said.

Her hand tightened on me, and then her other hand came to join it. She pushed up the hem of my shirt, tracing her finger along my belt buckle.

"How should I do that, sir?" she said. She didn't fool me with that sweet, simpering tone. I didn't need to look at Manson again to know he was excited, eager for us to put on a show. I was happy to give him some entertainment.

I adjusted my position, pulling open my belt one-handed as I said, "You know what to do, girl."

I was nearly choking on those words in a moment, because goddamn, she *really* knew what to do. After twenty seconds with my cock in her mouth, I was seriously regretting that I had to watch the road instead of her. Manson was the lucky one, and he leaned against the door with one leg up on the seat as he observed her, smirking all the while.

"Record her," I said, bracing myself for a moment when she moaned around me in her throat. Manson pulled out his phone, giving Jess's ass a squeeze as he recorded her. "I'm going to watch this back later, Jess. I want to see how sexy you look gagging on my dick."

She was using her mouth and her hand in unison, taking her time as she bobbed her head on me. She buried me in her throat, then popped me from her mouth as she said, "The piercing feels funny in my throat. I like it."

She took me down again, and I clenched the wheel until my fingers ached. Having Manson watch made it even better, and knowing it got him hard made me salivate with the want for a taste of him.

Jess probed at my jewelry with her tongue, causing the curved bar to move back and forth. It took considerable effort not to moan as she did that, but she must have noticed something because the next time she lifted her head, she said, "Do you like that? When I play with it?"

"Yeah." My voice came out as a tightly restrained snarl. "It feels good when you move it around. And when it's in your throat..." I pushed her head back down, resting my hand on the back of her neck.

"Such a good girl, Jess," Manson said, his hand rubbing between her legs. "Make him feel good." She moaned on me again, and my foot jerked on the gas. It took every shred of self-control to remain focused despite what she was doing.

The road was hazy — but the things she was doing with her mouth, hand, and tongue were perfectly vivid. It was shocking that we made it to the speedway in one piece, because I couldn't remember the rest of the drive if my life depended on it.

The second I parked in the large lot outside the Fairgrounds Speedway, I clenched my hands around the back of my seat and closed my eyes, head tipped back as she finished me off. Manson was praising her, and she was grinding down on his palm for pleasure. The sound that came out of me as I spilled in her mouth was more animal than human, and for a moment, I swore I felt my soul leave my body.

"Fucking hell…" I exhaled slowly as I opened my eyes, just in time to see her swallow.

She wanted a fast car? I'd fucking give her a fast car. What else did she want? Makeup? Jewelry? Clothes? A goddamn kitten? I'd give her that too.

Manson snapped me out of my foolish thoughts. Still recording with one hand, he flipped her over with the other. Jess's head was in my lap, right next to my cock, with her eyes wide and slightly dazed as Manson moved over her.

"Get her shorts down," he said, and I helped him do it, tugging them open so he could pull them off of her. I was still trying to catch my breath when he entered her, his cock stretching her pussy in a way I could only describe as stunningly sexy. She groaned, her eyes rolling back as he fucked into her. I held her legs up for him, keeping her spread.

"Fuck, that's going to make me come," she gasped. I couldn't decide which of them I wanted to watch more, as Jess's face softened with pleasure and Manson's grew harder.

They both knew how to get under my skin, how to rip me apart from the inside out and make me like it. I expected that from Manson, but her? How the hell could she read me so well?

How did she figure out the little things that drove me wild? I could always feel her watching me when she was near, but it was like she was reaching into my soul, taking a casual look around, and figuring out exactly what made me tick.

She made me feel like I was going to fucking lose it, even more than usual.

Her eyes squeezed shut as she came, and I was right there to see every expression as she fell apart. Manson braced his hand against the window next to my head, fucking her until he shuddered and came inside her with a groan. We'd watched each other fuck before, but God, there was something about seeing him with *her*.

There was something about the way she looked at him, and how manically enraptured he was with her. Was this how he felt when he watched us? I'd never fully understood the voyeur thing, but I didn't have his level of self-control. I could hardly bear to watch without participating, while he got off on exactly that.

He eased out of her, catching his breath for a moment before he leaned back and took her with him. He turned her around, so her back was against his chest and her legs were splayed open on the seat, facing me.

"Eat her," he said, his voice still rough.

Even having just orgasmed, those words riled me up all over again. I leaned forward, not giving a fuck about anyone else who happened to be in the parking lot around us. They could damn well look away if they didn't like it. Jess tasted amazing with Manson's cum dripping out of her. Every time I stroked my tongue over her clit, she bucked up against my mouth.

"Tell him how it feels," Manson said as her beautiful green eyes stared down at me between her legs. I wanted to feel her come again. I wanted her thighs to squeeze around my head as her body convulsed with pleasure.

"Your tongue feels so good," she moaned, wiggling against me and grinding on my mouth. Manson's hand pressed down on the back of my head, encouraging me to keep going. "Oh God, Lucas, yes…"

I pressed my tongue into her, savoring the taste of Manson inside her and her desperate little cries. She shuddered, thighs tightening. She clenched them around my head, and I lost myself in the moment. Who could care about oxygen when her pussy tasted so fucking good and she sounded like that — so sweet and helpless and full of need.

I barely lifted my head, licking the taste of her off my lips. Manson watched me, his eyes narrowed with sadistic glee as he murmured to her, "Tell him he's a good boy."

He grinned at me like he knew how wicked it was to tell her that. Sadistic fuck. But I still shuddered when her soft lips formed the words, "Mm, good boy."

My fingers dug into her thighs, my teeth bared as I loomed over her. Crushed between Manson and I, she looked vulnerable but also far too clever. She knew exactly how to get what she wanted, and we knew exactly how to deliver.

"You'd better be very careful using those words with me," I said, and she nodded rapidly, her pupils dilating.

"I'll be careful, sir," she said, but there was mischief in her eyes.

I tucked myself away and gathered my things, stuffing my

wallet and keys into my pocket. I had no idea what expression was fixed on my face, but Jess giggled in a way that betrayed both fear and excitement before she stepped out of the car after Manson, slinging her bag over her shoulder.

I didn't know if I wanted to spank her or fucking kiss her again.

Probably both.

Definitely both.

Jess walked ahead of us as we made our way to check in. The Fairgrounds Speedway was surrounded by trees on all sides, with a convention building at the forefront of the property that held merch and concession booths. Beyond that, the track occupied the rest of the property, with bleachers overlooking it. Vincent and Jason had driven the Bronco down to the pit, a curved expanse of asphalt right next to the track, where all the drivers and their crews were gathered to prepare for the day's competition.

The warm air was tinged with the scent of burned rubber and cigarettes, and I took a deep breath. I didn't feel comfortable in many places, but I was comfortable here. It was my home away from home, but we weren't only there for moral support; Jason needed mechanics to ensure the Z made it through the day. Drifting was hard on a car, and without maintenance, the Z wouldn't last past the qualifying rounds. We had our equipment in the back of the Bronco; tools and any necessary items for repairs. If something went wrong on the track, we had to fix it quickly or forfeit the competition.

"Amazing that you can scowl after a blow job like that," Manson said, walking beside me. Jess was far enough ahead of us not to overhear — or so it would seem. But I could have sworn I saw her head turn slightly toward us, trying to listen in.

She was too clever. Too observant.

Manson slung his arm around my shoulders, pulling me toward him and kissing me. He was in a good mood today; in fact, he'd been in a great mood ever since he spent the night at her house.

"I think she knows how to play the game too well," I said, when he pulled back but left his arm around me. "You're already getting too attached."

His smile faltered, but only for a moment. "She may know how to play, but we made the rules. Have fun with her. She plays to win, you know that. The more you challenge her, the more she'll push back."

Goddamn it, but that was what I was afraid of. I couldn't resist competition either, so when Jess pushed back, I pushed harder. It was a cycle that I couldn't see ending in anything other than an explosion.

And maybe that was how this whole thing was destined to go down anyway. A fierce competition to a fiery finish. I just didn't know how many of us would get destroyed along the way.

39

JESSICA

The moment I stepped into the pit, I was surprised
at the amount of noise and activity all around me.
Some groups were assembling canopies to cover their
work area, while others were simply arranging their tools and
supplies in front of their trailers. There was a plethora of cars,
some models I recognized and some that looked too strange to
be from any manufacturer I knew of. They were built light and
low to the ground, their interiors gutted down to bare metal.
Manson explained that it made the car lighter, faster, and easier
to maneuver.

Like Jason's Z, these cars weren't built for comfort; they were
built for performance.

The vibe was overwhelmingly positive. Multiple people

greeted the boys as they passed us by, some drivers stopping to chat. I kept out of the way, perching myself in the front seat of the Bronco with the door open and my feet propped up in the open window. I could watch the action from there, eating a corn dog Vincent had bought me from inside.

The excitement in the air reminded me of the energy of a pep rally before a big game. Except I didn't see any animosity from the various drivers, despite them all being about to compete against each other. I saw lots of people smiling and laughing, playing music on portable Bluetooth speakers. Some of the drivers had even brought their families along.

Jason appeared in the Bronco's open door, leaning against the frame as he smiled at me. He was wearing a black jumpsuit, the style of it reminding me of a certain Halloween party and the costume he wore that night. I remembered him zipping it down while I was on my knees, revealing his brightly tattooed chest and stroking his thick cock in front of me.

Oooh, I did not need to be thinking about his dick right now. My panties were wet enough.

I was still so uncomfortably turned on from that blow job. I didn't know why Lucas tried so damn hard to pretend he didn't enjoy anything. It made me want to rattle that hard-ass exterior and get into his head. Maybe my discovery of his little kink would enable me to do that.

Who would have thought that big bad Lucas wanted to be called a good boy? The thought filled me with wicked glee.

"Some of the guys are about to do a few practice runs," Jason said, grasping my outstretched leg. I was wearing denim shorts today so my skin was bare, and he turned his head to kiss my ankle, keeping his sharp blue eyes on me as he did. "Want to watch?"

Unsure of what exactly I was about to see, I nodded. He walked with me to the front of the Bronco and helped me climb up, sitting beside me on the hood with our feet resting on the bumper. A chain-link fence and a low embankment separated the pit from the track beyond. It was a wide, vaguely oval-shaped expanse of asphalt, marked with white paint and orange traffic cones. On the side closest to us, a curved road led out of the pit and onto the track, leading toward a starting line. A pole with a series of yellow, green, and red lights was affixed into the ground just beside the line.

An older, deep gray BMW pulled up to the starting line, and Jason leaned closer to me as he explained, "The drivers will be judged on three things: line, angle, and style. The line has to do with how the car is positioned. See those squares and diagonal lines on the track? Those are inside clips and fill zones. We're required to get our front or back bumpers into those zones as we move through the track."

He pointed them out, white squares and lines positioned either on the inside of tight turns or around the edges of the wide one. Suddenly, with a massive roar that made me clap my hands over my ears, the old BMW flew from the starting line and onto the course. Clouds of thick white smoke poured from its tires as it slid into the first turn, its back bumper gliding through the painted zone that curved along the first wall.

"We're judged on angle," Jason shouted over the engine's blaring scream. "See when he turns, how smooth it looks? His car isn't wobbling around, he isn't overcorrecting his steering. Last is style. The judges will look at how you initiate going into the first turn, and how well you transition through the course."

The driver sped through the course in mere seconds, leaving clouds of smoke and the aroma of burning rubber drifting through the air. The noise and speed were stunning, and I watched with rapt attention as more drivers lined up to practice.

"They're going so fast," I said. "It's amazing they don't crash."

"It takes a lot of practice," Jason said, giving me a toothy grin. "I'm going to get in a few rounds of my own before the competition starts." He leaned closer, his eyes flickering down to my lips. "Will you be cheering for me?"

I scrunched up my mouth in thought, as if it was even a question. "I don't know...That driver over there in the Corvette is pretty cute..." His eyes flashed dangerously, and I laughed, kissing him. "Of course I'll be cheering for you. You'd better win."

"I'm not going to lose against a fucking Corvette, that's for sure," he said, excitement in his voice as he slid down from the Bronco and headed toward his car. But he gave me one last wink over his shoulder before he got into the driver's seat. "I'll win just for you, princess."

The stands had filled, crowds gathering along the fence for a better view of the action as the first segment of the competition began. Lucas and Manson had come equipped with tools, extra parts, and even spare tires. Our area of the pit was set up like a miniature version of their garage.

"Excited?" Vincent said, coming to join me on my perch atop the Bronco. It was the perfect spot to watch the action, and was partially shaded from the sun by the canopy the men had assembled to work underneath.

"Very," I said. Jason was about to start his first official run through the course, and nerves were making my hands sweat. I couldn't remember the last time I'd felt so anxiously invested on someone else's behalf. I'd really meant it when I'd said I wanted him to win today. "I wasn't sure what to expect, but all these drivers seem so good."

"Believe it or not, this isn't even a professional-level competition," Vincent said. "All these drivers are considered amateurs."

"What?" I looked at him in disbelief. "Holy shit, I can't imagine what the pros are like, then!"

"Their cars are a hell of a lot louder, for one," he said, reaching into his pocket. "Speaking of which, I was supposed to give you these." I held out my hand, and he dropped a pair of plastic earbuds into them. "They're earplugs. They'll block out the worst of the noise, but you'll still be able to hear conversations up close. Try them out if you like. It can get pretty loud."

There was something exciting about the noise though, so I left out the earplugs for the time being. When Jason moved up to the starting line and revved his engine, burning out his tires and spewing clouds of smoke, I loved feeling the rumble of the engine through my limbs and how the deep sound reverberated in my chest.

When he shot forward from the starting line, I couldn't look away. I held my breath as he entered the first curve, his car sliding sideways as his back tires stayed perfectly within the lined zone along the wall. The next turn required him to wrench his wheel in the opposite direction, changing the angle of his slide. As he came into the last turn, I could barely see him through the smoke, so I balanced myself on the Bronco's front bumper as I tried to see.

He came flying out of the cloud, swerving through the final turn. The audience cheered, the metallic voice of the announcer calling the run "impressive."

Impressive wasn't a good enough word for it. It was incredible, heart-stopping. To control a vehicle going at those speeds through turns like that was stunning.

Jason went again, and this time, his driving was even faster and tighter. I was too enthralled by the excitement of it all to realize he'd hit every mark he was required to until Vincent pumped his fist victoriously.

"He's on it today," Manson said, smiling proudly as Jason slowly drove the Z around the backside of the track and back toward the pit.

"Heading for first, baby, I can feel it!" Vincent said excitedly, clapping his hands as Jason backed the Z under the canopy.

"You'll get into the Top 32 for sure, man," Lucas said, offering Jason his hand to pull himself out of the car. He pulled off his helmet, smiling widely as he shook his hair out of his face. Lucas and Manson were immediately getting down to business, opening the hood and beginning the process of replacing the tires.

"How's she driving out there?" Manson said, pulling on his gloves.

"Might be running a little rich. I was idling rough after the first run," Jason said, unzipping his jumpsuit as he stood in the shade. He poured half a bottle of water over his head, and the liquid dripped down his chest. I used a pamphlet I'd found like a fan, waving it to help cool him down. The sun was out in full force today; he was probably sweating his balls off in that jumpsuit.

The announcer gave Jason's final score, and Vincent cheered again. "Ninety-three!" he exclaimed, shaking Jason's shoulders in his excitement as the smaller man laughed. "I knew you fucking killed it out there."

With the top half of his jumpsuit tied around his waist, Jason came over to rest beside me in the shade. They were selling beers inside and Vincent had gotten one for me, although none of the men were drinking. But I was having a great time, sipping an ice-cold beer and watching the competition.

"Rub that on my back, would you?" Jason said, leaning against the hood as I ran the cold aluminum can over his shoulders. He shivered in contentment, sighing as he closed his eyes. "It's hot as fuck in that car."

"You were amazing to watch out there," I said, my breath hitching for a moment when he opened his eyes. I didn't think I would ever quite get used to how blue they were. "What happens now?"

"I qualified for the next stage of competition," he said, humming gratefully when I slid the can down his back. "Next up is tandem drifting."

"Tandem? What's that?"

"You'll see. I'd hate to spoil the surprise for you." He straightened, the two of us watching Lucas and Manson work. Vincent had brought a small speaker along and Manson had his phone hooked up to it, playing "Hunting Season" by Ice Nine Kills. It was the first time I'd watched him and Lucas working together, and it was clear how practiced they were. It was like they could read each other's minds, grabbing tools for each other before a single word had been said.

At one point, as they both fiddled with something under the hood, Manson leaned close and whispered in Lucas's ear. Lucas looked up at him with wide eyes, freezing for a moment before he shook his head and scoffed, his face reddening. I had no idea what had been said, but it still made me smile.

"What are you grinning about?" Jason said, resting his arm on my thighs.

"Just watching you guys," I said, leaning back on my hands. "It makes me feel happy when Manson and Lucas flirt with each other, or you and Vincent…I don't know, it's nice to see. I'm not sure if I can explain it."

"Sounds like compersion," he said. "It's when you feel happy for someone else's happiness. Like when Vincent flirts with you, I know he's enjoying himself and enjoying your company. So it makes me happy."

"I had no idea there was a word for that," I said. "It's like the opposite of jealousy."

"Yeah, it's like that. Finding joy in other people's joy. That's part of why the four of us get along so well. We really want to see each other happy."

This was something I'd never experienced before. Having a partner flirt with anyone besides myself had always been a threat, not something to be joyful over. But this was different. It genuinely did make me feel happy to see their closeness to each other, or to see how absolutely hyped Vincent was as Jason prepared for the next phase of the competition to start.

"You've got this, babe. Easy shit," he said, hugging Jason close. Jason zipped back up his suit and pulled on his gloves, flexing his fingers. But before he put his helmet on, he came over to me again and cupped my face, leaving me with a long, slow kiss that made my knees weak.

"Good luck," I said.

"I told you I'd win for you," he said. "I still plan on doing that."

The drivers lined up for the next phase of competition, but this time, they were paired together. Two drivers came up simultaneously to the line, and I frowned in confusion.

"Are they racing?" I said, and Lucas shook his head. "Then what—"

The lights blinked and the cars flew forward, one pulling ahead of the other as they came up on the first turn. To my complete shock, the two cars drifted through the curve side by side. Tires squealing, engines rumbling, the two vehicles skidded within inches of each other before switching up their angle and flying into the next turn.

"No fucking way…" I said, eyes wide as I leaned forward on the hood, staring in disbelief. "Are they on a team together? How the hell aren't they crashing into each other?"

"Same way they aren't crashing into the walls," Lucas said. "They'll switch off for the next run, and the other car will lead instead."

"You're telling me they haven't practiced with each other? Like those two drivers haven't worked together before?" It was hard to believe something so flawlessly, terrifyingly smooth could possibly have been done without hours of practicing together to get it right.

"They may have competed against each other before," Lucas said. "But drivers are paired up according to their scores in the qualifying runs, so they couldn't know ahead of time who they'd be paired with." He glanced back at me, his cigarette dangling from his lips. "They're just that good. You may see a few drivers tap each other, or even crash, but they're here for a reason. They're really damn skilled, and Jason's one of the best."

He sounded proud, the words not leaving even a shadow of a doubt that Jason was going to win. But my heart still hammered as the white Z pulled up to the starting line. I stood up on the bumper again to try to get a better view, but this time, Vincent noticed and came over to me, squatting down in front of me.

"Get on my shoulders," he said. "We'll go to the fence."

I climbed on, wavering for a moment when he stood up. Holy *shit*, he was tall. He walked with me over to the fence, giving me a perfect view of the competition. Manson and Lucas came up alongside us, and together, we watched the lights flash, counting down to the start.

Jason and the other driver rocketed from the starting line. I cheered as they whipped through the turns, Jason chasing the car in the lead. He stayed so close, I couldn't understand how they didn't collide when the vehicles changed their angle and their tires screamed, leaving long streaks of black rubber on the track.

"Fuck yes, that was good," Vincent said, leaning closer to the fence. The only thing I had to hold on to up there was his head, so my fingers were tangled in his long hair. But he didn't seem to mind at all. "That was a really solid run."

The two cars went again, with Jason in the lead this time. But his opponent faltered behind, struggling to keep up with Jason's speed and securing him the win.

The competition was whittled down from thirty-two drivers to sixteen, then eight, and finally down to only four drivers remaining. Manson and Lucas worked quickly in between runs, changing tires and refueling as Jason cooled off in the shade. He hadn't eaten a thing all day, but when I offered him some fries, he just bounced on his feet, shaking his head.

"Can't eat, too excited," he said. He was absolutely thriving here, all smiles as he zipped up for the next run.

Jason remained solidly consistent through every match-up, even when the lead driver in his last run lost control and spun out, swerving across the asphalt in front of him. He had to move quickly to avoid them, and my heart was in my throat as he executed the remainder of the course alone. His opponent was eliminated, and the competition had come down to the final two drivers.

Jason and the driver of the old gray BMW I'd watched practice when we first arrived.

Anxious energy vibrated through me as I sat on Vincent's shoulders, waiting for them to begin. Lucas was pacing along the fence, and Manson had his arm braced against the wire, his foot tapping rapidly as he watched.

The first run started, with Jason chasing the other driver. His opponent's car was clearly powerful, pulling ahead of him at first. But he readjusted and closed the gap. The two cars were impossibly in sync, as if they were controlled by the same person as they flew through the course. My throat was raw from cheering so loud, but I couldn't contain my excitement as they finished and lined up for the final run.

"Trying to pull my hair out, Jess?" Vincent said, and I hurriedly loosened my frantic grip on his hair.

"Sorry, I'm really excited," I said, and he laughed, giving my leg a squeeze as it dangled over his shoulder.

"You can pull as much as you want," he said. "I don't mind."

It was a good thing he didn't, because as soon as Jason's tires touched the starting line again, I was right back to gripping his hair. When the Z launched forward, I was screaming at the top of my lungs.

I was no expert by any means, but from my viewpoint, Jason made it through the course without any flaw. The crowd erupted into cheers; the announcer claiming that the run was stunningly close. Manson was smiling wide, giving a high-five to Lucas and clasping his hand. Vincent squeezed my legs. Everyone's excitement was palpable in the air as Jason drove back into the pit to join us.

Vincent let me down from his shoulders, and the moment Jason stepped out of the driver's seat, I flung my arms around him. He lifted me completely off my feet, holding me with just one arm as he pulled his helmet off with the other.

"That was amazing!" I exclaimed, breathless as I kissed him. He put me back on my feet, but kept his arm gripped around my waist as Vincent kissed him.

"You nailed that," Vincent said, smiling wide. "That was a

first-place run, no doubt about it."

"We don't know that yet," Jason said, but I could see the hope on his face. He knew he'd done well, but he reserved celebrating until everyone had gathered at the podium in front of the stands. The day had flown by and the sun was now set, the track's massive overhead lights illuminating the podium as the announcer introduced the third-place winner before turning his attention to the final two drivers.

"We had a very close run between our two top drivers today. I know it came down to the details for our judges." As the crowd's cheering for both drivers settled down, I stood between Vincent and Manson, waiting with bated breath. "But there can only be one winner, and I've got the final scores from the judges here. First place is…"

I was practically crushing Manson's hand in anticipation.

"Jason Roth!"

The crowd erupted, but I could barely hear them over my own cheering and the excited yelling from the boys as Jason accepted his trophy from the announcer. We surrounded him the moment he stepped off the podium, other drivers coming up to congratulate him and shake his hand.

It was the first time I'd seen them all look truly, unabashedly joyful. This was their world, this was where they found happiness. And they'd invited me into that, they'd brought me to share in their joy.

As it turned out, the things they loved made me happy too.

40

JESSICA

Everything felt perfect…at least, it did until the next day.

We stayed out late that night, the five of us stopping for dinner at a nearby bar and grill to celebrate Jason's victory. Vincent bought him a shot, then I did, and we kept going until we'd gotten Jason completely blasted.

I'd been a little tipsy myself by the time we left, but I could remember Jason grabbing me before he got into the Bronco, slurring slightly when he said, "You know, you're beautiful…so fucking beautiful…most beautiful woman I've ever seen. I'm so glad you came."

Those words had stayed with me long after they'd dropped me off at home, sitting like a little ball of light within me. Something had changed yesterday, something important. I wasn't sure what it meant, but it made me feel more hopeful than I had in a long time.

Except now, I had to deal with my mother.

"This is unacceptable, Jessica, do you hear me? Unacceptable!"

She had started on me first thing in the morning. I'd managed to fend her off during work, but now that I was done, she'd launched straight back into her tirade. Telling her the boys were "just friends" had done nothing other than make her start lamenting my terrible taste in friends and how my "standards" had fallen so low.

"You have friends," she insisted. "Friends who aren't criminals, who aren't trying to take advantage of a beautiful young woman."

My sister had already fled the scene, and even my dad had quietly crept away, probably to hide in his office. Cowards. Why was I always expected to be the bigger person here, to deal with this by myself?

"Whatever happened to Danielle?" Mom said, her eyes wide as she looked at me from her big cushy chair in the living room. "Or Candace, or Vanessa?"

"Vanessa moved to Kentucky," I said, purposefully avoiding discussing the other two women she'd mentioned. "Look, I know you don't like them, and you don't have to. But they're not dangerous. Don't act like I'm some naïve little girl."

"Oh, honey, that's exactly what you're acting like." She had her wine glass cupped between her fingers, and she took a large sip before she said, "You know better than this. You used to tell me those boys were creeps, that they were always getting into trouble. Good grief, Jessica, were the assaults they committed not enough for you? What happened to your sense?"

"Mom, they are literally fixing my car," I said. "I can't avoid them. I'm not going to *try* to avoid them."

"Avoid them…" She scoffed. "You sat your butt down in that man's car without a second of hesitation. You are far beyond them only being your mechanics." Her eyes narrowed. "Sweet Jesus, please don't tell me you're sleeping with one of them."

Mom didn't used to be like this, but things had changed as I'd gotten older. When I was little, I was her perfect little "Jessie Sunshine," a doll she could dress up in sparkly dresses and big bows. I was a chronic high achiever who couldn't fail to make her proud, and when I did, it was devastating.

But a teenager wasn't a cute little doll you could play dress-up with. Once I started gaining independence and making my own decisions, Mom lost her perfect toy and had to start finding other ways to remain in control. Shame, guilt, relentless nagging…

The years I'd spent away at college hadn't made her loosen her chokehold. She was only squeezing tighter, as if she knew how fragile her control was.

She'd taught me to accept nothing less than perfection, to be bold no matter what. Why did it surprise her when I used those same traits to make my own decisions?

"Mom, you need to stop." I tried to keep my voice as reasonable as possible. The screaming matches we'd have when I was a teenager had been completely unhinged, and I didn't want to hit that level again. But it seemed as if the calmer I was, the more upset she got. Like she wasn't getting the reaction she wanted.

"Oh, I see." The sarcasm dripped thickly into her words. "I'm the bad guy now. I'm the villain for looking out for my daughter's safety. Well, I'll tell you one thing, Jessica Marie Martin." She leaned forward in her chair, manicured fingernails spread on the table. "I will not have them coming to my house. If they show up here again, I'll call the police."

I rolled my eyes in exasperation. "No, you won't. You're not going to call the cops on them just for showing up on a public street. That's ludicrous."

"Excuse me? What did you say to me?"

Abruptly, I got up from the couch. This argument was never going to end if I didn't get out of here. "You're not going to call the police, and you're not going to dictate who I spend time with. I'm done with this."

"Well, I'm not *done*, Jessica. Don't walk away from me!"

But she couldn't stop me. I grabbed my phone, slamming the front door and putting a blessed stop to her arguing. God, some days I couldn't stand her. It tore me apart, because for so long, I'd done *everything* with her. I'd hung on to her every word. I'd thought she was so beautiful and fierce. A strong, capable person.

Then I realized it wasn't strength I was seeing; it was the ability to make others feel weak so she could control them. She could put someone down over weeks and months, chipping away at them until they bent to her will.

But not me. Not anymore. I was so done with this place. I could see the New York City skyline whenever I closed my eyes, waiting for me to get there.

Except…there were some things here I wasn't done with. Not even a little bit.

Putting in my earbuds, I tucked my phone into the tight pocket on my armband. While it sucked not to have a car, my favorite cafe didn't take very long to jog to. I hadn't been able to finish my breakfast since Mom wouldn't quit nagging me, and avoiding her meant I didn't even go downstairs for lunch.

My stomach was growling with hunger as I ran through the neighborhood park. The trails here were nice, with large trees providing some shade. But the sky was filled with thick gray clouds today, although the heat was no less intense. The air felt so thick that I was drenched in sweat within a few minutes.

If only Mom knew the truth, if only she'd accept it without completely losing her temper. I had no friends left to speak of, but it was largely by my own choice. No one that I'd grown up knowing was still close to me. Not a single person I'd once called a friend was trustworthy.

No one except…

I slowed my jog as I neared the cafe, smiling as I pulled out my phone. Ashley Garcia had been my friend longer than anyone else I knew. We'd met in fourth grade and been inseparable ever since — at least until she landed her dream job and moved to New York without me. We had always been a lot alike, and although she was a gossip queen, she'd never made me feel like I risked our friendship by doing my own thing.

I gave her a call, and it was so good to hear her voice that I almost choked up. She was living her best single life, partying on the weekends and grinding hard at work during the week. She'd gotten a job as an advertising consultant and loved it nearly as much as she loved trying a new cocktail bar every night.

"Anything new in Wickeston?" she said, after relaying all her weekend shenanigans. "Let me guess, it's still boring, boring, boring."

"Pretty much." I laughed. The cafe was packed that morning, and I was keeping an eye out for an open seat as I waited for my food. "It's exactly the same. Backstabbing bitches and assholes everywhere. I can't wait to get out of here."

Maybe she heard the little hint of a lie in my voice, because she said slyly, "Yeah, can't come soon enough. Nothing much to look forward to in Wickeston, except...well, you know."

I sighed. "What do I know, Ash?"

"You know," she insisted. "Your favorite boy toys are still there, aren't they?" When I said nothing, she explained, "Manson Reed? Vincent? Their weirdo friends?"

"Oh my God, girl, no." The denial came instantly, but the moment I'd said it, a pang of regret tightened in my chest. What was I so afraid of? It was Ashley I was talking to. She wouldn't judge me! Or at least if she did, she wouldn't make me feel bad about it. But I kept seeing Danielle in my mind's eye, smiling at me as she said with fake sweetness, *"It's our little secret, babe."*

I didn't think Ashley would betray me like that. I hated to even think about it.

She clearly wasn't buying my denial. "Riiight, sure."

I sipped my coffee, as if the caffeine would somehow help me relax. "What made you think that anyway?"

"First off, because you actually sound really happy. The last time I remember you being so upbeat was after a certain Halloween party a few years ago." She giggled. "Also, you were *so* not subtle about how hard you stalked them in college. I swear, every time I looked at your phone, you had one of their socials pulled up. But, okay. I believe you. You definitely haven't seen them, right?"

"Right," I said quickly, but her long silence afterward broke me. "Okay, fine, I saw them at a party."

Her shriek almost burst my eardrums. I had to hold the phone away from my ear, earning some weird looks from the people seated around me as the high-pitched scream emanated from my speakers.

"Oh my God, I knew it, I knew it!" she exclaimed. "You have to tell me everything — Ah. Shit. Never mind. My boss is calling me. Call me later?"

"Sure thing, girl. Love you."

"Love you, bitch, byyyye."

My order was up and I still hadn't found an open seat. I wandered out onto the patio, which was shaded by trees and surrounded by vine-covered trellises. I was scanning the tables when a bright red head of hair caught my eye.

Julia, the woman from Satin Novelties, saw me at the same moment I spotted her.

"Jessica! Hey!" She waved me over, a big smile on her face. She had an empty chair at her table and she motioned to it. "Need a seat? I promise I won't talk your ear off. I can't believe how busy it is here today."

I accepted gratefully, taking the chair across from her. She was halfway through a sandwich and a coffee, an open textbook in front of her and a notebook under her right hand.

I was hesitant to reconnect with anyone from high school at this point. But Julia and I had been in different grades and in entirely different circles. She'd seemed nice enough at the shop, so maybe I could risk getting to know her better.

440 | HARLEY LAROUX

"What are you studying?" I said, trying to read her massive book upside down. There were some complicated diagrams that looked like organs.

"Human Physiology," she said, sighing heavily. "I'm a nursing student. As much as I love selling porn and dildos, it doesn't pay quite enough to live on. Did you already graduate?"

She spoke loudly, without a care about who heard her. Some folks sitting beside us shot her a dirty look, but she brushed her hair over her shoulder and paid them no mind.

"Yeah, I graduated in June," I said. "Architectural Design."

"Oooh, so you're like, artsy *and* mathematically inclined," she said. "Are you going to design skyscrapers? Will you build the next Burj Khalifa?"

I laughed. "Damn, wouldn't that be a dream? Actually, I'm more interested in designing houses. Especially restoring older homes."

"You must love what Lucas and the guys have been doing with their old house, then," she said, leaning forward in her seat. "I've only seen it a couple times, but damn, I remember what it looked like before." She grimaced. "I'm pretty sure it was almost condemned when they got it."

"I believe it," I said. "I think that old place could be really beautiful. It seems like they're putting in a lot of work."

"Sooo, how are you and Vincent?" she said. "Or you and... the guys...all of them." She laughed awkwardly. "I never really know how to ask. Sorry."

I raised my eyebrows in surprise. "Wait, you know about all that? About them sharing with each other?"

"Oh, yeah." She waved her hand as if it was old news. "They've always had their own unit going on, as long as I've known them. Lucas has always been open about it, being polyamorous and all that. I think it's cool. Love should be free and ethical, in my opinion."

"Do they date much? I mean, have you ever seen them try to bring anyone else in?" It was a question I probably could have asked of them directly, but it felt like demanding information I didn't have a right to. After all, we weren't dating...technically.

That technicality was hanging by an increasingly thinning thread.

Julia screwed up her face in thought. "Not really. There was a girl last year, but she didn't stick around very long. And there was a guy the year before that, but the same thing. Didn't stick around. They keep to themselves, but I don't blame them. People around here aren't very open-minded." She leaned even closer, lowering her voice. "When Satin Novelties opened, people literally stood outside with picket signs. Like they thought we were corrupting the town or something."

She was easy to talk to and quick to laugh. No matter what topic we switched to, she never skipped a beat and I never heard a negative word from her mouth about anybody. It felt like hardly any time had passed as we finished our food.

"Here's my number," she said, handing me a folded sticky note. "If you ever want to hang out or grab breakfast, shoot me a text. I'm not really into jogging, but I love a good hike. We should go together sometime."

I was still smiling as I took my plate and cup back inside, dropping it off at the counter before I left. Julia seemed like a genuinely kind person, not like she was simply putting on an act or trying to get on my good side. When she asked questions, she acted sincerely interested. It still stunned me that the whole reason she knew the boys was because she'd managed to get on Lucas's good side.

I hadn't even realized how desperately I'd needed this. Just some time to decompress, and genuine conversations with women who weren't eager to stab me in the back the second they got the chance.

I'd only just made it out the door to head home when I ran smack into someone coming in the opposite direction.

"Oh! Excuse me, sir, sorry," I apologized hurriedly to the man I'd bumped into, edging around him on the sidewalk. But then I lifted my eyes, looking at him for the first time, and a flood of ice-cold fear washed through my veins.

He was in his fifties, at least. Tall and skinny, a tattered t-shirt and jeans hung loosely from his frame. His hair was grown out, streaked with gray, shiny with grease. His hollow cheekbones and dark eyes were far too familiar.

It was Reagan Reed. Manson's father.

I stuttered for a moment, my mouth gaping at him, before I hurriedly tried to turn away. But he grabbed my arm, yanking me back toward him so hard that I gasped. His hold was like a vice, and I could smell alcohol and cigarettes on his breath.

But as quickly as he grabbed me, he let go.

"Sorry about that, ma'am. I mistook you for someone else." It sounded as if he'd been gargling with rocks. "You'll have to forgive an old man for his poor eyesight."

"Oh, yeah…sure," I said, rubbing my arm where he'd gripped me. Was I supposed to run? Stay? Call for help? Did I *need* help?

Vincent had said Reagan "freaked him out," and I knew he'd been abusive toward his wife and son, but he was an old man now, thin and frail looking.

His grip had hardly been frail though.

"You're Jessica Martin, aren't you?" His use of my full name jerked my attention back. I nodded, before quickly realizing I shouldn't have confirmed it. "I thought so. I recognize you from church. You used to go with your mama."

The last time I'd attended a church service was at least ten years ago, despite my mom trying everything to get me to attend. "I haven't been to church in a long time, sir."

He smiled. His teeth were brown, gums red. "Neither have I." His eyes roamed over me, giving me an uncomfortable feeling, as if his gaze was covering me with slime. "You've grown up into quite the beautiful young woman. That blonde hair..." He reached out, confusion and surprise keeping me rooted in place as he caught a strand of my hair in his long fingers. "Like an angel."

Hurriedly backing away, I said, "I have to go," and walked away without another word.

Getting my keys out of my purse immediately, I nestled one of them between my fingers like a weapon, thankful for all the shops and people nearby. Reagan didn't follow me, but I heard what he called after me.

"Have a good day now. You be careful out there."

My feeling of unease remained for the entire walk home. I kept looking over my shoulder, expecting to see the old man again every time I turned my head. Thankfully, my mom's car was gone as I approached the house. Only once the door was shut and locked behind me, and I'd double-checked that the security system was set, did I feel any better.

Why was Manson's dad still hanging around? His son wanted nothing to do with him, and as far as I knew, he didn't have a house here. What did he want with *me*? Why and how did he even know who I was?

I pulled out my phone, staring at my reflection on the screen. I didn't like to go crying to anyone for help, but I had a terrible feeling in my gut that something was really off. Who the hell grabbed a stranger like that? The way he'd talked about remembering me, the way he'd touched my hair...

I shuddered, then pulled up Vincent's number and dialed.

He answered after only a couple rings.

"Hey, baby." He sounded sleepy despite it being midway through the afternoon. The huskiness in his tone was instantly alluring. "What's up?"

"Nothing much," I said, wandering through the house with my phone at my ear. I took a quick peek at my dad's office, but the door was shut, and I could hear the news playing from inside. I didn't want to blurt out *I called you because I was scared!* but I also wasn't sure what else to say. "Just, uh...called to see what you're doing, I guess."

"Oh, you know how it is. Sleeping in, getting high, eating snacks in bed. Thinking about your sexy ass. Degenerate things." He chuckled. "I started a new painting today. I'll show you next time you come over."

It was remarkable how quickly he could put me at ease, how the stress felt as if it was melting out of my muscles. I grabbed a water bottle from the fridge and trudged upstairs, flopping down onto my bed.

"Why'd you really call me, Jess?" Vincent said, his voice gentle. "Don't lie."

I sighed, feeling guilty that he didn't believe me about calling to chat, then feeling even guiltier that he was right. "I saw Manson's dad again today."

His voice was instantly more alert. "Where?"

"At the cafe. It was The Toasted Bean, off Fair Street and Westlake. I don't know what was up with him. I ran into him when I was leaving and he grabbed me —"

"He fucking *what*?" There was a thump, as if he'd suddenly moved or dropped something. "Where are you? Are you all right? Are you somewhere safe?"

"Yes, yes, I'm okay. I'm at home." I was surprised by the alarm in his voice. "But it freaked me out and I didn't know who else to call."

He sighed heavily. "I'm glad you did. Manson knows he's back in town and he's not happy about it. I actually…I kinda fucked up, Jess. I forgot to tell him and he found out because he saw his dad's truck parked near your house."

My eyes widened as I sat up. "Near my house?"

"Don't worry, don't worry, I'm sure it's not…I don't think it meant anything. I think it just scared Manson, you know?"

"Yeah, well, this old man is starting to freak me out too," I said, pulling my curtain aside and staring out at the street. "He knew my name, Vincent. He knew exactly who I was."

"Fucking hell." Vincent took a deep breath, sounding as if this was the last thing he'd wanted to hear. "Look, Jess, you have to be careful, okay? Reagan isn't safe. I don't know how much Manson has told you, but that guy is a fucking shitbag. I wouldn't put it past him to start something if he knows you've been spending time with us."

Dread roiled within me as I replayed the incident in my mind. The way Reagan had looked at me, how hard he'd gripped me — yeah, he wasn't a safe person. And he'd seen me that day with Vincent, so it was likely he'd made the association between me and them.

Vincent went on, "If you need to go someplace, call us and one of us will drive you. Seriously."

"I'd be calling almost every morning," I said, shaking my head. "I'll be careful."

"No." His voice was firm. "It's not enough for you to be looking over your shoulder every time you walk somewhere. I'm not going to risk that guy catching you alone. He's the reason I have a gun in the house, Jess. I need you to understand that."

This was even worse than I'd thought. My fingers clenched on one of my pillows, and I dug my nails into the fluffy surface.

"It doesn't make sense for you guys to drive me back and forth from the gym at 7 am every other day," I said. "That's too much."

"I'll talk to the others. For now, if you go anywhere besides the gym, tell me. Location and address. I know that sounds overbearing as fuck, but I'm serious. Do that for me, please?"

He sounded genuinely concerned, even fearful. The fact that

he was so protective of me, when I shouldn't have meant much of anything to him at all, made my growing fear lessen a bit. At least I didn't have to deal with this alone. "Okay. Okay, I will."

"Promise me."

"I promise, sir."

Finally, I heard a smile in his voice. "Good girl. All right, I'll talk to you soon. L—" He cut off abruptly and cleared his throat, as if he'd stumbled over the word. "Later."

41

VINCENT

If there was ever something serious going down, we handled it together. I'd fucked up when I hadn't told Manson about his dad right away; that was my bad. But I wasn't going to make that mistake again, not now.

Not when things had already escalated.

We were all gathered in the living room after dinner, tired after another long day. Jojo had wedged herself between Manson and Lucas on the couch, her mouth hanging open as she slept. Little Bo was curled up on Jason's lap, as usual, and as for me?

I had a big bag of weed.

"I find it concerning that you call for a meeting and then immediately start rolling joints," Manson said, watching me with his arms folded. He didn't smoke very often, but God, he was going to need it tonight. Talking about his dad was never any easy topic for him, but I had a feeling this would be worse.

When it came to Jess, Manson couldn't keep his cool as well as he could in other situations. It was like she disarmed him, shaking the careful hold he had over his emotions.

"Everything's better with a bag of weed, right?" I said, passing around the joints. Jason already knew why I wanted to have this discussion, but Lucas and Manson were in the dark.

Jason had been as upset as I was when I told him about Reagan. "Who the fuck does he think he is, messing with our girl?" was the first thing he blurted, not even realizing what he'd said until it was already out. But he was right, for better or worse: Jess was *our* girl. Even if we called it a game, even if we weren't playing for keeps — which I increasingly doubted — Jess was under our protection and we were going to look after her safety.

Everyone lit up, the sour herbaceous odor wafting through the room. The open windows let the cool night air seep in, and I waited until everyone was looking a little more relaxed before I said, "Jessica ran into Reagan today. He talked to her. He knew her name. I'm pretty sure he knows she's spending time with all of us."

Lucas's face darkened with anger, and he shook his head as he took another hit. But Manson looked as if I'd said I saw zombies in the front yard.

"He talked to her?" he said, disgust in his voice.

"Yeah. He grabbed her, apparently. Seemed like he was aggressive, and he was on a public street." I exhaled, the smoke clouding around my face. "He's escalating things, and obviously not leaving."

"We need to figure out what we're going to do," Jason said.

"We keep our heads down and mind our business," Lucas said. "If he wants something, he can come knock on the door."

"It's not that simple." Manson's voice was riddled with tension. "We need to figure out how to keep him away from Jess."

Lucas's frown deepened and he looked away, glaring out the window. His mood had been even more unpredictable than usual lately — brooding in his thoughts all day but barely saying a word.

"I told Jess to tell us when she leaves the house," I explained. "And send us the address for wherever she goes."

"As if she'd agree to that," Lucas said. "She probably laughed at you."

I shook my head. "She agreed. She was scared, dude. This is freaking her out."

"All the more reason for her to cut her little vacation to the losers' side of life short," Lucas said. "A hundred bucks says she'll have a tow truck over here by tomorrow to haul that damn BMW away to get it repaired somewhere else, after we've already bought the fucking engine —"

"Hey." Manson tapped the back of his hand against Lucas's chest. "Quit it. She's not bailing. She could quit the game any time she wants, but she hasn't."

"Well, now's the perfect time, isn't it?" he snapped. "Shit's getting real; it's not just about kinky playtime anymore." He laughed bitterly. "Do you think she's going to want to stick around now that Daddy Dearest is involved? Fuck no."

Manson was staring at him, his expression so hard I almost expected him to raise his voice, but he didn't.

"You're wrong." His tone was perfectly even, angry in a way I rarely heard from him. "And even if you weren't, we helped get her into this. She's involved whether she likes it or not, whether she ghosts again or not. My dad isn't going to care about the details. If he thinks he can hurt me by getting to her, he will."

"She shouldn't be alone," Jason said. "She goes to the gym every morning, doesn't she?"

"Every other day," I said. "Or something like that."

"I'll switch to her gym and start going there to workout instead," Jason said. "That way, at least she has someone with her in the morning."

Lucas tipped his head back, rolling his eyes in disbelief. "You're going to start waking up early to get to the gym with her? Really? You can barely even get out of bed by 10 am!"

"I'll set an alarm," Jason said easily. "I need to get into a better routine anyway."

"I can give her rides on my days off," I said. "She works during the week, so I don't think she's running around to very many places."

Manson was nodding, his eyes downcast as his mind churned. "We'll figure it out. Between the four of us, at least one of us will be able to find the time to go with her."

"Y'all are fucking ridiculous," Lucas said. "We have shit to do, we have *work* to do! Jessica is fine. So Reagan scared her a little, big deal. What's he going to do?"

"Don't fucking ask what he can do," Manson said. His tone was as sharp as a blade, but that didn't do a thing to intimidate Lucas. "You *know* what he can do."

"She's not even going to fucking stick around," Lucas grumbled. "You're acting like this chick is our girlfriend. She's not. She's not dating us. I wouldn't call her a paramour. We have a mutually beneficial agreement and that's it. As soon as she gets that job offer she's waiting on, she's going to be gone."

"Then we'll protect her until she's gone," Manson said fiercely. He got up from the couch, abruptly rousing Jojo from her sleep. "It's not an argument; it's what we're doing. Is everyone clear on that?"

Jason and I both nodded, but Lucas stayed where he was, glaring at Manson. Finally, without a word, he lowered his eyes and got up, stalking out of the living room. The front door slammed a moment later.

Manson sighed, his shoulders deflating as he sat back down. It wasn't often the two of them argued, but I hated to see it when they did. Tapping out my joint in the ashtray, I left him and Jason in the living room and went out to the front porch.

Lucas was pacing in the yard, obviously too pissed to have a normal conversation quite yet.

"Hey, so —"

"Don't start that shit." He cut me off, pausing to take a long drag on the joint. "You already know I'm going to hear it from Manson later. How I need to *let my guard down* and *work through my issues.*" He snorted. "Fucking therapist bullshit."

I let him pace for a bit, working out a little more of that nervous energy before I said, "I was going to suggest that you smoke more weed, but uh, yeah, those other things would be a good idea too."

He growled in frustration, sitting down heavily on the front porch and rubbing his hand over his head. "I don't get it, man. I don't trust her. Why should I? After all this time, suddenly she's feeling so friendly? Going out in public with us? Celebrating with us? Acting like a little flirt? I don't buy it. Jess is just getting what she wants, so why the *hell* should I get attached?"

Ah, so there it was. That was why he was so damn moody this week.

After taking a seat beside him, I pulled out another joint from my pocket once he'd smoked his down to the filter. I had it ready and waiting for him by the time he'd flicked the old one away.

"Damn, you're on it," he said, taking the lighter when I offered it. He passed the joint to me after he'd taken a hit, and we sat like that for a while in silence.

"You're attached to her," I said finally, when I felt he'd smoked a sufficient amount to hear it. "You're falling for her."

He scoffed, grumbling something under his breath.

"I get it," I said. "It's hard when there's so much history between all of us. But people can change. You have, I have…all of us have changed since high school."

"Not Jess," he said determinedly. "She's the fucking same."

I laughed, although I tried to make it gentle. "You know that's not true. It's different this time. She's different. I think she's trying."

"Trying what?" He looked at me, and I could see the desperation on his face. The confusion. "What the hell does she really want?"

"Ask her," I said simply. "Talk to her, Lucas. If you need to hear something from her to help you feel better about this whole thing, then ask for it."

"Don't need shit," he said, but he didn't sound very confident.

"I don't…fuck…" He stared at the ground; mouth pressed into a thin hard line. "What I need to know…all I fucking need to know…is if she'd choose us over them. Over those assholes she thinks are her friends."

I understood the feeling, the anxiety of impending betrayal. I tried not to dwell on thoughts like that, but there were things Lucas dealt with that I didn't — mentally and emotionally. I couldn't expect him to have the same easygoing approach I did; he had to find his own way.

"I think she'll prove herself," I said. "If you give her the chance."

"And how exactly would I do that?" he said. "Put Alex on one side of the yard while I stand on the other and see which one she runs to first?"

I chuckled. "At least you still have your fantastic sense of humor. I don't know, man, I'm sure you'll think of something. Hell, you and Jason have been plotting that whole scheme to get back at Alex's merry band of assholes, why not invite Jess to come along? See what she'll do."

He was silent as he thought about it for a moment. "That might be a good idea…we could bring her along on the revenge mission and really put her to the test. See who she's loyal to."

I clapped his shoulder. "There ya' go. Very healthy method of communication, totally normal." He glowered at my teasing, but hell, I was the one who'd suggested it. *Nothing* about our lives was totally normal — we were weird fucks through and through.

And although Lucas had his doubts, I knew Jess wouldn't let us down. Call it a hunch, intuition, whatever. But this time…

This time was different.

42

JASON

I don't know what kind of psychopaths willingly got out of bed before the sun was up, but apparently, I was one of them now. I felt half dead when my alarm went off, and I came within inches of chucking my phone across the attic before Vincent reminded me sleepily, "It's for Jess, just remember it's for Jess."

It was enough to finally push me out of bed.

I understood why Lucas was so irritated about the whole thing. He was fiercely loyal, but only once you had his trust, and that was extremely hard to come by. Jess was confusing to him, likely in the same ways she confused me. Every time I expected her to pull away, to fall back into her old habits of sneering at everything we did, she managed to surprise me.

Seeing her cheer for me during the competition had me

flying so high I hadn't had the slightest doubt I'd win. She didn't need to do that. Our agreement had nothing to do with dating, or supporting us in our endeavors...but she still did. She was still genuinely excited to see me do well, and I was struggling to understand why.

The only reason I could think of, the one that kept running through my brain again and again, was that she was falling for us as much as we were for her.

Not even in a sexual way. The lust was already there; we'd all acknowledged that a long time ago. It wasn't about that. This was different. It was like she was falling for *us*, for who we were and what we brought to her life.

I saw the way she looked at us, and the way the others looked at her. Even Lucas wasn't exempt. I'd seen the furious, pining looks he shot her way.

It was dangerous to feel this good. Defaulting to pessimism usually felt safer, especially today.

There was a bad feeling in my gut, telling me something else was coming. I didn't know if it would be Reagan, or more shit with Alex McAllister and his group, but something was stirring up alarm bells in me and I didn't like it.

I arrived at the gym early, getting inside as soon as they opened. It was a massive place, still new enough that everything smelled like plastic and disinfectant. It was going to cost me double the monthly rate as my old gym, but whatever. I'd just been handed my new membership card when an incredulous voice said from behind me, "Jason? What are you doing here?" and I whirled around.

Jessica had her pink gym bag slung over her shoulder, and her long hair pulled up into a ponytail. She wore leggings and a sports bra; her face bare of any makeup. It was easy to forget how many freckles she had when they were usually covered. No mascara, no false lashes, nothing on her lips…

God, she was beautiful.

"I go here," I said, holding up the card.

She stared at it in confusion, as if she suspected some kind of trick. "Uh…since when?"

"Since now." I picked up my bag from beside the sign-up desk, heading back so I could find a spot to start stretching. Jess followed right on my heels.

"I thought you went to the gym closer to the house," she said.

I grinned, although she couldn't see it from behind me. "I needed a change of environment. This place is nice. Pool, sauna, a yoga room — I should have upgraded a while ago."

There was a smile in her words as she said, "Vincent put you up to this, didn't he?"

I turned to face her. "Vincent? Nah, he could care less about the gym."

Her hip cocked as she folded her arms. "So it's a coincidence that you're here to watch me the day after I run into Manson's creepy dad?"

Shrugging, I said, "Can't hurt to have someone to keep an eye on you. Don't worry, I won't interrupt your flow. I've got my own routine. I'm not going to be following you around."

Her face fell so drastically I thought I'd offended her. But she wasn't looking at me — she was looking over my shoulder.

"Morning, Jess. Need someone to spot you today?

Oh fucking hell.

Alex's face stiffened when I turned around. I was pretty sure I was the only guy with blue hair in this goddamn town, but he still looked at me as if he was stunned to see me.

I waved a quick peace sign at him. "Mornin', buddy. She's good. I'll spot her today."

For a second, I thought he was going to punch me in the face. His hands clenched into fists, his lip curling in disgust as he looked me up and down. He had several inches of height on me, but height wasn't everything. I had no doubt I could kick this guy's ass if it came down to it.

But I wasn't trying to get kicked out of my fancy new gym on the first day.

"Later." I gave him a dismissive nod and walked away, leaving him there to stew. Jess followed right behind me, but a prickling feeling of irritation was bubbling up in me. I'd had no clue Alex went here too. Did he work out with her? Jess didn't even like the guy!

I was overreacting. But why the hell had he assumed he'd spot her? What the fuck was this bullshit?

I found a space to stretch out and lobbed my bag into the corner. There were lockers here somewhere, but I'd gotten distracted and didn't want to go hunting around for them.

It was petty, but I said, "Am I interrupting some bonding time with good old Alex?"

"I don't *bond* with him, Jason," she said, bending at the waist to reach for her toes. Her ass looked good in those leggings. Juicy as hell. "I try to *avoid* him. Trust me, I wish he didn't go here either."

I stretched out my quads, alternating between legs. I believed her. I didn't think she had any interest in Alex; it wasn't *her* that was the problem.

"I get it, I get it," I said, as I realized she was still staring at me, waiting for a response. "Pissed me off, I guess, him assuming you'd want him to spot you."

Her face softened as she smiled. "Don't tell me you're jealous?"

"Nope," I said quickly. "It's not jealousy." She tweaked an eyebrow at me skeptically as I clarified, "It's determination that you are way too good for him, and him stealing a second of your time pisses me off."

That small smile remained on her face. "Well...thank you. For saying that, and for showing up here. I didn't want you guys to feel like you had to go to the trouble for me."

"It's no trouble." *Lies.* "I don't mind doing it at all." *This morning was hell.* "It feels good to switch up my routine." *Nope, it felt awful.*

But it was worth it. Waking up early, going to a different gym, dealing with Alex. All of it was worth it if it meant keeping her safe.

Honestly, it was worth it because it meant spending time with her.

I didn't want to crowd her though. I knew that having someone insert themselves into my routine without any warning would be jarring and irritating as hell. After we stretched, I kept my distance, positioning myself so I could keep an eye both on her and Alex. But I was obviously distracting both of them. Alex looked suspicious, and he had every reason to be.

Lucas and I had been having a lot of discussions about how we were going to get back at him. We'd settled on a plan of attack but needed to work out a few logistics. After what Alex and his friends had done, it only made sense that he'd expect a response from us, and he'd get one.

Until then, I enjoyed the thought of him stewing in his own anticipation.

But that motherfucker didn't know when to quit. I was on the bench press, lowering the bar toward my chest when he appeared above me. I had to complete the rep before I could tap my earphones and mute them, allowing me to hear what he had to say.

"The fuck do you want?" I didn't sit up from the bench; I wasn't going to move an inch. He leaned against the bar above me; the stench of his sweat was truly repulsive.

"You freaks really can't stay away from her, can you?" he said, nodding his head toward the other side of the gym, where Jess was on the leg press. "It's creepy, man. What are you stalking her for?"

I laughed, the sound rough with the effort to get it out at all. "I think it's creepier that you dumped her on our property personally. And I think you should mind your goddamn business."

"You think y'all have a chance with her? Seriously?" He shook his head as he stepped back, whipping his sweat towel at the side of the bench. "She's fucking you because she's bored. And when she's done, she'll find a *real* man to take care of her."

Fuck him and his fucking bullshit bait. This was why Alex was such a bane to Lucas, because Lucas couldn't control his temper over jabs like that. But I was in the zone. I was zen. Nodding and grinning at him, I tapped my earphones and shut him out again. He could run his mouth all he wanted, but there wasn't a damn thing he could say that I hadn't heard before.

Instead of making me angry, it made me excited. How goddamn original to try to attack the fact that I could take dick as well as I could give it. Alex's preoccupation with my sexuality said far more about him than it did about me — but hell, if he was so curious, I was willing to assuage his "fears" that Jess wasn't getting taken care of right.

About forty-five minutes later, she and I headed toward the showers at the same time. A sheen of sweat was on her forehead, her muscles shivering slightly as we walked side by side.

"You have an intense routine," I said, and she smiled at the admiration in my voice.

"I like pushing myself," she said. "If I'm not shaking by the end, then it wasn't hard enough." She glanced over at me quickly, her smile slightly mischievous.

My cock swelled, which was a fucking problem when I was about to undress in a public shower. "Careful, Jess. I can't exactly hide a boner right now."

"What did I do?" she said innocently, pausing outside the women's shower room as she batted her eyes at me. Okay, she was blatantly asking for it now. I stepped closer to her, crowding her, pressing her back against the wall. Her eyes were bright, the scent of her sweat downright intoxicating. I wanted to take her like that, taste the salt on her skin…

"If you're going to try to turn me on, then you'd better be prepared to do something about it," I said. She tensed with anticipation, holding her breath for a moment…but I stepped away and headed into the showers.

Just in time to see Alex getting into one of the stalls.

I waited until he'd flicked the lock to "occupied" before I stripped down. My dick was at half-mast and the moment I allowed myself to think of Jess showering on the other side of this wall, I was rigidly hard.

There was a soft sound as I shoved my things into a locker for safekeeping during my shower. I glanced toward the door and stilled when I realized it was Jess who had come in. She no longer had her bag, and she looked around curiously before her eyes fell on me, standing there entirely naked and erect.

She grinned. "Wow. You weren't kidding about being turned on." Suddenly realizing we weren't alone, her eyes darted toward the one occupied shower stall, and she mouthed, *Who's in there?*

Alex, I mouthed back in silence. She wandered further into the locker room, taking her time as she made her way over to me.

"What are you doing?" I whispered.

She stopped in front of me and reached out, tracing her fingers slowly across the tattoos on my chest.

"You said I should be prepared to do something about turning you on," she said, the fake innocence in her voice driving me wild. "So here I am. Prepared to do something about it."

Oh, hell fucking yes. I looked around, spotting a wet floor sign leaning against the wall nearby.

"Put that outside the door and close it," I said. She complied, moving quickly to put the sign right outside the locker room. It wouldn't buy us much time, but I could work fast.

I only needed a few minutes.

When she returned, I was wedging a rubber doorstop I'd found under Alex's door. I didn't know how long it would keep him in there, but I figured it would buy us enough time before he broke out by sheer brute force.

Jess gasped when I grabbed her, slamming her up against the shower door and kissing her. Her lips parted, her hands grasping me as her tongue slipped eagerly into my mouth. I gripped her throat in one hand and slid the other between her legs, growling when she whimpered with pleasure. The shower was still running inside the stall, but when I turned Jess roughly and pressed her hard against the door again, I knew it was only a matter of time.

I ripped down her leggings and panties, the tight spandex keeping her legs squeezed together. Holding her against the door by the nap of her neck, I used my free hand to grasp her hip, but she was already arching her back for me. I nudged my cock against her entrance, groaning softly when I found her wet.

"Fuck, have you been thinking about this the whole time?" I said, bearing down against her, thrusting slowly against her slick folds. I readjusted, tugged her hips back a little more, and pressed inside her. Her groan was loud, and I immediately moved my hand from grasping her neck to covering her mouth.

"I love how you take it for me," I moaned, fucking her with hard, punishing thrusts. Her sounds were muffled against my hand, but certainly not silent.

The shower suddenly turned off. "Hey, it's occupied in here!"

Jess's eyes widened, but I didn't stop. The sound of my hips slapping against her ass as I pounded her was definitely loud enough for Alex to hear it. He threw back the deadbolt, and the door jolted slightly as he tried to open it — but the doorstop did its job.

"What the fuck!" His fist pounded against the door, and I switched up my pace, filling her with long, slow strokes. Her eyes fluttered closed, her pussy clinging to me like she was trying to keep me inside.

"That feel good, princess?" I murmured, and she groaned in response, nodding her head as I kept her mouth covered. I released my hold on her hip, wrapping my arm around her to rub her clit instead. She arched back against me, eager for those deeper strokes, her thighs clenching around my hand.

"Open the fucking door! Hey!" Alex's voice was growing louder and he was really trying to get the door open now. Even though I'd already worked myself into a sweat, I had more energy than ever as I slammed into her. My balls tightened, and my back tingled.

I was going to spill inside her delicious cunt and Alex was going to listen to every moment.

"Come for me," I growled the command in her ear, and her muscles spasmed greedily around me. Her legs trembled, her breathing choppy with desperate gasps as I rubbed her clit. I could *feel* her come on me, warm and slick and throbbing with pleasure.

I bottomed out inside her, pumping my cum deep. I hooked my fingers into her mouth and she opened, her ragged cry of bliss like a cherry on top of my pleasure. Alex was cursing, and it sounded like he was about to kick the door down.

Jess gasped when I pulled out of her and hurriedly tugged up her leggings. I kissed her quickly, grabbing my bag from the locker before I took her hand.

"Looks like you won't be getting a shower," I said. "Because we'd better not be here when he gets that door open."

She smelled like sweat and my cum, and it made me feel like I was on top of the world. It was some primal animal kingdom bullshit, but fucking her while Alex could do nothing more than listen was possibly the greatest ego boost I'd ever given myself.

I think I was going to like this new gym.

43

JESSICA

Those early morning workouts with Jason soon became a routine. He'd meet me outside my house, luckily before my mom was awake, and we'd jog together through the park and to the gym. It was clear he wasn't used to the early hour, and some days he arrived looking half asleep. But he was there every morning regardless, bleary-eyed until the jog woke him up.

I thought a confrontation with Alex was inevitable after what happened. But he didn't come to the gym at all for the rest of the week. Either he was going at a different time or had stopped coming altogether. Either way, I wasn't complaining. I was glad to no longer feel the heaviness of his gaze following me around.

It was nice to have a dedicated gym partner. Jason pushed himself hard, and he clearly knew his stuff. Having him there, matching my enthusiasm and challenging me with a little friendly competition, had me feeling eager to roll out of bed in the morning.

It was easy to forget he was there to protect me. The entire idea of needing protection was strange. The boys knew better than me what Reagan was capable of, but I still cringed at the idea of asking them for rides around town when I could simply walk. I was usually able to borrow my mom's car for my midmorning coffee runs, but on Thursday, she had gone to visit a friend.

I didn't think I could get through the rest of the day without my espresso. A brewed cup of coffee from our kitchen wasn't going to cut it. But I still winced when I pulled out my phone, trying to decide who to ask.

I'd always been independent. I'd gotten my driver's license as soon as I was legally allowed to, and before I got the BMW, I'd been driving around my mom's old Jetta. No longer having to rely on my parents or boyfriend for rides had been a relief. I never had to ask for permission or wait around for anyone else.

So texting the group chat, **Hey, can I get a quick ride to the coffee shop?** felt like going back in time. I hated to *ask*. Besides, this surely had to be annoying to them. I was supposed to be paying *them*, not getting chauffeured around.

But it had been their idea in the first place.

I can. Manson was the first one to text me back. **Give me fifteen minutes, I'll be over.**

I immediately hurried into the bathroom to touch up my makeup. It took several minutes of obsessive preening before I recognized the jittery feeling in my stomach as nervous excitement, like that sensation of anxiety before a first date. But Manson was just picking me up for coffee. It was nothing serious, nothing to get all worked up over.

I put down my mascara, staring at my reflection. I looked different than I had a few weeks ago, but I wasn't sure how or why. It was like my face had relaxed, as if I'd been holding tension there and hadn't even known it.

It was relaxing to finally be getting fucked right; that was for sure. No one else I'd been with had ever satisfied me like these men did. It was more than merely their casual dominance, their filthy words.

They made my life exciting. I never knew what to expect. I no longer knew if I was facing a regular day or if one of them would call, text, or come by and pick me up for a debauched adventure. It took my mind off work and buried all my petty day-to-day stressors.

I enjoyed spending time with them far more than I'd ever thought I would. I liked being in their company, conversing with them, learning from them. And they seemed to genuinely enjoy being around me too — except maybe Lucas, but he was impossible to get a read on.

My cell buzzed, and I picked it up, frowning when I saw a notification from Danielle. It was a Facebook invite to a party at her house this weekend, with nearly a hundred people on the invite list.

A few weeks ago, I would have RSVPed without hesitation. I'd always been a party girl; I loved going out. I loved the laughter and antics of being in a big group of people, all looking to have a good time. Even now, as I shoved my phone into my bag without responding to the invite, I feared I was missing out on something important.

But I wasn't sure if there was a place for me at parties like that anymore. If I had to go there and lie to make people accept me, why bother?

I passed my sister on the stairs as I was coming down, and she said, "Hey, your boyfriend is outside. Or…" She wrinkled her nose. "One of them is."

Manson had texted me he'd be arriving soon, but I remained frozen on the stairs, staring at Steph. "Why do you think he's my boyfriend?"

She cocked her hip and made a face — God, I could swear I used to do the exact same move. It was so weird to see your own sibling turn into a miniature version of yourself. "Um, let's see…you're always coming home with hickeys, so obviously you're seeing *someone*. Also, Mary Volkov told me you're dating her brother, so…" She shrugged. "I don't know why Mom ever fell for your whole *They're just my mechanics!* story. You're losing your touch, sis. You have to be sneakier."

She walked away, flipping her long blonde hair over her shoulder. I'm sure she knew all about being sneaky; I'd done everything in secret when I was a teenager. At the time, it had felt fun, risky, like stealing freedom I wasn't supposed to have.

But having to sneak around as a twenty-two-year-old woman was tiring.

I met Manson at the curb, sliding into the front seat of his Mustang and giving him a kiss on the cheek. It felt natural to do; I hadn't even thought about it. But he still looked at me in surprise as he put the car into gear.

"What's that look for?" I said, taking my mirror out of my

bag and preening more in an attempt to hide the blush that tinted my cheeks.

"You're in a good mood today," he said, chuckling as we pulled out of my neighborhood.

"You should see me after I have my caffeine," I said, turning up his music. "I'll really be in a great mood then."

I recognized the song as one he'd played the night we went to the lookout, and I found myself humming along as we drove. He parked outside the coffee shop instead of going through the drive-through, explaining, "The engine is too loud and they can never hear me order over the speaker."

We ordered and took our coffees to go; a white mocha latte for me, a regular mocha latte for him, and six shots of espresso over ice.

"For Lucas," he explained. "Black as his heart is."

He took the long way home, driving us through the back roads that wound past farms and fields. He avoided the dirt roads, however, unlike Vincent. But I couldn't imagine the Mustang would do very well bumping along the rutted dirt.

"Did I take you away from work?" I said as we cruised along at an easy speed. He had one hand on the wheel and the other dangling out his window, relaxed as he kept his eyes on the road. Another summer storm was rolling in today, the thick gray clouds blocking the sun but not its heat. There was electricity in the air, and lightning flashed in the distant clouds.

"I needed a break anyway," he said. "Your new engine should be arriving soon. At the end of next week, or possibly the week after. Lucas and I just have to get it installed after that."

I bounced in my seat. "Yes! Oh my God, finally, my baby is almost home." I didn't say anything about the pang of uncertainty that knowledge caused in me. Getting my car back was the entire point of all this, wasn't it?

Manson turned, pulling off onto a little winding road that led back into the trees. I noticed a sign saying the road was closed, and weeds were growing through the cracked asphalt.

"This is near the old bridge, isn't it?" I said. Right on cue, I spotted the bridge ahead through the trees. It was built entirely of wood — an old covered bridge that led over Wickeston Creek. It was narrow, only wide enough for one car to drive over at a time, but it certainly wasn't safe for cars to drive on anymore. A chain with a dangling *Caution – Do Not Enter* sign was strung across the bridge, preventing us from going any further.

"They say it's haunted," Manson said, nodding toward the bridge as he parked and turned off the engine. Birds chirped in the trees, the breeze rustling the leaves as we sat in the shade.

"I heard that rumor," I said, taking a sip of my coffee. "Ashley and I came out here one Halloween with a Ouija board and tried to make contact. Nothing happened, but I definitely don't recommend coming out here after dark. It's creepy."

He smiled. "Did you really? You're full of surprises, Jess."

He'd pushed open his door to let the breeze flow through the cab, leaning back in his seat as he sipped his coffee. His hands and arms were blackened with grease stains from work, and he smelled like motor oil and rubber. He was wearing black coveralls, but the top half was unzipped and pushed down so only his undershirt covered his chest.

He looked so damn good I practically salivated.

"So my car is almost done," I said. "What about my bill?"

His eyes brightened, a crooked smirk tugging the corner of his mouth. "You've made good progress with your payments. But you still have a long way to go."

That smile turned me on even more. "Do I? Damn, I guess I should start trying harder, then."

The leather creaked as I leaned toward him. His lips parted slightly, his eyes caressing down my body as if his gaze alone could peel away my clothes.

"I was looking at your list again the other day," I said. I trailed my fingers down his arm, watching a smattering of goosebumps break out over his skin. I absolutely loved knowing when I had an effect on people. These men, as dominant and overwhelming as they were, had little weaknesses I was slowly beginning to figure out.

Manson liked a challenge, but I knew what he liked even more.

"Worship," I said softly, my lips leaving the word like a caress near his ear. "You like it, don't you? To have someone on their knees for you, worshiping you, pleasuring you, savoring…" My fingers had trailed down to his hand, and he caught my wrist, using it to jerk me even closer.

"I do like that," he said, his voice having darkened to a growl that made my spine tingle. "An angel should worship her God."

"Tell me how to worship you," I said, so close I could kiss him, but I didn't dare. I waited for permission, for instruction, ignoring the inner voice that wanted so badly to remain in control.

He set aside his coffee and caressed his hand over my face. "Strip for me. I want to see that beautiful body."

Getting out of the car, I watched his face as I walked around to the front of the vehicle. I faced him, the wooden bridge behind me, as I pulled my shirt over my head. Every movement was slow, sensual, and I revealed every inch of skin like it was a present to be unwrapped. He watched me through the windshield, his fist resting against his mouth, his gaze heavy. My nipples hardened as I took off my bra and the breeze swept over me. I slipped my shoes off, then reached under my skirt to pull my panties down and then dangle them from my finger.

He got out of the car, tension in every step he took toward me. Like he was trying to hold back, as if part of him wanted to rush at me and grab me.

"Bend over the hood," he said. "And pull your skirt up."

I obeyed, my eyes lingering on him as I pulled the skirt up over my ass and bent down on the hood. The metal was still warm as I laid my bare tits against it. He stood behind me and squeezed my ass with both hands.

"Worship means letting me use you as I please," he said. One moment, his touch was soft; the next, it was tight and rough. "If I want you to suffer for me, you suffer. If I want you to endure pain, you endure it. If I want you to pleasure me, touch me, offer your body up for me…then you do it."

"Yes, Master." The title felt strange on my tongue, frightening and nerve-wracking, but somehow so right. He paused, his breathing going still for a moment. Then he laughed softly, the sound sending goosebumps prickling over my back.

"I'm going to hurt you," he said, leaning over my back as he spoke to me, the palm of his hand rubbing over my ass. "And you're going to thank me. Do you understand?"

"Yes, Master." Ooh, it made me tingly every time. I gulped and then shifted my position so my legs were spread a little wider.

"You're learning to be such a good girl," he said. His hand stroked over my thigh, then snapped back, and his palm smacked against my ass with enough force to make me gasp.

"Thank you, Master…" He pulled his hand back again and landed another sharp smack on my cheek. I groaned, forcing out the words, "Thank you."

He kept going, spanking me until my skin was hot and stinging. I kept my legs spread, my skirt pulled up, but before long, I'd begun to shake. Every biting impact fed my arousal a little more, and my pussy was wet after a dozen smacks. He kept going, pausing only to say, "It's beautiful when you suffer for me. When you endure because you know it pleases me. You're doing well, angel."

The praise fueled me. The next dozen swats made me cry out, and I whimpered, waiting for the next smack to land. It was humiliating in exactly the way I craved, making me feel small and blissfully overtaken.

"Does that hurt?" he said sweetly, rubbing his hand over my stinging skin. His palm was so warm, even warmer than my own burning flesh.

"It hurts…but I like how it hurts." I arched my back, pushing my ass back against his hand. I gave a desperate moan as I did it, anticipating the sting, but wanting it so badly. "Please…may I have another, Master?"

He laughed, and I thought he sounded so fucking sexy that

I squirmed. He spanked me again, right on the curve between my ass and my thigh, and my cry of pain quickly dissolved into a moan of pleasure.

"God, you're so sexy," he said, dragging his nails down my skin and leaving burning scratches behind. "Such a good little slut for me. So wet from your spanking…" Two fingers slid into my pussy, and I bowed my head at how good it felt.

He pumped his fingers inside me, continuing to spank me with his free hand. My pleasure was growing, my core swiftly heating as my breath came faster. "Oooh, that's going to make me come…please…please, let me come…"

"I'm going to bring you right to the edge," he said, his tone leaving no room for argument. "Then I'm going to stop, and you're going to get on your knees. You're not allowed to come yet."

I wanted it so badly I could have cried.

"Don't stop…" My voice was heavy with need. "Please… please…"

He withdrew his fingers, bringing them to my lips. "Open," he said. "Use your tongue and get me clean, filthy girl."

I did as he ordered, cleaning my arousal off his fingers as my pussy throbbed with the want for more. He wrapped my long hair around his fist and pulled me up, gripping it as he guided me to my knees. "You know I like you desperate…waiting…needing more. Needing *me*."

"I need you," I whispered the words as I gazed up at him, nuzzling my face into his groin. I could feel his hard length through the cloth, and I closed my mouth over the bulge as if I could tear through the fabric to get to him. "Let me worship your cock, Master. Please."

He zipped his jumpsuit down further, leaning back against the Mustang's grill as I massaged my hand over him, over the black fabric of his briefs between us. He pulled them down, and I leaned close, taking him in my hand and spitting on the head of his cock. I used my saliva to make my hand slick, stroking him slowly, watching his face contort with pleasure.

"Squeeze a little more," he said, his voice husky. "That's it, just like that…"

I kept my face close, inhaling his musky scent before I took him into my mouth. I bobbed my head on him, savoring him, humming as the taste of him filled my head. I was so turned on that any whisper of a breeze over my skin felt overstimulating, my every nerve so sensitive. Manson still held my hair, guiding my head, his hold tightening when he groaned.

"Fuck, Jess…your mouth feels so fucking good."

I loved to watch the pleasure on his face. His half-lidded eyes, his jaw clenching and then relaxing as he leaned his head back. Framed by the Mustang's shining chrome and bright paint, he looked unbearably sexy, too good to keep my hands off of. While my mouth pleased his cock, my hands moved over his thighs, my nails leaving teasing scratches on his skin.

After several minutes, he hissed softly and tightened his hold, pulling my mouth off him. I strained toward him, wanting the taste of him in my mouth, but he gave my head a little shake and said, "On your hands and knees, now. Get your face against the ground."

I obeyed, moving into position. I lay my cheek down against the rough old asphalt, keeping my ass up and my knees slightly spread. I felt so exposed out here — the sounds of nature all around me. Occasionally, I'd hear a car pass on the road and I'd hold my breath, certain that at any moment, I'd hear someone shout that they could see us. But the fear of getting caught was part of the thrill.

"So beautiful," Manson said, pushing my skirt out of the way. He buried his face against me, licking up my dripping arousal, his tongue probing my pussy, my ass. I gasped at the stimulation, groaning as I pushed back against him. I was so close to my orgasm I was shaking, but he stopped before I could plunge over the edge.

"You want to be owned so badly, don't you?" he said, his voice a murmur. I couldn't be sure if he was truly seeking an answer, or if he was merely talking to himself. "You want someone to take control, you need it. You don't want any more frustrating choices, you don't want to have to think about being judged or rejected. You just want to be a beautiful toy we use as we please."

There was a click, and I turned my head slightly so I could look up at him. He'd flipped open his knife, the shining blade catching the knife. I remembered the feeling of him slicing open my skin, how much it had excited me to see my own blood welling up.

I felt drunk on the scene he was setting for me — the pain, the edging pleasure, the surety that in that moment, I was entirely at his mercy. He could do anything he wanted to me, and I savored that feeling of merely being there to serve.

He knew what I wanted, the cravings I feared.

The blade traced lightly over the swell of my ass, taunting me.

"Do you want me to mark you, angel?" he said, ravenous desire in his words. "Do you want to bleed for me?"

There wasn't a doubt in my mind that not only did I want that but I trusted him to do it. "Yes, Master. Mark me, please."

He made a sound that was somewhere between a moan and a snarl. The blade tapped against my ass and he gripped my hip, holding me in place. Slowly, carefully, he cut into my skin. His pupils dilated; his expression completely transfixed as I whimpered softly at the sting.

I was submitting all control to him, but he looked in awe of me. As if I was something to be revered, my endurance admired, my service treasured.

There was no other feeling like that.

"Beautiful." His tongue stroked over the cut before he kissed my skin, whispering his praise, "Such a good girl, you look so fucking sexy..." He began to rub my clit, and I almost sobbed from ecstasy. I wanted more. I craved him to be inside me.

As if he could sense it, the head of his cock nudged against my pussy as he coated himself in my arousal. He plunged into me, immediately setting a hard pace as he pulled back my hips, jerking me onto him with every thrust. His hips slapping against my skin reignited the burn from being spanked, and I relished it, moaning with abandon.

A knot was tightening inside me, spurred on by every brutal thrust of his cock. I whimpered, the words shaking. "Please, may I come, Master? Please let me...please..."

Could I stop myself if he said no? Could I possibly hold back? The thought of even having to try was too much, but luckily, I didn't have to.

"Come for me, angel," he said, his cock punishing me, driving me relentlessly toward my peak. "Come on my cock."

His words shattered me into pieces. I couldn't think, I couldn't breathe. I could barely even manage to move. Pleasure washed over me in a suffocating wave, and when I finally rose back to the surface on the other side, I was gasping.

"God, you feel like heaven." Manson's voice was tight, breathless. "I don't want a single fucking day to go by that you don't have one of us filling you up. You should always feel us inside you, dripping down your thighs, every hole aching…"

"All I'm good for is your pleasure," I babbled, relishing how his breath came faster. "Use me whenever you want. Keep me sore, please. I don't want to forget what it feels like ever, ever, ah —"

His fingers dug into me, his hips giving one last thrust against me before he buried his face in my neck as he came inside me. He held me so tight, so close. Even after he'd pumped me full, he kept his cock inside me, sinking back so I could rest against him, holding me up even though his body was trembling.

"You're fucking perfect, angel. So perfect you'll make me lose my goddamn mind."

44

JESSICA

After a fuck like that, I wasn't ready to go home. I was done with work for the day, and now that I was thoroughly pleasured and worn out, I wanted to relax.

"I'll take you back to our house," Manson said, after he'd used a small disinfectant wipe from his glove box to clean the fresh cut on my butt cheek. "You can chill there as long as you want. Lucas and I will be finishing up work."

I was able to get a look at the cut for the first time in the Mustang's side mirror and found Manson's name etched into my skin. I'd expected to feel excitement and arousal at the sight of it. What I certainly hadn't expected was an overwhelming flood of emotion, a sensation of aching happiness.

"Don't worry, it won't scar," he told me. "The cut is shallow."

Maybe I wanted it to scar. Maybe I wanted his name on my skin forever, but I didn't say it. My ass stung as I slid back into the passenger seat, and I was glad I'd chosen a skirt today instead of denim.

The gate was wide open when we reached their house, and Manson pulled into the yard and parked in front of the garage. I spotted Lucas's legs under a vehicle as I followed Manson into the house, sighing in relief when the cool interior air hit me. As Manson put Lucas's espresso in the fridge, I sat on the stairway to greet the dogs as they snuffled excitedly around my feet.

But a sudden loud burst of singing from upstairs drew my attention. The voice was muffled, but someone up above was scream-singing at the top of their lungs.

Manson laughed. "I guess Vincent is awake."

"His room is in the attic, isn't it?" I said, unable to stop myself from giggling.

Manson nodded. "You can go up if you want. I have to get back to work, so make yourself comfortable."

As Manson returned to the garage, I went upstairs. There was another narrow stairway at the end of the second floor hallway, and the door at the top was open, music blasting from within as Vincent loudly sang along.

I went up the stairs and stopped in the doorway. The attic was spacious, although the angled ceiling limited its height at the edges of the room. A large bed was against one wall, the eclectic selection of patterned blankets and knit quilts rumpled. A couple freestanding clothing racks held shirts, jeans, jackets — also in a plethora of patterns and colors. A round window at the other end of the room allowed in the morning light, and it was in front of this window that Vincent was seated, cross-legged on the floor with a canvas in front of him and paints spread around him.

As the music's chorus began again, he leaned his head back, flinging his paintbrush to the side and splattering blue paint across the floor as he belted out the lyrics.

He noticed me standing there as he opened his eyes, and a wide smile spread across his face. "Oh, shit. Hey, baby." He got to his feet, uncurling his long limbs and enfolding me into a hug. As he let me go, I noticed a collection of spray paint cans in the corner, nestled on the floor behind a large canvas on an easel.

"Is this your new painting?" I said, crouching down to get a better look. The canvas was splashed with various colors, depicting a psychedelic sky over a field of tall green grass. The vague outline of a figure was walking through the field, their back to the viewer and their face turned slightly, as if they were about to look over their shoulder.

"Yep, started it on a whim," he said. "I took an edible last week and had this really vivid dream...I had to try to get it on canvas."

"It looks amazing," I said. The way the colors swirled together reminded me of the iridescence in a pool of oil, and the vastness of the field made me feel as if there was an entire world waiting on the other side of the trees along his horizon.

As I stood and had another look around the room, I spotted some hooks on the wall beside his bed. There were neatly coiled lengths of rope, in various colors and material, alongside a plethora of impact toys: big and small paddles, leather straps, even a slim wooden cane. There was a black chest on the floor beneath the hooks, and I bit my lip curiously.

Vincent noticed me looking.

"That's the toy box," he said, nodding toward the chest with a sly smile. "I've got all kinds of fun things in there."

I had no doubt he did, but a rapid popping noise from outside caught my attention. I stood on my tiptoes at the window to peer down and spotted Jason standing along the side of the garage. He lifted a gun to his shoulder and pulled the trigger, the popping sound pinging again as splatters of bright yellow paint hit a rusted car door leaned up against the side of the garage.

"Paintball?" I said. "Looks like fun."

"It'll be fun all right," Vincent said, coming to stand beside me. "He and Lucas have been putting their heads together for weeks, trying to figure out how we're going to get back at Alex and the others."

I turned, looking at him with wide eyes. "Like a revenge mission?"

"Oh, yeah. Those fuckers need to be taught a lesson. You should go talk to him. I have a feeling they have a very important role for you."

He gave me a wink, and curiosity got the better of me. Leaving him to his artwork, I went back downstairs and out into the yard, trudging around the side of the garage.

Jason saw me coming and paused his target practice, but at the same time, Lucas emerged from the garage's side door with another paintball gun in his hands. I couldn't read his expression as he looked at me; only that it looked pained.

What was his problem? He was always stand-offish, but he was looking at me like I was a grenade that could go off at any second. As if he wasn't sure how safe it was to have me close by.

Whatever. I wasn't going to let him ruin my mood.

"What's all this for?" I said, looking around at the various items they had set up around the yard. Besides the rusted car door, there were also several tin cans on cinder blocks, and another metal panel propped against one of the trees.

"Target practice," Jason said, propping his gun against his shoulder. Lucas had already looked away from me, focusing his attention as he took aim. He fired, the paintballs whizzing across the yard and knocking down three of the cans.

"Next target is Alex's Hellcat," Lucas said, squeezing the trigger again. Another paintball struck the glass in the rusted door, but this one didn't splat. It hit the glass with a sharp sound, cracks spreading from its point of impact.

"Woah…" My eyes widened slightly. "Can I try?"

Lucas handed over the gun. I'd shot my grandpa's BB gun when I was little, but didn't have much experience otherwise. I didn't think a paintball gun would be too different as I took aim at the door, firing off several shots.

I was pleased to see all but two of them hit their target.

"Nice shooting," Jason said, sounding impressed.

Lucas grunted, his eyes narrowed as if he didn't believe I'd done it. "Not bad," he said, taking back the gun. "Looks like you're already prepared for this Saturday, then."

"Saturday?" I said. "Is that when the revenge mission is?"

Jason laughed. "The revenge mission, right. I see you've already talked to Vincent about it."

"Don't sound so excited about it, fucktoy," Lucas said. "What we're going to do is far from legal, but you've never had a problem with that, have you?"

"Not when it's for a good cause," I said easily, getting Jason to smile again and Lucas to look even grouchier. "What's the plan?"

The two of them exchanged a look that spoke of nothing but trouble. Lucas stepped toward me, the strap of his paintball gun over his shoulder. He looked at me like he was sizing me up, and I automatically straightened my shoulders and stood up a little taller.

He noticed me do it, and his nostrils flared.

"All those fucks are going to be at a house party this Saturday," he said. "It's at Nate and Danielle's house in the Heights. Since they thought it was funny to come and thrash our shit, we think it would be pretty damn funny to return the favor."

Of course — the very same party I'd gotten an invite to that morning. But there was a problem they may not have considered.

"How are you going to get in?" I said. The entire community of Wickeston Heights was gated, and you were required to have your name put in at the guardhouse before you'd be allowed inside.

"Well, you got an invite to the party, didn't you?" Jason said. A door clicked shut, and I glanced back to see Manson had emerged from the garage and was making his way over to us.

"Yeah, I got invited," I said. "Let me guess: you want me to RSVP, get my name put in, and then I'll get you all inside?"

"Exactly," Jason said, speaking rapidly with excitement. "I've got paintballs sitting in a cooler with dry ice, and we'll have all the tools we need stored in the back of the Bronco. The last thing we'll need is a distraction."

"I'm great at being distracting," I said, and Manson chuckled.

My brain was already churning with ideas, but Lucas was still glaring at me.

"You're volunteering to come along and fuck up your friends' night?" he said. "Really?"

"They're not my friends," I said quickly, and Lucas rolled his eyes. "I mean it, they're not! They destroyed your cars and left me here to take the blame. Alex is a complete asshole creep and Danielle is a backstabbing bitch." I folded my arms. "So no, they're not my friends, Lucas."

He held up his hands. "Hey, whatever. But you're sounding defensive. Maybe a little guilty…maybe a little uncertain…"

"Lucas…come on, man." Jason shook his head. "She wants to come."

"Never said she couldn't," Lucas said. He leaned close to me again, the challenge obvious in his posture. "All I'm saying is that I don't think she's going to rise to the occasion. I don't think she's down."

"I think she is," Manson said. "You love a challenge, don't you, Jess? Because this is going to be a big one."

"I'm ready for it," I said. "You'll see. You guys aren't the only ones who want payback."

Lucas still didn't look as if he believed me. But Jason sounded excited when he said, "Perfect. We've got this in the fucking bag." He fired a shot, hitting the window right where it was cracked and shattering the glass. "Saturday is going to be fun."

45

JESSICA

That Saturday, I found myself waiting in line to get into the Heights behind the wheel of Manson's massive rumbling Bronco.

It was way more fun to drive the beastly vehicle than I'd expected. The big tires and lifted suspension made the entire thing shake and bump as we drove down the road, jostling us in our seats. Manson sat up front with me, while Lucas, Jason, and Vincent were in the back, their heads ducked down so the guard wouldn't see them as he checked my ID.

It was the same old guard who'd been working that gate for years, although it was far more difficult for him to leer at me when I was in a massive SUV instead of a tiny car.

"Welcome back, Mr. Reed," he said, giving Manson a wave

before he opened the gate and let us drive in. I wasn't surprised he remembered Manson, who used to live in this neighborhood with his former social worker, Kathryn, and her family.

I breathed a sigh of relief once we were in. The boys straightened up as I drove through the Height's winding roads. Some of the houses here were truly massive, mini mansions on every corner. Danielle and Nate's house wasn't so grand, but it was still large. It sat on a one acre lot, a rambling farmhouse surrounded by trees. The only way they were able to afford it was because they had Matthew and his girlfriend as roommates.

I made sure not to drive by the house, but parked down the road so Manson and I could get out. We'd discussed how we could best stage this distraction; we wanted to give the others plenty of time to do everything they needed to, but we also needed to scope out the place before they could move in.

I'd come up with the plan we finally settled on, the perfect way to get and keep everyone's attention at the party. We just needed to do something they'd never expect.

That was why Manson laced his fingers through mine as we walked up the driveway toward the house. My stomach was in knots, my palms clammy with nerves. I usually dressed to the nines for a party, but I couldn't be slowed down by heels and restrictive clothes today.

"I can't believe I wore flats to a party," I whispered as we approached the front door. Vehicles were parked around the yard, but my eyes zeroed in on Alex's Hellcat parked in front of the garage. Nate's truck was next to it, and Danielle's pretty little Lexus was there too.

Manson squeezed my hand. "Feeling nervous?"

"A little," I admitted. Any number of things could go wrong tonight, but I'd already decided it was worth the risk. We looked for any cameras around the exterior of the house, and finding none, Manson texted the group to let them know.

"Ready?" he said. He was about to walk into a party where half the people used to bully him relentlessly, yet he didn't seem worried in the least. Considering I was a bundle of nerves, I was amazed he was so calm.

The two of us were going to walk in there and shatter the entire vibe. Despite how nervous I was, I sincerely couldn't wait to see the look on Danielle's face when we did.

"Ready," I said, and I reached over to ring the doorbell.

The music grew even louder as Candace opened the door. The smile on her face instantly froze when she saw us.

"Oh, Jessica, wow, hi!" she said, her enthusiasm poorly faked. She had a red plastic cup in one hand, and she sounded tipsy despite the early hour. It was only 4 pm, the party was just getting started. But she'd never been able to handle her alcohol very well. "I had no idea you were coming. I, uh…" She looked at Manson, her eyes combing up and down his body in a slow appraisal. "You brought a plus one…cool…"

Manson had exaggerated his outfit on purpose. It was closer to what he used to wear in high school, back when he had the mohawk and everything he put on looked like it had survived a cataclysmic event. His tight acid-wash jeans were covered in patches and ragged holes, his Black Flag t-shirt similarly thrashed. But my favorite part of the ensemble was, obviously, the boots.

They were large, and laced up to his knees, with a thick sole that made his already tall height closer to Vincent's. It made me look particularly small beside him, dressed in my pink crop top and jeans.

"Yeah, it was a spontaneous decision," I said, smiling as I pulled Manson along behind me into the house. Candace was looking at us like I'd allowed an extremely dirty dog to walk in. "I really needed a night out. Work is *killing* me. You know how it is."

I turned away from her with a little wave. Top 40 songs were blasting from the sound system, and people were gathered in every room, yelling to each other over the music. The kitchen was crowded, bottles of liquor and open pizza boxes littered across the countertop.

People looked twice as we passed, and when we stepped into the kitchen to get ourselves drinks, a group of guys who already looked wasted spotted us.

"Holy shit, Manson? What's up, man?" One of the guys grasped Manson's hand, pulling him into a bear hug as he did. The others clapped his back, asking how he'd been, quickly striking up a conversation.

When they eventually moved on, distracted by someone's shouted invitation to open a keg, I looked at Manson in surprise. "That was Rob Davis, wasn't it? I thought he…"

"Shoved my head in a toilet freshman year?" Manson finished for me, pouring a shot of vodka into a plastic cup. "Yeah, that was him. A few of those guys were there for the toilet incident actually." He opened a can of Sprite, emptying it into his cup. "Good times."

"God, they're so *fake*," I hissed, ladling sangria into my own cup. I sipped it as I said, "I don't know how you can stand it."

"I rarely ever see those guys, so I can manage to be polite," he said. "Besides, people change. So long as they aren't giving me or my family a problem, then I don't have a problem with them. We've all done fucked up things when we were young and dumb. You did. I definitely have."

"What did *you* do that was fucked up?" I said, genuinely curious. I could remember him getting into trouble for smoking, tardiness, skateboarding on campus, and obviously, the knife incident. But otherwise, he seemed to always keep his head down.

"Murder and mayhem," he said, putting his arm around my waist as we left the kitchen. We had a mission to accomplish, but we also needed to blend in for at least a little while so no one got suspicious. "You know, stereotypical punk rat shit."

"Murder?" My eyes widened. "No way…"

"I'm joking. Come on, Jess." He gave me that crooked smile that made my heart flutter. "Do I really look like I'd murder someone?"

"Well…" I let it hang, then leaned toward him and said quietly, "You look like you could murder this pussy, so yeah, you do look like a killer."

His smile was barely restrained as he shook his head. "Damn, you've barely even had a drink yet. Flirting with me already?"

"I don't need alcohol to flirt with you." We'd entered the living room, where the large sliding glass door was open, leading to the back patio. Crowds were gathered around the beer pong table outside, and I spotted Danielle and Nate among them, subtly pointing them out to Manson. He pulled out his phone again to let the others know we had eyes on them.

Now we had to find Alex. We needed to know where they all were before the boys made their move.

"Funny, isn't it?" Manson said as we watched the excited crowds. "The last time we were at a party together, I had to dare you to get close to me." He laughed softly. "Now, this time..."

"I'm here because I want to be," I finished for him, smiling gently as I leaned over and kissed him. He stiffened for a moment in surprise before he leaned into the kiss, cupping my face in his hand and smiling against my mouth. I could feel eyes on us and even hear a few murmurs. But I didn't care.

For those people who bothered to care, I hoped it pissed them off. They could all die mad about it if they thought they could dictate who I kissed or who was at my side.

But slowly, the sensation of being watched made a prickly feeling run up the back of my neck. I pulled slowly away from the kiss, turning to look at our audience. Danielle had come back inside and was staring at me — at us. Candace was close behind her, and on the patio, Nate had his eyes narrowed in our direction.

Perfect. We were getting their attention now.

I smiled sweetly, keeping one hand against Manson's chest as I said, "Hey, girl! Feels like it's been ages! Thanks so much for the invite."

By the look on Danielle's face, she was sincerely regretting the invitation now.

"Sure," she said, her teeth clenched. She and Candace proceeded into the kitchen, but they still watched us. My ears burned from wanting so badly to listen in on their conversation.

"...think she's doing? I can't believe..."

"So fucking weird. And what's up with..."

"...whatever. Just keep an eye..."

I tuned them out. This was what it felt like to be on the other side, I guess, but it didn't kill my confidence like I thought it would. In fact, being here in opposition to them made me feel better than ever. Their hatred and disgust fueled me.

Why had I ever been afraid of their rejection? I didn't need them; I didn't need these parties. Lucas didn't think I'd be able to do it, but I was determined to prove him wrong.

I'd changed, and it was for the better. I wasn't the same Jessica they used to know. I wasn't the version of myself that I'd been in high school. This was my chance to abandon all that, to wash my hands of it once and for all.

We still needed to find Alex, but he wasn't out on the patio, nor in the living room. It wasn't until we'd done a slow circle through the house and came back into the kitchen that we finally found him. We walked in, and at the same moment, he turned from pouring himself another drink and spotted us.

"What the fuck?" His voice was loud enough to carry above the other conversations and silence them. People stared between him and us; some with confusion, some with expectant looks that something was about to go down. Alex's shirt was off, showing off his sweaty muscles, and he was wearing a red baseball cap backward on his head. His eyes locked onto Manson and he snapped, "Who the hell invited you?"

"Um, helloooo?" I twiddled my fingers at him. "I did. He's here with me."

Alex worked his jaw, clenching so hard I was surprised I didn't hear his teeth crack. "Right. And why are you here, Jessica?"

"Why wouldn't I be here?" I said, as if the answer was painfully obvious. "Where else would I be on a Saturday night?"

"Probably fucking the losers," Danielle said. She and Candace had walked into the kitchen behind us, with Nate and Matthew in tow this time. It was clear they'd brought the men along to try to intimidate us. But no matter how much they postured and puffed out their chests, Manson remained entirely unbothered. His serene demeanor soothed me, keeping me calm despite how nerve-wracking this was.

"It's a little weird how concerned you are with my sex life," I said. Usually, their insults would have had me on the defensive. The urge to raise my voice was strong, but I wasn't going to let them see me lose my cool.

Danielle clicked her tongue, casually examining her nails. "You know, Jessica, it's sad that you think everyone cares so much about you. You're like a little kid who put on a great big performance and didn't realize that everyone was clapping out of pity. Like right now. Look at you! Did you come here just to parade your freak around? Do you need attention that badly?"

My veins felt like they were on fire. I wanted to fly at her, to claw her face and rip out her ugly extensions. But instead, I looked down at my phone and sent off a quick text to the group chat, **Found Alex. The gang's all accounted for. Move in.**

I tucked my phone away, and lifted my head to find all of them — Alex, Danielle, Candace, and the guys gathered around — staring at me as they waited for a response.

With a laugh, I said, "Oh, I'm sorry. Were you all waiting for me to say something? I thought you'd have better things to do."

Danielle looked absolutely *livid*.

"You know what your problem is?" she snapped, stepping away from Nate to get in my face. People in the living room and on the patio were taking notice now, beginning to gather closer for a look at the fight. "You're so convinced that the world revolves around your little finger, but it *doesn't*, Jessica. The only thing people are revolving around is your cunt, since apparently, you'll give it away to any creep off the street."

Manson made a guttural sound, and I glanced over to find him laughing. He didn't care about his reputation, or gossip, or even the fact that there were people here willing to physically do him harm just for being present.

That was far sexier to me than any of these people mindlessly following the crowd.

I'd known Danielle for years. We'd shared secrets, we'd shared our dreams. But we'd also fed off each other's toxicity, we'd encouraged the worst in each other. That wasn't a friendship. Our relationship with each other had been parasitic, not supportive.

I had to wonder why I made her so angry. I didn't want her man; I'd never intruded in her space. But then I thought of all the people I'd hated without reason. The horrible things I'd said about people I barely knew. How I'd judged people so harshly without ever giving the benefit of a doubt.

It made me feel powerful. It felt good to be the gatekeeper, to hold power over the social lives and decisions that others made. Doubtlessly, Danielle felt the same way.

"Maybe you should take some of your own advice," I said. I didn't want to hate her. But if she kept pushing me, I wouldn't hold back. "The world doesn't revolve around you either, and neither do I."

"God, you are pathetic!" Her voice lifted to a shriek. "You're whoring yourself out to Wickeston's trash. Four guys at once, Jessica? How many more do you need?"

"Apparently Manson likes to get cucked by his own boyfriend." Alex sneered, encouraging some jeers from the people around him. "Where is your dog anyway, Reed? I thought Lucas was always sniffing around your heels."

"Can't bring him around crowds," Manson said. He'd leaned his elbows back on the countertop, so chill you'd think he owned the place. "He bites. *Apparently*, people get pissed about that."

Alex's face darkened, his hands clenching. The tension in the room was thick, and people were starting to get antsy. They were all exactly where they needed to be, focusing on us rather than anything happening at the front of the house.

Danielle's lip curled as she said, "Maybe you want to put on a little show for everyone like you did a few years ago, huh? At Daniel Peters' house?" She pulled out her phone. "I still have the video."

I knew exactly what video she was talking about: me on my knees at Manson's feet, during the drink or dare game we'd played almost three years ago. I'd kissed his boots in front of everyone. I'd soaked in the humiliation like the first hit of a drug and I hadn't been able to shake my addiction to it since.

Bizarrely, I didn't even feel angry. This entire situation was ridiculous, with grown adults giving me a hard time for who I chose to form a relationship with. They were trying so hard to cling to this faux dichotomy, determined that there had to be a hard division between "us" and "them."

"You can put on the video," I said, draining my cup and tossing it in the trash. "Go ahead, stream it to the TV if you'd like. I think it's a classic at this point, but in case anyone doesn't know…" I raised my voice a bit, so everyone could hear me. "It's the video of me kissing Manson's boots at Daniel's Halloween party. We gave each other some wild dares that night, but do you know what's even *wilder*, Danielle?"

She looked like she wanted to hit me.

"It's wild that you think I care what you think of me," I said. I felt such a profound sense of relief once the words were out, I almost laughed. I *had* cared; I'd cared so much that it hurt, that it almost broke me. But not anymore. That paralyzing fear was gone.

My phone buzzed in my pocket, likely the signal from the boys that they were almost ready to bail. Looking at the crowd gathered around us, I said, "Look at all of you! The moment I stepped inside, all your attention was on me. *Me*, Danielle. I don't think the world revolves around me. No, I know it doesn't. But I think you, and all of you other pathetic petty bitches, do revolve around me. You can't help it. You can't even mind your own business long enough to realize that nothing you say matters to me."

She snarled like a shrieking wildcat as she launched at me. In one smooth motion, I reached back, grabbed the bowl of sangria from the counter, and threw the entire thing in her face.

Deathly silence fell. Manson looked stunned, his mouth open in an expression that was dangerously close to bursting into laughter. Everyone stared, wide-eyed, their mouths hanging open as Danielle stood dripping on the kitchen tile. She was gasping, blinking slowly as her mascara began to run.

A sudden loud sound from outside snapped everyone out of it, and I knew instantly that we had to *go*. Manson heard it too, and as soon as I glanced over at him, he grabbed my hand, pulling me with him as we ran. We shoved through the crowd, sprinting for the door. I had no idea who all was behind us — Danielle was screaming like a banshee, Alex was yelling, and I could hear multiple footsteps in pursuit.

We burst out the front door and the Bronco was there, the back hatch open. Vincent was in the driver's seat, and Jason and Lucas were crouched in the back, ski masks over their faces and paintball guns in their arms.

I leapt into the back as Manson sprinted for the front passenger seat, and the moment I was safely between them, Lucas and Jason opened fire.

Frozen paintballs pinged off the cars, peppering their windshields and leaving tiny dings across the metal. They'd thrown a few regular balls into the mix too, as bright paint splattered across the Hellcat's shiny red exterior.

With a whoop of excitement, Jason hauled the back hatch closed and yelled, "Go, Vince, step on it!"

Vincent slammed on the gas, the big tires quickly gaining traction. I watched out the back window, my heart pounding out of my chest as people spilled out of the house. Alex came outside, took one look at our Bronco fleeing the scene, and sprinted for his car. His headlights came on, and I said, "He's going to follow us!"

Lucas smiled grimly beside me. "He won't get very far."

He was right. The red car lurched toward us, and for a few seconds, it seemed like Alex was quickly gaining speed. But his front tires began to wobble, then shake, then —

"Holy shit!" One of Alex's front tires bent inward, his car swerving to the side and spinning out in the dirt. The headlights on Nate's truck were on too, but we were gaining momentum and were quickly too far away to see what exactly was happening. I turned, looking at Jason. "What did you do?"

"Loosened the lug nuts on their wheels," he said. "And put sugar in their gas tanks."

Lucas continued, "We snipped a few wires, pulled a few hoses…"

"And cut their brake lines," Vincent called from the driver's seat. He glanced back at me, shoving his hand excitedly against Manson's shoulder. "Did you two have a good time in there?"

I shrugged, as if it had just been a casual night out. "I threw a bowl of sangria in Danielle's face."

Vincent burst out laughing, and Jason grabbed me and squeezed me into a hug as he said, "That's our girl! I fucking knew you'd kill it."

I'd never thought that hearing "our girl" from his lips would give me butterflies.

46

LUCAS

S he'd done it. I never would have believed it if I hadn't seen it with my own eyes. Jessica walked into her friends' party and came out as a traitor. Seeing the smile on her face, the enthusiasm as she cheered at our victory, felt like stepping into a parallel universe.

I'd been certain she was faking it at the track. Cheering for Jason, acting excited for the win — it had to be fake. She'd been told to submit to us and to think of our pleasure, so what better way to do that than to pretend she was invested in our victories?

But now…now I didn't know if I believed that anymore.

We sped through Wickeston Heights, slowing only when we reached the gate and tried to look casual as we drove past the guardhouse again. But that old guard couldn't be bothered to even glance up as the exit gate opened for us and we were free.

"Aren't you guys afraid they'll report this?" Jess said. "I mean, Nate's dad is a cop…"

"If they report us, we'll report them," Jason said. "And we have a hell of a lot more evidence against them besides what they did to the cars. If Nate wants to go crying to Daddy, then he'd also better be prepared to explain all the party drugs he's bought from Vincent over the years."

Vincent chuckled from the driver's seat. "There's benefits to being everyone's dealer. Prime blackmail material."

"If they want it to get ugly, I can make it fucking ugly," Jason went on, with a grim smile. That was the only reason we'd been able to be so bold with this. Getting the police involved would work out badly for everyone, but if that's what they wanted to do, we could do far worse than simply fucking up their rides.

"We have plenty of ammo with us that isn't frozen," Manson said as we drove. "We should go over to Crookston. We still have enough light."

"What's Crookston?" Jess was seated between Jason and I, and she was still vibrating with energy. Her green eyes were bright, and her posture was rigid as her fingers tapped rapidly on the shoulder of the front seat.

What was her deal anyway? What did she want? Why was she doing this?

Why did she keep playing these games?

"Crookston High School," Jason said. "The whole building has been abandoned for decades. We use it for paintball games."

"I'd be down to play a round," Vincent said. His tone changed as he gave Jess a mischievous look in the rearview mirror. "And what do you know, we have enough guns for everyone. Even you, Jess."

"Really?" Her voice came out squeaky, and I thought she was about to say she wasn't interested. "Oh, hell yeah! Let's go!"

I didn't know what the hell she was thinking.

We kept driving, eventually taking a turn and heading back into the trees. The old high school couldn't be seen from the road anymore — its yard was overtaken by tall grass and overgrown trees. In the dusk, it looked particularly eerie with its broken windows, its chained doors halfway off their hinges. The white plaster exterior was now a dingy gray, with streaks of brown that seeped from the window frames like dried blood.

"It was abandoned back in the 70s," Vincent explained to Jess. She was edged up on the seat next to me for a better view as the Bronco bounced along the rutted road, the asphalt buckled and cracked from years of neglect. "Attendance was too low. They locked it up and left everything behind."

I glanced to the side, just in time to see Jess's eyes dart away from me. I was the first one out of the vehicle as we came to a stop, shoving open the door before the car was even in park.

"Ready for a little urban exploration, fucktoy?" I said, leaving the door open so Jess could climb out behind me. We all piled out, stretching our arms and rolling the stiffness out of our shoulders.

She looked at the old building sprawled out before her, half overtaken by creeping vines. "Looks pretty creepy. Is it haunted?"

"Probably," Jason said, and she laughed, playfully shoving his shoulder. My frown deepened even more.

"Technically, it's private property, but no one bothers to check for trespassers," Manson said as he opened the Bronco's hatch and pulled out our guns, tossing one to each of us. Jess caught hers easily.

"Are we going against each other?" she said, watching as Jason and Vincent reloaded their hoppers.

"That's right. Player versus player," Jason said.

"We'll spread out through the building," Manson said. "Last man standing without paint on him wins."

"Or woman," Jess said, and I gave a low laugh that made her fix me with a narrow-eyed glare. "What do you think is so funny?"

"That you think you have a chance at winning," I said, resting my gun against my shoulder. "Or that you're playing at all. Honestly, I can't decide which one is funnier."

Manson was giving me a *don't start shit* look, but it was too late for that. Jess marched up to me, jabbing her purple nail against my chest.

"Not only am I going to play and win," she said viciously, "but I'm taking you out *first*."

"Oooh, she's coming for you, Lucas," Vincent said, and Jason snickered. I glared down at the tiny woman in front of me, her gun strapped over her shoulder, her hip cocked.

"You'll be *coming* for me," I said, and her eyes flashed. "Just not in the way you think."

"All right, all right, let's go!" Manson clapped his hands sharply to get us all focused. Jess and I gave each other one last biting glare before we walked across the old parking lot toward the building, and Manson explained our rules to her as we went. "If you get shot, you're out. Text the group and wait back at the Bronco. The building's layout is pretty simple. It's a square with one long hall down the middle and two halls straight across, on both floors. Structural integrity is pretty good, but watch your step. Oh, and keep an eye out for squatters."

Visibility was getting low, with barely enough daylight remaining that we wouldn't need flashlights as long as we were near the windows. Vincent showed Jess how to turn on her flashlight just in case, which we all had attached to our scopes.

We were able to get in through the front door, squeezing into the dark hallway beyond. Rows of lockers and classrooms stretched ahead of us, leaves, dirt, and debris scattered across the floor and piled in the corners.

"All right, set your timers," Manson said, pulling out his phone and the rest of us followed. "Five minutes to spread out and find yourself a good position to defend…or start hunting." He grinned, only his teeth catching the light. "You didn't refill your ammo, Lucas, do you want us to wait?"

"Nope." I trudged on ahead, brushing Jess's shoulder as I did. "Unlike you fucks, I can actually aim."

Jess exhaled with a sharp sound behind me, her tone sarcastic as she said, "I bet you only need one paintball for each of us, right? You're just that good?"

I kept walking. That little brat was going to regret trying to taunt me.

Who the hell did she think she was? After years of looking down her nose at us from the other side, Miss Martin suddenly wanted to play delinquent. She wanted to run around with us like she'd never laughed in our faces, like she'd been here all along.

Damn it, and I'd brought this on myself. I was the one who'd insisted she come along today, and for what? Because I'd hoped to see her chicken out. I'd wanted to see her bail on us because it would prove me right. But she hadn't. She fucking hadn't, in fact — she'd been brilliant. She'd smiled and laughed at Alex getting what he deserved, and she'd come along without even hesitating.

I took the stairs two at a time, boots crunching on old broken glass. Graffiti covered the walls in the stairwell, light pouring in the broken windows in narrow shafts. Maybe the others were quick to forget who Jess really was, but not me.

Fat fucking chance I'd forget. I had too many scars for that.

I didn't understand the point of forgiveness. Where the hell did it get you? Right back where you started: naïve and vulnerable to the same shit happening again. This deal with Jess was supposed to be a game, but the others were getting far too cozy. Sleeping at her house, driving her around, working out with her?

No. Hell no. This is how we'd get fucked over, this was how Manson was going to end up with his heart broken all over again. This was how I...

Shit. This was how I was going to get myself in trouble. Getting these stupid *soft* feelings for her. Feeling *proud* of her. Feeling like I wanted to kiss her every damn time I saw her, or make her laugh, or see her smile.

God fucking damn it.

I slipped into a classroom and checked my timer. A little under a minute remained. I stood near the window and peered out at the courtyard below, spotting Vincent as he crept past a few rusted lunch tables. I lifted my gun, locking my aim on him. It was definitely shady of me to take aim before our time was up, but whatever. He shouldn't have been out in the open.

My phone vibrated in my pocket as the timer ended, and my finger tightened on the trigger.

A sound from the hallway made me freeze, like the clatter of an aluminum can being kicked. I immediately shifted my aim to the doorway, crouching low behind a desk. I slowed my breathing and listened, my twitchy finger ready to fire. Come on...push open the door...

There was a creek, a soft step...then nothing. From down in the courtyard, I heard someone fire once, twice, then three times. But there was no cry of dismay to tell me anyone had been taken out, and I rolled my eyes as I slowly stood up.

I'd meant what I said about having better aim than all of them.

I nudged the door open wide as I crept back into the hall, sweeping my gaze from one end to the other. It could have only been a critter scrambling around, but I stayed low, peering carefully into the next classroom. Nothing, but I did catch a brief whiff of a familiar scent: strawberry and vanilla. That one little sniff made me salivate, and I continued on, my steps quickening.

Where the hell was she?

The better part of my brain told me I was acting like a child. Taking Jess out in this game wouldn't prove shit, it wouldn't stop what was happening. It wouldn't stop the way the others looked at her, and it wouldn't change the way I felt. Manson would say I needed an outlet, a way to release my frustration. Well, that was exactly what I was doing.

Venting some fucking frustration.

But Jess was cleverer than I'd thought. As I passed a row of lockers, I paused again, faced with an upcoming stairway on either side. My eyes narrowed as I lowered my weapon. It was so eerily quiet I could have heard a needle drop.

Suddenly, with a popping spray of paintballs, Jess burst out of one of the lockers. They peppered my chest, hot pink paint splattering over my shoulder and across my right arm. I tensed so hard I almost lost my footing, stumbling back as I stared at her in disbelief.

"Woooo! Yes!" Jess bounced on her toes, pumping her hands as I stared with wide eyes. Her grin was huge as she continued her victory dance. "Ha! I told you I'd get you!"

My hands tightened on the gun. No way...no fucking way did she actually...

"Hey! Hey, wait a minute, you're out!" She backed away as I advanced, her victory celebration cut short. My vision was tunneling, narrowing in on that freckled face whose smugness was quickly shifting to worry. "I shot you, Lucas! You're cheating!"

She almost stumbled over debris, dodging into the first classroom on her left. I came in after her, immediately greeted by another paintball straight to the chest. Damn it, that one was going to leave a welt. She shrieked as I took aim, barely dodging the paintball that exploded against the wall beside her.

"Why...won't...you...go...down?!" She fired with every word, each ball hitting me square in the chest as I kept coming. Her eyes grew wider with every step, realization dawning on her as she was torn between fight or flight.

She didn't get to win this. Not against me.

She leapt away as I lunged for her, sprinting back out of the room as I gave chase. I aimed again — missed. Damn it. She scrambled halfway down the stairway and then leapt, landing in a crouch before she kept running. Why was she fucking fast? My lungs were aching as I chased her at full speed down the dark hallway below, then through the open doors into the courtyard.

She kept glancing back over her shoulder, eyes wide, panting for breath. God, that expression on her face made me want to grab her, dig my fingers into her skin, feel her writhe and struggle against me. I spotted Jason peering down from one of the windows above and heard him fire, but we were both running too fast to be hit.

Jess burst through the doors on the opposite side of the courtyard and we were back inside. She turned so fast that I skidded on the floor, bracing myself against the lockers on the wall as she turned to face me.

Her face was red, her hair wild, her chest heaving for breath. I felt like I'd run a goddamn marathon. I was gasping for air as my eyes narrowed in on her.

"Give up," she demanded, taking aim at me again. "I have plenty more ammo and you haven't hit me once, loser!"

Loser. Oh…oh-ho, she'd done it now.

I fired, striking her shoulder. She yelped, clutching where she'd been hit, and I took full advantage. The next paintball hit her chest, the next hit her thigh, and she yelled, swearing at me furiously.

"That fucking hurts, you asshole!" She ducked into a classroom and crouched behind the large desk in front of the blackboard. I was out of ammo anyway. I tugged the strap on my gun until it was resting against my back, out of my way, before I went to grab her.

Little brat was still fighting. She had her finger on the trigger, and she started firing the moment I stepped around the desk. Paintballs at close range hurt like a bitch, but I didn't care. The pain got my dick hard, and I suddenly didn't give a fuck about winning or losing this stupid game. I cared about putting Jessica in her place.

I disarmed her, pinning her down, and wrenching the gun out of her hands. I shoved it away, sending it skittering across the floor before she could manage to grab it again. She was so damn slippery that she almost got away, but I hauled her to her feet and held her back against me, my hand gripped around her throat.

"You're fucking cheating!" she snarled furiously. The way she was wiggling was rubbing her ass on my cock, and I couldn't help grinding against her. She growled again when she felt me do it, snapping, "God, you're such a pervert, Lucas! You sicko!"

Every furious word spurred me on. She fought with all her strength, pouring out her fury, but she could have simply called her safeword and gotten away. She could have, yet she didn't.

"Call red, Jess," I said, my voice tight as I struggled to keep her in place. She was fighting so hard, but if I wasn't careful, I'd hurt her, and I didn't want to do that. "Call it, now. Give up."

She laughed, the sound maniacally mocking. "Give up? Oh yeah, I bet you wish I'd give up." She did it again, grinding her ass against me. She was doing it on purpose now. "You lost! I got you just like I said I would."

She almost wrenched herself out of my hold, but I snatched her back. I pressed her against the wall, pinned there by the throat. There was nothing but defiance in her eyes as she looked at me, our bodies pressed so close that I could feel her chest rise and fall with every breath.

"Why won't you fucking call it?" I said. "Why don't you stop trying? You're not going to win."

Her lips pulled back from her teeth. "I already won and you cheated! You — Goddamn it!" She rested her head back against the wall, eyes closed for a moment as she panted. "Why don't you admit it? I got you. Why don't you…I wish…"

She opened her eyes again. Those green irises stared into mine, full of confusion and sincerity and something so strange I didn't dare put a word to it.

"You wish *what*?" I said. "That I'd play fair? Because I don't fucking play that way, sweetheart."

She was still pushing back against me, but I could tell she was wearing out, her arms beginning to shake. Thank God for that, because I didn't know how much more energy I had left to try to fight her.

"I wish you didn't hate me," she said, and it felt as if my entire world ground to a halt.

"Hate you?" I said. "You think…you think I hate you?"

Her nails dug into my wrists as she nodded. She looked so angry, so…hurt. Fuck.

I moved my hand up, from gripping her throat to gripping her chin. She was so strong it stunned me. Every time I moved her, I had to fight for it. We were close enough to breathe the same air, and I didn't want any more space between us.

"I wish I hated you," I said. Her face tensed, tightened — contorted with confusion. "Everything would be so much fucking easier if I hated you."

There was a long moment where we merely looked at each other. Her eyes roamed over my face, uncertain, disbelieving.

"You don't?" she said softly, and her words shook as if the answer meant everything to her. But why should it? Why would she care? I was a fucking loser and she was...

I couldn't be sure which of us went for the kiss first. She grabbed me, using all her strength to pull me closer, but I was already surging against her as if I could melt into her. Her kiss was wild, almost rabid as she raked her nails down my arms. She bit my lip. I crushed her against the wall until she moaned.

But that moan broke me. God, I couldn't get enough. I couldn't breathe without her. I was tugging her shirt over her head and she was pulling at the button on my jeans, finally yanking it open and squeezing my bulge.

There were still rows of desks in this old classroom, and I pushed Jess over one of them. Bent over, legs splayed, I wrapped her ponytail around my hand and held her there, giving her beautifully round ass a hard smack.

"Goddamn it, Lucas..." She groaned as I pulled her pants down. She was wearing a thong underneath, and I paused for a moment as I noticed the scabbed cut on her right cheek.

Manson's name was carved into her skin. It gave me a shiver of pleasure to see the way my man had already claimed her, and I brushed my fingers over the cuts, before hurriedly tugging down my boxers.

"Is this what you used to think about?" she said breathlessly. I bet she was trying to sound taunting, but her words came out as desperate. "When you sat behind me in biology, was this why you were constantly staring at me?"

"Damn right, it was." I sunk into her, her pussy deliciously wet and warm as she clung around me. Part of the reason I failed that class — besides the fact that I didn't care — was that I couldn't stop staring at the back of her head, fantasizing about her, imagining that stuck-up look on her face crumbling into the expression she had now.

Full of longing, pained with need, looking at me like I was the only way she could get what she so desperately wanted.

I pounded into her, the desk squeaking on the old floor as I used her hard. "I thought about this so many times, Jess." I ground out the words as she throbbed around me. "I wanted to bend you over in front of the whole damn class." She groaned as I lowered my voice and said, "I knew it would only take a few strokes and you'd be begging me for more."

Her mouth hung open as she cried my name. I pressed down on her lower back, arching her into me. Her thighs shook, squeezing so damn tight around me, every hard thrust brought a moan from her.

She cried out again as she came, clenching so hard my vision sparked. I scratched my nails down her spine, curling over her like a beast as I came inside her.

"This is what you've fucking done to me," I growled right in her ear as I pressed as deep as I could get. I wanted every drop of my cum in her. I wanted her to feel the heat of it for the rest of the night. "I'm not good at letting go of things I want, and you...I have wanted you for so goddamn long."

I went still at last, both of us out of breath. My heart was pounding so hard I was surprised it didn't burst. I pulled her up and against me before I weakly sunk down against the wall, taking her with me. She sat on my lap, my cock still inside her, her legs twitching as she rested against my chest.

"You won," I finally said, once I had enough air in my lungs. "You won, you little brat. Happy?"

I swear the way she wiggled was another victory dance. "Yeah. I'm happy, Lucas."

That statement shouldn't have made me feel so good. Like I'd done something right, like her happiness was a gold star and I'd won first prize. Damn it all, I was pathetic. Falling for a woman I should have detested, having thoughts of domestic bliss and imagining beds big enough for all of us.

I knew better, and yet…apparently, I didn't. I was screwed like the rest of them.

But then Jess turned on my lap. I slipped out of her, but she still straddled me, chest to chest, her fingers caressing over my lips as she looked into my eyes.

"I don't hate you either, Lucas," she said. "Even when you irritate me, or glare at me, or cheat at games…" She kissed me, and it was so much slower and gentler than any kiss I'd ever been given. It made my body melt in a way I really wasn't used to.

I liked it. More than liked it. Far, far more.

"Well, I'm glad to see you two didn't kill each other."

We both glanced up. Manson stood in the doorway, with his paintball gun propped on his shoulder. Vincent's head popped up behind him, and I glimpsed a flash of blue hair in the hallway.

"I am in fact mortally wounded," Jess said dramatically,

motioning at the splatters of paint on her clothes. I didn't feel like getting up yet; I needed another couple minutes before my legs would be willing to work.

"It was a bloodbath," I said, resting my head against the wall as I tightened my hold on her waist.

"Don't tell me she got you?" Vincent snickered. I finally found the strength to get myself up, helping Jess with me. We adjusted our clothes, and the boys got to see how many bursts of paint I had splattered across my chest.

"Shit, you weren't kidding." Jason circled me, nodding his head. "Not bad, princess."

She beamed, looking proud of herself. When she glanced back at me, I scowled to hide my smile.

"Don't get used to it," I said. "You got lucky." She just lifted her chin, smirking.

"Well, who won then?" Jason said.

Manson raised his hand, grinning. "No one got me."

But I shook my head. I hated to admit defeat; I really did. But Jess had played fair and I hadn't. "I only shot Jess after she shot me multiple times. She never got eliminated."

"We'll call it a tie, then," Manson said, slinging the strap of his gun over his shoulder. "Are you all ready to head home? I'm starving."

"Let's pick up pizza on the way back," Vincent said as the five of us left the classroom and made our way out of the school. "Oh, wait, no, hot wings…or maybe burgers…or all three?"

Jess laughed softly at his indecision. We were walking close, our arms bumping into each other. I slipped my arm around her side, encircling her waist and pulling her closer against me.

"I'll admit it," I said. "You're a damn good shot."

She smiled as she leaned into my side. The chaos in my brain had calmed, but instead of leaving me confused and irritable like it usually would, I felt okay. Content.

I felt happy.

47

VINCENT

"Drinks are up, fuckers!"

I shoved open the backdoor with my foot, my arms full with cups as I emerged into the backyard. Sparks rose into the darkness as Lucas tossed more wood into the fire, the night air potent with the rich scent of smoke. We'd hauled ass to the nearest pizza place, returning to our house with three large pies and an order of hot wings. It felt nice and cool outside so we'd decided to get a fire going and eat in the yard, our folding chairs set up in a circle around the flames.

"For the lady," I said, passing a drink to Jess as she sat with her feet up in her chair.

"Oh, I'm a *lady* now, am I?" she said.

Manson reached over from beside her and gave her face a

squeeze. "You still hold the official fucktoy title. But I have to say, hearing you laugh like the Joker when Alex's car got fucked was one of the sexiest things I've ever heard. You've earned the honor of being *Lady* Fucktoy."

Jason snickered. "It's a very elevated position."

Jess shook her head, dramatically rolling her eyes. "God, you're all terrible."

"And you like it," I said, raising my cup in a toast. "Gentlemen — and Lady Fucktoy — I propose a toast. To whatever poor bastards have to try to repair Alex's Hellcat."

They laughed as they drank. Jess took a long sip, her eyes widening before she swallowed.

"Damn, this is good," she said. She looked over at me, nodding as if impressed. "So, you can do more than just tell terrible jokes."

"My jokes are fantastic," I said, taking my seat. "Not my fault you don't understand the highest level of highbrow humor."

"Truly the *highest*," Jason said, laughing when I reached over to smack his arm.

"I'm surrounded by brats," I said. "Honestly, what have I done to deserve to be surrounded by brats?"

"Can't do shit about it either," Lucas said, shaking his head as if he was disgusted. But I could see the mischief in his gaze when he looked at Jess. "You can chase a brat down with a gun and they still won't submit."

Jess stuck out her tongue at him across the fire. We dug into the food, holding paper plates and napkins on our laps. Jojo came to beg, of course, resting her head on Manson's lap with the biggest puppy-dog eyes she could muster.

"You're a bartender, right?" Jess said, looking at me in between bites of pizza. She lifted her cup and took another sip. "You clearly know how to make a good cocktail."

"Yep. At Tris," I said. "It's a club in Memphis. Can't say I'm a fan of driving an hour to get there, but the tips are good."

"What kind of club is it? I can't really imagine you serving up drinks to honky-tonk."

"I can get down with all kinds of music," I said. "But it's not a country club, no. They play a lot of electronic, and occasionally they'll put on a metal show. Tris is a little unusual. It's not exactly a BDSM club, but they do work with the local kink and LGBTQ communities. They'll hold munches there sometimes, but mostly it's just a fun place for music. And obviously, the drink selection is superior."

Jess tipped her head curiously. "Munches? What is that?"

"It's a gathering for people interested in BDSM," Manson said. "A way to meet the local community and like-minded people. The first munch Vince and I ever went to was at Tris." He laughed softly, and I knew even before he said it that he was thinking of how embarrassing that first meeting had been. "We went into it so damn cocky, too. Tris is supposed to be 21+, but we were 18 and snuck in. I don't think we fooled a single person there."

"Everyone was side-eying us like we were kids," I said. The memory still made me cringe, and I wasn't one to be easily embarrassed. "We thought we were hot shit, big bad dominant dudes."

"They set us straight pretty damn fast," Manson said. "The woman who runs the munches pulled us aside and warned us to behave or we'd never set foot there again. She knew we really wanted to learn, but we needed to humble ourselves a bit. We didn't get to call ourselves Dominant just because we felt like it."

Mistress Rachel and her husband, Mark, had set us on the right track. It was lucky we'd had someone to call out our bad habits early, before we got too involved in the scene. Someone could have gotten hurt if we'd gone on thinking that all you needed to tie someone up or wield a whip was the desire to do so. It took a hell of a lot more responsibility than mere desire.

"We'll take you there sometime," I said, and Jess smiled excitedly. She looked like she'd be right at home in a club, dancing under the neon lights. "I think you'd enjoy it."

"I love going dancing," she said. "I feel like I hit every club in Nashville during college." She looked between us, eyes narrowing slightly as she thought. "Which one of you is the best dancer?"

She looked at Lucas and his expression was completely appalled.

"Me? You think it's *me*?" he said, nervously rubbing his hand over the back of his head. "I can't dance for shit."

"Have you ever tried?" she said, and he vehemently shook his head again.

Manson was snickering at him. "Closest he'll come to dancing is a mosh pit."

"Pft, as if you're any better," Lucas said.

Manson innocently put up his hands. "I didn't say I was better, trust me. I'm happy right there in the pit with you. Sorry, Jess, I'm no good either."

"Aw, you've just never tried," she said. "We'll get you both on the dance floor when we go to Tris."

Not *if* we went to Tris — *when*. I shot a quick glance at Jason, and as he returned the look, I knew he'd caught it too.

"What about you, Jason?" she said, and he gave her a cocky smirk after he'd sipped his drink.

"I'm the best dancer," he said, and not a single one of us denied it. "And I actually enjoy it."

Jess glanced at me next, and I quickly shook my head. "Nope, not me. I'm a musician, not a dancer."

"Oh, a musician?" Jess leaned back in surprise. "Another hidden talent from you?"

"I'm full of them." I gave her a wink as I got out of my seat. "Give me a minute."

I went back inside and up to the attic, retrieving Miss Daisy from her case and bringing her outside. Jess's mouth dropped open when I returned.

"Oh my God — is that fiddle?" she exclaimed.

"This is Miss Daisy," I said, holding out the instrument so she could see it. "She's been in the family awhile, as you can see…" I pointed to all the little drawings and stickers on the lower bout, including the simple daisies drawn on with a marker. "My sister, Mary, got ahold of it when we were kids and left her mark. I think it adds character."

"I had no idea you could play," she said.

"How else do you think I seduced this charming gentleman?" I said, motioning toward Jason as I sat down again. "I played him the song of my people and he simply couldn't resist me." Jason almost choked on his drink, sputtering as he tried to stop his laughter.

"The song of your people?" Jess arched an eyebrow at me. "And what would that be, exactly?"

I held up my hand for perfect silence. I tucked the instrument beneath my chin, positioned my fingers as I lifted the bow...

And began to play the Benny Hill theme.

They all burst out laughing. But that wasn't the only song in my repertoire. I transitioned to the Charlie Daniels Band, and Jess got out of her seat, holding her drink in one hand as she danced around the fire. She pulled Manson out of his chair and he gave her a twirl before he caught her close in his arms. Jason clapped to the tune as they danced, and even Lucas still had a smile on his face as he watched them.

Nights where we got to let loose and enjoy each other's company were too few and far between. But Jess had snapped all of us out of our heads. She'd made us adjust our reality and try something new. She even managed to get Lucas out of his seat for a dance, albeit briefly.

She eventually stumbled into Jason's lap, laughing drunkenly as she rested her head on his shoulder. I switched it up again and slowed the pace to something calm and mellow. That was one of my favorite things about music — how it could tug people's emotions and change the mood with only a few notes. Between my slow pull on the strings, the crackling fire, and the alcohol, I could tell everyone was beginning to tire.

As the fire died down, Jess yawned and stretched in Jason's arms.

"I think that's a sign, boys," he said, helping Jess to her feet with an arm around her waist. "It's probably time to tuck in."

Manson nodded as he got out of his seat, pausing to stretch. Lucas buried the last smoldering coals, and Jess blinked up at me sleepily, her head resting against Jason's chest.

"You're sleeping right here with us tonight," I said, leaning down to kiss her soft lips, then Jason's. She looked so comfortable in his arms, stifling a yawn behind her hand. Manson came up alongside her, taking her hand as it lowered and kissing her knuckles. She smiled, humming a drunk little tune as she trudged up the back steps.

Then Lucas swooped up behind her, snatching her from between Manson and Jason and scooping her into his arms. She gasped, her eyes going wide as she looked up at him.

"I'm not going to watch you trip and fall flat on your face trying to get upstairs," he said. "I'm carrying you to bed."

"My bed is the biggest," I called to Lucas as Manson opened the door for him to carry Jess inside. "Everybody can pile in."

"I'm going to be sweating my ass off with all you fucks," Jason said, but he was a sucker for cuddling and wouldn't have it any other way.

It took a while for everyone to shower and get into bed in various states of undress. Jess was swaddled in one of my shirts, and figuring out where she fit into this cuddlefest took another ten minutes of shifting around and swearing at each other. Eventually we settled in, with Jess in between Manson and Jason, and Lucas and me on either side.

"You'd better not kick me in your sleep this time," Lucas grumbled, even as he wrapped his arms around Manson's chest and rested his head against his back. We shoved away the blankets, our combined body heat more than enough to keep us warm. I'd always been a night owl and was used to staying up late, but even if I wasn't tired, I still didn't want to miss the opportunity to cuddle up in bed. I missed it too much on the nights I was gone.

Jason sighed against me, and I looked down to find him already drifting off to sleep. He was usually tossing and turning for hours. But Jess's arm was thrown over his back, her long nails slowly scratching soothing circles on his skin.

Soon enough, I was the last one left awake. But part of me felt like it was worth staying awake just to see all of us so close.

After everything that had happened over these past few weeks, it was nice to feel at peace.

48

JESSICA

When I first opened my eyes the next morning, blinking slowly in the golden light from the window, I immediately knew I wasn't ready to get up yet. I was too cozy, too comfortable. My legs were tangled with Jason's, my arm laid over his side and resting on Vincent's chest. Manson was against my back, so I closed my eyes and snuggled into the pillows, dozing off again until the need to use the bathroom finally drove me to get up.

Quietly slipping out of bed, I noticed Lucas was already gone. I wasn't sure whose oversized shirt I was wearing, so I pulled it over my nose and deeply inhaled — Vincent. Sour-sweet marijuana and citrusy brightness that left a smile on my face as I left the attic.

"Good morning, Jojo," I greeted her at the base of the attic stairway, where she was sprawled across the floor. Her tail wagged lazily as I patted her side, giving a little sigh of sleepy contentment.

I finished up in the bathroom and felt a bit more awake with my face washed and some of the tangles worked out of my hair. The scent of freshly brewed coffee wafted through the house, beckoning me downstairs and into the kitchen.

Lucas was standing at the counter, pouring into his mug from a full pot. He was shirtless and barefoot, wearing only loose red sweatpants. God, he looked sexy. All his hours of work in the garage had honed his muscles and roughened his big hands. But his face looked softer in the morning, as if it hadn't settled into his permanent scowl quite yet.

"Good morning," I said, after leaning silently against the doorframe for several moments to admire him.

He glanced at me over his shoulder. "I was wondering when you'd say something. You're not so sneaky, girl, I heard you come down the stairs. What were you doing back there anyway, staring at my ass?"

I snickered, coming to stand beside him. "Maybe. So what if I was? You have a nice ass."

He raised his eyebrows at me before quickly turning his head back toward the cabinets. "Do you want some coffee?" he said, already pulling down a mug for me.

"With cream and sugar, please."

My eyes roamed over his back as he prepared it. His elaborate back tattoo appeared to still be in progress; the outline was there but shading was absent. But the detail it already contained was stunning. A large tree was the main focus of the piece, the trunk following his spine, its branches sprawled across his shoulders.

"What inspired the back tattoo?" I said as he turned with both our mugs in his hands. He handed mine over, and I took a sip, the scent and rich taste instantly elevating my mood.

"Let's go sit on the porch," he said. "It's not too hot out yet."

The morning air was fresh and cool, but the clear blue sky told me it would be warming up swiftly. We sat in the shade of the porch; I took an old rocking chair that creaked slightly as I swayed, while Lucas sat on the bench seat beside me.

"Where I used to live, when I was kid, we had a big tree in the backyard," he said, after several moments of silence. "It was a massive old thing. Huge limbs, and a lot of them were low to the ground so it was easy to climb up. My brother and I used to make these shitty, hazardous forts in the branches. Like we'd literally take old scrap wood and sheet metal, and heap it all together with some rope and nails. Not much of a treehouse, but…I love those memories. They're good. I'm trying to focus more on remembering what was good instead of everything else." He sipped his coffee, nodding slowly. "So that was what inspired the tattoo. Good memories."

"I never knew you had a brother," I said. "When you moved here, he didn't…"

He kept his eyes focused ahead, but his hand tightened on the bench beside him. "He didn't come with us when we moved, neither did my mom. Just me and Pops, a match made in Hell." He shook his head, exhaling softly. "Pops really only brought me with him so he could have someone else to work and bring money into the house. Mama couldn't handle me; she was too sick. She's still in that same old house I grew up in. I send money back for her caregiver. She has to have someone come out and help her seven days a week."

I tried to imagine my own mom allowing someone to help her around the house. She'd probably nitpick their every move, disgusted that nothing was up to her standards.

"Your dad was hard to get along with?" I said, knowing that was probably the understatement of the year.

"Yeah, he was a dick," Lucas said bluntly. "He wasn't the type of person who believed in having conversations with his kids. You either did what he told you or he'd fucking make you. And I was a difficult little shit so I spent most of my childhood getting my ass whipped every other day." He stopped, then cleared his throat. "Anyway. Family seems to be more trouble than it's worth in most cases. Manson got fucked over by his folks, Jason practically escaped a cult." He glanced over at me. "No offense, but your mom sounds like a piece of work."

"My mom can be a *lot*. I think she has my best interests at heart…maybe." I sighed, settling back in the rocking chair. "She wants everything her way, always. And if not — damn, you'd better watch out because she'll never let it go."

"Struggles to give up control, thinks she's the center of the world…why does that sound familiar?"

"Hey, watch it," I said, stretching out my leg to kick at him playfully. "Don't start comparing me to my mother."

We both looked up as the door opened. Manson, Vincent, and Jason filed out, squinting in the sunlight with mugs of coffee in their hands.

"Mornin' y'all," Vincent said, plopping down heavily on the bench beside Lucas and slinging his arm around the other man's shoulders. He jostled Lucas enough that he almost spilled his coffee, but Vincent didn't seem to notice as he sipped his own down. "Beautiful day."

"It's gonna be a scorcher," Jason muttered, sitting down on the steps.

Manson came over to my chair, carefully taking my mug and setting it alongside his own on the railing before he squeezed into the chair beside me. He pulled me onto his lap, settling me back before grabbing our mugs again.

"That's better," he said. He looped his arm around my waist and rested his head against the side of mine, his voice husky with sleep. "I woke up and you'd left. I don't remember giving you permission to leave bed."

I giggled. "You couldn't exactly give permission if you were asleep now, could you?"

Jojo barked from inside the house, and Jason suddenly sucked in his breath. I looked over as Lucas slowly stood up, and at the same moment, Manson's entire body went rigid beneath me.

Someone was standing at the gate — a tall skinny man with gray-streaked hair. The smoke from a cigarette slowly curled into the sky above his head.

"Oh my God…" My words came out in a disbelieving whisper. "Is that…"

Manson stood up, bringing me with him. The moment I was on my feet, he stepped in front of me, physically blocking me with his body. Vincent was on the edge of the bench, his face grim.

Lucas's fists were clenched as he stood there staring, and Jason was on his feet now too.

"Lucas, take Jess inside." Manson's voice was hard, his gaze fixated on the man at the gate.

"Manson." Lucas's voice was tense. "I don't think I should leave—"

"Lucas, *now.*" The viciousness in Manson's tone shocked me almost as much as the look on his face as he turned. I had never seen Manson look like that before.

Terrified. Completely terrified.

Lucas nodded, taking my hand and pulling me from behind Manson. "Come on. Stay close." He kept his body between me and the yard, ushering me toward the door.

Blocking me. Hiding me.

"Manson?" I tried to reach back for him, fear beginning to spread through me.

"It'll be fine, Jess," he said, but the smile he offered was weak at best. "Don't worry. Lucas…"

"I've got her." Lucas's voice was firm, his hold on me unbreakable as he opened the front door and pushed me ahead of him inside.

49

MANSON

Itold myself I wasn't afraid of my father anymore. Vincent and Jason were right behind me as I walked across the yard toward the gate, but even with them right there, the panic was closing in. Every step I took was too loud, adrenaline pumping through my veins as I forced myself to suck in a slow breath.

I'd memorized which floorboards creaked in the house. I used to know exactly how wide I could open a door before it squeaked. I'd trained myself to walk silently, to breathe softly, to lower my voice. Like my dad was a bomb and the slightest sound would set him off.

My hands were sweating. I hadn't taken my pills yet because I'd woken up feeling calm for once, but now I desperately wished I had. Panic pressed up beneath my lungs, a slow-moving suffocation. I told myself I wasn't afraid, but the closer I got to him, waiting there with a cigarette hanging from his lips, the farther I got from myself.

I was gone and what remained was a terrified child, small and alone. Looking for an exit, desperate for a place to hide, sitting with his back to his bedroom door with the hope that his own body could serve as a barricade.

I stopped about five yards away from him and the gate between us. Vincent and Jason came to a halt right behind me. They had my back; they'd fight for me without a second of hesitation.

Dad pulled the cigarette from his lips, the cherry flaring as he flicked it away and blew out a cloud of smoke. God, he'd aged. Years of alcohol abuse and smoking had forged deep lines across his face; his blotchy cheeks a few days past his last shave. Still, looking at him was like staring into a terrifyingly distorted mirror. Like those horror films where the protagonist sees their own reflection transform into something sinister.

Our resemblance was a curse, but it was also a warning. His path could have been mine, and I'd done everything in my power to ensure that it wasn't.

"You're not welcome here," I said. My voice didn't shake, but I kept it low and rough with the effort to steady it.

Dad chuckled, a slight wheeze coming out with it. "That's the greeting I get? I come home to my boy telling me I'm not welcome? What kind of shit is that?"

That was all the greeting he deserved. No niceties, no small talk. He wasn't fucking welcome, and I wanted there to be no doubt about it.

The sound of his voice felt like getting punched in the chest. My body flushed rapidly hot, then cold.

At least Jess was inside, out of his sight. Lucas was always the most eager for a fight, but I didn't need that right now. I needed him to keep our girl safe, and I knew he would. I *knew*, but I still couldn't stop the rising panic. But I kept it hidden. I masked it like I always had.

"This is my property," I said. "And if I say you're not welcome, then you're not goddamn welcome."

He turned his head and spat, the sound triggering something in the back of my brain. The feeling of hot, thick saliva hitting my face. Coiling revulsion in my stomach from the rotten tobacco smell of it. He stepped toward me slowly, his eyes never leaving my face. Like he was testing me, daring me to run. He used to call me a coward for running.

I lifted my chin and clasped my hands behind my back. It probably looked like I was at ease, but I wanted to hide how tightly my hands were clenched.

"*Your* property," he drawled, glancing from me to Vincent, then Jason. "Is that how it is? No room for dear old dad, huh?" He looked up at the house, his eyes narrowing. To have him come here and look in on *my* family made me sick. "Well, ain't that something. Got a place all your own, moved all your friends in, even got yourself a girl. Or one of you does. I can't tell which one of you is fucking her."

How long had he been watching us? Was this the first time he'd been out here? Or was this only the first time he'd made himself obvious?

"I'm not interested in chatting." Rage blanketed my fear, drowning it out. "Leave, or we'll make you leave."

He stared at me, nodding slowly. His eyes kept flickering back to the house, like he was searching for something. "Big man now, I see. Got your own space and you think it's right to leave family out in the cold? You're lucky I'm not looking for a room tonight. I'm not looking for a goddamn handout. I want what I've got rights to."

"There's not a single thing on this property you have any *right* to. If Mom had wanted you to have this place, she would have left it to you. But she didn't."

In my mind's eye, I could see myself slamming my fist into his face again and again — blood spattering, his nose breaking, teeth cracking.

How many times had I thought about killing him? I used to dream about it, how I'd stand up to him one day, how I'd prove he never broke me. I'd relish the shock on his face before he died. I even used to imagine what would happen after I killed him; what I'd say in court, how I'd survive in prison.

But that would have made me just like him, capable of the same violence. It would prove that the cycle continued, pain begetting pain.

"You're wrong there, boy." Dad rolled back his shoulders and cracked his neck. My stomach twisted at the sound. "You know your mother wasn't right toward the end. Wasn't right throughout most of her life. Gave me plenty of reason to suspect you weren't even mine." He snickered. "Can't deny genetics though. Spittin' image of me."

He didn't need to fucking remind me.

50

JESSICA

Lucas's tension was obvious as he led me up the stairs. He was practically crushing my hand in his from holding onto me so tight, and he didn't let go until we entered his room. Only then did he drop my hand and immediately went to the window, his eyebrows drawn together as he looked out into the yard.

But the gate wasn't visible from that vantage point.

He hissed in frustration, his arms folded and his fists clenched. "Shit."

"Shouldn't you go out there?" I said. My palms were sweating, nervous energy making me pace. I'd never seen any of them look like that, as if they were genuinely frightened when they saw Reagan at the gate.

"Jason and Vincent have his back," Lucas said. He didn't sound particularly happy about it though. "If Manson wants me to keep you safe, then I'm fucking keeping you safe. So just relax."

He sat on the edge of the bed, elbows resting on his legs as he bowed his head. He looked far from relaxed himself; he looked more like a grenade whose pin was slowly being pulled loose.

"How dangerous is he?" My gut twisted as I recalled Vincent telling me that Reagan was the reason he had a gun. What the hell could have happened to make them so afraid of him? I understood why Manson was — I could only imagine the trauma of having a parent like that. But they were *all* freaked out and it was worrying me even more.

"Don't underestimate him." Lucas got off the bed again, pacing in front of it like he couldn't figure out how to settle himself. "The last time Manson saw him, Reagan threatened to kill him."

The knot inside me grew hard as a rock. "We need to call the police. This isn't safe."

"Police won't do shit, Jess."

He paced to the window again, scoffed, and paced back. He looked around the room helplessly, his frustration palpable in the air.

"Somewhere in that police station downtown is a file for the Reed family about three inches thick," he said. "Domestic disturbances, DUIs, public intoxication, domestic battery. No good came of it. Fucking nothing. His mom wouldn't press charges. Reagan would sit in jail for a night and come right back in the morning. Cops around here see the last name *Reed*, and they think trash. Criminals." He sighed heavily, rubbing his hand over his buzzed hair. "A kid like Manson isn't supposed to make it this far, Jess. He should be dead, or hooked on drugs, or already in prison. The police have had him on their radar ever since he brought the knife to school. Vincent has a record. *I* have a record. If the people the cops are supposed to help are already behind bars in their mind, then they don't care."

Criminals. Just like my mom had called them. But it was wrong, it was so wrong. Their entire lives were written off because of what they'd done to survive, because of circumstances beyond their control.

"That's not fair." I was so frustrated that my throat swelled, but I choked down the lump. This wasn't the time to cry, not now, not in front of Lucas. They were all worried enough. "That's so wrong, they shouldn't…fuck." I was so useless just standing there, not knowing what was going on. I wanted to help, but what could I possibly do?

"Life isn't, and never has been, fair," Lucas said. His voice was gentler than I expected, like he was imparting a valuable life lesson that he wished he didn't have to give. He stood in front of me, looking at me for a moment as if he couldn't figure out what he was supposed to do.

Then he wrapped his arms around me. Slowly and stiffly at first, as if he was hugging something prickly. But when I burrowed my face against him and wrapped my arms around him in return, he softened. It was like his chest caved in and he tried to draw me into it, clinging to me as if I would slip away.

"You chose some fucked up guys to play with, Jess," he said. His chin rested on top of my head, and I could hear his heart pounding so hard and fast it was a wonder he could stand still at all. "I'm sorry to say this shit comes with the territory. But you're safe with us, I swear that much."

"I'm not worried about myself," I said, not raising my head from his chest. "I'm worried about you. About Manson, and Jason, and Vincent. I want you to be safe too."

He exhaled softly — a half-hearted laugh. "I don't think we're going to find safety in Wickeston. But someday...someday we will. Somewhere else."

Without me. The thought sprang to my mind so hard and fast that it shocked me, the lump squeezing into my throat again. But I didn't want to think about that, not now. The more I thought about the future, the worse it would be. I needed to focus on the here and now.

And here, now, we had a bigger problem to deal with.

"Try not to worry." Lucas finally eased his hold, giving my arms a squeeze as he did. "Manson can handle himself."

My worry hadn't dissipated; I could tell his hadn't either. But I felt a little steadier at least. He went to stand in his doorway, leaning against the frame as he listened for them to come back into the house. In the meantime, I tried to occupy my nervous energy by having a look around.

The first time I'd seen his room, I'd assumed it was a guest room because it was so empty. But there were signs it was lived in; his bed was unmade and the laundry basket in the corner was overflowing. The dresser was old, covered in scratches and stains, but there were a few items on top that caught my attention.

There was a small wooden figure that looked as if it had been whittled by hand, a candle scented like chamomile and lavender, a deck of cards, and even an old GameBoy. I picked up the wooden figure, turning it over in my palm. It looked like a cat — I could see little whiskers on its face and claws on its tiny feet. The deck of cards appeared well-used, and the GameBoy had a Pokemon Red cartridge inside it.

Shoved toward the back of the dresser was a boombox, its plastic exterior cracked and scuffed. It was clearly old, equipped with a cassette player and AM/FM radio, but nothing else, not even a CD drive.

The front slot was open and a cassette was inside. I pulled out the tape, curiously reading the handwritten label on the front. *Best Mixtape Ever!* was scrawled with a red pen in messy, child-like letters.

The floor creaked softly as Lucas came up behind me. I turned, holding up the tape. "Did you make this?"

Something painful flickered over his expression. He took the tape, turning it over in his hands.

"My brother made it," he said. "But I named it. It's old, the audio is fucked up in some spots…"

He put it back into the boombox and pressed play. The volume was low, but after a moment, I recognized the tune of "Heaven's On Fire" by KISS.

"What's your brother's name?" I said.

He stopped the tape. The softness of his expression was still guarded as he picked up the wooden cat and rubbed his thumb over the rough wood.

"Benji," he said, keeping his eyes down. "He's five years older than me."

An older brother. It was difficult to imagine Lucas as anything other than he was now: hard as stone and just as immovable. But as he spoke, I was able to picture him differently. As someone far more innocent and gentle, a child that the world hadn't yet broken.

"I thought he was the coolest guy in the world," he said. "I followed him everywhere when I was a kid. Probably drove him fucking crazy. He'd sneak out with his friends and end up with his kid brother tagging along, but he was always nice about it. He'd keep me with him and make sure I was safe."

He cleared his throat and set the cat down on the deck of cards. His face was unreadable now, wiped clean of whatever emotion I'd seen there before.

"What happened to him?" I was afraid he'd close up, that I'd ask one too many questions and destroy this fragile openness between us.

To my surprise, he answered bluntly, almost numbly, "He's in prison. Been there for thirteen years."

His tone was so even that it didn't hit me right away what he'd said. Then my eyes widened, realization dawning, and I blurted out, "Thirteen years? What did he do?"

That question had required far more tact than I'd given it. I gasped the moment the words were out, grasping for an apology that I'd gone about this all wrong, but Lucas didn't seem bothered.

His voice remained detached as he explained. "He fell in love with a girl. I guess an older kid had a thing for her too; I'm not sure. A lot of the court case was…" He paused, rubbing the back of his head. "It was a lot. I was little. I didn't really get it. But apparently…" He frowned, as if he didn't fully believe what he was about to say.

"Apparently, Benji was really possessive of this girl, and he didn't like this other kid being into her. So he..." His frown deepened. "He lured the kid out of his house, hit him over the head with a brick, took him out into the woods...and killed him."

He said it so calmly, but the words washed over me with a cold chill. "Oh my God..."

"They put him away when he was fifteen," he said. "They kept saying he was so dangerous, but he was just my brother. He liked rock music, and Pepsi, and he could create shit like no one else could. He was an artist. He was patient. I never even heard him raise his voice." He exhaled heavily through his nose, shaking his head. "But they said he did it. Locked him up. The whole community knew, there was practically a target on my back at that point. So my dad took me with him, and we left. Mom got sicker..."

I didn't know what to say. My little sister could be a pain in the ass, but I couldn't imagine her being taken away. And for something so heinous, at such a young age...it was horrific. It was unimaginable.

I laid my hand on his arm. He was very pointedly looking anywhere except at me, but it was because the shield over his face was gone. I could see the sadness in his eyes, the confusion. As if he knew the story but refused to believe it was real.

"Do you miss him?" I said, and he finally looked up. His throat bobbed as he swallowed hard.

"Yeah, I miss him. Every damn day."

The sound of the front door opening made us both jerk our heads toward the hallway, footsteps tramping heavily into the house.

"They're back," I said.

Lucas took my hand again. He lifted it to his lips, kissing my knuckles tenderly. "Let's go see what happened."

We reached the bottom of the stairs right as Vincent was closing the door behind them. Their faces were drawn, the relaxed energy from not even an hour ago now completely sapped. Little Haribo was in the living room, up on his back legs so he could look out the window with Jojo toward the gate, both of them clearly on edge. Manson's eyes were hollow, sunken in shadow.

"What the hell did he want?" Lucas said.

Jason shook his head, going into the kitchen and grabbing a beer out of the fridge despite how early it was.

"He wants money," Vincent said tightly. "From the sale of the house. Fifty percent."

"Fuck that," Lucas snarled. "We're not giving him shit."

"That's what I told him," Manson muttered. Deep lines were chiseled into his forehead, like the weight of his entire life had suddenly caught up with him and perched on top of his skull. "He didn't like that."

"He threatened you," Jason said firmly, opening the beer as he leaned against the kitchen counter and spoke to us through the doorway. "All that shit about death? That was a threat, no doubt. We need better security cameras. Clearer picture, clearer audio. And electronic locks for the gates —"

Manson slammed his fist against the wall so hard I jumped. Jojo flattened her ears against her head, looking up at him with wide eyes.

"Why the fuck does he get to walk back into my life like he

owns it?!"

I'd never heard Manson's volume so loud. He wasn't looking at any of us as he yelled, his fists clenched, face reddening.

"Why the *fuck* does he get to come to my property and threaten my family? Fuck!" His fist slammed against the wall again, leaving behind a smear of blood as his knuckles split. Then he did it again, and again, each impact of his fist making the wall shudder. Haribo barked softly at the noise, and Vincent gently shushed him, reaching down to scratch his chest.

Manson was breathing hard. He roughly trailed his fingers through his hair to push it back, sucking in his breath as he turned. His eyes swept over me, narrowed with fury, and it was like he'd entirely forgotten I was there.

The moment he looked at me, he froze. His fury fled and in its place was an expression of utterly horrified shame.

"He doesn't get to do shit," Lucas said. "We'll figure this out."

"He can't force you to give him anything," Jason insisted. "Not legally or otherwise."

But it was as if Manson didn't hear him. His throat tensed as he gulped, shaking his head slowly as he looked at me.

"Jess…" His voice was a whisper. "I'm so sorry. I didn't…I didn't mean to…"

Any fear I'd felt was already gone, brought on by the shock of seeing him like that rather than any worry over my safety. But Manson looked down at his hand, his knuckles split and smeared with blood.

He sucked in a stuttering breath as his hands shook.

"You're bleeding," I said, reaching for him. "You need to —"

He flinched away from my touch. He was shaking his head, looking between his fist and then back to me.

"I'm sorry," he said. He looked at the dogs, watching him with flattened ears. "Fuck. Shit, I didn't mean to…"

"It's okay." Vincent's voice was calm, soothing. "You're upset, that's okay."

"No." Manson flexed his knuckles, watching the blood drip down his fingers. "No, this isn't fucking okay. Nothing about this is okay."

He wrenched open the front door. Lucas started forward. "Hey, Manson, come on, you don't have to —"

"I need some air," he said hoarsely. He looked at me again, as if there was so much more he wanted to say. But then he winced and turned away, slipping out the front door and slamming it behind him.

I immediately tried to follow him. But Vincent caught my arm before I could open the door, saying gently, "Give him time, just give him time." He held me against him, rubbing my back and somehow slowing my pounding heart. "He's scared. He never wanted you to see him like that."

"Then I have to go talk to him," I said fiercely. I didn't know what the hell I'd say, or if it would even help at all. But I couldn't hide in the house anymore. At least Manson had Vincent and Jason with him when he faced his dad. Whatever he was facing now, he was trying to do it alone and that didn't feel right.

Vincent loosened his hold but kept his arm around me. From the kitchen, Jason said, "Don't worry about it, Jess. This isn't your issue to deal with, it'll be fine."

"It *is* my issue," I snapped without meaning to, but it wasn't from anger. I just needed them to understand. "I'm not some delicate little flower, okay? We made a deal. I'm yours until my debt is paid and I meant that. *Yours.* But if I'm yours, then you're all mine too." I looked between them, trying to steady the worried shake in my words. "I'm not on the outside anymore. I'm part of this, all of it — even the scary fucked-up parts. I need to talk to him. Please."

Jason was watching me, his arms slack at his sides. For once, that icy gaze wasn't so sharp. Vincent squeezed me closer, leaning over to kiss the side of my head. "Okay. I get it. You're right. I guess we can't really try to shield you from this when it's right in front of you."

He let me go, and I looked back at Lucas. His jaw was clenched, his posture rigid.

"We're used to dealing with things on our own," he said. I walked back to him, laying my hands on his tightly folded arms.

"After yesterday," I said softly, "I think I made it clear that I consider myself a part of *we*." His expression faltered, torn between accepting it or automatically denying it. "*We* are dealing with this on our own. I'm dealing with it too."

He looked down at me, and his face finally cracked. He shook his head with a heavy sigh.

"You've got to be the most hardheaded woman I've ever met," he grumbled. "And I don't think you have much sense at all trying to be so damn involved…"

"Just tell her she earned your respect and go fucking find Manson," Jason yelled from the kitchen.

Lucas's lips pressed tightly together. He didn't need to say out loud what Jason had demanded. It was clear enough to me.

"Come on." He took my hand again. "I know where he'll go."

51

MANSON

It was shame that drove me out of the house. Shame for falling apart, letting my boys down when I should have been present. For letting Jess down, when she should never have been brought into this mess in the first place.

I'd let her see me lose control. I never did that, but of course when I finally broke, she had to be there to witness it.

Violence was like an infection inside me that I couldn't dig out. I couldn't fight something that was in my blood, seared into my brain through years of repeated exposure. I couldn't change the mold I'd been formed by, and failure felt inevitable.

The dirt road in front of our house led either to Route 15, or to a dead end. It was the dead end I walked toward, my boots kicking up dust as I went. I slipped past the metal barrier at the end of the road and into the trees, the path overgrown with weeds. The way still felt familiar, even though it had been a few years since I'd gone back here.

Places held memories, and most of mine were bad. This quiet spot back in the trees used to be where I came for peace, but over the years, it had come to feel more like a place to hide. Somewhere I could run away to when I couldn't face reality.

Coward. Fucking pussy. Running away like a pathetic little bitch.

I sat down, my knees drawn up as I rested my arms on them. My own inner voice sounded like him. Like he could never fucking leave me alone. Even when he was dead and gone, his voice would still be there.

My tongue felt thick, my mouth too dry as I swallowed hard anyway. I'd been selfish. I'd wanted Jess so damn badly. I'd wanted another chance, as if a second opportunity would allow me to prove to her that she belonged with me. With us.

I'd allowed myself to forget that Jess was surrounded by privilege, by safety. That by inserting myself into her life, I'd dragged all my problems along with me.

My father had seen her. He'd fucking *seen* her with us. It was a violation just to have his eyes on her. It was violent for him to merely know her name. Nothing was off-limits in his mind, not even her. And I'd exposed her to that. It was my own damn fault.

A dark, coiled knot of anxiety crawled around in my chest. It gripped my lungs with sharp claws and stuffed its ugliness into my throat, making my hands shake. It made sure that no matter how hard I tried, I didn't really have any control in the end.

I jumped to my feet, the sound of a twig snapping nearby

sending my hand flying to my back pocket and the knife I kept there. But it wasn't my father who came walking through the trees.

"Jess?" I cleared my throat, my voice barely audible. Her eyes were wide as she looked around, taking in the trees, the chirping birds, the soft grass beneath her shoes. But when her gaze fell on me, the worry in her eyes made me feel like a literal piece of shit.

I was scaring her; I was probably scaring all of them. They deserved better from me, but I couldn't function enough to be that person. Not now.

"How did you find me?" She came closer, looking me over as if searching for any more injuries. My hand ached from punching the wall, but it was a well-deserved pain, and I wished I'd broken my damn fingers.

"Lucas," she said. "He's back on the road. He's worried about you."

Unable to keep eye contact with her any longer, I said, "You should go home, Jess. Tell Lucas…tell him I'm fine. Have him drive you home."

Did I sound confident? Strong? Determined? Or did I sound fucking weak, like a coward, a man who couldn't face the world?

She inhaled deeply, lifting her chin in that familiarly defiant way that made my entire chest clench up. "I'm not leaving you alone out here."

"Don't worry about me." I wanted to hold her, but I didn't dare. If I couldn't even manage to explain myself, why did I deserve to touch her? I managed something like a smile, but the look on her face told me it was weak. "I'm okay. I just need some time alone."

"Bullshit," she said. "Look, you gave me a rule about communicating. You told me to always be honest, to speak openly. If you're not ready to talk yet, that's okay. But I'm not leaving. I'm not mad, I promise. You haven't —"

"You should be."

She stopped, frowning at me. "What?"

"You should be mad." I sat back down, leaning against the tree behind me as I gripped my knees, wishing the pressure would relieve some of the tension inside me.

She sat beside me, leaving a gap between us. But she reached over and laid her hand on top of mine, and the words spilled out before I could stop them.

"You should be mad, because you shouldn't have to see that. You shouldn't have some guy throwing his fists around like he can't control himself. Raising his voice like a child. It's not right. It's not safe."

She shouldn't have to see what I'd grown up seeing. The adult tantrums, fists thrown into walls; plates, cups, and valuables broken. Using violence as strength, as intimidation. It made me sick to see it come out of me, leaking like an infected wound. But that was all my dad had left me with: festering wounds that refused to heal.

"I'm safe with you, Manson," she said firmly. "There isn't a single doubt in my mind that I'm safe with you. You got angry. Everyone does. That's okay."

No. No, it wasn't. She was wrong. I flinched when she touched my cheek, turning my face toward her. That tightness in my chest was swelling to a breaking point. But she held my face there, and

I couldn't look at her and lie. She disarmed me so completely that it didn't matter how ashamed I was to be like this.

She deserved to hear the truth. All of it.

"I saw the way my mom looked at him," I said. "I saw how afraid she was every time he spoke, every time he *moved*. And I —" My voice broke, and I hated how it sounded. Hated the way my own mind berated me for it. "Every second of every day I spent in that house, I was afraid. I was never safe there. He couldn't control himself. He didn't *care*. He wanted to cause pain. It made him feel powerful. And you know what really fucking sucks? I loved him. Mom loved him. What do you do when you love someone so goddamn much that you'll let them hurt you and even let them destroy you? Just hoping they'll love you back? Hoping you'll *earn* it?"

The tightness had broken. I felt so raw I shuddered, and Jess's fingers swiped gently at my cheeks. Well, fuck, the tears were coming and they weren't going to stop.

"How am I any better?" The words tasted bitter in my mouth. "How am I any fucking better than him? It's like he infected me, Jess, his genes are a fucking cancer. The way we play...even though we call it a game...I hurt you and I like it. I like the way you sound, the way you look when I do it. I crave seeing you suffer for me. How the *fuck* is that okay?"

I was spiraling, and I saw no way out. The darkness around me was only growing, and I swore it would suffocate me.

I wanted to speak, but I hated my own words. I wanted someone to understand, but I also didn't want anyone to know. These weren't things that were easy to admit. They were dark, panicked thoughts that lurked at the back of my brain, packed away right next to tightly sealed memories of my childhood. I could try to lock them away, but I couldn't hide them when they lived in the same house, when they echoed in the walls, specters of pain lurking in every corner.

"I'm broken, Jess." I took her hands in mine, enfolding her fingers and kissing them.

I could smell Lucas on her, and it reminded me of all the times when it was only him and I. When he'd meet me out here in the dark, or I'd pick him up in the Bronco and drive around until we found somewhere to sleep. All the breakdowns neither of us knew how to handle, because we'd only been kids trying to figure out how to grow up alone. Holding each other through tears and rages, hoping that if we clung tightly enough, we wouldn't lose each other.

I clung to her hands the same way, with words I couldn't say. I'd lose her because I wasn't good enough, because I was too broken, too fucked in the head.

"I told myself I'd never be like him," I said, staring down at her small hands in mine. "I don't want to hurt people, I *don't*. But sometimes I feel so angry, I don't even know who I am. I could destroy everything I touch, even things I love. Even myself."

"Manson, you are *nothing* like your father."

Her voice was so fierce. She held my hands like she could squeeze the words into them, but that wasn't enough. She put her arms around me, pulling me against her. I was frozen, stiff and shaking with the effort to hold myself together.

"I was awful to you and you never hurt me back," she said, her voice soft against my ear. "You showed me what it meant to be taken care of, did you know that? No one had ever bothered to talk about a safeword with me. No one had even bothered to ask what I'm into. You won a silly bet at a party and you didn't do *anything* I didn't want you to. You *cared*, Manson. You've always cared."

My brain screamed that her words weren't true. She was lying, she pitied me, she hated me. There was no way I could ever be good enough for her. But she didn't let me go, and as fierce as she sounded, her words were thick as she said, "I trust you, Manson. Lucas trusts you, and he doesn't trust anyone. Vincent and Jason trust you. They'd follow you to the ends of the earth. You're not some evil, awful person. You're strong and kind, and you take care of people. But you can't only take care of other people all the time and have no one take care of you too."

Her chest swelled with a long, deep breath, and I lifted my head. She kept her arms around me as she kissed me, and the ugly darkness inside me died a little more.

"I'm here because I want to be," she said, leaning her forehead against mine. "Because I chose to be. And I really don't know what the hell is going to happen or how any of this will work out in the end. But the only things I'm scared of are the same things you make me forget."

"Fuck." Somehow, blessedly, the pressure released from behind my ribs. I could breathe again. I could *think*. Panic still ached in me, but it was manageable now. It wasn't the same raging storm as before.

Some things went beyond words, and we held each other until those things felt clear.

Lucas was sitting on the metal barrier when Jess and I came back. He stood abruptly when he heard us coming, stubbing out the half-smoked cigarette in his fingers and shifting from foot to foot until we'd reached him.

Then, he threw his arms around me and held onto me so damn tight he practically crushed the air right out of my lungs.

Jess stepped away, giving us a moment with each other. His heart was hammering, his chest swelling with every deep breath.

"Lucas —" I started slowly, but he wasn't about to let me apologize.

"Don't you fucking say you're sorry," he said. "Just don't... don't leave like that again. Please." He lowered his voice even more, barely above a whisper, but the pain in his words was impossibly loud. "I can't watch you walk out the door on me, Manson. I don't care what you have to do to stay. I'll listen to you yell all damn day if you need to. Just don't walk out on me."

I nodded against him, knotting my hands into the back of his shirt. It had hurt him, frightened him, probably far more than he'd ever say. "I won't. I'm not going anywhere."

He cleared his throat as we parted, hurriedly scrubbing his hand over his face so nothing remained but his usual stony expression. He nodded abruptly, reaching his arm out for Jess and slipped it around her shoulders as she took my hand again.

Jason was sitting on the porch when we returned, chewing his thumbnail down to nothing. Bo was beside him, and I expected him to bark at me again, but he wagged his tail and licked my hand when I scratched his head.

"Sorry, buddy," I said. "Didn't mean to scare you."

"Glad to see they dragged you back," Jason said, embracing

me as he got up from the porch. "I was about to go after you myself if you didn't show up in the next five minutes."

I clapped his shoulder, finally allowing myself a little laugh. "I didn't flee the country; I just walked down the street."

"Yeah, well, you went by yourself." Jason frowned. "That's not supposed to happen. If you're going to flee anywhere, you better damn well take us with you."

I'd shed enough tears for one day; I wasn't about to have him getting me in my feelings again. So I didn't say how much that meant to me. I couldn't find the words to tell them that they'd proven wrong every awful thing my brain wanted to believe. But if I couldn't say it, then I'd find a way to show it.

If I wanted to keep being here for them like they were for me, I needed to face my demons.

"Breakfast is coming up!" Vincent called from the kitchen as we came back inside. I could smell bacon and hash browns, and when I looked into the kitchen, there were multiple bowls on the counter and pans on the stove. He glanced over his shoulder at me with a grin, his long hair messily tied up as he added another pancake to the stack in front of him.

"God, Vince…you didn't have to…" He held up his hand.

"Don't. I don't want to hear a word unless it's *wow, Vincent, you're the best cook ever and so unbearably charming and attractive.*" He raised his eyebrows expectantly.

Jess slipped around my side and wrapped her arms around Vince, saying, "Ooh, wow, Chef Vincent, you're so charming and attractive I might swoon."

I snickered as Vincent looked at me pointedly. "See? She

knows how to do it."

Jojo had come to sit by my feet, leaning heavily against my legs as she looked up at me and her tail thumped on the ground. No fear, no hatred, no anger. Just her big, goofy smile as I scratched behind her ears.

I don't know where I'd be without all of them. I wouldn't have survived this long; I knew that much. No matter what had happened through the years, I'd always had someone to pull me back from the brink, someone to hold on to me when I thought there was nothing left to keep trying for.

When I'd met Lucas, he'd understood me better than anyone I'd ever met. He was a mirror of my own pain and rage in more ways than I'd been prepared for. But he'd been strong when I wasn't. He'd been there every time I needed him without hesitation, even when it meant facing his own fears to risk being close to me.

And Vincent? God, if he hadn't been there to bring a never-ending sense of optimism about the shit-show that was my life, I would have wallowed in misery forever. He had the kind of close, loving family I'd always longed for, but that didn't make him naïve. It made him caring, fiercely protective, willing to do anything and everything for the people he loved.

When we'd met Jason, I'd thought the quiet kid with his nice respectable family couldn't possibly want to be around losers like us. But I'd watched his entire life be torn into pieces so he could live authentically, all because he dared to stray from the life his parents had forced on him. He'd endured their rejection, all the pain of being abandoned, and not once did I see him falter. He'd been so damn determined to claim his life, to live as he wanted, that it had kept me going too.

And now Jess, whose presence in my life had felt like both an aspiration and a warning. This wasn't only a game, regardless of whatever silly rules we made or excuses we came up with. Jess had given me something to strive for, but it was more than that.

Her presence here was proof I was better than where I'd come from. I was stronger than the violence and the pain that had formed me. She felt safe here, safe with me — and that meant the world. That was what I'd always wanted for myself and my boys — safety, peace, somewhere we could exist without constant judgment, without fear.

I watched her with them and knew they would protect her as fiercely as they protected me. Whatever the fuck my father tried to do — if anything — we would never let him touch *her*.

Never.

52

LUCAS

The setting sun kissed the horizon, turning the sky pink and orange. The colors melted into the clouds, swirling like paint as the golden light touched my bare arms.

It made me feel nostalgic, although I wasn't sure why. Was it possible to feel nostalgia for something you'd never experienced? Bedtime stories, running through sprinklers, playgrounds, and holding your parents' hand — I longed for things I'd seen only on TV, or enviously watched others experience. I craved it as if it had ever been mine and not only a dream.

There was a pop and hiss as Manson opened a beer and handed it to me before opening his own. We were seated in the back of the Bronco, legs dangling over the tall weeds in the middle of the field we were parked in.

This gave me nostalgia too. Just the two of us in the back of his car, marveling at the approach of another long night. Shocked that we'd survived another day.

How many nights had we laid together in the back of this vehicle, telling each other every fucked-up thought in our heads because no one else would listen? How many nights had we fallen asleep in each other's arms, because parting felt like one of us might not be there the next morning?

How many times had we told each other to keep going, to keep fucking fighting, because if one of us gave up, there was no hope for any of us at all?

"Feels like a lifetime since we watched the sunset," I said.

Manson was seated close beside me, his arm pressed against mine as he lifted his can and took a sip. "Been too long. I feel like I'm losing track of time. The days keep disappearing."

I nodded as I took out a cigarette and lit up. I took a long drag, savoring the slight burn in my throat and the hit of nicotine. I passed it to him, and he looked at it between his fingers for a long time before he took a drag.

"I should probably quit," he said. The words made a pang shoot through my chest like a bolt. He was right, we both needed to quit. But sometimes, when I saw him getting better, when I saw how hard he was trying to be a better man, I felt like I was being left behind. He was able to do what I couldn't, and although he kept trying to drag me along with him, I still lived with the fear that eventually, he'd fix himself and I'd still be broken.

Too broken for him, for any of them.

We'd met each other at our lowest and risen out of that

together. We'd been desperate back then, searching for any reason at all to keep going, and we'd found that in each other.

How selfish was I to worry that he might not need me anymore?

It was weird how it seemed like he could read my mind. He passed the cigarette back and said, "Do you know why I wanted you with her? Why I sent you inside with Jess, instead of having you with me?"

It was like he knew that had hurt me. And I'd tried not to let it, I'd really tried. But it kindled my fear that he was pushing me away. I'd protect him, I would always protect him. But if he wouldn't let me…

"I have the worst temper," I said, inhaling slowly. "Your dad is volatile and I suck at keeping my cool. Figured you were trying to avoid the situation escalating."

I could feel his eyes on the side of my face, although I was still staring toward the setting sun.

"I knew you'd keep her safe. I knew that no matter what happened, if my father wanted to hurt her, the last person he'd have to get through was you. And he wouldn't get through you."

He wasn't the kind of person to say that out of pity or lie in an effort to make me feel better. Manson had always been careful with his words and he said what he meant.

He plucked the cigarette from my fingers, inhaling deeply. He cupped my face, his fingers tracing back over my jaw until he grasped the back of my head and pulled me close.

He kissed me, his taste so familiar, the sharp pinch of his teeth on my lip igniting a fire in my chest. I grasped his shirt, fingers knotted in the fabric as his tongue pushed into my mouth and the scent of him filled my head with need.

I'd thought I was losing my mind when I met him. When I met this boy who was so much like me, who shook with pain and rage like I did, who was looking for a reason to live like I was. The way he made me feel, like I'd finally found this glittering sliver of goodness in the world, was fucking terrifying. I'd never cared one way or the other about the gender of the people I slept with — although my dad had tried to beat it out of me when I told him I'd fuck whoever I damn well pleased, it hadn't dissuaded me.

I'd found someone I trusted enough to be vulnerable with, something I thought was impossible.

"I've missed this…" He ran his fingers along my jaw, traced them down my throat and then laid his hand there. He didn't squeeze, but I liked the weight of his hand. "I've missed you."

"I know," I said. I didn't like change, and it seemed our lives had been in constant flux for so long now. It made me anxious, and when I got anxious, I withdrew. I pulled away from the very people I was closest to. Like I needed to punish myself for feeling anything at all.

"You told me not to walk out on you." His breath brushed over my skin, and my lips parted with the desire to kiss him again. But I didn't struggle; I let him keep me under control even though I wanted to sink my teeth into his skin and taste his blood on my tongue. "Now I'm telling you the same thing. Don't walk out on me." He tapped the side of my head with his finger, his tongue running slowly along his lower lip before he said, "When you're physically in front of me but not with me mentally…I can't stand it. I need you with me, Lucas. Do you get it?"

"I get it," I said. He held the cigarette to my lips, carefully, allowing me to inhale.

"What do you need from me, pup?" he said. His hand squeezed my neck, and I let the smoke curl from my mouth. "You have that look in your eyes, you know. Like you need something, like you need…"

He let the question hang, his dark eyes searching mine.

"Hurt me," I said. His pupils dilated, his lips parting as his breath quickened. "I need you to hurt me. Control me."

Sometimes I needed to destroy myself, and I needed it done brutally, mercilessly. I needed pain to remind me I was human, to root me in a reality that oftentimes felt too chaotic to bear. There was no chaos in the way Manson could overcome me. It was the opposite; when I gave him control, I felt peace, clarity.

I reached up, tracing my fingers down his cheek. He really was a beautiful man. I loved the way he leaned into my hand, how his eyes never left mine. He said I often spoke silently, and that was why he watched my face so carefully. He was looking for the things I left unsaid.

"You're what I need," I said.

He gave me a crooked smile as he leaned down to kiss me. His kiss was deliciously slow, and I tangled my fingers in his hair as I held him close. He was intoxicating, a flawed god I couldn't resist worshiping. His imperfection made him sacred, his strength made him holy. But the lust he inspired in me made him wicked, and the ease with which he bent me to his will was the closest thing to divinity I could imagine.

He parted from me, taking another drag as he released his hold on my throat.

"Take this off," he said, tugging at the hem of my shirt before he got up.

I obeyed and followed him when he slid out of the back of Bronco. I tossed my shirt aside, and he pressed me against the side of the vehicle, the cold metal shocking on my skin. He stared at my chest as he pinned me by the throat, tracing the lines tattooed into my flesh with the cigarette, moving it slowly through the air. He brought the cherry close to my skin, hovering it above a small spot untouched by ink.

"Beg me for it," he whispered. He didn't want to have any doubt. He didn't want to fear that he'd done anything I wasn't already longing for. I was wound so tight I thought I would explode, waiting on the edge of desperation for him to give me what I craved.

"Please, fucking hurt me," I got the words out, harsh and heavy. "Use me. Fuck me. Show me that I can't ever get away from you."

His lips crashed into mine, and the cigarette pressed against my chest. It was only for a moment, only long enough for the burn to set in. The pain didn't scare me; in fact, I savored it.

It made me feel human. Flesh and blood, mind and soul finally connected into one complete being.

I groaned into his mouth, his hips grinding against mine as he flicked the cigarette down and crushed it under his boot. His tongue slid past my lips, his hand on my throat squeezing right below my jaw.

I used to make a game of putting cigarettes out on my skin. It was an ugly habit, destructive, full of hatred for my own flesh. Manson made me stop with the promise that he'd do it to me instead if I asked him. The control I was seeking in self-destruction was something I could find with him. Something I could trust him with.

Sometimes, I needed someone to tell me when enough was enough before I tore myself into pieces.

I fumbled for his belt buckle, wrenching it open and grabbing his cock through his briefs. He was hot in my hand, throbbing when I squeezed. He shoved me to my knees and I pressed my face into his groin, inhaling deeply. I was practically salivating, my head flooded with the musky scent of him.

He jerked his briefs down, and I dug my fingers into his hips, taking his cock into my mouth until my nose was buried in his dark hair. He thrust into my throat, one hand pressed against the back of my skull.

"Choke on it," he said, and the pleasure in his voice made me ravenous. "Get it wet for me, pup."

He held me down until I gagged, until my eyes watered and I couldn't breathe, my lungs aching for air. But I didn't care. I wanted to reach that edge of endurance and push past it.

He pulled out of my mouth, and my lips were still parted when he spat on my face.

"Thank you, sir." I grinned up at him, my chest tight with feral laughter at the bliss of having him over me. He hauled me to my feet and turned me around, dragging his nails down my spine.

He pressed against me, pinning me in place before he said, "Don't move. I'll be right back."

The seconds he was gone, rummaging in the front of the Bronco, felt like an eternity. I held my breath, counting each moment as it passed, resting my forehead against the window's cold glass.

When he returned, he had a little bottle of lube in his hands.

We kept that shit everywhere, just in case. Glove boxes, bedside drawers, jacket pockets. We weren't going to be caught unprepared.

He made me stand in place as he undressed me. Starting with the boots, he knelt to pull the yellow laces loose. He pulled my jeans down, slapping my hands away when I tried to do it myself.

"Be patient," he said, once I was naked and he was still dressed. My back was to him, my chest pressed against the vehicle. It was so hard to remain like that, to obey his orders not to move and just *wait*. I wasn't patient. The anticipation was nearly impossible to bear.

"Make it fucking hurt," I said, repeating the words like a prayer as he kissed my shoulder, dragging his nails down my arm. There was a sound, the click of a bottle cap, and then his fingers probed me, slick with lube. One pressed inside my ass as he gripped the back of my neck. He took his time before adding a second finger, and I groaned as it squeezed inside.

"Want more?" he said, his voice low in my ear as his fingers pumped into me. My cock was leaking against the Bronco, pre-cum beading on the metal.

"More...fuck, give me more," I snarled. I needed it now, *right* now. I didn't want to wait. I didn't want to fuss and simper about pain. I wanted to lose myself in hurt and agony until there was nothing else in my brain.

He moved us to the side and forced my head down until I was bent into the back of the Bronco. The tremble in his arm gave away how eager he was for this. A third finger pressed inside me, and I slammed my fist against the thin carpet hard enough to hurt.

"Do it," I murmured. "Do it, do it, do it, fucking *please* —"

He sunk his fingers in past the knuckle, pumping them until my cock jumped and I was gasping through clenched teeth. My hands were knotted into fists when he withdrew his fingers from inside me and the head of his cock pressed against me instead.

He hunched over my back, tongue gliding along my spine. "You'll call red if it's too much," he said, and I growled in frustration. He squeezed my neck in warning. "Promise me."

"Fine, fuck, yes, I promise —"

He pressed inside me, stretching me with a slow stinging ache that had me groaning harshly. His grip on my neck steadied me, keeping me in place as I adjusted to him.

"*Fuck*, goddamn it..." I panted, my legs shaking as he drew his hips back and thrust forward again, slamming against me. The sensation overtook me, melting into every corner of my brain like sticky goo that drowned everything else in its path. No fear, no frustration. No swirling, chaotic thoughts.

Only pleasure. Only agony. Only us.

"Is this what you needed, pup?" The words were guttural. He spoke them with his mouth against my back, teeth grazing my skin as if he meant to plant the words in my flesh. "Is this what you fucking deserve?"

I tried to answer. But he spat in his palm and reached around me, gripping my cock and stroking me. His fingers moved over me with a twisting and pulling motion that had my eyes rolling back. My usual efforts at stoicism were abandoned; the groans he forced out of my mouth carelessly loud. I thrust my cock in his hand, my breath hitching.

"I deserve it…" My voice was ragged and my muscles grew taut as I plummeted past the point of no return. I couldn't move other than to shake. I couldn't force another word out of my mouth.

A chill went through every nerve, from the tips of my toes all the way to my head. Cum spurted across his hand as I came, losing myself in ecstasy. I was unbearably sensitive almost instantly, gasping as he kept stroking me until I wanted to curl up into a ball to escape.

"Take it for me," he grunted, his thrusts coming harder, with new urgency. He leaned heavily against my back, his panting breath hot as he buried himself deep inside me. His cock pulsed as he came, his body shuddering.

For nearly a minute, neither of us moved. It was all we could do to stay on our feet, legs shaking, leaning there as we caught our breath.

Finally, although the words still trembled, I said quietly, "I love you."

He rested his head against my back, his breath warm on my skin. "I love you, too."

He pulled out of me, keeping a grip on my arm as we crawled into the back of the Bronco again and collapsed.

"I don't tell you enough," I said. "I think about it all the damn time. I look at you…" I glanced over at him — at the sweat on his skin, the blissful afterglow on his face. "And I think of how much I love you, but I don't fucking say it."

His eyes were half-lidded in the fading light. "I know you try."

"I need to try harder. I know I don't always get it right. Not with you or…or with Jess, or Vincent, or Jason. But I'm trying. And I'll keep trying. I want you to know that."

It used to scare me the way I loved him, just like it scared me to love Jason and Vincent. It was so much to lose, too much. And now…

Now there was Jessica.

God, she terrified me.

We laid side by side, curled against each other as we lit up another cigarette and passed it between us. The sun was gone and crickets chirped in the long grass. The air was cooling, the heat finally beginning to fade.

"I think she loves you, too," I said suddenly, and he shifted beside me.

"Jess? I doubt that."

"You shouldn't. You should have seen how worried she was about you when you left the house." My head was resting on his arm, and he curled it closer around me. "I think if I'd fought your dad, she would have joined me."

I hadn't expected much of her at first. A guy like me wouldn't be wise to expect anything at all from a woman like her. But she never failed to surprise me. She was ferocious, a force to be reckoned with — yet now, I could see the cracks in her armor, the insecurities, the worries, the fear.

She wasn't as different from me as I'd thought. Maybe that was why she made me feel this way, as if I wanted to cling to her and push her away at the same time.

"I don't think she could love me," I said, and Manson scoffed.

"If that's what you think, then I wish you could see how she looks at you," he said. "You're both too damn prideful."

"It's not worth dwelling on," I said, taking the cigarette when he held it out. "We won't have her around for much longer."

I didn't like the thought at all. In fact, I hated the idea of her disappearing from our lives again so much that it made my fingers shake with anger. She needed to stay and give us a chance to figure this shit out.

"Do you remember what I used to tell you?" Manson said. "When we were teenagers and we'd drive out here to talk about shit…you'd tell me you didn't want to see another day…"

I remembered that, of course I did. I remembered the despair I felt, the pain we shared, how hopeless I'd been.

"If you can get through the night, you'll see the sun again," I said, repeating the words he'd told me back then. "Keep chasing the next sunrise." I closed my eyes as I exhaled. "The night feels really fucking dark, Manson, but I'm still chasing sunrises."

He squeezed my arm, leaning his head over to press against mine. "Yeah. Shit has gotten a little darker lately than I'd like."

A few minutes passed in silence before he said, "We need to get out of town for a few days. Go somewhere else, give ourselves a break. Give my a dad a chance to fuck off."

"Yeah? I could go for that. Vincent's parents could watch the dogs." I couldn't remember the last time we'd taken a vacation, even a small one. It felt like we'd moved into that big house and had been working ourselves to the bone every day since. "What about Jess? It feels weird to leave her."

"We won't leave her," he said, his tone thoughtful as his lips curved into a smile. "I've got plans for her."

"I love it when you grin like that," I said. That sadist's smile on his face meant only trouble, and I was ready for it. "What's the plan?"

"She told me about her ultimate fantasy," he said, scratching his thumb over his chin. "She talked about how she wants to be stolen away, made to submit, to have all her worries and cares disappear. I say we make that fantasy come true."

A shiver went over my back at the thought of it. "Oh, fuck yeah. Snatch up our pretty little toy and take her away all for ourselves? Sounds exactly like the vacation I need."

It wasn't just lust that had me excited. The need to pull Jess close and never let her go, no matter how completely mad she drove me, was growing more intense by the day. I had some fucked up abandonment issues, and I didn't know what the hell Jess felt about us, but knowing that was her ultimate fantasy made a ridiculous burst of hope explode in my chest.

She wanted something we could give her. An escape, an outlet for her darkness, a safe place she could fulfill all her filthy desires. I *wanted* to give her that. I wanted to show her that regardless of her fears, she could have everything she wanted and more.

I needed it to be different this time. I'd break every damn rule necessary to win, to claim a prize that had been dangling in front of our faces for years.

This was *our* game, and I didn't care what it took to make her ours in the end.

TO BE CONTINUED. . .

ACKNOWLEDGEMENTS

When I published The Dare, I really didn't think a kinky, weird, Halloween-y novella would get much traction. But as more and more people read it, enjoyed it, and spoke to me about it, one thing became very clear: the story of Manson, Jess, and the clown boys couldn't yet come to an end. Readers wanted to know more, and I wanted to delve back into these characters, I wanted to give them the space to tell their story as it needed to be told.

So the first thank you I must extend is to everyone who wanted The Dare to go on. All those who knew that Manson, Jess, Jason, Vincent, and Lucas had a story that needed telling, all those who have waited SO PATIENTLY while I got this book written. I appreciate you endlessly.

To my husband, as always, you see the best and worst of me through this process. You comfort the breakdowns, the tears, and all my doubts. And you make sure I actually eat and get outside the house now and then. Thank you for always supporting me, caring for me, and showing me all the love that inspires these books. There would be no Manson Reed without you.

To Z, my lovely editor, thank you for all your work on this absolute brick of manuscript! I know I can always count on you to make these books shine.

Tasha, thank you so much for being my beta! And my part-time therapist, lol. This book would not be what is without you.

To all the amazing folks with JLCR Author Services, thank you for everything! I don't know what I would have done without you all.

To Bethany, I'm convinced you're literally Superwoman. Thank you for your tireless work and for believing in these books.

To my Wicked Dark Desires reader group and ARC team, you all help keep me inspired day after day, and drive me to always be improving as a writer. These books would never end up finished if it wasn't for the amazing support and kindness I've been blessed with from you all. Thank you!

To all the bookstagrammers, bloggers, TikTok creators, reviewers, and artists who take the time to share their love for anything I've written, I can never thank you enough. The creativity and love I see come out of the book community is truly amazing, and I'm so grateful to be a part of it.

And finally, to each and every reader who's picked up this book, thank you. Thank you for trusting me to take you along on a weird, smutty, wild adventure. I promise there's much more to come.

Until next time,
Harley

ALSO BY HARLEY LAROUX

The Dare

Dirty First Dates (Short Erotica Series)

Halloween Haunt

The Arcade

The Museum

Souls Trilogy (Paranormal Romance)

Her Soul to Take

Her Soul for Revenge

ABOUT THE AUTHOR

Harley is a writer of New Adult Erotica, Erotic Horror, and Dark Romance. She enjoys crafting steamy stories on the dark and kinky side, the creepier the better. Harley lives in Washington with her husband and three cats. She loves horror films, dry red wines, and almost always has a candle lit. Most days she can be found at her desk drinking tea with at least one cat on her lap.

You can find Harley Laroux on these social platforms:

Twitter → @harleylaroux
Instagram → @harleylarouxwriter
Facebook → @harleylarouxwriter

Join Harley Laroux's Facebook Reader Group, Wicked Dark Desires, for exclusive sneak peaks and info on upcoming books.